The Brat

Jim Loughran

Copyright © Jim Loughran 2024.

The right of Jim Loughranto be identified as the author of this work has been asserted by him in accordance with the Copyright, Designs and Patents Act, 1988.

First published in 2025 by Sharpe Books.

For Nenad

With grateful thanks to Mirjam, Linda, Katrina, Lucille and the members of 'The Real Writing Group.'

THE BRATINSKY AFFAIR

CHAPTER 1

Bray, County Wicklow, July 1975Just out of university with a BA in English, Politics and Russian, and a diploma in journalism, Tom O'Brien had no intention of following his father and brother Dermot into teaching. Journalism was the thing. This job with *The Wicklow Herald* was the first step on a path to greater things: breaking news, scoops, investigations into criminal doings and foreign assignments. He could see the headline: Tom O'Brien, War Correspondent!

Unfortunately, the daily grind of council meetings, planning objections and local politics didn't quite live up to his expectations and Tom was starting to get itchy feet. A junior reporter's job didn't pay much but at least living at home with his father made life easier. John O'Brien was the retired headmaster of the local secondary school and he knew everybody in Bray and everything that was going on. That was part of the problem. Tom could never escape from being John O'Brien's son. John's wife, Oonagh, had died just six months after he retired. They had thought they would have all this time to spend together and then, he was on his own with two sons who were making their own lives. He had always loved history and to fill the days he had done a degree in the history of art in Trinity. Now, he spent afternoons looking at second rate pictures in local auction rooms in the hope of turning up a lost masterpiece. He read non-stop, including every newspaper he could get his hands on and he listened to every news bulletin from early morning to the last headlines at midnight. His wife used to say to him:

"Dear God, John, do we have to listen to the same bad news ten times a day?"

He collected antique books, especially anything to do with the history of Wicklow. Tom had a good relationship with his father but there were certain things he knew not to ask him about, like being in the IRA and the things that had happened during the War of Independence and the Civil War. If it ever came up in conversation, his father would change the subject. "Won't do any good to rake all that up again."

Tom had arranged to meet his father in Kelly's pub for a bite of lunch. They had just sat down and were perusing the menu. The food in Kelly's was good but the choice was limited, fish or flesh?Trifle or apple tart? One thing for sure, the pint was always good. They were still debating what to eat when two girls walked in. One of them came over to their table.

"Hiya, Tom. Haven't seen you in ages. Are you going to Jane's party on Saturday?"

Theresa (Tess) Maguire had been in Tom's year in school. He had taken her to the school debs and they had dated for a while after that but they hadn't seen much of each other since then. He had gone on to University College Dublin (UCD) and she had gone to Cork to study art. She was pretty: tall and slim with dark brown hair and a nice smile.

Tom stammered and blushed. "I doubt it" he said. "I think I have to work late."

"Pity' said Tess. "Well, see you around and she smiled at Tom's fat she turned away. "Nice to see you again, Mr O'Brien.

"Well, that's a chance I wouldn't pass up", said John looking at his son over the edge of his pint. "I always liked that girl."

He was about to say something else when Bill Egan, the local auctioneer, walked in with a very elegant older woman and two prosperous looking men. The men looked like well to do farmers, but in her tailored navy blazer, crisp white trousers and with her sunglasses tucked up in her hair she looked as if she had just stepped off a yacht. Egan nodded dismissively to John but Tom noticed that his father, who usually had a friendly word for everyone, barely grunted a reply.

"What was that all about, Dad? You barely spoke to the man."

" Oh, I've no time for that fellow. I saw him in action in the war of independence back in the 20's. You'd need to be watching your back with him around. Before the war he hadn't an arse in his trousers and now he has one of the biggest farms in the county and an auctioneering business to boot, though for one I wouldn't be doing any business with the likes of him."

"How come?"

THE BRATINSKY AFFAIR

"A bit of a back of the wall man!"

"A what?"

"If something valuable turns up in the auction and nobody else has spotted it, he is known to take a bid off the back wall and knock it down to one of his cronies: They sell it on and split the difference. And you couldn't be too sure where half the stuff comes from. Friends of mine went on holidays and when they came back their house had been burgled. They lost a lot including a valuable Georgian dining table. A month later he was driving down Main Street when he saw a table that looked like his being loaded into Egan's Auctioneers. Then he remembered that when they had painted the dining room a splash of paint landed on the table: half on the main part and half on the spare leaf. The leaf was behind the door in the dining room and the burglars had missed it. He raced home and got it and went in to confront Egan."

"I bet he was thrilled."

Oh he huffed and puffed a bit and muttered about it having been bought in good faith. But when my friend showed how the two halves of the paint stain matched up and threatened to call the Gardaí (Irish police) he caved in and gave him the table back. Called it a gesture of good will! He thinks nobody knows about it but Bray's a small town."

"Who is that glamorous woman he's talking to?"

"Oh, she's another antique dealer, comes from Paris from time to time – Irene something - calls herself a Countess – Grabinsky or something. There was an antique fair in Bray a while ago and she was there talking to some people I knew. Very grand. She does an occasional swoop around the local auctions in search of lost treasures."

"Dear God!!" said Tom. "Is there anyone in these mountains you don't know?"

His father laughed. "Ah, now!" Then he leaned towards Tom confidentially, tapped his knee with a long bony finger and went on: "One of these auctions, she picked up an old silver box. It turned out to be Fabergé, silver gilt! The profit paid the deposit on the house over in Kilquade – Mik O'Connor, you know, the house agent, was saying it in the pub."

"She seems pally with Reilly."

"Hmmp! You know what they say – birds of a feather!

And the two others?

Also dealers – known as the ring. They turn up to all the big auctions and go through the catalogue beforehand, deciding who wants to bid on what so they don't bid against each other and keep the prices down.

"Isn't that illegal or unethical or something?"

"Who's to say? Either way you'll regularly see them in a huddle out in the yard before the auction starts."

Tom noticed that two of the men had set catalogues on the bar while they chatted.

They said no more about it but the conversation started Tom thinking. If he wanted to be an investigative journalist he needed to start making a bit of a name for himself. He needed to start digging. The week before, he had heard an interview on the radio about the need to regulate the property sector, especially auctioneers and estate agents. The words rampant corruption were being bandied about a lot. He knew he was on to something when a few days later he overheard two men in the pub complaining about how solicitors took deposits and purchase money and lodged the cash in their own special short-term accounts. "It took me 6 months to get the money." said one. "A cousin of the wife's works in his office. She told us that he lodges the money to a special short term account and pockets the interest. And, do you know what I did? When he sent in the bill I calculated the interest due on the money for the 6 months, and took it off the bill! He was bloody furious, but there was nothing he could do. I told him if he wanted to make an issue of it we could ask the Law Society for a ruling. There wasn't a word out of him after that."

Willi Regan, his editor, wasn't that interested but he was smart enough to let his new recruit have a run at a story, to sharpen his teeth, so to speak. Willi Regan was a tough old bird. Originally from Tyrone, he had been living in what he always referred to as "the Free State" for more than forty years, yet had lost nothing of

THE BRATINSKY AFFAIR

his northern accent. Willi had been editor of the paper for longer than anyone could remember. Despite the fact that every second word was 'fuck' and he sounded like an angry bear; he was a decent sort who would do you a good turn if he could – especially if you were a young journalist trying to make your way. Tom suspected that he had been hired because Regan and his father had fought on the same side in the bad old days of the War of Independence.

Over the next couple of weeks Tom kept digging. He got an interview with the head of the special Garda (police) unit dealing with stolen art and antiques, a young couple who had been gazumped on a house sale and an architect friend who had waited for four months to get the money from the sale of a house. His breakthrough came when, through a contact of his father's, he got the head of one of the big auction houses in Dublin to go on the record about how the activities of the ring were undermining public confidence in the antique trade. Another contact explained a regular scam to him: "huge Victorian wardrobes, that nobody wants, will be taken apart and reappear, reincarnated as 18th century hunting tables that are all the rage. As he explained, "The wood is old, the screws and hinges are old. Who can tell the difference? And if you buy a set of antique chairs from certain people you can be sure that each chair will have at least one original leg. As for all this gilded French furniture that's flooding the market. Louis Seize? More like Louis says who?"

Tom even included the tale of the stolen table but doctored it enough that it couldn't be linked to any one person. He was feeling pretty pleased with himself when the article finally appeared, albeit in the business section at the back of the paper, under the headline:

Buyer Beware? Stolen Goods, Exorbitant Fees and Your Money in Their Pockets. How Estate Agents, Solicitors and Auctioneers Collude in the Systematic Rip-off of Clients.

Even Willi Regan gave it a grudging nod of approval.

"You won't get a Pulitzer for this one but, overall, not bad."

The paper came out on a Thursday and that evening Tom and a few of the lads headed for Kelly's. After the third pint he badly needed to go to the toilet and was turning down the long echoing corridor at the back of the pub when he walked smack into Bill Egan.

"Well, look who it is? If it isn't our very own Inspector Clouseau. You know, Tom, you'd want to be a bit careful before you go around pointing the finger at people. Might have unfortunate consequences."

Tom just looked at him. "Go to hell, Bill. The civil war is long over!"

"Well, don't say you weren't warned, and, if you do get into a spot of bother that arse wipe of a father of yours won't be any use to you."

With that he barged past and headed back into the bar. Tom heard him mutter "ponsified fuck" as the door closed.

The confrontation had taken the taste off the evening and Tom headed home. His father was sitting reading by the fire in the dining room that doubled up as his study. Tom poured them both a glass of his favourite Red Breast whiskey and sat down on the other side of the fire.

"Had a bit of a run-in with Bill Egan this evening, about the article. Want to tell me what the story is between you two?"

John O'Brien sighed and closed his book.

"I was hoping that chapter was well and truly closed but I suppose you have a right to know. It goes back to the war of independence. I was a member of an IRA unit up in the hills near here and so was Bill, though he was more senior. I was a raw recruit. The British were carrying out reprisals and we took hostages in retaliation. One of them was a young officer, not much older than us, a decent sort. The order came through that he was to be shot. I mean, shooting a man in combat is one thing, but taking a prisoner out and shooting him in cold blood – well, it stuck in my throat. I objected and said that we should get confirmation of the order, but Egan said no, he was in charge and I had to do it. A test of loyalty or something. I refused and walked out. I heard later that Egan went ahead and shot the man himself. We never did find out where he buried the body. Since then, he regards me as some sort of traitor. Tom, you need to be careful with people like him. Bill Egan is dangerous. He has money and lots of political connections and he's completely ruthless."

"Bit late for that, Dad. Think I am well and truly on his shit list."

"Tom, you need to think about the future. Is this journalism thing really right for you? I mean, do you want to spend your life turning over the dirty secrets of men like Bill Egan? If you wanted, I could probably get you a job in the school. They always seem to be short staffed."

"No thanks, Dad. Journalism is the only thing I ever wanted to do. Someone has to tell people what is going on in this country."

"Very noble, I'm sure. Your mother always said you were ambitious but be careful. Remember what they say: lie down with dogs and you'll get up with fleas."

"You worry too much, Dad."

John had reached the bottom of the stairs, heading for bed, when he hesitated for a minute and turned back.

"You know, Tom, if there's ever anything bothering you, you can always talk to me. I'm not a complete dinosaur. Hard to believe it I know, but I was young, once upon a time."

"Thanks, Dad. I'm fine, I am."

⸸

A week later when Tom went out to the yard behind the office to get his bicycle, he found that both tyres had been slashed to ribbons. Message received, loud and clear! He was wheeling the bicycle under the arch when the back door opened and Willi Regan appeared with the light behind him. He took one look at the bike and asked:

"What's all this then?" In the light from the kitchen Tom could see that the tyres on Willi's Mercedes had also been slashed.

"Bill Egan's work I'd say.'

"He was always a snake. Well, I know a couple of boys will settle his hash!"

"Let it go, Willi. It's not worth it."

"Oh no, he's crossed a line. Put a beggar on horseback and he'll ride you to hell, but I'm the man to put manners on him."

He looked at Tom. "You: Take a cab home. Put it on the tab – and say nothing to your father. Better leave him out of this."

It was clear thatWilli Regan meant business.

Things settled down over the next few days and Tom had pretty much forgotten all about it when just as they were putting the paper to bed on the following Wednesday evening, they heard two fire engines roar up the street.

Tom followed the crowd that had gathered and they could see the flames shooting up over the roofs from the direction of Egan's Auction Rooms. Tom and Mark Wilson, the paper's photographer, raced down to see if they could get a picture. With a bit of luck, they could still manage to get it into the next day's paper. The shed across from the auction rooms where they stored stuff before a sale was an inferno. Set against the darkening night sky it would make a great front-page photo.

The next morning Tom and Willy were in Kelly's pub having coffee with the paper on the table in front of them, when Egan walked in with a face like thunder.

When he saw the two of them, he stopped dead and directed all his anger at Willi.

"Don't think I don't know for a fact who's behind this. But don't you worry, Willi Regan, there'll be a reckoning."

Willi didn't miss a beat. He stood up, folded the paper and put it under his arm.

"Here's another fact for you to digest, Billy Boy. If you so much as look sideways at me or mine, or anybody remotely connected to me, for that matter, it won't be the shed that will go up next time. Count yourself lucky that the fire didn't catch that lovely new house of yours. And wouldn't it be a terrible pity if the Gardaí found out about those "special deliveries" to the back door on a Sunday night and decided to take a look. You need to be more careful, Bill, there's always someone watching."

With that, he turned on his heel and walked out.

"Come on, Tom!" Tom trotted obediently along behind.

"Tell me, Willi, how did you find out about the "special deliveries?"

"You can't keep a secret in a town like Bray. Bill Egan has

money but he's not liked. There are quite a few people round here would like to see him come a cropper and are happy to pass on a bit of dirt. He thinks nobody knows about his girlfriend up in Dublin either but sure half the town knows. It's a wonder his wife hasn't heard about it. She's a holy terror, that woman. I wouldn't like to cross her."

"You know, Willi; I'm supposed to be building a network of contacts around here, not re-launching the civil war."

"Oh, don't mind him, Tom. Like most bullies he's all mouth and no trousers. Any rate, we'd better be getting back to the office. We'll need to drum up a few new advertisers. Something tells me the Herald won't be getting any more ads from Egan Auctioneers.

CHAPTER 2

Paris, Rue du Bac, New Year, 1976.
Irina picked up the gilded invitation and ran her finger over the rich creamy card and the embossed lettering, reading slowly. H.E. the Prime Minister of France, Monsieur Jacques Chirac, invites the Countess Irina Bratinsky to a New Year reception at the Hôtel Matignon, 31 December 1976. 8PM: Dress Formal. RSVP. *What was the point?* There had been a time when having that invitation tucked into the edge of the mirror over the fireplace would have been a badge of success. Now, she didn't care. She flung it back on the table, picked up her glass of scotch and walked into the bathroom. The house was quiet. No sound from the streets. That would come later with singing and exploding fireworks. For now, the only sounds were the clinking of ice in her glass and the crackling of logs in the fireplace. She was in half a mind to settle in for an evening by the fire – but no: *the show must go on.*

Irina brushed away the steam on the bathroom mirror to apply her lipstick. She raised her head to tighten the muscles in her neck and turned her head left and right, looking for signs of imminent collapse. *Not bad, all things considered.* Still, she was in no mood for a party. When Kerensky, her contact in the Russian embassy, went silent, she had been worried. Then a friend in the Minister's office tipped her off that people were asking searching questions about *a certain Irina Bratinsky.*

And now, this sudden demand from Kerensky. Irina didn't have time to think about that now. For the moment everything needed to go on as normal. The parisian world of politics and high society was a shark pool and Irina had survived so far by keeping her finger firmly on the political pulse. Now, for the first time in years, she no longer felt in control. Fifty years on and here she was again, struggling for survival. The party would be a bit of a bore but it was important to be there and even more important to be seen to be there. Anyway, the alternative was to sit at home, alone, staring into the fire.

THE BRATINSKY AFFAIR

Irina left nothing to chance: her hair was softly waved à la Dietrich, her makeup flawless, her dress a column of dazzling blue sequins. When she walked into the ballroom of the Hôtel Matignon, wearing one of the original costumes from Diaghilev's Scheherazade, she almost got a round of applause. She would play the Russian role to the hilt: aristocratic exile, romantic victim of revolution, iconic beauty of a vanished world, enterprising business woman. She had played all these parts and they had served her well. They had given her money and status. Above all else they had given her security, or so she had thought. Now, swathed in a sable cape over layers of midnight blue chiffon, diamonds on her wrists and with her head wrapped in a silver turban Irina looked sensational. She was ready to face the world.

#

At 75, Irina had kept her figure and in the right lighting with her elegant clothes and discreetly coloured ash blond hair she could pass for twenty years younger – more on a good day. As she went up the stairs to the ballroom, she glanced in the mirror to make sure her image was perfect. What was that line from the Oscar Wilde play she had seen in Dublin last year? Twenty-nine when there are pink shades, thirty when there are not! *Let's hope they've dimmed the lights. Now to work: shoulders back, head up, smile.*

When she was a teenager back in Russia, before the revolution, her diplomat father Count Victor O'Rourke de Breffny, with the strange Irish name that no one ever knew how to pronounce had taught her how to work the room. "First, be sure to make contact with your hosts, and be seen doing it. "The art of making an entrance," he called it. "Next, scan the room, making a mental note of anyone important or useful. Finally, work your way around the room, ticking them off as you go: then, a discreet exit. That way you don't waste valuable time on people of no importance." The car was waiting outside;afterwards she would call into the Ritz where some wealthy clients were hosting a party. Thirty minutes max, then home. Home? It didn't matter what time she got back, there was no one waiting there for her anyway. Sometimes she still found herself listening for the door bell to ring in the early hours of the morning when Suzy would arrive after the club closed, dripping sequins and swathed in furs. They would sit up to daylight wrapped in each other's arms chatting and laughing at all the latest gossip and the absurdities of Paris life. Suzy's night club La Vie Parisienne was the coolest club in Paris before the war, the place where artists and poets, the gay and the straight and everything in betweenwent to play. Forty years: a lifetime ago.

#

Irina continued her progress into the party. Was there a slight chill in the Prime Minister's smile? Was his welcome less effusive than normal? Probably her imagination. Maybe she was just tired.Irina accepted a glass of champagne from one of the impeccably dressed waiters and moved from gilded room to gilded room, stopping here and there to smile, say hello and move on.

"Mwah mwah – you look ravishing, darling. You must come for dinner sometime soon." How often had she heard that line? This week, next week, sometime, never.

When she had completed the circuit of interconnecting rooms she would arrive back at the top of the stairs and be able to make her escape, unnoticed. It was all so elegant, so charming - so fake. Every person in this beautiful room had an agenda and if, like Irina, you had the inside track on what was going on in Paris it could be amusing to analyse the groupings and assess who was on the way up, or who was moving, inexorably, in the direction of the door.

As usual there was a scattering of distinguished older men chatting to handsome young men as they navigated their next move in a bed-to-bed career. After all, boys will be boys and some things never change in the eternal game of sex, money and power. The key was to watch the eyes: one moment looking intently into yours, the next flicking discreetly over your shoulder looking for a better opportunity. Her father had also showed her the strategic use of mirrors. In a room like this with its enormous sparkling mirrors a casual and completely natural turn of the head, to adjust an earring or push back an errant lock of hair, enabled you to get a complete sweep of the room and plan your next move. Shimmering in blue, Irina glided through the shallows on the edge of the larger groups, watching out for predators, and opportunities. There was the Lebanese arms dealer chatting to the Russian Ambassador. The Ambassador made a point of ignoring Irina, but as she crossed the room she could feel his eyes tracking her every move. There was Lillian Betancourt, owner of L'Oréal, being fawned over by a group of aspiring politicians and Catherine Deneuve chatting to Yves Saint Laurent, who looked as if he wanted to make a run for the door;he had promised her a preview of his new Russian themed collection. They waved a greeting but Irina wasn't in the mood. She just blew a kiss and drifted on.

There was a sudden ripple of excitement as Fiat boss Gianni Agnelli arrived with his very beautiful wife. Irina noticed she was wearing Chanel. Very politic! There was no doubt that he was the star attraction. What was it Suzy had called him? *A great white among minnows!* The muscular body, year round tan and oh so white teeth attracted every eye in the room, male and female. He was easy on the eye but there was nothing kind in his expression. You could hear the wheels turning behind the smile. She watched as Marella Agnelli drifted discreetly but steadily in the direction of the Prime Minister. Ah! The Italian gambit: King's pawn forward two squares.

A picture from the past flashed into her mind: a winter landscape, a firelight room and two children playing chess while their father looks on. *Block it out;don't go there, not now, –not ever.* For a moment Irina stood marooned in time staring at the candles, remembering. Fear coiled in her stomach as she looked at the flushed faces reflected in the fragmented light from the chandeliers. She knew most of the people in the room, at least to see, but there wasn't one she could call a friend. The hum of voices and the perfume of lilies rose around her and for a moment she felt dizzy. *Pull yourself together, Irina: breathe. Snap out of it.What was it about the Agnellis?* Now, she remembered. *Fiat has its eyes on Peugeot and needs to start the courtship. Smart. And she's so beautiful, so elegant – and such a bitch.* Once, she had enjoyed playing this game, but not tonight. Irina knew that if she dropped dead in the middle of the floor most of these people would step over her lifeless corpse to get to the bar and when the Prime Minister's wife pretended not to see her, she knew there was trouble brewing.

Maybe it was time to give it all up. Money was no longer the issue, but what else was there?She handed her glass to a waiter and took a final look around the room. *Time to exit, stage left!* The rumble of voices faded behind her as the cool air in the staircase rose to greet her from the hall below. Irina had almost reached the top of the stairs when a burly figure stepped out of the shadows into her path. Oleg Kerensky, officially, the First Secretary in the Russian Embassy, was tall and well built. He had the look of a cross country skier and in his elegant tuxedo and highly polished shoes he looked as though he spent his life moving from one diplomatic reception to another. But Irina knew that under the polished veneer he was a ruthless thug who to her certain knowledge had killed at least one man. His presence at the reception was no coincidence.

"Kerensky! What are you doing here?"

"Is that any way to greet an old friend, Irina?"

"I don't have time for this. What do you want?" she asked, glancing over her shoulder to see who was watching.

"Nothing, just a friendly word of warning; remember where your loyalties lie."

"And where exactly would that be, in your humble opinion?"

"With the people who hold your life in the palm of their hands."

Irina stared at him without saying a word and turned to walk away. She could feel the jaws of the trap snapping shut. When the heavy glass door closed behind her Irina pulled the fur up around her neck and glanced up at the first floor balcony. There was a man standing there, smoking. He had the usual square shoulders and shaved head of the security services and he was not trying to be discreet;he wanted to be seen. The message was not subtle: I'm here. I see you. I know who you are. He stood watching her intently, indifferent. Finally, he nodded, flicked the cigarette out into the night in a flurry of sparks and went back inside.

The vultures were circling. As she settled into the soft leather seat of the Mercedes Irina wondered about the future. She could retire to the South of France and become one of those beautifully dressed old ladies sitting on the terrace of the Hotel Negresco in Nice, admiring the view and waiting for death. Maybe, one day, but not yet. In the meantime, she needed to find out what was going on. Life had been different when she arrived in Paris in 1923. But that was a different time – and she had been a different person. That girl was dead.

\#

By the time she got home Irina knew she wouldn't sleep much. Her head was spinning trying to work things out. She did fall asleep briefly but the sound of an explosion woke her up with a start: *Fireworks!* She relaxed, relieved to find herself in her own warm, comfortable bed instead of back in Saint Petersburg in the middle of a revolution. Sometimes, when she couldn't sleep, Irina would find herself lying in the dark replaying images from the distant past: the days before her world shattered in a shower of broken glass and blood. She had spent her life trying to put the pieces back together: for what? Her mother Ana and her daughter Masha were dead and her granddaughter Olgawas almost a stranger and there would be no ring of the doorbell in the early hours.

When the revolution erupted in February 1917, everything changed overnight. One day Irina was rehearsing quadrilles on the polished parquet of the Smolny Institute for Young ladies of the Nobility, the next stepping over bodies in the street with the smell of smoke in the air and the crunch of broken glass underfoot The young men she had danced with had all been sent to the front. Many of them were killed in the first weeks of the war. None of them had realised that their privileged world would never be the same again. One by one the servants disappeared and the shutters on the front of the house were kept permanently closed. Her father warned her: "Never open the front door unless you know who it is and never stand with your back to the light - it will make you a target for a sniper." She had heard her father and mother talking in the study late at night, her father's reassuring voice telling her mother, "don't worry so much, Ana, everything will be ok. Things will settle down."

But they didn't. Every night for weeks after that Irina had lain awake listening to the explosions interspersed with the rattle of gunfire and the sound of people running in the street. She would hold her breath in case they stopped outside their house and only breathe again when she heard them running on. She heard her brother Pavel crying and asking: "mummy is that more people being killed?" when he heard a particularly loud explosion. He had made the connection between the gunfire he was hearing at night and the bodies he was seeing in the street next day. The first group of soldiers who came to the house had been reasonably polite. They said they were looking for guns. The second group threatened her father and stole his watch. By late August the violence had escalated out of control. The turning point came when a group of drunken soldiers shot the old lady next door. She had shouted at them for pissing on her doorstep. One of them called her a bourgeois parasite and shot her in the head. When her family came out onto the street screaming the soldiers threatened to shoot them as well and went off laughing. The last of the group stooped down and pulled the gold cross from around the old lady's neck, stuffing it into his pocket as he ran. He didn't look much older than Irina.

Next day, the O'Rourke de Breffny family packed up what they could carry and went to the house in the country near the palaces at Tsarskoye Selo. Her mother packed the portraits and the family silver into the secret cupboard under the stairs. "With a bit of luck it'll keep them safe until we get back in October," she said. They dressed as inconspicuously as possible and left the house at first light to avoid the soldiers in the streets. There was still an occasional train running, but now there was no well heated waiting room or deferential porter to handle the luggage and show them to their seats. Nor was old Sergei waiting with the carriages at the village station in Pushkin: one for the family,

THE BRATINSKY AFFAIR

one for the luggage. They trudged along the side roads to the old O'Rourke estate at Babalakovo, staying as far away from the palace as possible to avoid the groups of bored revolutionary guards who were standing outside the gates smoking.

The weeds were starting to take over the previously manicured gardens and some of the broken windows had been roughly boarded up. The whole place was silent, empty, abandoned. Nobody knew anything about the whereabouts of the Imperial Family. Some said they had fled abroad; others said they had been taken to Siberia. A mangy dog sat in the middle of the courtyard scratching himself before going over to raise his leg against the statue of Tsar Alexander 11. Strange, the little things you remember when everything else fades into a blur. Irina remembered one of the guards laughing, his voice carrying across the courtyard:

"That's a good revolutionary dog. Go on, Boris, piss on them all!"

It was a long walk through the woods to the house and Irina remembered the sense of relief when they turned through the gates into the park. The grass on the avenue was knee high and every so often a gap appeared in the line of trees. "Probably taken for firewood," her father said. It was still high summer and the air was full of bird song and the deep verdant smell of slowly ripening grass. Normally, the fields would have been busy with farm workers getting the hay in before autumn. The house stood long and low with its two-story pillared portico in the centre. The verandas along the front connected to the orangery at one end and the kitchen atthe other end of the projecting wings. Still there! It was only then that Irina realised that she had been holding her breath as they came round the final bend into the courtyard in front of the house. Home! Before the war, the staff would have been lined up outside to welcome the master and his family. Now, the door was closed and leaves had piled up in the porch. As her father turned the key in the lock, they all wondered what would greet them: a friendly welcome or a bullet? The door creaked open. Silence: but everywhere signs of a hurried exit: doors gaping open, overturned chairs and just inside the front porch a bag with the silver from the dining room. Forgotten or just too heavy to carry?

They settled in. Ana got to work putting things to rights and for a while everything had superficially gone back to normal: summer lilac, the heavy smell of linden trees on the avenue and the familiar, reassuring routine of life in the country. Except, now there were no friendly servants to cater for their every need and Irina could no longer go galloping on horseback through the surrounding forests with her little brother, Pavel. "Stay close to the house," her father had warned them and "don't go near the village."Weeks went by and the only news was from the few visitors who called to the house and even that seemed to consist mainly of rumours. In truth, nobody knew what was going on. When news finally reached them of the Bolshevik takeover they knew that the writing was on the wall for people like them.

Previously Irina had never had to wonder where food came from. It had always appeared by magic in the dining room. Now, she had to help her mother with the chores, peeling potatoes and chopping cabbage. They were in the kitchen preparing lunch when Irina decided she had had enough.

"I'm sick of this muck!! I'm sick of cabbage. I want to go back to Petersburg and my friends." Her mother put down the knife she was holding, looked at her daughter and without saying a word slapped her across the face, once, very hard. It was the first and only time her mother had ever hit her.

"You're such a spoilt princess. Don't you know there's a war on and we're trapped in the middle of a revolution. People down in the village would kill for a loaf of bread. You should be grateful for what we have. Now, go to your room and stay there."

Irina ran up the back stairs to her room and buried her face in her pillow, sobbing. Gradually she fell asleep. Later, she heard her father come into the room and heard the bed creak as he sat on the edge of the bed. He began to stroke her hair.

"You mustn't be angry with mama. She's upset and worried about what will happen. You know – she hates cabbage too! Now, come!" They went down into the kitchen together and nothing more was said. Her mother kissed her as she put the food on the table.

The replay always ended with the same image. Her father and Pavel being marched off down the avenue and her mother screaming.

\#

On bad nights when she could not pull herself free of the grip of the past there were other, darker images that Irina tried hard to bury: the humiliation of having to sell her confirmation cross and being offered more money if the dealer could put his hand up her skirt, the soldier with the rough hands and the sour smell of vodka on his breath and the sickening feel of the knife as she stabbed him. He had tried to rape her in the woods near the station outside Tallinn. She had stepped behind a clump of trees to relieve herself when he grabbed her from behind. She remembered the look of astonishment on his face as he fell. Irina had stood in shock looking at the knife in her hand and the blood, until her mother shook her.

"Hurry, we have to get out of here!"

As they got closer to the coast there were more and more people on the roads pushing prams or bicycles, even wheel barrows, with whatever they could carry. For the moment the road was empty but they had to get rid of the body. If soldiers found them, they wouldn't ask questions, just shoot them on the spot. The first snow was beginning to fall and Ana helped her to roll the body to the edge of a ditch where they could cover it with loose leaves and branches. Hopefully, the snow would cover him soon and nobody would see the body until spring. Irina swallowed hard and went through his pockets:a few coins, a packet of cigarettes and his papers. His name was Mikhail and he was twenty years old. From Vladivostok; on the other side of the country, a continent away. *How in God's name did he end up here?* His coat was ragged and she noticed a hole in the sole of his boots. *Probably a deserter, and probably just as lost and hungry as we are.* Irina shrugged and kicked him over into the ditch. She noticed the splash of blood on the toe of her boot and wiped it clean on a clump of dry grass. Ana looked at her seventeen-year-old daughter as if she had never seen her before.

Irina could still remember the look on her mother's face: part astonishment, part revulsion. "Don't think about it, just keep moving", her mother had said. Always that: don't stop, or think or feel, "just keep moving, never look back." That was easier said than done;down all the years Irina had never been able to shake off the feeling of desolation and sometimes in dreams she would find herself standing alone in the middle of that cold,silent forest listening, as flakes of wet snow landed on her face.

It had taken a gold chain and a pair of diamond earrings to get them on the boat to Helsinki.From the minute they arrived they could feel the tension in the city. If the Bolsheviks managed to seize control they would need to move on quickly. Ana and Irina had been standing frozen for several hours in the queue to get through the checkpoint when the commanding officer arrived. They were used to the ritual by now; Ana even had the handful of coins ready in her pocket in case they needed to bribe one of the soldiers. This time was different. He glanced along the line, picking people, apparently at random, demanding to see their papers. If they kept their eyes down maybe he wouldn't notice them. They heard the crunch of snow as he walked down the line. He stopped in front of them. Irina held her breath: "papers?" They handed over the documents. He looked at them for a moment and said nothing. Then he nodded to one of the soldiers who pointed his gun at them and forced them to one side. They were taken to the old harbour master's office near the docks and separated, Irina in one room and Ana across the corridor in another.

"You can't separate us; she's only a child," Ana screamed.

The guard clicked the safety catch on his rifle and pushed herinto the cell. The metal door clanged shut behind her. She was alone in the dark. Somewhere at the top of the building a door slammed and a man screamed in pain. The cell smelt of sweat and urine. There was nothing she could do so she sat huddled on the filthy bench and waited.

Across the corridor Irina looked around her: a couple of chairs, a desk with an overflowing ashtray and a half smoked cigarette still burning. A spiral of smoke curled up towards the ceiling.

THE BRATINSKY AFFAIR

The officer in charge looked about the same age as her father, except that his eyes were bloodshot and he smoked constantly. He didn't say anything for a few minutes, just sat there smoking and looking at her with her papers open on the desk in front of him. He stood up, pulled the chair round to her side and sat astride it, facing her. He started to play with one of her plaits.

"You don't want to go back to Russia, do you?" he asked.

Irina shook her head.

"Then you know what to do."

He stood up and unbuttoned his trousers. There were no preliminaries. He pushed her back against the wall, pulled up her dress and ran his rough hands all over her body, before ramming himself into her, grunting and slobbering on her neck. Irina heard the fabric of her dress tearing and felt the buckles of his uniform pressing against the soft skin of her thighs.

He smelt of stale sweat and tobacco. There was a window on the other side of the room and Irina could see a church spire in the distance. She focused on the spire and tried to ignore the pain and pretend that this was happening to someone else. There was nothing to do except wait for him to finish with a final shudder. When it was over, he wiped himself clean on her dress and patted her on the cheek. "First time I've fucked a Countess, and a virgin as well. My lucky day! He turned back to his desk and as he picked up another cigarette he half turned back towards her and dismissed her with a flippant, "You can go," as if what had happened was the most natural thing in the world.

Irina and Ana gathered their belongings, without looking at each other and headed down the long corridor towards the entrance. She could hear the guards sniggering as they went past. They knew what had happened; her mother knew what had happened – everybody knew; but Irina would not look down as if she were some sort of criminal. She held her head up and looked straight ahead.

As they set off into the city, it was already beginning to get dark. All civil authority had collapsed and they needed to be off the streets before night fell. If they ran into a random patrol who knew what would happen. Ana had been given the address of a woman who might take them in. At first sight the house looked abandoned; it took several knocks before anyone answered the door. Finally, they heard shuffling as someone came slowly down the hall and the door opened a crack. When Ana said who she was the door opened further but the woman still looked them over suspiciously.

"Payment in advance – cash."

The tiny room smelt of mould and wood smoke. They sat on the damp bed and Ana took her hand and pulled her close, stroking her hair. "Don't worry, my darling. It's over. We'll get through this together. You are my beautiful daughter and that will never change." Ana put her to bed and took away the stained and torn dress. "I'll make us some tea, if I can get this stove going."

She fumbled with the matches but when the third match blew out she gave up, put her hands over her face and started to sob. Irina got up, put her arms around her mother and after a moment they set about putting the room to rights. Something had broken in Ana and gradually Irina took charge, organising their trek across Europe to get as far away from Russia as possible. Ana knew that they needed to leave for Sweden as soon as possible before the reds took over but it was almost Christmas before they were able to get a boat to Stockholm. The night before they left Ana managed to find the ingredients to make a small pot of borscht and some dumplings. It would be their last Christmas in Russia. Ana and Olga sat at the window waiting for the first star to rise in the night sky, as they had done so often in the past as a family. Then they blew out the candle, shouldered their rucksacks and headed to the harbour.

THE BRATINSKY AFFAIR

CHAPTER 3

Wicklow 25 January 1976
Sunday night in the newsroom of *The Wicklow Herald:* the graveyard shift, left to the baby journos. The most pressing issues locally are the deaths, the doggies and the gee-gees. Breaking news is an alien concept.

Tom had thought that his article on corruption in the property business would lead to greater things but one year on here he was, back reporting on car crashes and the debates in the local council. His next deadline was a piece on the collapse of cattle prices in the local mart. On this Sunday at the end of January, he was thinking about how to escape from this rural backwater when things began to change at a pace that even he could not have expected.

Just before midnight the phone began to ring with other papers asking questions about a fire in Wicklow – a house burnt to the ground, reports of at least one death.

Tom rang the local Garda station but they weren't forthcoming – hardly a story for the morning news. He was about to head out the door when his direct line rang. It was Frank O'Neill from *The Irish Times* wanting a suss on the Wicklow fire. *What's got their tail up?* Tom thought. All he could get out of O'Neill was that the fire was in a house in the Russian Village in Kilquade – home of an elderly Russian aristocrat who lived alone.

Hardly a coincidence – there couldn't be that many Russian Countesses roaming around Wicklow. Had to be the woman he had seen in Kelly's pub with Bill Egan. As for the Russian Village – never heard of it. He rang his brother Dermot, a history teacher in London who gave him the full bill of the races: "Built in the 1940s. The builder was a White Russian architect who'd survived the Revolution and then the Blitz in London. He and his wife built an echo of his homeland in the Wicklow Hills. She was the first ever female member of the Dublin Stock Exchange. – Unusual in those days. An interesting couple all things considered.

He came over here to farm, bought some land and built a house. It was new and modern looking and after a while people startedasking him to build houses for them. Soon there was a colony of Russian-looking houses. Cedar shingled roofs, white walls with wood trim and large gardens. The President used to have a place there, I think. There are around twenty houses in the village. Why do you ask?"

"One of the houses burnt down, and there was supposed to be an old lady from Russia living in it. There might be a body, nobody's sure."

"You're the news hound, and you're ringing me!? Get on over there!" said Dermot, and hung up on him.

Maybe he could stitch something out of it: Escape: first from Lenin, then Hitler. Now, tragic death in a blazing ruin in Wicklow. He had to subdue a rush of purple prose and remember that the mart report was due on his editor's desk on Tuesday morning. It wouldn't do to upset the paper's biggest advertiser, or his editor.

Deadlines are sacred in the newspaper business so he decided to get that particular stick off his back before he headed home. Latest developments in cattle breeding, the direction of prices and the scarcity of fodder. That would surely do the trick, especially if he stuck in a few quotes from his Uncle Paudy, who had a hill farm up near Glendalough in the Wicklow Mountains. A touch of creative licence about the sorry state of modern Irish farming would round it off nicely, and Paudy would be amused at seeing his name in print.

Tom shivered when he left the office. It was bitterly cold and there was an occasional flake of snow. He threw his leg over the bike and was heading for home when curiosity got the better of him and he changed direction. Kilquade was three-quarters of an hour away; he used to go there berry-picking with his mother and a gang of friends not so long ago. His hands were icy – he hadn't bothered to his bring gloves in to work today. His father's old Crombie coat flapped back over his knees letting in the cutting wind as theice-white smell of the snow filled his nostrils. There was nothing else for it. He leaned forward and pedalled hard. It was a quiet country road and hopefully there wouldn't be much traffic. Luckily he had got the lamp fixed on the bicycle.

When Tom arrived opposite the old church in Kilquade he had no need to ask for directions; a pillar of smoke still rose from the ruined house. He cycled up through the laneways towards it. The smell of smoky steam reached him as he turned the corner and saw the ruin. Not a sinner in sight. No, he was wrong, a lone garda stood puffing smoke in the lee of the shell of the building. Tom didn't know him; he must be from Wicklow station. Tom propped his bike against the wall and approached. The Gard glowered at him from under the glossy peak of his uniform cap. *Poor lad must be freezing.*

"Cold enough," Tom said. The cop grunted.

"Looks like a bad fire. No one hurt, I hope?" Still no reaction. Tom cursed himself for not bringing a flask of tea with him. Tom didn't smoke any more but he pulled out the packet of cigarettes and shook them forward to offer one – 'cigartreats', his editor called them, advising him to have a packet with him at all times, on the basis that having a smoke with someone would make them loosen up and talk.

Not this time, though. "I don't smoke, and if you had any sense neither would you. Now, you may be about your business. I have nothing to say to journalists."

"What makes you think I'm a journalist? I mean, it's just a harmless question."

"Do you think I came down the Liffey in a bubble? I know your sort, so NO COMMENT, now on your bike."

The cop turned his back and walked away.

Tom pocketed the smokes and got back on his bike. At least there was a moon. He turned and headed for home, thanking the heavens at least for the tailwind that propelled him along the coast road towards Bray Head. It was past midnight by the time Tom got home but his father was still up drinking tea in the kitchen, a book on his lap and his spaniel Mungo snoring at his feet. His favourite seat in the kitchen was the armchair in the corner. With the window on one side and the range on the other he could see who was coming up the garden path and keep his mug of tea warm on the corner of the Aga. He spent a lot of time watching the antics of the birds in the front garden and thinking about the past.

They sat for a while by the range waiting for the kettle to boil to make a fresh pot of tea. "You heard about the fire up in the Russian Village in Kilquade? Sounds like that woman you knew – the antique dealer."

"Ah yes, poor woman, it was on the news headlines and I reckoned it must be her. I hear they found a body. Looks like she smoked one too many cigarettes in bed. It could happen to any of us."

"I'm thinking I might be able to get a story out of it; you know: escaping from the jaws of revolution only to die in a blazing inferno in Wicklow – something like that. It's a bit sketchy at the moment. I need more detail like that yarn you told me about the silver box."

"Well, if you hold on a minute, you may be in luck. The story made the front page of The Irish Times and I cut it out at the time. It's around here somewhere. Probably stuck in a book to mark the page." When he came back triumphantly from his study a few minutes later he handed Tom the yellowed cutting. God bless Ireland. Somebody always knows somebody who knows somebody.

They had a bite to eat, melted cheese on toast and a couple of whiskeys by the fire. The old man was lonely since his wife had died. "Oonagh used to love this view," he murmured. The Wolf Moon was at its height and they could see the full length of the wintry garden.

"I know it well," Tom said. He tipped the bottle of Red Breast into both glasses again. "Mam loved it best in winter, though. She'd sit there reading Yeats and looking out. That and spring – last March she rang me up mad with excitement and said there were two hares boxing on the hill!"

The two of them sat gazing at the fire, each lost in their own thoughts.

\#

The next morning Tom was trying to sidle past the editor's

half-open door when he heard: "O'Brien, you wee shite, come in here." It turned out his creative licence had not gone unnoticed. "Listen, you. As it happens, I know your uncle, Paudy fucking O'Brien, and what he knows about trends in modern Irish farming would fit on the back of a fucking stamp. So, in future, stick to the facts and maybe we'll get along."

He got up from the desk and came out of his office. "And by the way, what's the story on this fire in Kilquade? Do something useful for a change and get me some facts. Now piss off, Dostoyevsky."

Regan had a series of mad rules. Always carry a flashlight was one of them – you never know when you'll need it. Never ask a question that can be answered yes or no. Take notes in shorthand so your source can't gainsay a quote – shorthand jots the exact words down faster. And get the story and get it in, don't be fiddling around with great writing.

Tom practically skipped down the corridor. He was thinking about borrowing his dad's car to head up to Kilquade again, but he was ravenous. He decided on a mug of coffee and a sandwich in Michael Kelly's pub. Kelly's was the beating heart of communications in Bray – beside the bookies, two doors up from the paper and four doors up from the *Garda Síochána* barracks where the police looked after the town.

He saw Bill Egan going out the side door as he went in. *Thank God for small mercies*!

Using the age-old technique of throwing a trout to catch a salmon, Tom casually mentioned "the terrible accident up in Kilquade."

Michael Kelly turned back from shouting an order into the kitchen. "Accident! Not so sure about that. I hear the Gardaí have been looking closely into what caused the fire. Not much left of the poor woman, by all accounts. There were three of them in here this morning in a huddle – all very intense. I asked the Inspector what the deal was and he nearly took the snout off me. Told me to mind my own business. I'll remember that at the end of the month when he has to clear his slate!"

Tom's journalism lecturer had once told him that the secret of being a good reporter was to play dumb: act as if you know nothing and listen. As Kelly finished speaking, the local doctor came in for his regular mid-morning coffee.

Tom stared at his doctor's bag trying not to think about what might be inside. He was sometime assistant to the new State Pathologist, and was known to use it to bring samples from the morgue for analysis in the hospital. He thought he'd try the same tack again. "Terrible accident up in Kilquade," he said. "I hear the poor woman was burnt to a crisp."

Dan O'Brien looked at him over his half-moon glasses. "I suppose being hit in the side of the head with a lump hammer, or something similar, could theoretically be considered accidental."

"So, she was murdered?"

"I'm saying nothing, but this lady was well dead before the fire started, *and* you did not hear this from me, *and* if you quote me, it will be the last bit of information I ever give you."

It can be useful having an uncle who works with the State Pathologist.

#

This was beginning to look like a real story. Tom stuffed the remains of the sandwich into his mouth, ran down the street and up the stairs, into Willi Regan's office.

"The woman in Wicklow," he panted –"spoke to Uncle Dan. Looks like murder, and at least for the moment all the Gardaí will say is that they are treating the death as suspicious and have called in the forensic people."

Regan grinned. "Contact Inspector Fitzgerald. Ask for an on-the-record comment, then write up as much detail as you can get. Then ring production, tell them you need 200 words on the front page. We have to nail it as our story before anybody else gets to it."

He ran for his typewriter. Regan yelled after him, "You're the lead on this story, and if anybody rings up, tell reception all calls are to be put through to you or me. No exceptions." Lead! Tom liked the sound of that.

Next morning Tom's first headline appeared on the front page of the *Wicklow Herald*.

THE BRATINSKY AFFAIR

Mysterious Russian Countess Found Dead after Blaze in Wicklow

"The Gardaí investigating a fire in Kilquade have revealed that the body of a woman was found in the ashes of an elegant cottage in the Russian Village.

"It is believed that the victim was international antique dealer and expert on Russian art, 75-year-old Countess Irina Bratinsky. The Countess was found dead after a fire which Gardaí suspect may have been started deliberately."

"CountessBratinsky's family fled Russia after the Revolution. She lived in Paris but was a regular visitor to Ireland, and had bought a house in the Russian Village, Kilquade. Next of kin have been notified and Gardaí are carrying out door to door enquiries in the area.

Inspector Aidan Fitzgerald told our reporter, "Gardaí are keeping an open mind on the cause of the fire, and all possible avenues are being investigated. We have no further comments at this time."

Tom had padded it out with quotes from the old *Irish Times* article on the discovery of the silver Fabergé box, and was even able to copy in the photograph of CountessBratinsky – the *Wicklow Herald* had bought a copy of the photo at the time. It was blurry, but better than nothing. The piece ended up with the 200 words on the front page and a follow-up on page three, below the editorial.

"Yes!! Tom O'Brien ace reporter," Tom blurted out. Regan gave him a look, but turned away grinning.

When Tom got home, his father had gone out for a walk, but the paper was on the rack over the Aga, open to page three. He was sitting rereading it when his father came back in with Mongo, the ten-year-old springer spaniel that followed him everywhere.

"Well done. I suppose you'll be insufferable now." From the tone in his voice, though, Tom could tell that he was pleased.

CHAPTER 4

Paris 1920

In Paris, Ana reverted to type as the aristocratic Countess O'Rourke de Breffny. What else could she do? That was the part she had been brought up to play but the reality was that they were no longer important. The friendships with members of the imperial family and their political contacts no longer counted for anything. The French were too busy rebuilding their own lives after the war to worry about some penniless foreign refugees. The jewels Ana had stitched in between the stays of their corsets would keep them afloat, at least for a while. It was them against the world.

The big surprise of life in Paris was to discover that the tenuous Irish connection of the O'Rourke de Breffny name opened the doors to some very grand houses. Ana became even more enthusiastic about her husband's remote Irish ancestry when she discovered that there were at least two eligible bachelors, of Irish descent with titles, and substantial fortunes, either of whom would make an excellent match for her beautiful daughter. After a while Irina began to feel like a prize pony, trotted from afternoon teas to lunches or one of the occasional balls that were starting up again after the war. If Ana could organise a good match for Irina all would be well. What Irina wanted really didn't come into it.

One afternoon as they were on their way to an exhibition of Russian art in the Louvre Irina stopped dead. "I'm not going to another dog and pony show to be treated like some prize thoroughbred. I'm surprised some of the mamas don't ask to see my teeth or trot me round the room to see if my wind is sound!"

One part of Ana wanted to laugh, the other part wanted to shake her rebellious daughter hard. She decided to confront the issue head on. "Face facts, Irina. We have money for, at best two years, if we are lucky. And then, what? You can't sing; you can't dance, and from what I can see you certainly can't cook. Do you know what happens to girls like you when the money runs out?"

THE BRATINSKY AFFAIR

At that moment they were crossing the bottom of the notorious rue saint Denis when Ana stopped and looked across at a group of women standing on the corner.

"Do you see that girl over there? The blonde one who turned her back and is pretending not to see us by looking in the shop window. I recognise her. Her father was an admiral in the imperial navy and she is the only member of her whole family who escaped, with just the clothes on her back. Now, here she is walking the streets of Paris. Look at her, Irina and then tell me what your great alternative plan is; I'm all ears. What? Nothing to say? Well then, wake up my dear and play your part."

Irina wasn't prepared to back down without a fight.

"Is that what you did, mother, played your part?"

"That's exactly what I did. I was twenty eight with no sign of a husband, but my father was rich. Your father had a title, good connections and an estate that was sinking in debt. Our families made a deal, but we were lucky. We didn't marry for love but we fell in love over time and if you're lucky you'll find the same happiness."

Irina looked at the girl who could have been her older sister and felt ashamed.

There was still an Imperial Russian Embassy in the magnificent Hôtel d'Estrées and when Irina met Egon Bratinsky at one of their regular Sunday afternoon dances and fell madly in love, it had seemed like the answer to prayers, both hers and her mother's. Finally, someone to stand between her and the world. Count Egon Bratinsky was young, handsome, and rich. The Bratinskys had been one of the richest families in Russia, with houses in Moscow and St Petersburg and such huge estates that Egon's father hadn't visited some of them; he just collected the rents. As Ana said to one of her friends: "they're not as rich as they were but you can't be too picky these days."

When Irina married Egon in the spring of 1922, the wedding was small but stylish, with some of the most distinguished names from the Russian aristocracy in attendance. There were Sheremetevs and Obolenskys and Paleys. Ana was fairly bursting with pride and relief at having got her daughter so well settled.

As Irina and her handsome husband walked around the church under the wedding crowns she felt dizzy with happiness. During the reception Irina overheard old CountessBratinsky chatting to her mother. "It's such a relief Egon is marrying a nice girl like Irina. Imagine - he might have married a dancer!"

Life for Irina, and Ana, now picked up where the war and the revolution had interrupted it. There was money for new clothes and trips to the races at Longchamp and Deauville. Even the Grand Duchess Zenia and her insipid daughter would condescend to nod a greeting if their paths crossed; she might even crack a smile if Irina were paying for lunch. When their daughter Masha was born in 1924 Irina's happiness was complete and life settled into a comfortable routine. The future was bright and some of the people who had snubbed her and her mother previously now became amazingly friendly. Irina and Egon were the picture of the young couple in love. There were invitations to art exhibitions and dinners in some of the large houses on the boulevard Saint Germain. Even so, money was a constant worry and Irina had to be a bit careful with the cash while they waited for one of Egon's business deals to deliver.

Irina couldn't afford Chanel or Lanvin, but she had a dressmaker who could copy their latest designs to perfection – almost. She had the magazine with the photograph of the summer dress in her handbag. She went into the shop and sat in a corner where she could see who was there and what they were buying. When the vendeuse finally came over, Irina thought she was a touch offhand, but didn't pay much attention. She took out the photograph and explained what she wanted. "Wouldn't it be lovely if we could do this in blue with a hat to match? A drop-waist? What do you think?"

"Yes of course, Madame, that would not be a problem, but first, there is the slight matter of Madame's account."

Irina was startled. "But I sent you a cheque last week, for the full amount!"

"Unfortunately, Madame, the bank declined to accept the cheque – I'm sure it's a mistake, but perhaps Madame would like to take it up with the bank? In the meantime, perhaps Madame would be interested in a pair of stockings?"

To cover her embarrassment, Irina bought the stockings, paying with the last cash in her handbag. When she went into the bank it was the same story. The Manager looked her up and down as if she were some kind of criminal.

"I regret, Madame but we are unable to help. Perhaps the Count would be good enough to get in touch. We have written several times but have received no reply."

When Irina went back to the apartment Egon was slumped in an armchair, chain-smoking with a half-empty bottle of Slivovitz in front of him.

"Darling, I need cash to pay some bills but that silly man in the bank wouldn't cash my cheque."

"There isn't any money."

"Don't be silly, darling – I need some money to pay the dressmaker!"

He looked up at her. "You don't get it, do you? – The money is gone – finished. The party is over, Irina. Looks like you backed the wrong horse."

It was on the tip of her tongue to say that backing losers was more his speciality but she held back. Things were starting to make sense. The letters on the hall table that he rushed to pick up in the morning and the hurried conversations on the telephone when he thought she was out of earshot. Irina looked at her husband and said nothing. Egon Bratinsky was handsome and charming but he had a problem with three things; alcohol, gambling and an allergy to work. He was a gambler, but a very unsuccessful one, and his ill-advised investment schemes, each of which was going to solve all their problems, had swallowed money with no return. Clearly, he was not as smart as his father.

Egon was gullible as well as lazy and had been persuaded by a supposedly wealthy Argentinian he had met at the polo to invest a lot of money in a cattle ranch in Argentina; "it was a golden opportunity." Unfortunately for Egon while the land in question was cheap, it was also a mosquito infested swamp and the whole thing was a fiasco, eating up the last of their money. The Argentinian disappeared shortly afterwards.

It then turned out that the apartment had been mortgaged to fund this last "golden opportunity" and would now have to be sold to clear the debts. Even the money they had been living on was borrowed. Egon had floated along in the belief that his charm and good breeding would see him through. Like many exiled Russians, the Count Bratinsky had assumed that sooner or later things in Russia would settle down and he would go back to his elegant apartment in St Petersburg. The civil war was a temporary inconvenience. The final retreat of the White Army from the Crimea was a shock to the system. No going back and no more rich and indulgent family to honour his debts or cover up the fact that behind the veneer of perfect tailoring and good manners, Egon Bratinsky was in fact a bit of a shit.

Irina held onto the back of a gilt chair to steady herself. "How much do you owe?"

"Two hundred and fifty thousand." He lit another cigarette.

"A quarter of a million francs? How could you be so stupid?"

"A quarter of a million *pounds*, my dear. We are royally screwed."

There was no avoiding it, they were broke. With the apartment sold, the little money that was left would have to stretch a long way. The immediate priority was to find somewhere smaller and above all cheaper to live. A pearl ring went in search of a new owner, and produced enough cash to rent a tiny apartment on the attic floor of their building. The higher up you went the cheaper it got until finally, you reached the maids' rooms. No mirrored doors and marble floors up here, just painted floorboards, poky windows and the smell of fried food.

"One room for us, one room for Ana and the baby, and a combined kitchen and bathroom," Irina said gaily, lifting up the kitchen sink to reveal the bathtub underneath. "Look, darling, I can cook dinner and scrub your back at the same time!"

She thought it was rather amusing but Egon was horrified. He was even less amused by the shared toilet on the landing and the fact that the mirrored doors in the hallway were firmly closed and they now had to use the service stairs. As far as Irina was concerned it was grim, but at least it was in the same building, and would give them time to catch their breath and make plans. Somehow, they would manage and as far as their friends were concerned, they would still be living on the Avenue Foch.

"Don't worry, darling, it will all work out. You can get a job and I can help. I can speak to the vendeuse in Chanel and see if I can get some modelling work. They seem to like Russian aristocrats. It'll be fine, you'll see."

Egon looked at her as if she had lost her mind. "You expect ME, to live HERE?"

It was like trying to placate a petulant child, and Irina's patience was wearing thin. "Egon: we have no money, so we have no choice. Now, grow up and get a job." Previously Irina might have gone to Egon's parents for help but they had invested all their remaining money in an annuity that barely kept them afloat.

\#

It was not long before things between them began to unravel. Egon had never been the perfect husband, but compared to what Irina and her mother had been through during their escape from Russia, life was good, so Irina ignored the fact that he would regularly disappear mid-morning and often not come back until the early hours. He was silent and sulky and they barely spoke. As Ana had effectively stage managed the wedding she could say nothing and sat, silently watching her daughter's marriage fall apart.

In the December of 1929 the final blow came. Irina had gone early to the market to buy the food that would have to last them to the end of the week. As she came in through the front door, she found her mother and Madame Rostand, the concierge, sitting chatting in the sunshine while Masha played nearby with Madame Rostand's little dog, Milou.

"Hello, Madame Rostand. Is Egon in, Mother?" Irina thought she saw a quick look pass between Ana and Madame Rostand.

"I think I heard him going out earlier," murmured Ana.

Irina was quietly relieved. She would prepare the potatoes and cabbage and have a rest before she started to cook dinner. She went into the kitchen and dropped the shopping on the table: a small package of meat, for Masha, a large bag of potatoes and even more cabbage. If things ever picked up, Irina swore, she would never – ever – eat cabbage again. She went into the bedroom to take off her hat and fix her hair. The wardrobe was open and her clothes were spilling from a jumble of open drawers. She knew immediately that Egon was gone. When she turned to go back into the kitchen, she saw that the jewellery box on her dressing table was open and the few pieces of hers that hadn't already been sold were gone.

"You shit – you complete and utter shit!" The only things left were her engagement ring, which she happened to be wearing, and the tiny egg on a gold chain that she always wore. At least he had had the good manners to leave the remaining cash. There was no note or explanation, just two words scribbled on a piece of paper:

"Sorry, darling."

Irina was sitting on the bed crying when Ana came back into the room with Masha.

"Please don't say anything, I couldn't bear it."

Ana spoke quietly and for once her steely resolve came to the rescue. "My darling, we women have to be tough to survive. You should know that by now. I saw my husband and your brother Pavel walk out and never come back. I thought that was the end, but I survived and so will you. And you have your daughter to think about."

Ana sat on the bed and silently rocked her daughter as she had when she was a child. After a few minutes she took Masha by the hand and they went back down to the courtyard, leaving Irina alone. It wasn't supposed to end like this.

THE BRATINSKY AFFAIR

CHAPTER 5

Bray, County Wicklow, Ireland
It would be weeks before the inquest, so Tom headed up to Kilquade to see if he could rake up any new angles. He borrowed his father's car and brought the staff photographer along.

"Come on, Mark, it'll get us out of the office."

Mark Wilson was a photographer's photographer. He might drive you crazy taking a hundred shots, but if there was one perfect shot that would capture the essence of the moment, he was the man to get it. It was one of those bitterly cold days at the beginning of February, with a blue sky and a scattering of clouds. With luck they might get some useful shots to do a holding piece while they waited for things to develop.

The two-storey house was an almost total ruin, though the front door, the entrance hall and part of the stairs looked more or less intact. The back of the house where the fire was most intense had largely fallen in, and you could see up through the rafters to the sky.

"Hey, Mark, get some shots of this" said Tom pointing to some burnt book bindings and the frame of a broken mirror. They were standing in what had been the drawing room of the house with charred paper everywhere and the remains of a badly burnt desk lying on its side. Tom jumped as out of the corner of his eye he saw a figure standing at the window looking in. "Holy moly you scared the shite out of me" he burst out before correcting himself. "Pardon my French, but who are you?"

"As I suppose this is probably my house now, I could ask you the same question."

"What do you mean?"

She stepped through, and struggled across the jagged, blackened floorboards, ignoring the dirty water staining her elegant boots. "Olga Radcliffe. Irina was my grandmother." She was young and pretty and as he looked at her more closely, he could see the resemblance.

"And so, who are you?" she asked.

He felt himself blushing. "Tom O'Brien, a journalist with *The Wicklow Herald*. I did the first report on the fire. And Mark Wilson here is our photographer." He called up to Wilson to get her picture. "Mark!" But Mark had already included her in the shots he was taking from a precarious perch halfway up the broken stairs.

"Do you know what happened?" She lifted a water-stained picture from the wall.

"Looks like it was deliberate, but I don't know what else to say." He didn't know what she knew or didn't know and didn't want to upset her – or get in trouble with the Inspector.

"What are you looking for now?"

"I wanted to get a feel for the place and get a sense of who this woman was for a possible follow-up article. She seems to have had a very adventurous life but I haven't been able to find out much about her."

Olga looked around. "I was only ever here once before. Irina liked to escape here every so often and I came for Christmas one year. It was such a beautiful room."

Tom was standing beside the half-burnt desk and instinctively reached out to turn it right side up. As he did so he caught a glimpse of something red shining among the ashes. He reached down and pulled it out. It was a tiny gold egg on a broken chain.

Olga looked at him and held out her hand. "It was Irina's. She always wore it."

He dropped the egg into the palm of her hand. It looked intact. The table must have protected it from the flames. Olga blew the dust off and as she held it up to the light a tiny ruby glowed in the winter sunshine. "It's Fabergé, a gift from her father."

It was bitterly cold and there were a few flakes of snow. Olga shivered. With her fur hat and her collar turned up he thought she looked like Anna Karenina. Olga brought the gold egg in her palm up to her cheek. "The smell of snow: Irina used to say she could smell snow in the wind," And she started to cry.

Tom glanced over at the photographer giving him the nod to keep clicking. At the same time, he said to himself: *Calm yourself, Tom. It's the story you're after, focus on the story.*

"Why don't we go and get a coffee and warm ourselves up? I don't know about you, but my feet are like blocks of ice. And maybe I could talk to you about your grandmother. It would be nice to know more about her as a person."

She gave him a half-amused smile. "That could take a long time."

Tom didn't push it, but over coffee Olga told him about Irina's early struggles, the shop in Paris, about her mother and the Irish connections of her great-grandparents, Victor and Ana O'Rourke de Breffny. He could feel the story shaping up in his mind, the front-page beckoning to him again.

"Could I get a picture of you standing by the house and one of you holding the Fabergé egg? A close up of it in the palm of your hand" Mark winked at him.

"Then we'd better drop by the Garda barracks to hand this over or Inspector Fitzgerald will have me arrested for withholding evidence."

When the two cars pulled up in front of the station the Inspector was coming down the steps.

He looked from one to the other

"And to what do I owe this honour, O'Brien?" Tom introduced Olga who then handed over the gold egg. They had had the good sense to drop it into one of Mark's empty film canisters.

"Nice to meet you, Miss Radcliffe. My condolences on the death of your grandmother." Then he looked at Tom "Don't know why I bother with an investigation at all, when all I have to do is wait for the next exposé by the intrepid Tom O'Brien."

The tone was sarcastic. He was clearly annoyed at having been beaten to the punch. He turned to go but then thought better of it.

"Oh, and by the way, next time you want to go interfering with a crime scene you might think of asking for permission – it is in fact a criminal offence, as I'm sure your editor is aware, or he will be when I tell him." The threat was clear; hostilities had been declared.

Tom needed to get back to the office so after a quick exchange of telephone numbers Tom raced for Willi Regan's office shouting as he went "I'll call you later to run through what I've written."

This time it was five hundred words on the front page and a half-page inside. Someone had sent Olga a photograph taken at the New Year's Eve Ball in the Hôtel Matignon and she gave Tom permission to use it. The picture of Irina looking resplendent got pride of place in the middle of the article. Willi Regan was practically purring, "Good boy! way to go!"

#

The story was coming along nicely. Tom was now the recognised lead but there was one thing he needed to do that made him feel slightly sick. There was now no doubt that the CountessBratinsky had been murdered. It was the lead story in Ireland and on the front pages of all the international papers. Even the New York Times had run a piece on it and Tom was now the go-to man for updates on the case. So far, so good. Willi Regan had even given him a raise.

However, there was one fly in the ointment, and a large one at that: Bill Egan. The Countess was a regular visitor to Ireland and the one person she had definitely been connected to was Egan. Tom was experienced enough to know that if he wanted to be taken seriously as an investigative journalist he had to cover all the angles.

As far as he knew, Willi and his father were the only other people who knew about Egan's connection to the Countess. But if the question came up and he hadn't asked it, his career as an investigative journalist could be over before it got properly started.

After the Monday editorial meeting Tom stayed on in Willi's office.

After one look at Tom Willi got up and closed the door.

"What's up?"

"It's Bill Egan."

"Not him again. What is it this time? I've had about as much of him as I can take."

"No, nothing like that. I think I need to interview him."

Willi looked at him in silence for a full minute.

"Are you out of your tiny effing mind? He's more likely to

THE BRATINSKY AFFAIR

smack you round the head with a monkey wrench than give you an interview. And why in God's holy name would he agree to talk to you?"

"Well, this is the way I see it. He is up to dodgy business, as we know, and so by implication was the Countess. After all, she was known to have made several valuable discoveries in his auction rooms, not to mention the famous Fabergé box. If we can put two and two together so, presumably, can the Gardaí. Don't you think it might be in his interest to get his version of the relationship out in the open before Inspector Fitzgerald comes knocking on his door?"

"It might. I still think it's 50/50 whether he talks to you or knocks you out cold."

"I guess there's only one way to find out."

"You want any back-up?"

"No thanks - the phrase red rag and bull springs to mind."

Tom walked slowly down Main Street to Egan Auctioneers. The place was a hive of activity with porters getting ready for a forthcoming auction. He nearly tripped over a snarling tiger's head on a rug as he went through the door. Egan was standing at the door to the back office as he went in. He was in the middle of a conversation when he saw Tom. He brushed off the girl he was talking to and watched as Tom walked the length of the office.

"You have some nerve coming in here!"

"We need to talk."

Tom could see Egan clenching his fists and had a feeling that he was about to exit head first through the front door.

A glimmer of a smile flashed across Egan's face.

"You have more guts than your father anyway."

"Let's leave my father out of it."

"I have nothing to say to you. No comment – isn't that the appropriate answer?"

"Well, you can talk to me or answer the same questions from Inspector Fitzgerald."

Egan scrunched up his eyes and looked at Tom quizzically. Tom could see him weighing up his options. Finally he spoke: "I'm busy – but ok, you have five minutes" and he nodded into the office. He sat on the edge of the desk and crossed his legs at the ankles looking at Tom. Tom could see his mind ticking over wondering what Tom knew, or didn't know. There were no niceties or small talk, just straight to the matter at hand.

"Now tell me, what's this about? Why would Inspector Fitzgerald be interested in talking to me?"

"I need to know what you know about CountessBratinsky – and her murder."

"What makes you think I know anything?"

"Enough games! Here's what I know, plus what I think I know. Tom tried to maintain an air of bravado as if he did this kind of thing every day but his stomach was doing somersaults.

"For starters, I know that some of the stuff that goes through these auction rooms is as crooked as a dog's hind leg." He put up his hand to forestall Egan's objection. "I have that information first hand – and in writing."

Egan shrugged.

I know that you and the Countess did business, regularly.

I also know that she and you were part of what is known as the ring, creaming off the best pieces for yourselves at knockdown prices.

I know that she made some valuable discoveries here and made a lot of money with objects of, shall we say, dubious provenance.

I suspect that at least some of those pieces were stolen abroad and given a false paper trail through Egan Auctioneers."

Egan stared him down. He was completely relaxed and had obviously decided to let this conversation run its course to see where it would end up.

"A lot of if's and maybe's there, Tom. Now, let's say any of what you say is true. What are you going to do about it?"

"Cards on the table? I have zero interest in any of that. I want the story. I want to know all about CountessBratinsky – who she knew – why she came to Ireland - what happened."

"You don't want much do you? Why would I tell you, of all people, any of that, supposing I knew?"

"Up to you. On the other hand, I could just wander down to the station and tell Inspector Fitzgerald what I know. He's bound to be interested and I'm sure he will have some searching questions to ask. Wouldn't look too good if your premises were searched for stolen property, would it? As he spoke, Tom let his eyes linger on a fine pair of early eighteenth century mirrors that were leaning against the wall. He had taken the precaution of stationing himself on the roof of the building opposite Egan Auctioneers on the previous Sunday night, and had seen them being carried into the building.

"Why, Tom, that sounds surprisingly like blackmail. Mr nambypamby Lillywhite gets his hands dirty. Welcome to the real world. Maybe you'll grow a pair, finally."

Tom ignored the sneer in his voice.

'It's a trade off. You tell me what I need to know and I keep your name out of it. As far as the paper is concerned you are a protected source."

Egan sighed and started to talk.

"Not that much to tell. It all began after one of the auctions. We had a few drinks and she opened up. She had this source for items from the Soviet Union. All good stuff from historic collections. Apparently a few families who had survived the revolution and its aftermath had pieces stashed away that they wanted to sell abroad, discreetly. She didn't offer any further explanations and I didn't ask any questions. Simple as that.

"So, you were doing these poor people a favour?"

"Something like that."

Very noble! "Did you believe her?"

"I chose to believe her and as long as the story held up I couldn't care less. It was easy money and as far as I could see no harm done."

"Do you know who her source was?"

"Some guy called Dmitri but that's all I know. It went well for a few years but recently she had started getting jittery – said someone was putting the squeeze on her, that she had been getting threats - political stuff -I don't know the details. That's why she bought the house in Ireland. Said she was thinking of retiring."

"Do you have any idea who might have killed her?"

"I have no idea and if you have any smart ideas about trying to drag me into all this, you can think again. On the night of the fire I was playing poker with a group of friends and I can produce four witnesses to back me up. Anyway I liked the woman and I'm sorry she's dead. Now, we're done. I have work to do."

Back in the office Willi Regan looked at Tom in open mouthed admiration. "You more or less asked him straight out if he killed the Countess, or knew who might have, and you're still alive, sitting there, talking to me?"

"As far as I can tell" said Tom, laughing as he headed back to his desk to write up the article.

He was closing the door when Willi called him back. "Great work, Tom, but you know you've done a deal with the devil, don't you? A word of warning though. Don't get too close to the fire or you might get scorched."

Tom nodded and went back to his office. He had to tread warily this time so as not to bring the wrath of either Bill Egan or Inspector Fitzgerald down on him. What he knew and what he could prove were two different things.

Mystery Surrounds Death of Murdered Russian Countess

"Countess Irina Bratinsky was an acknowledged expert in Russian art, especially the work of renowned imperial jeweller, Fabergé. In recent years she had been involved in the sale, outside Russia, of objects belonging to former noble families who opted to keep below the radar. It appears that many of these objects had been hidden for generations to escape the attentions of the authorities. According to an informed source this activity was seen as political in some quarters and the Countess had allegedly received threats prior to her death."

He had fudged the real story but there was enough truth in it for him to stand over it without revealing his source. He knew that as soon as the article appeared Inspector Fitzgerald would be banging on his door wanting to know who that source was. Tom was standing outside the office chatting to Willi when he saw Fitzgerald barrelling up the street towards him.

"Here comes trouble," Tom whispered to Willi.

Fitzgerald looked as if he was about to explode. "You know, O'Brien, I could do you for obstruction of justice."

"Haven't a clue what you're talking about."

Fitzgerald had the new edition of the paper rolled up in his fist and started banging it against his thigh. He proceeded to quote from the article: "the *Countess was involved in the sale of articles hidden for generations.* Now, how would you happen to know that?"

"Can't reveal my sources, Inspector. Journalistic ethics and all that!

Fitzgerald looked in mute appeal to Willi who just shrugged. "Can't help you, Inspector – the kid's right."

"I won't forget this, O'Brien" he muttered and strode off in the direction of the station.

CHAPTER 6

Paris 1929

It was months before Irina had any news of Egon. Before he left he had been so unpredictable and angry that it was almost a relief for Ana, Irina and Masha to be on their own. One afternoon Irina was coming out of the bakery when she ran into Pauline de Fougère coming towards her, a determined glint in her eye. Pauline always had something to tell you that you absolutely needed to know. Irina hated the way she revelled in other people's misfortune. But there was no escape, so she braced herself for the onslaught.

"Let's go for coffee, Irina – we need to talk."

"What's so urgent? Can't it wait? I have to fix Masha's tea." It was the daily afternoon ritual when Ana, Irina and Masha would sit down together. Irina and Ana would sit drinking Russian tea as Masha dipped her croissant into hot chocolate and managed to make a mess of whatever she was wearing. Money was rapidly running out as one by one the crocodile jewellery cases that her mother had stashed away disappeared. It was the one luxury they kept up to make Masha's childhood as normal as possible and reassure her that she was loved, despite the absence of her father. Sometimes the only food left for Ana and Irina to eat was some fried left over potatoes. Ana could smell the warm croissant in the bag and her instinct was to hurry home rather than get drawn into a bitching session with Pauline. Irina was also conscious of the last few francs in her purse, but Pauline insisted. She caught Irina's hesitation and smiled.

"Don't worry, my treat."

The one thing Pauline could always be relied on for was the latest gossip. She was the widow of a prominent general and seemed to know everybody and everything that was going on in Paris. If she didn't know, she would make it her business to find out. Pauline kept chattering aimlessly as they walked down to the café on the corner. While Irina was glad to have a break from the normal routine of cooking and cleaning it was also humiliating to know that she could no longer afford even anything as simple as a cup of coffee in a café.

"Have you heard about poor Princess Menshikov?" Pauline asked.

"What about her?

"Too much of the silver syringe, darling, and now she's completely smashed broke and driving a taxi. Good job they kept the car!"

They grabbed a seat in the café on the corner and Pauline glanced at the mirrors around them to make sure no one was within earshot.

"What's all this drama about, Pauline?"

"It's Egon!"

"Is that all? You know, Pauline, at this point Egon is the least of my worries."

"Be serious, Irina – he's your husband."

"Unfortunately, yes"

"My friend Aileen was in Monte Carlo staying with some people, you know, those Germans, the ones with three castles and no manners – when who did she meet…?"

"Let me guess – the Shah of Persia?"

"No, silly!" Pauline looked hurt. "You're not taking this seriously!"

"Seriously? How can you ask me that?" The anger surged out of nowhere. " Egon gambled away all our money and then walked out, abandoning his wife and daughter to fend for themselves when he sniffed a better opportunity. He's nothing better than a gigolo!"

As quickly as it had surged the anger dissipated itself in a weary sigh.

She looked at Pauline. "Alright you might as well tell me, whatever it is."

"It was Egon of course, with that woman, de Villeneuve – well, she calls herself de Villeneuve, but I'm not convinced. She's Jewish you know. Anyway, it seems her industrialist husband died and left her an absolute fortune and now she's going around telling everyone that she's going to be a Countess. And she was beautifully dressed and positively dripping in jewels – including your earrings."

Instinctively Irina reached up and touched the lobe of her ear. She hadn't thought of Egon in weeks, but the idea of someone else wearing the earrings Egon's mother had given her on her wedding day was too much and the tears started. It was part disappointment and part humiliation combined with the stress of worrying constantly about how money. The tears wouldn't stop.

"I knew you'd be upset but I felt that you *had* to know. Better to hear it from me than a complete stranger!"

Part of Irina wanted to laugh, and she tried half-heartedly to make light of the situation. "You're a good friend, Pauline. Anyway, poor Egon, now he's going to have to choose."

"Choose? What do you mean? Seems to me he's already made his choice."

"A lawyer friend told me that if he wants a divorce, he has to choose one of three grounds: adultery, bigamy or impotence. He can't sue me for divorce on grounds of adultery and bigamy doesn't apply. Madame de Villeneuve's Jewish family won't want a scandal – which leaves…impotence." Irina started to laugh, and kept laughing until her side hurt. She couldn't tell why she was laughing. Hysteria or the release of all the tension? Irina thought she caught a glint of satisfaction in Pauline's eyes at this reaction, and knew that she would dine out for weeks to come on the details of *how devastated poor dear Irina was* when she heard about Egon.

If she only knew! Thinking about Egon made Irina feel tired and she walked slowly back to the apartment in the late afternoon sun. She had been young and naive, but she had loved Egon and tried to make him happy. Now the struggle for survival took up all her energy and she no longer knew what she felt any more. She switched on her happy face for Masha and her mother as she went into the kitchen but straight away Ana knew something was up.

As they sat at the battered kitchen table watching Masha make a mess Ana looked at her daughter?

"What's happened? I can see that you're upset."

THE BRATINSKY AFFAIR

Irina was tempted to side step the question but her mother was having none of it.

"Tell me!"

It all came tumbling out.

"Egon is getting married. He's met a rich Jewish widow and she will be the new Countess Bratinsky."

The more Irina talked the angrier she got.

"I can't believe it. He's swanking around Monte Carlo without a care in the world while we struggle to put food on the table. Whatever about me he doesn't even care about his own daughter. It's shameful!"

Masha looked up and Ana gave Irina a warning shake of the head as if to say "not in front of the child."

"At least she paid for the coffee and cakes!," Irina said, forcing herself to laugh.

When the divorce papers came, Irina didn't even read them at first. *"Good luck to her – but if they think I am going to make it easy for them they have another think coming,"* she thought. The package of papers tied up in brown paper sat on her bedside table for weeks, unopened. In the end it was Anna who forced the issue.

"What are you going to do about those?" she asked, nodding at the bundle of legal documents.

"I don't know what to do for the best. I know he's gone but, signing them feels so final. He is Masha's father after all!"

Ana sighed. "I know I pushed you into this marriage but you have to face facts. Egon is neither useful nor ornamental and even if he did come back he would drag you down. Better to draw a line under it and move on."

"I know you're right but I feel so alone."

They held hands across the table and said nothing. The problem was Masha who kept asking "when will daddy be coming home?" Irina could only try to distract her and hope that she would gradually begin to forget, but she knew that the hurt ran deep. Despite the fact that her own father had been dragged away by the Reds against his will, Irina had never completely got over the feeling of abandonment: that somehow he had let her down. The feeling of loss and anger never disappeared. She could tuck it away in the back of her mind for months at a time but it always came floating back to the surface.

Meanwhile, there was the slight problem of survival. Unlike Princess Menshikov, she didn't have a car, so setting up as a taxi driver wasn't an option. She had heard that Grand Duchess Maria Pavlovna was making a lot of money doing embroidery for Coco Chanel – but Irina couldn't sew to save her life. Her grandmother had tried to teach her the needle skills considered important for a young lady of her class, but even she gave up in despair when she saw the tangled results of Irina's handiwork. Irina still smiled to herself when she remembered her grandmother's rather caustic comments when she saw all the dropped stitches in Irina's attempt at knitting: "it's a sweater you're knitting, darling, not a fishing net." That was the end of her knitting career. Despite everything she treasured those moments spent sitting with her grandmother on the balcony of the house in Crimea, looking out over the blue sea. She tried not to think about it now. It made her too sad. At least her grandmother had died before their world fell apart. Her funeral had been the last big family event before the revolution. When Irina then had to sell her grandmother's emerald bracelet she realised they couldn't keep going on like that; she had to get a job.

In the end Renault came to the rescue. Irina had gone to the market early to buy some of the damaged fruit and vegetables that the traders sold off cheap. She had just picked up her bag of salad when she looked up and there he was, Colonel Yuri Kuznetsov, formerly of the Russian Imperial Guard. The last time she had seen Yuri was in the palace of the Dowager Empress. Irina was almost the same age as the Grand Duchess Tatiana and she and her mother had been invited for tea, "so the young people could get to know each other." Irina had been bored to tears but she remembered clearly how in the middle of tea, the Tsar had suddenly arrived escorted by Yuri. She had been dazzled by the glamour of his uniform and his twinkling eyes. Even her mother had commented afterwards on how handsome he was. In the car on the way home she had laughed as she told how Yuri had left a trail of broken hearts between Moscow and Saint Petersburg. Now, here he was, wearing blue overalls and workmen's boots.

"Countess O'Rourke – a pleasure to see you again," and instinctively he kissed her hand and clicked his heels. It was so absurd, given their present circumstances that they both burst out laughing. While she filled him in about Egon and Ana and Masha, Irina could feel him taking in the shabby clothes and the bruised contents of her basket.

"How are things?"

"Could be better – probably couldn't be much worse. "

He had started to say goodbye when he stopped and turned back. "If you wanted, I could probably get you onto the assembly line at Renault. It's the new factory out onIle Seguin at Meudon - a bit out of the way but it might keep you going until something better turns up. Since the war we're always short of people on the night shift. Pay's not great but it's a job?"

Irina could have kissed him. At least the factory was on a direct metro line, though it meant almost an hour's travel at either end of her shift. The next week she put on her oldest clothes and turned up at the factory gates. Yuri was waiting for her.

"You'll be on the piston assembly line in the new part of the factory."

"Yuri! I'm not sure I can do this. I mean, I don't even know what a piston is."

"Don't worry. It's not that complicated. You'll get the hang of it soon enough."

Renault had gradually taken over an island in the river Seine and the whole site reverberated with the sound of building work and steel being hammered into shape. Irina could hardly hear herself think as Yuri took her in and introduced her to the other people on her shift. A lot of them were women and from the very first minute she could feel the hostility. They had her sussed immediately. The way she spoke, the way she moved – everything about her betrayed her class, despite the shabby clothes. By the end of the first shift they knew exactly who she was. The foreman at least was straight with her.

" You needn't think you can pull rank here. Just do your job and keep out of my way."

As he walked off, she heard him saying to one of the other men: "Heaven help me, - another one of Yuri's lame ducks. Bit of a looker though.!!

From the word go Irina knew the supervisor didn't like her. Her name was Blanche and when she was showing Irina how to fix the parts together she spoke so fast and did it so quickly that she might as well have been speaking mandarin. She was always hovering in the background waiting for Irina to make a mistake and when at her first attempt she put the components in the wrong order Blanche didn't miss her chance."

"Speed it up, there, you're holding up the whole line. I'm not going to lose my time bonus because you don't know what you're doing."

Fortunately for Irina the woman on her left took pity on her.

"Don't mind her," she said with a smile. "She hates everybody. By the way. Name's Jeanne. Just watch what I'm doing."

"When Irina gushed 'thank you so much, you're very kind", in her posh upper class voice Jeanne raised an eye brow and laughed.

"You have a lot to learn, girl."

She was a good hearted older woman and she and Irina got on well. She had two children and during the breaks they sat together bitching about Blanche and talking about their children. The work was boring and repetitive but after a couple of days she got the hang of it. At least she was doing something constructive instead of sitting in the kitchen worrying about money and gradually she began to relax. When Yuri tried to kiss her on the way home at the end of the first week, she slapped his face.

"You mind your manners, Yuri! My mother warned me about you." He laughed good-naturedly and shrugged it off.

"You can't blame a fellow for trying, now, can you?"

He was a big bear of a man and so good natured that Irina couldn't be angry with him. After that, he became her guardian angel and kept an eye out for her. It was hard, dirty work but better than starvation. A lot of Russians worked in the factory, but unlike Irina they weren't aristocrats. Most of them were ordinary people who had got swept up in the turmoil of the war, and they were bitter, blaming people like her for the nightmare of violence that had swept across Russia. "Would your highness care to sweep the floor? Would your duchessness like to hurry up or we'll be here all bloody night?"Sometimes they would deliberately put the components in the wrong order and complain about her to the foreman. If it hadn't been for Jeanne she wouldn't have lasted a week. Irina let it all wash over her and kept her eyes fixed on the clock. Every five minutes seemed like an eternity until she reached the end of the shift and could escape into the fresh air. One or two of the women were friendly and she would stand chatting with them and Jeanne as they smoked at the back door during the breaks. Irina never smoked but she enjoyed those fleeting moments of camaraderie. To her surprise she discovered that she had a lot in common with these women: worries about useless husbands, the price of food, children who always needed new shoes or a visit to the doctor and the deadly monotony of work.

By the end of the first week Irina was exhausted. Working all night and then trying to get a few hours of sleep in the afternoon, in between shopping and cooking, was taking its toll and she didn't know how long she would be able to keep it up. She did the food shopping in the morning on the way home but the hardest part was dragging the heavy bags up the seven flights of stairs to their dingy room.

The thing she hated most was the smell of lubricating oil that was used on some of the engine parts. It had a heavy viscous smell that clung to her clothes and even when she was sitting in the metro on the way home, she could still smell the oil all around her. On Saturday morning Irina would get up early, clean the shared bathroom and heat the water. A long hot soak washed the grime and the smell of the factory away and she would relax, dreaming of living somewhere warm and safe and luxurious. It was the one time in the week when she could be completely alone and focus on herself. Afterwards she would dab on a few drops from her precious, and rapidly dwindling bottle of

QuelquesFleurs by Houbigant and begin to feel more like herself. It had been her grandmother's favourite perfume and she had always kept a bottle of it safely out of the sunlight in the top drawer of her dressing table, with her gloves and her prayer book. Every morning she would emerge from her room trailing the faint smell of roses.

At other times Irina would find herself thinking about the future. The factory was ok, for now, but the prospect of staying there indefinitely didn't bear thinking about. She needed a real job. Something where she could earn real money and plan a future for the three of them.

THE BRATINSKY AFFAIR

CHAPTER 7

Bray, County Wicklow, Ireland February 1976
Olga had flown back to London on the early flight. Tom hadn't expected to hear from her until the inquest and he still wasn't sure what to tell her about what he had found out about her grandmother from Egan. On balance, better to keep stum for a while. After all, he didn't know her that well and, unlikely though it seemed, maybe they were all in this together – a family business. Meanwhile, it was back to porridge and an interview with the bishop about the opening of a new school, and chasing the local politicians to get a comment about the number of people currently on the county's housing list. He was peering into the fridge to decide whether it would be pizza or a rasher sandwich when the phone rang. It was Olga.

"I'm sorry for ringing you at home but I wasn't sure what to do."

"What is it?"

"Well…when I got home there was a card from Irina – from Paris. It must have got held up in the Christmas post. She said she was going to Ireland for a few weeks – that if anyone came asking questions, I was to say nothing. Then she said if I didn't hear from her, I was to call the police."

"It sounds like she was scared of something. Where are you?"

"I'm at home in Devon with Dad."

"And what does he make of it?"

"Oh, he thinks I should stay out of it and let the police get on with their job – what do you think?"

"To me, it sounds as though she was trying to lie low in Ireland. As to why, I have no idea'

"What should I do now?"

"First thing, get onto Inspector Fitzgerald – he'll want to see the letter – and keep the envelope. Oh, and make sure to copy out the wording exactly. Anyway how are you feeling?"

"It's very stressful. My grandmother is dead and then it turns into a murder investigation and then, as if that wasn't bad enough it looks as though she was involved in some seriously dodgy business. I'm so busy worrying about all this and trying not to upset my father that I'm not able to think about her. Then I find myself thinking about my mother and I realise that now I've lost both of them."

"Mind yourself, I'll keep you posted if I hear anything."

Tom tossed and turned all night trying to make sense of what was happening. The next morning he was up early and went in to see Willi Regan to get a steer on what to do. He was in the office before 9 and stuck his head round Willi's door.

"Fancy a coffee?"

Willi looked at his watch.

"Mirabile dictu! You, in at nine o'clock! What's seldom is wonderful."

"Enough with the sarcasm – I need to talk to you."

Willi opened his mouth to say something, then thought better of it and grabbed his hat. As they walked down to the coffee shop on the corner Tom filled him in on the latest developments and told him about the card that Olga had received.

"Looks like this story has legs, Willi. Question is: do we run with this now or hold off for a bigger piece to coincide with the inquest?"

"Run it now. As soon as Fitzgerald hears about it it'll be all over *The Irish Independent*. That Garda station leaks like a sieve. And by the way, be careful with Fitzgerald. He wasn't one bit happy about you stomping all over his crime scene. Especially as you finding the necklace made him look like a bit of an idiot."

"Fuck him – he's an arrogant prick."

Willi grabbed him by the arm.

"And you are an arrogant pup with a lot to learn. You don't need to make an enemy of someone like Fitzgerald. He could be useful to you, or, a big stumbling-block. He's ambitious, he doesn't forget – and he doesn't forgive. I've met his sort before. Meanwhile, forget Fitzgerald and get on with the story."

Tom couldn't lead in with the card from Irina, and wasn't even sure he should mention it at all in case it was confidential information. He decided that Ana was the key to the story. The

THE BRATINSKY AFFAIR

only problem was that he knew next to nothing about Irina's mother, and Olga couldn't tell him very much. He was going round in circles and around five o'clock he decided to call it a day. "That's it, I've had it – I'm off home." He would have something to eat with his father and watch a bit of telly to clear his mind.

John O'Brien was a good cook, and in fact, even when Oonagh was alive he had done the lion's share of the cooking – when he was in the humour. However, on a Thursday evening it was a lucky dip as to what was left in the freezer. Today, Tom was in luck: it was steak and chips, with onion rings! And a glass of red. They rarely used the dining room anymore. When Oonagh was at herself she had liked to entertain and she and John had liked nothing better than to have a few pals in on a Saturday night for a bite to eat and a game of cards.

None of that now, though. John had lost the heart for it, and immersed himself more and more in his books. Bit by bit the books had invaded the dining room and it had become his study. As a result they normally ate at the round table in the bay window in the kitchen. With the heat from the Aga, it was warm and cosy and easier for John to manage when he was on his own. However, they usually lit the fire in the dining room in the evening and left the door into the kitchen open so they could feel the good of it.

They were chatting over dinner when Tom mentioned the trouble he was having digging up anything on the O'Rourke connection. His father stood up with a grin and went into his study. "I think I might have something – if I can find it."

John O'Brien's bookshelves covered three walls in the room and included everything from ancient history to the latest science fiction. Tom could hear him pulling out books and muttering. A few minutes later he came back and handed Tom a heavy tome. *"The Irish Brigades– Fighting in a Foreign Land.* You could start with this – there are a few references to the O'Rourkes in the index.

" Dad! you're like the Encyclopedia Britannica!"

"Sign of a rag-bag mind. Either that or a sign I have too much time on my hands; Anyway, my reward is – another glass of red – and you get to do the dishes!"

As he headed back next door to enjoy the fire and his glass of red, he added, "It might be worth a trip up to Dublin to the Chief Herald's office. They have a lot of information on these old Irish families. If they don't have it, they should know where to find it."

\#

Tom got the early train that chugged along the coast and sat enjoying the warmth inside, interrupted at every station as a burst of people came in with icy mist blasting off them. He walked along by Trinity College and turned up Kildare Street. The Chief Herald's office had wall-to-wall leather-bound volumes on every aspect of the Irish diaspora from the sixteenth and seventeenth centuries. It was a roll call of all the ancient Irish families who had fled the oppression of the penal laws to seek fame and fortune abroad: Brown, Burke, Butler, de Lacey, Dillon, McMahon, and O'Brien. Finally O'Rourke. *Who knew there were so many!*

The family history read like an adventure story, and it certainly would by the time Tom had finished with it. First the exile in France, then joining the Russian army – then General Count O'Rourke de Breffny, owner of a large estate and 1,000 souls.

Tom was putting the books back when the librarian asked him

"Did you find the section on the Battle of Leipzig – stirring stuff?"

He hobbled off and got another volume on the Napoleonic Wars.

"See here – General O'Rourke led one of the crucial charges which helped carry the day for the allies. When Napoleon fled the battlefield to rally his troops, the allies emerged victorious and afterwards the King of Prussia presented General O'Rourke with a dress sword studded with diamonds."

There was even a line drawing of the famous sword. The blade was slightly curved and as far as he could tell from the drawing the flat part was heavily encrusted in gold, as was the scabbard. Would be worth a pretty penny if you could get your hands on it.

THE BRATINSKY AFFAIR

This was what he needed for another piece to flesh out the background to the fire. Then when the inquest came round, he would get another crack at it.

Tom was becoming the recognised lead on this story and RTÉ, the state radio channel, had already been on to him twice to do interviews, giving him a contact in the newsroom. Profile: that's what Tom needed if this story was going to take him anywhere. Another reason to stay close to Olga Radcliffe. With a bit of luck by the end he would have made a name for himself with the national papers. There was even the chance of a bit of international coverage. He took the train back to Bray and walked up to the newspaper office. When he went into the newsroom, Willi looked up from his paper

"Ah here he comes, the conquering hero, star of stage and screen."

He sounded amused, but Tom couldn't help wondering if Willi wasn't a little bit miffed about him getting so much attention.

\#

The inquest was a week away and Tom was finalising the article when out of the blue he got a call from Olga. She sounded upset. "I'm not sure if I can make it for the inquest."

"What's up? Are you ok? You sound a bit stressed."

"It's my father – he's not well. He was attacked – fact is I'm not sure what happened. I was up in London for a job interview and Dad was at home in Devon, alone. He had gone to bed early and was reading when he thought he heard something downstairs. He turned into the hall and saw a light on in the library. As he went in something hit him on the head. When he came to, the French windows were open and the room was in a mess. Strange thing is, nothing was taken."

"What did the police say?" Tom asked, and then added hastily: "Is he ok?

"He's fine –shaken and he has a shiner of a black eye. Of course, he's making light of it, telling everyone he fought off a gang of intruders! I don't know what to make of it, and I'm wondering if it has something to do with Irina."

"Probably some opportunistic thief who saw an open window,"

said Tom.

"That's what the police are saying. But we live in the middle of nowhere – people don't just wander past!"

He said slowly, "Let Inspector Fitzgerald know – he'll probably want to talk to you – and your father." He gave her the inspector's number. He knew it by heart now. "By the way I've done a profile on Irina's background and the O'Rourke connection. It's a pity your great grandmother isn't still alive. She could be famous."

There was silence on the end of the line.

"Sorry, I didn't mean to be so flippant."

"For you it's a story. For me it's my family, what's left of it."

"I'm sorry. Is there anything I can do this end?"

"It's ok, don't worry. I'm a bit weepy at the moment – anyway I probably will come over next on Monday."

"I could collect you at the airport if you like."

"That's kind of you, but it's such a long way."

"No trouble at all, and as it happens, I have to be in Dublin that day anyway," he lied. "I'll see you on Monday then?" He liked Olga. She was smart and funny and he felt comfortable with her. Tom whistled loudly as he walked down the stairs. The story was going well and his article would be in the paper on Thursday morning.

\#

On Monday morning Tom was finishing his breakfast in the kitchen when the phone rang. It was Willi Regan.

"I wasn't planning to come in this morning, Willi – I've borrowed Dad's car and I'm collecting Miss Radcliffe from the airport."

"Are you indeed? Well, you better come in anyway."

"What's this about?"

"You'll see when you get here."

Tom shared an office with another reporter, Brendan Sheils, who was usually out covering the local court cases and human-interest stories, so most of the time Tom had the office to himself. When he got in Willi was standing by the window.

"We've had visitors."

THE BRATINSKY AFFAIR

Everything had been turned upside down. The drawers had been emptied and it looked as though someone had gone through all the files.

"Or rather, you've had visitors. Looks like you might have stepped on someone's toes."

"Why do you say that?"

"None of the other offices have been touched. They weren't after money – all the cash from the charity collection is still in the drawer – so it looks like they were looking for something specific."

At that moment they heard footsteps on the stairs and Inspector Fitzgerald came into the room. Tom's heart sank as Fitzgerald started to go through the sequence of events.

"So, let me see – first CountessBratinsky does a runner from Paris to Wicklow. Then she sends a postcard suggesting that she's scared of something or someone, then she gets murdered – then Miss Radcliffe's father gets burgled and bopped on the head, and to top it all off your office gets done over. Now, what, I wonder, have you two been doing to get someone so upset?"

Doing your job for you Fitzgerald he wanted to say, but Regan's glance warned him to keep his mouth shut. "Willi, I'll talk to you later," he said. "I have to get to the airport."

As Tom went down the stairs Fitzgerald shouted after him "And I do not want to read any of this on the front of the *Wicklow Herald* – or hear it on the lunchtime news either, for that matter. Do I make myself clear?" Tom banged the front door in response.

\#

Tom polished his shoes with unusual care in the morning, and made sure to put on his good tie and his best tweed jacket. He was fixing his tie and brushing his hair when he thought to himself: "cop on to yourself - what in God's name are you doing? "He put the jacket back in the wardrobe and pulled on his usual anorak.

The flight from Heathrow arrived on time and as they drove out to Bray, Tom and Olga had time to catch up. The UK police had made no progress in finding out who had broken into Olga's house and attacked her father, and regarded it as another minor instance of rural crime. Since nothing had been stolen and no one was injured, it was hardly worth pursuing.

"I told them about Irina's death and the postcard from Paris, but they didn't treat it very seriously. Said he couldn't see any connection. The officer in charge said he would speak to Inspector Fitzgerald, but there's not much else they can do. He looked at me as if he thought I was some kind of hysterical fantasist. I thought they'd take it more seriously, given that Dad is an MP and a member of the Defence Committee.

I'm worried about leaving him on his own – "and he's worried about me. I catch him watching me when he thinks I'm not looking. He had a stroke the year after mother died, and he's not able to travel much. He didn't want me to come for the inquest, said 'let it go', but I feel I owe it to Irina. It's the end of an era, now the whole Bratinsky line has come to an end."

Olga looked at him in dismay when he told her about his office break-in

"I have no idea what they were looking for," he said. "Is it a coincidence, or is there some connection? I have no idea."

Tom looked at Olga wondering: what did she know that she wasn't telling? He'd never come across a family like this before: part Russian, part French, part English with a dash of Irish thrown in for good measure. They were very different: his father had a bookcase – her father had a library. His family lived in a detached bungalow in the suburbs of Dublin: her family lived in a country house on an estate in the country. And they didn't mean a housing estate. Still, he liked her.

"Of course, it's bloody well connected – there's no other explanation. First Irina gets killed, then the postcard arrives with its cryptic message, then my father is attacked during an attempted break-in and now your office is trashed. What does Fitzgerald make of it?"

"He asked exactly the same questions you did. Word for word. He seems to think that maybe I knew something that I'm not telling, and that maybe I'm holding out for some big newspaper exposé. I only wish! Beyond that, I didn't get much information.

THE BRATINSKY AFFAIR

But then he and I are not exactly on confidential terms at the moment."

He pulled in on the Main Street. "I'll drop you at the hotel. You can have a rest and if you like we can go for a bite to eat. I can show you the sights of Bray."

"That would be great, but I'm tired and I'm nervous about tomorrow, so I need to get an early night."

"OK I'll call for you around six."

Tom arrived on the dot of six to find Olga sitting on one of the cane sofas in the porch of the Royal Starlight Hotel. The old hotel had been revamped in the sixties and gave a fairly good impression of being on the Costa del Sol, though when you looked closely it had seen better days. But it was central. In the morning they could walk up to the end of Main Street to the District Court.

"There was a wedding on inside so I thought I'd sit out here to escape the noise," she said, standing.

"It's early yet and it's a lovely evening. Let's go for a walk along the seafront – and if you're lucky I'll buy you an ice cream!"

"Are you flirting with me, Tom O'Brien?" and she laughed. Tom cringed inwardly. One part of him wanted to kiss her. The other part wanted to run away. They walked in silence for a while. When they reached the seafront they stopped and looked at the view. The dodgems had closed up for the winter but there were still quite a few people out and about walking their dogs or enjoying the sunshine. He could reach out, put an arm around her shoulders and pull her to him but something stopped him. Something always stopped him.

"Kind of like Brighton, isn't it?" she said.

"I don't know, I've never been. Haven't travelled much, except ten days in Moscow and Petersburg when I was in second year."

Olga was startled. "You've been to Russia – how come?"

Tom stopped and stood with his back to the terrace looking out across the promenade.

"I did history and politics with an optional language. So I took Russian for the first two years. I wanted to do something new and different. I could have done French but I hated our French teacher at school and have avoided it ever since. All we ever seemed to do back then was recite lists of irregular verbs and practice making vowel sounds through our noses. The Students' Union was very left-wing in those days and they organised one of these subsidised cultural exchanges. You know the kind of thing – solidarity of the workers across international borders!"

"Me too!" said Olga. "Or rather, I did Russian language and literature but I've never been to Russia. I've mixed feelings about the whole Russia thing and my Russian leaves a lot to be desired."

"Why?"

"It's a long and complicated story, but the short version is that my mother and Irina hadn't seen much of each other for several years, at least until I was born. Irina always felt that Mum could have done better for herself, and my father resented that. In fact, until my mother was diagnosed with cancer Irina was more or less a stranger, even though she loomed over our lives from a distance.

Isn't it odd? I never think of her as granny or grandmother – always Irina. She was definitely not the grandmotherly type! No knitting and making borscht for her. Ana was my real grandmother. I was only six when she died but I think of her often. I still have her cookery book. In fact, one of the few times we were all together was when we went to Paris for Ana's eightieth birthday. It was just the four of us: Ana, Irina, mother and me in the house in Auteuil. Dad made some excuse not to go – an international delegation or something like that, but I think he wanted to leave the four of us to enjoy the time together. It was one of the happiest times I can remember. We sat in the kitchen reminiscing and telling stories. Ana made my favourite cake – chocolate sponge filled with chocolate butter cream and filled with fresh strawberries from her garden. If I close my eyes I can almost taste it.

A week later we got the phone call. Ana was dead. One of her old Russian pals had called around and found her sitting in the garden with the book of Akmatova's poems in her lap. There were bits of bread around her feet. She had clearly been feeding the birds. Her heart had been bad for years and it looked as though it had finally given out and she had slipped quietly away.

Of course, Irina couldn't resist the opportunity to make a gala performance out of the funeral in the Russian cemetery. Every duke, prince or count within 500 miles was there. I was small so it was all a bit of a blur. My father went reluctantly but even he had to concede that Irina had given her mother a fitting send-off."

"What was Irina like?"

"Is this an interview for the paper?"

"Nooooo! I'd like to know – that's all."

Olga paused and thought. "She was tall and beautiful and dressed elegantly – couture, always Chanel. I think it was her payback for the days when she didn't have money. I mean, you can see that in the photos. She was always … distant – not quite cold, but she had a way of looking at you, with her head slightly on one side that made you feel you were being weighed up. It took me a while to get used to her."

She paused and thought. "She was tough, and secretive. Sometimes, though, especially if she'd had a couple of glasses of champagne, she could loosen up, and be quite fun. And of course, she was smart and knowledgeable – antiques and all that. I *loved* her apartment in Paris – so chic in that very French way. I worked for her in the shop for the last two summers. I stayed in the apartment over the shop and she stayed in the apartment on rue du Bac, my other favourite part of Paris.

After my mother died in 1973 things got a bit complicated. First, we all retreated into our respective shells to deal with our grief. Ana and my mother were the glue that held the whole thing together. Then my father had his stroke and I thought I might lose him as well. He became my priority and there was almost no contact with Irina which was also unfair on her because she had lost both her mother and her daughter. She must have felt a bit abandoned.

Then, out of the blue we fell into each other's lives again: I was in my final year of Russian Art and Literature and I needed to do a placement. I wanted to focus on modern Russian art so I applied to Sotheby's who handle a lot of the big Russian sales. To my surprise they accepted me. Just before the big spring Russian sale they announced that we were going to have a lecture from a leading expert on Fabergé. When Irina walked into the lecture room, she pretended to be as astonished as I was. Of course, she knew I was doing the course which was probably why she agreed to give the lecture in the first place. Irina dazzled everyone with her knowledge and her style. The others on the course couldn't believe me. "She's your grandmother!!! I thought maybe your aunt, but grandmother!! Some of the snobby girls who work in art galleries instead of going to finishing school, and who had largely ignored me up until then, became terribly friendly.

We went for lunch and after that we would meet up any time she was in London. It was hard not to be impressed by Irina. I mean, she had it all: –looks, brains and so much style. However, there was always a slight distance and she never wanted to talk about the things that mattered, Ana , mother, life in Russia, how she survived the early years. A series of closed doors. Instead she wanted to know what my plans were: what I planned to do: what career I wanted to focus on: did I have a boyfriend – on and on. Then she suggested I come to Paris for the summer. She needed help in the shop. Her assistant had gone off on maternity leave and she was stuck, or so she said.

Dad wasn't keen but if you wanted to learn about Russian art, Irina was the woman to teach you, and boy was she a tough teacher. She always used to say, "Never forget, Olga, it's a business, it's all about the money." I think my father was afraid that she would try to manipulate me as she had my mother. And he was right. Irina was always trying to work on me, bringing me to her favourite clothes shops or encouraging me to get my hair done. There was this boutique called Light on the Champs Elysées and she was forever dragging me in there and getting me to try on things. She would say: "it fits you perfectly, you have to buy it." I had to buy a new suitcase to take all the loot back to London." She thought my Russian was atrocious and I thought

THE BRATINSKY AFFAIR

she sounded like something out of a nineteenth-century novel! I did have one major bust up with her. She had been on at me for days and days about this party she wanted me to go to in some big country house. I knew exactly what she was up to. She was matchmaking. She never stopped: what was I going to wear? Did I not want to lighten my hair? Did I not need a new evening dress? I finally snapped one day in the middle of Galeries Lafayette. "Irina, stop trying to turn me into my mother. I can't be her," I shouted. We were both mortified but after that she did back down and we got back to normal, eventually.

At the same time it was such fun! I was 23 and working in the most beautiful parts of Paris and we always got invited to openings and parties and embassies. I think she was pleased to show that she did have a family: that she wasn't just this lonely old lady. Behind it all I think she was lonely. In the end, I did become fond of her and now, it's hard to believe that they are all gone: Ana, mother, Irina. I'm the last of the Bratinsky women and I only know part of the story.

Tom stayed quiet, letting Olga's flow of reminiscence go on. He could tell that she needed to let it all out. He was surprised that despite her background she wasn't at all snobby and they chatted away as if they had been friends for years.

Olga stared out over the sea.

"Irina was a great one for the grand gestures – like a beautiful icon at Christmas or a piece of jewellery for my birthday or my name day. But most of the time she was very much the CountessBratinsky. My father couldn't stand her, felt she had bullied Mother, and I sometimes felt that being her only granddaughter I didn't quite measure up. Another disappointment."

Olga smiled: "sorry to burden you with all this but I don't have anybody else to talk to. My father doesn't want to talk about it and my friends in London are only interested in going to parties and having fun."

"I know the feeling said Tom. "I was so angry after my mother died. She hadn't been sick but we all noticed that she seemed to get tired easily. Then out of the blue, lung cancer. The doctors said she might get 5 years. In the end she barely got 2. I didn't want to talk to anyone. My father is great but I didn't want to make it harder for him. As for my brother, Dermot, he didn't want to go there. 'No point dwelling on it" he said. "Just get on with your life. Shit happens."

It's never easy, is it?" Olga said briefly nudging his shoulder, "but come on, let's move; I'm getting cold."

"What did you mean when you said you felt were a disappointment to Irina?"

"That's another long story… and I'm starving… let's find somewhere to eat."

Olga wanted something light so Tom suggested Kelly's pub. As well as being the oldest pub in Bray it had also recently developed a great name for food. Tom led Olga into the snug. You could go in either from the bar or the lounge and it had a fire blazing in its own fireplace, so it was a great spot for a quiet chat. Olga had a glass of white wine and he had a pint of Guinness and they both ordered the seafood platter with prawns, smoked salmon and salads.

"My lord, Tom, this would feed a family of four!"

One of the advantages of the snug was that there was a mirror on opposite the hatch into the bar and if you leaned the right way you got a good view of who was in the lounge. Olga had squeezed lemon on her prawns and reached for a napkin when she froze.

"That man."

Tom leaned over to look. "Where?"

"The two men in the corner by the window – the one on the right – he was on my flight."

Tom sensed that Olga was getting jittery so he did his best to downplay the significance of the man's appearance, though he made sure to get a good look at him through the hatch.

"No big deal – so were a hundred and twenty other people – and after all Ireland is a small country. It's hard to avoid people, even if you want to."

Then Inspector Fitzgerald walked in with Willi Regan and joined the men. There was a lot of handshaking and manly

THE BRATINSKY AFFAIR

laughter before they ordered a round of pints.

"See what I mean, Tom? I think he followed me."

"You're becoming paranoid, Olga"

"Well, you know the old story – the fact that you're paranoid doesn't mean that you're not being followed."

They both laughed and clinked their glasses: "touché" said Tom.

At that moment the young bar man arrived to see if they were happy with their food. Tom had been at school with him. "Mikey, any idea who the boyos are, over in the corner with Fitzgerald. It's embarrassing. I know I've met them but for the life of me I can't place them."

"Unlikely. They're cops. Foreign I gather. Something to do with the murder of that Russian woman up in Kilquade. The one on the right is French. The other one is Russian though what he is doing here is anybody's guess."

"Thanks, Mikey. I must be thinking of someone else."

Mikey looked at him knowingly. "You're a journalist and I'm Father Christmas." Barmen miss nothing.

Olga couldn't relax and after waiting a few minutes to see if they could catch any of the conversation they decided to slip out through the bar, leaving their food behind them.

"Sorry about that," said Tom. "How about fish and chips out of a newspaper instead? You can have fresha cod or freshafresha cod!"

"What in God's name is freshafresha cod?"

"Fresha cod is square, box-shaped cod, and freshafresha cod is fish-shaped cod."

"No thanks, Tom – I think I lost my appetite. Anyway I'm a bit tired and could do with an early night so if you don't mind, I'll head back to the hotel. I'll see you in the morning. By the way, thanks for listening to my tale of woe."

≠

Tom headed home along the seafront and the side road that would take him up towards Bray Head. When his parents had bought the house in the 1940s it was still out in the country. Now, the new houses were closing in around it, but from the field at the back of the house you could still look out to sea. The walk would do him good. He needed to think things through and work out what was going on.

And what on earth was Willi Regan up to? He had never known Willi to be friendly with Fitzgerald…though Willi made it his business to know everybody in Bray, especially anybody who had influence with the owners of the paper. It wasn't a fluke that Willi Regan had held onto the editor's job for the last thirty years and in the process made *The Wicklow Herald* one of the most profitable newspapers in the country. As for the grey men…maybe Uncle Dan would know who they were.

He tried to analyse what was going on. What was behind the murder of CountessBratinsky? There was the Irish connection, the French business connection, her French political connections and the Russian connection. The Irish connection seemed the least likely. That left French politics, French business or possibly some vague Russian connection from sixty years ago. Realistically, the answer had to lie in Paris. He kept moving the options around in his head like a game of find the lady until he began to develop a headache.

Tom took the long way round by the seafront. He told himself that the fresh air would do him good. The case wasn't the only thing that had his head spinning. Tom had dated a couple of girls in college but nothing serious. There was always something that made him pull back. Tess Maguire was the closest he had ever come to a real girlfriend, but even that hadn't worked out. He thought it would all sort itself out if he had sex but even that hadn't helped. A few frenzied grapplings in the back of his father's car with tourists down from Dublin during the summer season hadn't changed anything. He had hoped the right girl would come along and save him from himself but he still found himself noticing the good looking guys in his class or the handsome Italian who worked in the ice cream parlour on the sea front. He glanced up the promenade to see if it was still open but the shutters were down. He looked at his watch – almost midnight. These days he found himself thinking about sex all the time. In the bus last week he hadn't realised he was staring until the conductor asked him "what are you looking at?"

Tom walked further up the promenade and stopped to look out over the bay. Out of the corner of his eye he could see movement 100 yards or so away, up near the gents' toilets. He knew what went on there, though he had never had the courage to do anything himself. Walk up and down – sit for a while on the bench beside the toilet – pretend to admire the view - a short conversation then drift off together. Even though he didn't have the nerve to do anything the thought of it made him unbelievably horny. Tom had walked along the promenade a million times but recently he kept ending up at the same spot. He was so engrossed in his thoughts that he hadn't heard anyone approach until a voice beside him said

"Nice evening."

He nearly jumped out of his skin.

"It is. Maybe we'll get a bit of decent weather." God that sounded so lame.

His heart was beating ninety to the dozen, part fear, part excitement. He didn't know what to say or do. A quick glance sideways told him he was a youngish man, may be a few years older than Tom himself. He was a good looking guy with a tache, wearing denims and a check shirt with the sleeves rolled up. He was gripping the railing with both hands. Their hands were barely an inch apart and all it would have taken was a single casual movement to make contact. More than anything else Tom wanted to reach out and touch the golden fuzz that curled around the watch on his tanned wrist. He had the kind of tan that you only get from working outdoors in all weathers. Tom found himself wondering if it was a farmer's tan that stopped half way up his arm. He smiled.

"And what's going on here?" The voice froze him to the spot and he turned to see two Gardaí standing a few feet away.

"Nothing, Gard, just stopped for a smoke, to admire the view." Tom's legs were shaking so much he thought he was going to vomit.

"Well, you'd better be moving on."

As Tom turned to go the Gard flashed the light of his torch

across his face.

"You're John O'Brien's son, aren't you?"

"I am," said Tom. There was no point lying.

"A decent man your father. You wouldn't want to be seen hanging around here in future. There's all sorts of unsavoury characters about. You don't want to get a name for yourself."

"Yes, Gard"

Tom legged it out of there as fast as he could and didn't stop walking until he got to the beginning of Bray Head. He had no idea where the other fellow went. He sat for a while on the bench at the top of the hill waiting for his blood pressure to settle and his knees to stop shaking. He could vaguely hear the sound of the distant waves and wished he had a cigarette. He had given them up the year after his mother died to please his father. Oonagh had been a heavy smoker and his father blamed the dark green packs that were always on the kitchen table for her early death.

Jesus, Mary and Joseph that was a close run thing.

Tom knew that sooner or later he would have to make a choice and in his heart of hearts he knew that the choice was already made. Part of the problem was that, besides the obvious thing of being a gay man in a small town, he was John O'Brien's son. His father knew everybody and everybody knew him. Every conversation started or ended with "How is your father doing?" He loved his father and enjoyed being at home with him, but if he was serious about being a journalist then the chances were that he would soon be leaving Bray. He had no intention of doing mart reports for the next twenty-five years. He could be the next Willi Regan, but he wanted something more. Meanwhile, the thought of his father knowing about him made him feel sick. The Bratinsky story had brought all these issues into sharp focus. It was a big world out there and he wanted to be part of it. He needed space to be Tom O'Brien.

THE BRATINSKY AFFAIR

CHAPTER 8

Paris 1930

Ana looked after Masha while Irina went to work, and she would spend the day talking to the baby, reminiscing about the good old days and telling stories of the heroic exploits of their noble ancestors.

Masha always wanted to hear the story of their Irish ancestor General Count O'Rourke de Breffny leading the charge against Napoleon at the battle of Leipzig, and how he had been presented with a diamond-studded sword by the King of Prussia. The story was enacted with a box of toy soldiers and a wooden figure of the hero on horseback. As a child Irina had heard her father tell that same story to her brother Pavel many times, but now she wanted to shout at her mother "It's all over – forget it." Instead, she bit her lip and went for a walk.

Those were the hours when she got to know Paris: walking along the Seine, through the park behind Notre Dame, or if she was stressed, the full length of the Champs-Élysées, across the Place de la Concorde and into Catherine de' Medici's Tuileries Gardens. She always kept a book in her pocket and would pretend to be reading it if there was a predatory male lurking. The Louvre was her great resource as the days got colder especially on Sundays when she didn't have to pay. After a while she had a mental list of all her favourite paintings in the collection.

Sometimes, if she didn't have much time she would go straight up the main staircase, past the enormous statue of the winged victory of Samothrace, to see the Botticelli's on the first floor. There was something serene in these visions of beauty that helped to steady her nerves, and she would walk out feeling better able to face the world. One Sunday she had arranged to meet her friend Sofia there and was sitting waiting for her on the edge of the statue where she could see who was coming in through the main door. A sleazy looking middle-aged man sidled over to her and muttered "lots of people here today, heh? petit chat."; Normally Irina would have panicked but just at that moment she saw Sofia coming up the staircase towards her and the two of them walked off up the stairs giggling like two school girls.

As winter drew on Irina would sometimes buy a paper bag of roasted chestnuts as a treat. They helped to keep her hands warm and stopped her thinking as she walked along, looking at the shop windows and the clothes she could no longer afford.

\#

The only good thing about the room they were in now was that no one, apart from the concierge, would see her leaving home in the evening and coming back early in the morning. Madame Rostand was different from the Parisian tradition of dragon concierges and had been kind to her. Her own husband had been killed in the first war, a year after she was married, and she knew at first-hand how tough it was to get by. She tipped Irina off about which butcher sold the cheapest cuts of meat and which grocer sold off fading vegetables cheaply at the end of the day.

Irina and Ana did their best to keep up an aristocratic facade. They went to Mass in the Alexander Nevsky Cathedral, even though this meant enduring the knowing smiles of the Russian ladies. Irina still had some decent clothes that would pass muster. Her taste was classic, so things didn't date, and she and her mother were more or less the same size so they could swap their skirts, shawls and blouses. She pulled out her navy crêpe de chine shirt dress, printed with bunches of cherries and the red hat matching her red lipstick when she needed to look her best.

Sometimes Irina met her friend Sofia for coffee, but no cake, at the MuséeJacquemart-André. Its palatial rooms were still furnished like a private house, and for an hour she could pretend that the revolution and the war were something she had dreamt. She was back in her home with its gracious rooms, stepping out into the forest surrounding the family dacha for an hour with her father, learning to shoot with one of his many hunting guns or galloping through the trees on one of her mother's glossy Cossack ponies.

Before the revolution SofiaKonstantinova had been a star in the Bolshoi Theatre and MariinskyOpera Company. Now, she was lucky to get an occasional recital or some teaching. Every so often she would appear with a different admiring gentleman. They would invite Irina to join them for dinner to meet some of their friends. Irina usually said no, she was tired and had to get up in the morning.

One beautiful spring evening Irina finally gave in and accepted an invitation to join Sofia and some of her friends for dinner. She needed to remind herself that she was still a young, attractive woman and to escape the monotony of worrying about money, scrabbling around for cheap food and looking after her mother and Masha. She needed some fun!

It was a small group: Sofia and her beau, Antoine; one of Antoine's friends, Serge, a journalist, with his girlfriend, Odile or Odette, something like that; and another man, Gerard – a policeman and former army officer. He had fought in the French forces in the Crimea and still floated around the edges of the Russian community. Some people thought he worked for French Intelligence, keeping an eye on the Russian exiles. He was good-looking, in a fleshy sort of way, but his easy charm and eager smile appeared too contrived. *What was the word? Smarmy – that was it.*

Still, Irina felt flattered by his attention. It was a chance to sit back, have an adult conversation and focus on herself for a while. Irina had been too busy struggling to survive since Egon left to have time for romance but surely there was no harm in a bit of harmless flirtation. The restaurant was a simple bistro but the food was good, and to Irina, after such a long struggle, it was the height of luxury. No cabbage! As dinner wound down, Serge and his girl drifted off, while Sofia and Antoine were so engrossed in each other that Irina and Gerard were left to their own devices.

"Why don't we go on somewhere else– leave these two lovebirds on their own?" Gerard moved his chair closer than was strictly necessary. Irina felt it was time to make a strategic exit.

When he persisted, Irina stood up to go." My daughter is at home and my mother will be worried."

"At least let me drive you home, my car is round the corner."

Irina hesitated, but... at least she would get home at a reasonable time. She reluctantly agreed. As she leaned in to kiss Sofia goodnight, Sofia whispered, "Careful with that one, he has a reputation."

Irina settled into the passenger seat, wondering if this had been such a good idea. When the car turned in the opposite direction to home, she began to be worried.

"Where are we going? This isn't my way home."

"Don't worry, this is a short cut." He drove on and when he pulled into a narrow street beside the river Irina knew she was in trouble. As the car slowed to a stop by a park, in the shadow of a church, she said, "Let me out – I'm leaving now."

"What's the matter? I thought you liked me?" Gerard leaned across and Irina thought he was going to open the door for her. Instead, he pulled her towards him and mashed a kiss onto her lips.

She had kept her nails perfect, manicured and buffed to a shine. Now he seized her hands and kissed the palms wetly. "You pretend you're classy, but you have the hands of a working woman." His breath was thick in his throat. Irina tried to push him away. He tightened his grip on her arm and she cried out. He sneered. "Don't play so hard to get. You know the score – like your friend Sofia. You be nice to me; I'll be nice to you."

By this time, he was on top of her and pulling at her dress. As Irina fought back, he slapped her across the face, and she felt a trickle of blood from the corner of her mouth. "You're not in Saint Petersburg now, missy, and a girl has to pay her way."

He panted and pushed against her, at the same time pushing down his trousers. The smell of sweat and cheap aftershave brought her back to Helsinki. No way! This was not going to happen again. Irina fought and kicked as hard as she could but that seemed to excite him all the more. As she writhed out of his way – Irina felt something cold and hard pressing into her back – a gun, stuffed in between the seat and back. She dragged it out by the handle and pressed the muzzle against his forehead. "If you don't get off me now, I'm going to blow your brains out."

Gerard froze. "What the hell do you think you're doing, you stupid bitch?

Give me that." He made to grab the gun, but Irina whipped it away and stuck the muzzle up under his chin, clicking the safety into the firing position.

THE BRATINSKY AFFAIR

Her heart was beating nineteen to the dozen, but outwardly she appeared calm and completely in control. She spoke slowly and clearly. "I am getting out of this car now, and if you try to stop me, I will shoot you." It hadn't occurred to her before, but instinct told her he was married. "Imagine how your wife will feel if you're found dead in a car, late at night with your trousers round your ankles. But then, something tells me this isn't the first time you've pulled this stunt."

Gerard slumped back in his seat but Irina knew he was weighing up his chances of grabbing the gun. "Don't try it. My father taught me to shoot and I rarely miss. The only question is whether to shoot you in the head or shoot you in the balls. I think I'll aim for the balls – that way you'll take longer to die. And I'll keep the gun as a souvenir of this little adventure. You can explain to your boss how you lost it."

Irina backed out of the car and ran towards the lights of a café she could see facing the church on the other side of the park, stuffing the gun into her bag as she went. As she walked into the patch of light from the café, Irina heard the car accelerate and screech off round the corner.

When Irina was sure he had gone her nerves gave way and she threw up against a wall. After she had pulled herself together Irina went up to the bar and ordered a glass of white wine, to steady her nerves. She pulled her hat down over her eyes and avoided looking around at the other customers. The barman was sitting on a stool at the end of the bar chatting to a girl and out of the corner of her eye Irina could feel them watching her. After a few minutes the girl came over and stood beside her: "Are you alright? I mean; I couldn't help noticing and she glanced down at Irina's torn dress. Irina knew that if she said anything about what had happened she would fall apart.

"I'm fine, honestly. Just a bit upset – had an argument with my boyfriend." The girl smiled, "Ok, if you're sure." As she turned to go she put a square white hanky on the zinc counter, looked at Irina and pointed to her own lip. Irina glanced in the mirror behind the bar and noticed the smudge of blood in the corner of her mouth. Irina nodded at her sadly, a silent communication between women and got up to go. "Thank you, you've been very kind." Later, she was about to drop the gun into a canal as she made her way home when she thought better of it. The way things were who knew when she might need it.

As she clicked open the door into the dim light of the hallway Irina walked straight into Madame Rostand, who was putting out the rubbish. She took one look at the torn dress and the bruises and dragged Irina into her cosy apartment. Without asking any questions she poured her a glass of brandy and went to get a basin of warm water and a cloth. When she came back, she sat beside Irina and wiped her face, her hands gentle. The water smelt of antiseptic and stung when she touched Irina's cut lip.

"Some things never change, my dear." The warm cloth moved up over her face, stroking away the terror. "You know, some men think that if you are poor and vulnerable, they can do anything they want. I know that story all too well. For them it's a game of winner takes all. People like charming Monsieur Marchand up on the first floor. You know him, the nice, stylish lawyer. Thinks he looks like the perfect English gentleman. Nice is as nice does, I say. Just don't ever find yourself alone with him." She kept talking quietly until Irina had calmed down and fixed her face as much as possible. "But a pretty girl like you, you need to be more careful."

As Irina was about to go, she turned back. "Madame Rostand, please, don't…" but Madame Rostand forestalled her "Don't worry – I see everything but I know nothing."

Irina tiptoed into the apartment without switching on the light and slipped into bed. She could tell that Ana was still awake, but the last thing she wanted was to have to explain to her mother what had happened. She lay awake for a long time, thinking about what lay ahead. Before the war everything had been so clearly mapped out. She was young and beautiful and the O'Rourkes, if not hugely rich, were well connected at court and in army circles. She would study art or music, maybe spend a year in Paris or Rome, after which she would marry someone suitable and raise a family. Now, here she was: twenty-nine and divorced, an exile with no money and no prospects.

THE BRATINSKY AFFAIR

CHAPTER 9

Wicklow March 1976: Coroner's Court
The inquest started the next morning at ten sharp. Olga and Tom were heading up to the District Court when they walked into Tom's Uncle Dan. Tom introduced him to Olga as they shook hands.

"Miss Radcliffe, I'm sorry we have to meet in such circumstances," said the doctor, doffing his hat in gentlemanly fashion. He told Tom he would be representing the State Pathologist's office, as he had done the post mortem on Irina's body.

As they took their seats in the court Olga nudged Tom's knee. She nodded towards the front of the court. "Look who's here? It's Captain Haddock and the Thompson twins"

Inspector Fitzgerald was sitting in the front row with the two men from Kelly's pub. He spotted Tom and Olga immediately but all they got was the barest nod.

"Friendly sort, isn't he?" said Olga.

It was all Tom could do not to laugh.

The coroner came in and the proceedings were brisk.

Inspector Fitzgerald gave his evidence. Then it was Uncle Dan's turn. Tom could feel Olga stiffening in the seat beside him as Dan described his examination of the body. After the fire officer gave his report it was pretty much all over.

It didn't take the coroner long to reach his conclusion.

"Unlawful killing! said Olga. "What was the point of all that? I could have told him that! We waited all this time for a statement of the blindingly obvious – it's as if we are all going through the motions and no one is interested in finding out who killed Irina. At seventy-five years of age, having escaped a revolution two steps ahead of the Red Army, crossed Europe without papers and made a life in France – to die, murdered in the middle of nowhere, in Ireland of all places. It seems a dismal ending."

Tom thought it best to let her anger run its course and said nothing. They met Uncle Dan on the way out again. "There you have it, Tom, your first murder case. My condolences again, Miss Radcliffe."

Olga looked at Dan, "Oh – please call me Olga. One thing, though. Can you explain what happens next, Dr O'Brien?

"I'll call you Olga if you call me Dan. A file will go to the Director of Public Prosecutions, who will see if there is enough evidence for a prosecution. In the meantime, the Gardaí will continue their investigation."

#

The funeral a few days later was a low-key affair. In the end Olga had decided to bury Irina in the old cemetery in Kilquade, just down from the Russian village. Ana had been buried in the Russian cemetery in Paris, but it was now closed to new burials so that was no longer an option. To bury her with Masha in England made no sense, and after all Irina had found some kind of peace in Ireland.

The church in Kilquade was quiet and peaceful. Olga had picked a spot near a grove of birch trees that were an echo of Russia. There had been a church there for more than two hundred years and the building had a quiet country elegance that had escaped the heavy hand of reforming curates. She had even been able to find an orthodox priest. Father Couriss, like Irina, had been born in Russia before the Revolution and had lived in Ireland for many years.

"I think Irina would have approved even though she wasn't religious– the right kind of Russian."

There were as many press as mourners at the funeral. There was even a photographer from Reuters covering the funeral for the French media. Olga had put the announcement in *The Irish Times* more for form's sake than thinking anyone would turn up. In the end the church was packed. All the neighbours from the Russian Village came, an attaché from the French Embassy, a scattering of antique dealers and, astonishingly, the community of exiled Russians had turned out in force. Even old Count Tolstoy came over from Delgany.

Like Irina they had fled the Revolution and by some quirk of fate ended up in Ireland. They were all getting on now, but

THE BRATINSKY AFFAIR

coming to the funeral was a way of connecting to a time when they were young and did not know that everything they knew would soon be obliterated. They were a collection of ghosts, remnants of a world that no longer existed.

Olga stood at the graveside in the icy wind receiving condolences from people she had never met. Inspector Fitzgerald and the Thompson Twins stood discreetly out of the way but in a place where they could see everything that was going on. Olga was stepping away from the grave when she turned to Tom and grasped his sleeve.

"See that man standing other there opposite the churchyard gate? There's something Russian about him, but he's making no attempt to join the old Russian expats who all seem to know each other."

Tom looked over. The man was a stranger, standing with his face muffled up in a scarf, and a hat pulled down over his brow. He didn't look particularly Russian to him – a big coat, strong shoes, could be Irish, could be anything.

In the pub afterwards Count Tolstoy came over to speak to Olga. He took her hand and pressed it. "I didn't even know Irina lived so close. You know, I knew your grandmother in another life. I was twenty-one and she was sixteen and all we wanted was for the war to be over so life could go back to normal. Little did we know what lay in store. And after all that, to end up here, like this. Such a pity. Now, would you do an old man a favour and walk me out to my car. Nice to have a young arm to lean on. Arthritis, you know, the bane of my life."

Count Tolstoy was quite sprightly for his age and showed no evidence of arthritis. Before he got into his car, he turned to say goodbye. "A word to the wise my dear – I assume you saw our friend from the Embassy?"

"Embassy? Oh, do you mean the French attaché?"

"No, no – our dear comrade from the Russian Embassy. He was the one standing outside the gate –moustache, square shoulders, and cheap coat – trying to look as inconspicuous as possible but sticking out like a sore thumb. They all do."

"But why on earth?"

"They keep a discreet eye on us old relics, just in case. Listening for whispers of conspiracy, I suppose, and of course your grandmother's death has been in all the papers so it was bound to attract attention and bring the community together. You know what they say: where two or three Russians are gathered together at least one of them is bound to be a spy. Can't see any of this lot storming the barricades though, can you?"

As he got into the car, he kissed her hand and said goodbye. There was something so sincere and courtly about the old-fashioned gesture that tears came to her eyes. When the last of the mourners had drifted away Olga was telling Tom what Count Tolstoy had said when Inspector Fitzgerald and the twins came up.

"My sympathies again, Miss Radcliffe. I wonder if you wouldn't mind calling to the station whenever it's convenient. There are a few things I want to clarify – nothing major."

He nodded to Dan and ignored Tom.

"Certainly," said Olga. "How about tomorrow morning? Around ten?"

The next morning, as Olga was shown into Inspector Fitzgerald's office she found the Twins already there.

"How can I help you, Inspector?"

"A few points I need to clarify. You mentioned previously that your grandmother…"

"Sorry, Inspector," Olga interrupted. "These two gentlemen are…?"

Fitzgerald was taken aback that she had the nerve to interrupt him.

"This is Captain Balmot of the French Sûreté and this is Major Semenov of the Russian Ministry of the Interior."

Olga adopted her most aristocratic tone. "I see – and may I ask what interest the Sûreté and an officer ofthe Russian Ministry of the Interiorhave in the murder of a French citizen in Ireland?"

"It's normal procedure when a French citizen is murdered abroad, and the Russian police is keeping a watching brief on the case… because of the ehhhemmmvarious international angles. It seems your grandmother had a lot of influential friends," he

THE BRATINSKY AFFAIR

added hastily changing the subject.

The dynamic of the meeting had changed and it was Olga who was interviewing Fitzgerald, but he was not so easily put off. "Can you tell me about your grandmother's business?"

"What's to tell – she was an antique dealer specialising in Russian art and jewellery. She was a recognised specialist."

"Your grandmother made a lot of money in this competitive business. Would you have any idea who she did business with or where she got some of the pieces?"

"I didn't know my grandmother well, and I certainly didn't know the ins and outs of her business."

"Let's leave that for a moment. Do you by any chance know of anyone who might have had a grudge against your grandmother?"

"In terms of grudges I imagine there would be quite a few. She was a tough businesswoman, ruthless even, and she didn't entertain fools, but I wouldn't know them. If you mean enemies, I can't think of any. I don't know why anyone would go so far as to kill her. She wasn't political, and the whole Russian thing was a lifetime ago. So, in short – no."

"But your grandmother had a number of political friends."

"She certainly knew a lot of wealthy and prominent people – but that was business – as to them being political, I couldn't say."

He flicked a newspaper cutting across the table to her. It was Tom's article in the *Wicklow Herald* with the photograph she had given him.

"Notice anything?"

"It's a beautiful photograph of Irina at a ball."

"Not any ball. It was the New Year Ball in the Hôtel Matignon– *the official residence of the Prime Minister of France*. Now, look more closely –do you recognise the two gentlemen beside your grandmother?"

"I haven't a clue."

"Let me enlighten you. One is the Prime Minister of France and the other is the head of the French intelligence service."

"But why is this so important – you meet all kinds of people at these big social events– it means nothing."

"*Au contraire*, Miss Radcliffe." The tone was sarcastic and altogether tougher now. The gloves were coming off and the use of the French term was clearly intended to irritate her. "This event in the Hôtel Matignon wasn't any old party – it was restricted to a select and well vetted list of people, all with high level security clearance."

"I still don't see what this has to do with my grandmother's murder."

"I was hoping you might be able to enlighten me. After all, at a time when the Russians, the Chinese, the Americans and the French are all at each other's throats, and testing nuclear weapons to beat the band, we have a Russian friend of the Prime Minister of France, a woman whose background is, shall we say, a tad vague, murdered in Ireland in unexplained circumstances."

"I have no idea about any of this!"

"Clearly someone else thinks that you do. Your grandmother is murdered, your home is broken into and your father attacked, followed by the ransacking of O'Brien's office. Hardly a coincidence."

"Oh, for goodness sake – I told you already, Inspector, until recently I hardly knew my grandmother. It's only recently that I have got to know her at all."

"So you say."

"What exactly do you mean by that?"

"This woman you claim you hardly knew paid for your education and seems to have been in the habit of sending you cheques for quite large amounts of money. And, you worked in her shop for the past two summers, six months in total. Hardly strangers. Of course there's also the link to your father."

"What link? Dad despised Irina and had as little to do with her as he possibly could."

"Am I correct in stating that your father is Sir William Radcliffe, MP, chair of the Parliamentary Defence Committee?"

"Former chair – he stepped down two years ago."

"But he remains a member of the committee, which handles some quite sensitive security matters, isn't that right?

"Look Inspector, if you're trying to establish some spurious link between my father's committee work and Irina's political connections in Paris, you are wasting your time. As I keep saying, they didn't get on and they seldom saw each other, so I doubt this will prove a fruitful line of inquiry."

"In that case, let me ask you a slightly different question. Who would benefit from your grandmother's death?"

"Benefit?"

"Your mother is deceased, and in any case, as I understand it she and your grandmother were not on good terms. Is that correct?"

"Pretty much, though after my mother got sick Irina and she were in contact much more often and towards the end spent a lot of time together."

"But following your grandmother's death you are the only remaining blood relative – is that not so?"

"Yes. But why is this relevant?"

"You know the saying, *cui* bono."

Olga was baffled.

"Otherwise expressed as 'follow the money.'"

Captain Balmot broke in. "As I understand it, Mademoiselle, your grandmother was a very wealthy woman. Apart from the house in Wicklow; which I gather was well insured, there is a shop with its valuable contents, and the apartment in one of the most expensive locations in Paris, the place des Vosges, plus another apartment in the *très chic* rue du Bac – all of which would amount to a fine sum– and which one assumes you stand to inherit."

Olga held her nerve and stared him out. "As I don't yet know the contents of my grandmother's will, I can't answer your question. So maybe I stand to benefit, as you put it– or maybe not. Now, I think we're finished here."

She stood up to go. "Before I leave however, can I clarify one or two things with *you*, Inspector? Apart from making veiled insinuations, can I ask what progress you have made in finding my grandmother's murderer? I mean, you have the postcard from Paris, which I gave you, and you have Irina's necklace which Mr O'Brien found for you, and apart from that – well, there doesn't seem to be any progress – does there?"

"Early days yet, Miss Radcliffe – everything in due course."

"A nice turn of cliché, Inspector, but all in all, not informative. Perhaps the next time you need to 'clarify any small points" you could give me more notice – and I will be happy to attend – with my solicitor."

Olga walked out of the office but didn't bother closing the door behind her.

After she left, Fitzgerald whistled and grinned at the two men. "And she says the grandmother was a toughie!"

As she headed up the long corridor towards the front door Olga paused for a moment. Maybe she had been rude and should go back and apologise. She was still debating what to do when she heard the wooden floor creaking as someone walked over to close the door. Clearly Semenov, judging by the heavy smell of black tobacco that wafted out into the corridor. His deep base voice boomed out into the corridor:

"That girl's hiding something. Personally I'd bring her in and shake her until her teeth rattle. A couple of nights in a cell and a few slaps and she'd talk."

Olga stood still, afraid to move and equally afraid of being caught eavesdropping. When she heard Fitzgerald's reply she was so angry she wanted to march back in and put him straight. "Doesn't quite work like that here, Semenov, but for all that we'll keep an eye on her: the father too for that matter. He's a player on the UK's Defence Committee. Big on notions – short on cash. Might make him vulnerable. If we need to, we can bring her in later."

"And ask me precisely what?" Olga seethed inwardly.

Semenov grunted. "I'm not that interested in the father: it's what this girl knows about the Bratinsky woman's business that interests me. She's the key to it. It's not just a few pieces turning up here in Ireland: there's a chain of dealers in Europe selling antiques smuggled out of Russia from small provincial museums where the collections have never been properly catalogued. In most cases nobody even notices when something disappears: small stuff – a pair of silver candlesticks or a small picture.

THE BRATINSKY AFFAIR

Nothing too big that would attract attention."

Olga thought back to the famous story of the silver Fabergé box that had turned up in Egan Auctioneers.

"We stumbled on it by accident. A young research student saw an icon in an auction catalogue and knew it was from a monastery in Ekaterinberg where she had done the research for her thesis. When we started looking we could see the pattern but not who's behind it. .Personally I'd shoot the bastards."

At that point Olga wanted to run away. This was all too incredible to take in. For a moment she was terrified that Semenov was going to step out into the corridor but he stopped just inside the room before continuing.

"We lost so much during the war and now we're being robbed again by our own. Not that most of my colleagues give a shit. They'd have their hand out for a share in the take. But I'd make that girl squeal until we fit all the pieces of the puzzle together. It would be no harm if you came to Petersburg to meet my team and help us fit it all together, one piece at a time. This investigation will take time and I don't want to do anything that will scare off the big boys. Softly, softly catchee monkey: isn't that what you British say?"

Olga could almost hear Fitzgerald grinding his teeth in irritation, but he said nothing as she

stood still and held her breath until the door finally clicked shut.

≠

Olga had arranged to meet Tom in Kelly's. He was sitting by the fire in the snug with the newspaper and a pint of Guinness in front of him when she went in. "Well?"

"God almighty, Tom, I need a drink – a gin and tonic."

"That bad, huh?"

"Oh, it was nothing! Merely an interrogation by the combined forces of the Irish police, the French police and a Russian police officer. Semenov seems to think I should be locked up straight away for interrogation about Irina possibly being part of an international ring selling stolen antiques from Russia and

Fitzgerald is having both me and Dad watched. He casually asked if maybe Irina was a spy and maybe I could remember whether or not I might have murdered her to inherit all her property."

"Well, was she? Did you?" asked Tom mischievously. At that moment the barman put Olga's drink on the table. She nodded thanks, then flicked an ice cube at Tom and said, "You, Tom O'Brien, are skating on very thin ice."

She took a gulp of her drink and started to relax.

Tom went silent for a minute and eventually Olga asked: "What's up?"

"There's something I never told you. I met your grandmother." Olga looked shocked.

"Well, I didn't exactly meet her. I was in the pub with Dad one day and she came in with a few other people so I only saw her from a distance. She was with a local auctioneer called Bill Egan and a couple of other antique dealers. Egan is more than a bit dodgy. It seems that your grandmother was using him to sell antiques that were smuggled out of Russia. She apparently had a contact, some guy called Dmitri and he was supposedly moving stuff on behalf of families who had kept their treasures hidden since the revolution and now needed hard currency. Not exactly criminal but not exactly kosher either. Now it looks as though that may have been just a cover story."

"And when were you planning to tell me all this?"

"I wasn't sure what to make of it but now it's beginning to make sense."

"Dear God. Have you any more little surprises for me? MY grandmother! the international antique dealer, maybe a spy and now an antique smuggler. The only thing missing is for her to have been an assassin working for the Gestapo during the war!!"

"Funny you should mention that" said Tom.

"Don't even go there, Tom. I need another drink after all that. On second thoughts I think I'll just go for a walk along the sea front before I head back to the hotel. I need to absorb all of this."

Tom walked up home, and sat up late chatting to his father and filling him in on all the developments in the case. John was

THE BRATINSKY AFFAIR

especially interested in the French and Russian involvement.

In the morning, despite the late night, John was up at seven and out to walk Mungo and get the paper. Then he sat in the bay window with a mug of coffee and opened his *Irish Times*. Mungo was contentedly sprawled on the floor in front of the Aga when the phone rang.

Tom was still in bed when his father came running up the stairs – "Tom, call for you –says it's urgent."

"Who is it? What time is it anyway?"

"Half past eight. It's that Radcliffe girl."

Mungo opened one eye to glance up as Tom flapped into the kitchen in his slippers. He wagged his tail a couple of times and went back to sleep.

"Olga! You're up early!"

"The police rang me." Her voice sounded panicked.

"What did Fitzgerald want at this time of the morning?"

"No! The French police! There's been a break-in at the apartment on the place des Vosges – they want me to go over."

"This is becoming a habit!" Tom accepted the mug of coffee his father handed him. "Hey, are you all right? Can I help?"

"Tom, I need to ask you something – would you come with me? My father isn't able to travel, and while there are a few people I could normally ask, I can't very well ring up and say 'fancy a weekend in Paris with a mad murderer on the loose? 'What do you think? Anyway……there might be a story in it!"

"Oho – that's sneaky – but I'd have to run it past Willi."

Later on, Tom went in to Regan's office. As he flopped into the chair Willi looked up from his paper. "What's up with you? You look like you have the weight of the world on your shoulders?"

"It's Olga – I mean Miss Radcliffe – she has to go to Paris – there's been another break in, at her grandmother's apartment this time – she wants me to go with her – what do you reckon?"

"Well now," Regan said slowly, putting his paper down. "That would all depend on whether the attraction was the story – or the lovely Olga, I mean Miss Radcliffe." He laughed.

Tom had the good grace to blush.

"I suppose so – why not –it's your first big story and it still has legs– but remember, this is on my tab so I get first dibs on the story, whatever it is. No running off to *The Irish Times* or Reuters with it."

"Thanks, Willi – of course!"

Tom stood up and turned for the door.

"One more thing: be careful, Tom – this is a murder investigation, not a game of Cluedo, and someone is definitely not playing by the rules."

Willi Regan wasn't the only one to be concerned. When Tom told his father he was planning to go to Paris and what Willi had said, John put down the fish slice he was using to poke at the salmon steaks he was cooking for dinner. "Are you sure you know what you're getting yourself into, Tom? Willi is right: this is a murder investigation, and you are a journalist not a policeman. Are you not in danger of getting too close to the story?"

They sat for a long while over dinner and John had another go at warning Tom off. "At the end of the day what do you know about these people – this Radcliffe girl and the Bratinskys? They're not our kind of people, Tom. Better let the police deal with it."

"Dad, I want to do this. I know it's a leap in the dark but it's my first chance at a big story – this can take me somewhere."

His father sighed. "I see you've made your mind up, so there's no more to be said."

John went through to the sideboard in the dining room and came back with the bottle of Redbreast and two glasses. "You'll take a drop?"

They sat for a while in the heat of the stove, sipping the whiskey in silence. Tom knew his father was thinking of Oonagh, and of Dermot teaching over in London, probably wondering if Tom would be next to head off. He got up and patted Tom on the shoulder. "Good luck with it. I hope it takes you where you want to go. But be careful!"

Tom listened for the bedroom door clicking shut as he settled down to think. "Where exactly do I want to go?"

THE BRATINSKY AFFAIR

CHAPTER 10

Paris 1931

Irina worked every hour that she could get but it still wasn't enough. Her mother had never been strong, and the strain of their escape from Russia had left her deeply depressed. When they finally left Finland, some vital spark had gone out of Ana. Their roles had switched with Ana the child and Irina forcing them on. One morning, as Ana stood at the window holding a cup of tea in both hands to warm them, the weak morning sun shone full on her face and Irina realised for the first time that her mother had turned into an old woman. She had shrunk and her skin was waxy.

"Mother, you look terrible. You need to see a doctor."

"I'm fine, a bit tired with all those stairs." But Irina had heard her coughing in the early hours. The thought that something might happen to her mother filled Irina with panic. She knew that she would never be able to manage without her.

The doctor was expensive but he had to be paid – in cash. Her engagement ring was a large sapphire with a border of rose-cut diamonds – the one expensive gift Egon had given her on the day they got engaged. It would have to go. Sofia had told her about Berenson, a jeweller who specialised in Russian pieces.

"He's a decent man and he won't rip you off. You'll get a fair price."

Irina decided she would go to see him the next day. Exhausted from her shift on the assembly line, she dressed in her smartest clothes and pulled on her mother's worn kid gloves to cover up her calloused hands. She prepared her story as she walked up rue du Faubourg Saint-Honoré: *"My husband was killed in the war and now I need to pay my son's school fees. That's the only reason I'm selling it."*

She walked through into place des Vosges, once the home of royalty, now sadly faded. Irina hesitated outside the shop, then squared her shoulders and stepped in. It was small and dark, but the cabinets around the walls with their sparkling contents spoke of discreet wealth and good taste. As her eyes adjusted to the dim light, she took off the ring and laid it on the counter.

"How much would you give me for this?"

"Nice: a Ceylon sapphire – about 8 carats. The diamonds are nice quality, very clean stones, and good workmanship."

Old Mr Berenson looked at Irina appraisingly. He noted the dress that was smart but several seasons old and the shoes that had been repaired once too often. He had heard all the stories before and knew all the fictions that people used to protect their dignity in exile, though he didn't know why they bothered. Pride, probably. He had been there too, not so long ago, fleeing pogroms during a different revolution. He had arrived in Paris from Odessa with ten gold coins stitched into the lining of his hat and a letter of introduction to a cousin of his father's who was in the business. He had been lucky. The cousin was a decent man and gave him a chance. The wheel had turned again.

But business is business: "Five hundred francs."

"But that's nothing – it cost many times that!" Her voice broke. She would not cry! She clenched her teeth.

"It's the market" the old man said. He spread out his hands, shrugged. "Refugees have brought down the value of jewels! Between the Germans, the Austrians and the Russians, the market is flooded. Half the royal families in Europe are selling, and prices have dropped." The price made her feel like a beggar but she accepted; she had no choice.

The old man hesitated, and said kindly, "If you waited a while, you would probably get a better price, when things pick up."

Ana's cough would not wait, and the doctor wouldn't wait for his money. Irina thanked him, and gathered the bundle of notes. She had her hand on the door, about to leave, when he asked her name.

"Tell me, what's the real story?" There was always a story. He could spot a liar and a fake a mile off, but there was something about this young woman, an intensity, a style, that made her stand out. There was no longer any point pretending, so she told him the whole sorry story.

"My husband is Count Egon Bratinsky. He is also a gambler

and a drunk. He lost all our money and to add insult to injury he walked off with another woman. I have to support my mother and my daughter, and I need cash to pay a doctor for my mother."

There, she had said it and she looked him defiantly in the eyes. Make of it what you will, she thought, I don't care anymore.

He looked at her for a minute, before asking, "Would you like to do some work for me? I am getting too old to be climbing up and down the stairs to the storeroom every ten minutes. I need an assistant to talk to the customers, the ones who come to look but never buy anything and waste my time. And the women, like you, who come early in the morning or late in the evening to sell. An attractive young woman with your background and looks could be useful to me. No promises, now, but we could try you out for... a week?"

Irina was so stunned she couldn't say a word. Apart from Yuri he was the only person to offer her a single act of kindness. She would have to leave Peugeot – or 'fall ill' for a week. Then if she could keep this work—

"What do you say?"

"Yes! Yes, of course!"

"One thing: get yourself some new shoes." He opened the drawer under the counter and pulled out a banknote: an extra hundred francs. It was enough for a pair of the scarlet ankle-strapped kid shoes with diamante buckles and adorable chunky military heels she had been craving in the window of a shop she crossed the road to avoid. And a few pairs of the glossy silk stockings – she snapped herself back to reality. Shoes, yes. A pair of stockings with no darns. A manicure to smooth her calloused hands. One of the new drop-waisted dresses in deep green with red touches. A little clutch purse—

But first, the doctor for Ana, and the medicine she would have to buy.

And so, Irina's introduction to the antique and jewellery business began. The week became two weeks, then months. She gave in her notice at Peugeot, in front of the envious glances of her former workmates.

"Landed on her feet, that one! Or maybe her back, hahaha!"

The one person she would miss was Yuri. He had thrown her a lifeline when she needed it most.. On the last day she went up to him and stuck a small enamel pin in the lapel of his jacket. It was a badge of the Imperial Guard and had belonged to her father. She had found it stuck in the lapel of one of her mother's jackets. The motto round the edge read, God is with us. "It's not worth much but I'd like you to have it." He gave her a sad smile: "Always a pleasure; Countess."

The doctor listened to Ana's chest, smiled at her and told her to wait outside while he spoke to her daughter. 'Your mother's heart is gradually failing. There's no immediate danger but she needs to be careful. The medicine will keep danger at bay – but no physical strain, and as little worry as possible." He wrote out a prescription, and she went out and told Ana, "It's fine! But you have to take the medicine."

Ana made a face when Irina spilled out the powder the pharmacist had twisted into a paper knot for her, but when Irina tipped it into a glass of sweet wine and mixed it in, she drank it up, and smiled for the first time in months.

CHAPTER 11

Dublin to Paris, March 1976
On the flight to Paris, neither Tom nor Olga said much, each pretending to be engrossed in their books while inwardly stressing about what was awaiting them. Tom couldn't make up his mind whether the tingle in his stomach was anxiety or excitement. Here he was, Tom O'Brien from Bray, flying into Paris on assignment. The stuff of dreams. It started to become real when he looked out the window of the plane and saw the S bends of the Seine curving away into the distance and as they got closer to the city the Eiffel Tower stabbing up through the clouds. Tom glanced over at Olga. He could see from the rigid set of her shoulders that she was worried. Not only had her grandmother been murdered, but everything she had known about her seemed to be a lie. To make matters worse, whoever had killed Irina was still around and the police didn't seem to be making any progress. What chance did he and Olga have of solving a mystery that had defied the best minds of the Irish and French police. This story could be make or break for Tom and if he messed it up, he might not get another chance. Olga at least knew her way round Paris while he on the other hand was the original innocent abroad. If he was going to make it as an investigative journalist, he would need to toughen up.

Olga looked up. "I've read this chapter 3 times and I still can't remember anything. My brain seems to have turned to cotton wool."

He tried to reassure her: "Don't worry it'll be fine."

She nodded in reply, unconvinced.

The hustle and bustle of the airport at least took their mind off things as Olga took charge, shepherding them safely through customs and down to the bus terminal.

"Ok, Tom, you get the bags and I'll change the money."

"Yes, boss."

Tom felt a real surge of excitement when Olga handed him the bundle of colourful notes with the faces of famous people he didn't recognise. This was real travel, no package tours for them. The bus in from Orly dropped them at the bottom of the rue de Rivoli and then it was just a short metro ride to the place des Vosges.

The metro was a revelation to Tom. He had been on the tube in London but this was something else. They walked at speed down one long tiled corridor after another and descended multiple stairs down into the depths of the labyrinth until they reached their platform. Tom kept looking around him in a daze trying to follow the signs but Olga sped along, turning left and right without a second's hesitation. All the Parisians seemed to be rushing to meet some impossible deadline: no stopping, and no eye contact. From time to time they came upon a group of classical musicians or a solitary busker booming out music in the vaulted spaces, but nobody was paying them any attention. He felt the suction of air when the train sighed into the station and they rushed to drag their bags into the compartment before the automatic doors closed and they hurtled off into the dark. Tom didn't know where to look: whether at his fellow passengers or the people he saw on the station platforms as they passed through Palais Royal, Louvre, and Hôtel de Ville. It all felt very glamorous, until that is they reached their stop at Saint Paul and had to drag their bags up what felt like three hundred steps before emerging with relief into the fresh evening air.

"God almighty, Olga, that was a bit of a marathon. Does everybody in Paris always walk at a hundred miles an hour?"

She just laughed. "You'll get used to it!"

Tom looked around him. It was rush hour and the city was humming with cars and traffic and lights and people everywhere. "I have absolutely no idea where we are – except that we are somewhere in the middle of Paris."

"This is the rue de Rivoli– it goes all the way back down to the Louvre. The place des Vosges is just up here. For me it's the most beautiful square in Paris. Irina's shop is under the arcade in the square. No point going there tonight and anyway I need to psych myself up for it. I have to meet Commandant Jourdain there at ten tomorrow morning. Our hotel is round the corner from the shop." In the excitement of being in Paris Tom had almost forgotten why they were there, but the mention of Irina and Commandant Jourdain brought it all back.

Olga led the way and as they turned in under the arch leading into the square Tom looked around him at the four-storey houses of cut stone and brickwork that had faded over the centuries to a soft rose pink. Arcades ran all the way round the square and as they walked along Tom got an occasional glimpse though grills of the glittering contents of shops whose shutters had been pulled down for the night. The shops were a mix of art galleries, antique shops and jewellers and some of them had a light on inside so that passers-by could catch sight of their wares. None of it looked cheap. There was a park in the middle, and in the distance, he could see the outline of an imposing statue of someone important on horseback.

"Welcome to Paris, Tom."

The large and comfortable Hôtel de la Place des Vosges was a small cosy hotel in what had been part of the original royal stables. Like most of the great houses in the Marais it had been sliding slowly into dereliction for the last hundred years until rescued by tourism.

"You know, Tom, Irina told me that after the war place des Vosges had been more or less forgotten about. That's why this area ended up full of artists and antique dealers. Now, every time I come back it seems to be even more chic – and expensive." Irina's investment had paid off handsomely.

They had two rooms not far from each other. Tom dumped his bag and was brushing his teeth when the phone rang. "Since it's your first night in Paris let me invite you to dinner – see you downstairs in 30 minutes. I'll bring you to one of the best bistros in Paris. "As Olga and Tom walked into Ma Bourgogne, an ancient restaurant tucked in under the vaulted arcades on the corner of the square, the Maître D recognised Olga and rushed over to offer his condolences. Some of the diners sitting on the terrace turned to see who this celebrity could be.

Olga, flustered, apologised and backed out again. She took Tom by the arm and muttered, "Let's keep going. I can't go in there. I'd forgotten that Irina was kind of a celebrity round here, and this was one of her favourite places – everybody knew her. We used to come here for a drink after work and she would know half the customers. Let's walk for a while– it's still only eight o clock."

Spring had not arrived in Paris, and even though it was still bitterly cold there were lots of people about: couples strolling or busy smartly-dressed people who looked as though they were rushing home late from work. Tom and Olga walked down towards the Seine and the Île Saint-Louis. As they crossed the bridge, they could see the towers and the spire of Notre Dame in the distance and stood for a minute looking out over the river. One of the Bateaux Mouches tour boats floated by with dozens of happy tourists having dinner and taking photographs of the sights of Paris.

Olga clearly had a destination in mind; she didn't hesitate for a minute until they found themselves outside the olive-green-fronted Brasserie Vagenende on boulevard Saint-Germain. Inside the walls were lined with mirrors reflecting crisp linen and shining silverware. There was even an old fashioned nickelodeon against one wall that for an old franc would clink out a rather mechanical waltz. The waiter in his black jacket and ankle-length apron showed them to a table near the window where they could see the people sitting outside on the terrace and the full length of the restaurant inside.

Tom felt intimidated. "I feel underdressed! If I'd known I would have made more of an effort."

"Oh, don't worry – look around you – half the people are wearing jeans and polo necks."

"How do they do it? I mean, how do they pull on a sweater and jeans and still look chic? Makes Grafton Street look a bit down at heel."

Olga turned serious. "I'm sorry to drag you all the way over here, but I didn't appreciate the shock of being back in Irina's local restaurant knowing she was gone. When the Maître D started to offer me his condolences I wanted to run away. Anyway, at least you got to see a bit of Paris, and I love walking around the city at night. It's almost the best time to see it. Even so, it's sad. The last time I was here was with Irina for my birthday."

"It's normal, Olga. In fact I'd be astonished if you felt any other way. After my mother died a friend told me that grief is like a wave. One minute you are sailing along, everything is fine and the next minute you are totally swamped by grief."

Tom could see that Olga was having difficulty holding back tears. He offered her the hanky from his breast pocket which fortunately was clean and ironed.

"Never apologise for your grief, Olga. It's not just about Irina. Bad and all as that is; it's also probably bringing up all the other stuff about your mother and Ana. I think you're being brave and I'm sure your mother would be very proud of you. Most people would just crumple into a mindless heap."

It felt good sitting here like this with Olga. She reminded him a bit of Tess. Maybe that was why he liked her. That was the problem, he liked her. The mood lifted when the waiter arrived with the menus and they could focus on enjoying dinner in one of the nicest restaurants in Paris. The food was delicious – she had oysters cooked in a cheese sauce, Tom had fillet steak with golden fries – and the carafe of wine helped them both to relax.

"Tom, this whole situation is a complete nightmare. I have no idea what is going on, and the police seem to think that I know something I'm not telling. I keep waiting for Fitzgerald to turn up with handcuffs but I have no idea what I am supposed to have done. I wish my father were here."

"You mentioned before that you father didn't like Irina."

"That's another long story – let's order coffee first." Olga smiled at Tom. "You're a very good listener. It's easy to talk to you."

They got tiny cups of espresso and a crème brulée with two spoons. Olga settled in to talk, and Tom to listen.

"It wasn't so much dislike – in fact I think he rather admired Irina – but he felt she tried to control my mother, Masha, whom he absolutely adored. You see, they were this tightly-knit group of three women. My great-grandmother Ana, Irina, and my mother. Ana and Irina had arrived in France with nothing, and it was them against the world, even though at times they fought like cat and dog. Shortly after mother was born my grandfather did a runner, and after that they had nobody else to depend on. None of them ever mentioned Egon. It was as if he had vanished into thin air. I often wonder what became of him."

Olga sat for a moment in silence drinking her coffee before she picked up the thread of her story.

"Ana and Irina loved each other but Irina always felt that she had been pushed into marrying Egon because he was the right class, the right family and he had money – or so they thought. I don't think she ever quite forgave Ana for that."

"Understandable enough," Tom said, and poured her another glass from the carafe.

Olga took a sip and went on. "Then Irina tried to do exactly the same thing with my mother! You would think she would have learned her lesson from her own disastrous arranged marriage. But no! Irina was ambitious and tough. In fact, that was her mantra: *To survive in this world you have to be tough. You have to take what you want, because nobody will give it to you.* And she was ambitious for my mother, wanted the best for her – education, perfect clothes, and in the end marriage, with a carefully chosen young man of perfect lineage and prospects. Chosen by her that is. After the war Paris became very social again and Irina was always organising parties to introduce mother to the most eligible young men. Eligible for her meant money, and preferably a title but in the end, it was all about stability, having a position that nobody could take away from you. It's like that for a lot of refugees: not belonging, trying desperately to fit in and at the same time battling with this constant yearning for home."

"I'm waiting for a disaster here," said Tom, then bit his tongue, realising he had been rude. But Olga went on regardless.

"Then mother met this charming, older, and in Irina's book, impoverished English diplomat, and fell madly in love. In fact, he was from an entirely respectable and very well-off army family with a beautiful country house in Devon. The Radcliffes were not unlike the O'Rourkes, army, politics, public service but nothing short of the Duke of Westminster would have satisfied Irina. In many ways she was quite conventional.

She did everything to keep them apart. In the end she even used her wiles on the British Ambassador to have Dad sent back to England. It did no good. Mother followed him and they were married six months later. Irina and Mother hardly spoke for years, and for most of that time Ana was the link. Things warmed up when I was born and then when my father became an MP and ended up as Sir William Radcliffe she warmed up even more. She loved being able to say, this is my daughter, Lady Radcliffe. But four generations of Russian women! My poor father!"

One of the advantages of Brasserie Vagenende is that there are so many mirrors you can watch people without being seen. As he glanced up to ask for the bill Tom caught the reflection of the man sitting at the next table. Their eyes met briefly in the mirror before the man looked away. Judging by his guilty reaction it was clear he had been listening in on their conversation. Then Tom noticed *Le Figaro* open on the table in front of him. The newspaper was folded open to a photograph of Olga standing beside Irina's grave in Wicklow. The French attaché was shaking her hand and he could clearly see the wreath with the tricolour on one side.

Pretending to look down at the menu, Tom muttered to Olga, "Don't look now but you've been spotted – we should leave."

But then their spy got up and went to the back of the restaurant towards the toilets. A few minutes later he left and Tom started to relax again. Maybe his imagination was working overtime. Tom moved to pick up the bill but Olga intercepted him.

"No, this is my treat - a thank you and a welcome to Paris at the same time." She sorted the bill and added a nice tip. The waiter slipped it into the pocket of his apron and leaned over confidentially.

"The gentleman who was sitting beside you is a journalist. I heard him talking to his office on the phone at the back just now. He is standing outside with a photographer."

As he walked away he spoke directly to Olga; "My

condolences Mademoiselle." He had obviously also recognised her from the newspaper.

Olga looked at Tom in a panic. "What do we do now? I wasn't expecting this."

Tom nodded to the friendly waiter and asked him to call a taxi. "Ok, here's what we do. As soon as we see the taxi – we walk out, head up, but look straight ahead – don't look at the camera – say nothing – leave the rest to me."

By now Olga had put her hair under a beret and was wearing a large pair of sunglasses. He couldn't help laughing "Very Jacky O– sunglasses at midnight!"

Then the taxi pulled up. "Ok, let's go."

They walked out keeping their eyes straight ahead. Tom put the palm of his hand out towards the cameraman, took Olga firmly by the elbow and steered her into the taxi in the blinding light of flash bulbs. The journalist tried to doorstop them but Tom brushed him off with a crisp, "Non merci."

Once the door of the taxi was shut tight, he told the taxi driver "place des Vosges."

Neither of them said anything as the taxi sped through the streets of Paris. Back at the hotel Tom picked up copies of all the papers as they went through the lobby. "Let's have a drink and think about what to do."

They went into the hotel bar, and both ordered whiskey to steady their nerves. Then they went through the papers. They all had the same prominent picture of the funeral in Wicklow. And there, standing directly behind Olga and looking straight at the camera was one Tom O'Brien. One paper also ran a photograph of Father Couriss officiating at the graveside and one of Count Tolstoy kissing Olga's hand.

Tom groaned. "Nothing like making a discreet entrance is there! Willi Regan will be so pleased. I'm supposed to be on the story – not in the story!"

Olga raised the glass. It chattered against her teeth as she took a sip. "It never occurred to me that there would be so much media interest."

Tom felt sorry for her. "There's nothing we can do," he said.

"For now, you are clearly a media celebrity and we have to brazen it out over the next few days."

\#

Next morning when they went in for breakfast, the situation got even worse. *Le Matin* had three photographs side by side: Irina at the Hôtel Matignon ball, Olga at the graveside and Olga and Tom leaving the restaurant. The tagline read: *"Estranged granddaughter of murdered Countess returns to France as investigation widens into possible political connections."*

The article elaborated on the details of the postcard from Irina, the break-in at Olga's house and the attack on her father. The journalist was clearly well informed and had taken in every detail of their conversation in the restaurant.

Olga put down her coffee and looked at Tom. "As the French would say – *merde!"*

Tom and Olga were still debating their next steps when a tall, thin man walked into the dining room and looked around. He came straight over to their table. "Mademoiselle Radcliffe? I'm Commandant Jourdain. Given this morning's papers I thought it might be better if we met here first, since your arrival in Paris has been so…" he shrugged and waved a hand at the newspapers scattered on the chairs around their table.

Commandant Jourdain was beautifully dressed, about fifty, tall with a neatly clipped beard, not at all like your usual policeman. He was wearing a trench coat, a navy suit and a dazzling white shirt with a purple silk tie. Tom particularly noted his shoes, which looked shiny and expensive. He tucked his own battered, but lovingly polished brogues out of sight under the chair.

"There may well be newspapermen at your grandmother's shop." Jourdain looked meaningfully at Tom.

Olga, flustered, said, "My apologies, Commandant, this is Tom O'Brien a… friend of mine."

"Monsieur Tom O'Brien of *The Wicklow Herald*? Inspector Fitzgerald mentioned you by name. I see, Mademoiselle, you travel with your own press secretary." His tone was not friendly.

"It's not like that all, Commandant! Tom agreed to come because my father is ill and he knows all the background, and

last night that journalist happened to be sitting at the next table."
It all sounded so pathetically amateur.

"Let's get something clear, Monsieur O'Brien. You are present merely as a friend of Miss Radcliffe. Anything you hear is confidential until cleared for publication by me – otherwise – no dice, as they say in the movies. Are we clear?

"Yes, Commandant." Tom took an instant and barely concealed dislike to the policeman.

Jourdain looked at Olga

"Yes, absolutely."

"Before we go to the shop, here's the drill." What strange English he had: fluent, slangy. Tom wondered if he had spent time in the US or simply watched a lot of movies. "There is a policeman there already. He will watch for us. He will open the door and we go straight in, saying nothing to anyone. On the way out, we will use a police car, which will take us to rue du Bac. But if there are reporters, you will need to give them something. Slow down but don't stop. Enough for them to get a photograph: then straight into the car.

"If they demand a comment say you thank the French and Irish police for their diligence, there is no clear line of investigation at the moment but your lawyer will issue a statement in due course, if there are any developments. If they have heard rumours of the break-in and ask you about it, say investigations are at an early stage and you can make no comment at this time. You, Monsieur O'Brien, will stay completely quiet, and will say nothing to nobody." The deliberate use of the double negative made Tom grind his teeth. *Thank you Mr Cagney*, he thought.

Tom and Olga glanced at each other like two naughty school children and nodded agreement.

As planned, they walked around the square to Irina's shop and were in before anybody even realised they were there. The shutters on the front window were down and the shop was in semi-darkness.

Tom looked around. The shop consisted of two large rooms divided by a pair of columns. Irina's desk was discreetly tucked away at the back of the second room beside a pair of double

THE BRATINSKY AFFAIR

doors that led out to a lobby and the staircase up to the apartment. Its position had allowed Irina to see the full length of the shop, which was full of cabinets, occasional tables and objects piled up in what could only be described as carefully contrived disorder. Three glass cabinets beside Irina's desk had empty shelves.

Some boxes had been opened and some tables had been knocked over, but the thieves had mainly focused their attention on Irina's desk. Each drawer had been emptied out and papers left in piles. Whoever it was had been methodical.

Commandant Jourdain turned to Olga, "Would you know if anything was missing?"

"Not that I can see straight off. Irina always emptied those glass jewellery cabinets in the evening. There's a floor safe under her desk. If you lift the carpet tile, you will see the lock. She used that for smaller pieces, and I have a key for that. Anything larger or more valuable went in the big safe, but I don't have keys for that, though she did leave a spare set in the bank. She had a safe deposit box there, too. I suppose you will have to contact her lawyer, Maître Beranger." about that. His number will be in that diary on the desk."

Olga knelt down, opened the floor safe and took out two velvet bags. Each had about ten smaller individual bags holding bracelets, earrings and brooches. "In terms of the number of pieces for the three glass cases this looks about right, though I couldn't be absolutely sure."

Olga hesitated, before going through the double doors and up the stairs. They were now stepping into Irina's territory and the sense of her personality was strong. For an antique dealer the interior was surprisingly modern, painted in shades of white with a mix of art deco and modern pieces. The art was almost exclusively modern and the whole atmosphere was one of relaxed and stylish luxury. In the drawing room and dining room everything looked intact. Only the contents of a bookcase had been scattered.

The next floor was a different story. The bedroom had been torn apart. Everything was such a mess it was impossible to see what might be missing. As she looked around Olga had a strong feeling of something missing but she couldn't put her finger on what it was.

Commandant Jourdain gave her the name of a local locksmith who came round immediately to change the locks and make the place secure. He promised to wait until the police were finished and then drop two sets of keys round to Olga's hotel. A police technician was busy dusting for finger prints and a photographer was systematically making a record of the damage. There wasn't anything that Olga could tell Jourdain.

It took about twenty minutes to drive from place des Vosges to the rue du Bac, and as they pulled up to the door Tom's eyes were out on stalks. He had never seen anything like it and he felt like the country mouse come to town. First there was the entrance through the double front doors into a spacious but severe stone flagged lobby, then up the sweeping marble staircase to the door of the apartment. He hardly had time to appreciate the panelled elegance of the apartment before he heard Olga's gasp as she took in the scene of devastation.

It took Tom a while to get a sense of the layout of the apartment. The door from the outside landing led into a spacious lobby with a long corridor leading off left and right. In front, another set of double doors led into a series of three interconnecting rooms. All had been left open, so Tom could see that the three rooms had been turned upside down. But the worst damage had been inflicted on the sitting room and the bedroom at the end. Every book had been opened out and thrown on the floor, cabinets emptied and pictures pulled off the wall and thrown on the floor.

Commandant Jourdain called his colleagues and within minutes the apartment was a hive of activity. "Don't touch anything," he warned Olga sharply, just as she was stretching out her hand towards a table for support. "They came up the service stairs and in through the kitchen. The door opens into the side street, so they could take as much time as they needed."

Olga looked stunned and sat in an armchair surveying the devastation. "What in God's name are they looking for? Maybe

THE BRATINSKY AFFAIR

if they told us straight out, we could give it to them? Why didn't they leave a note?"

"Maybe they did, in a kind of way," Tom said. "This tells us it wasn't a robbery. There's silver in the dining room, some pieces of expensive-looking jewellery in the bedroom, and this art doesn't look as though it came cheap."

Commandant Jourdain picked up on this train of thought. "Same story in your father's house, I gather – and the same story in Monsieur O'Brien's office. Most of their attention has been on books, drawers, cabinets. They were looking for something very specific – documents –papers – information of some sort."

"But why would they kill Irina for something like that?"

"Did your grandmother have anything of exceptional intrinsic or historic value that someone would kill for – perhaps connected to her past?"

"Not that I know of." Olga shook her head slowly.

"Can you think of anything in your grandmother's background that would tie all this together? Surely there must be something," he insisted.

Jourdain was starting to get on her nerves.

"Clearly there is, but I have no idea what it is." Olga's voice mixed despair and irritation as the Sûreté man pressed her for answers.

"What about your father – would he know anything?"

"You can speak to him, for all the good it will do. As I told Inspector Fitzgerald, he had very little contact with Irina, in fact as little as he could possibly manage. He had no interest at all in the whole Russian story. It bored him, quite frankly. Except for Ana. He had a soft spot for her and he was very upset when she died."

"Well, think: could be the missing link?"

"That's impossible – she's been dead for years –I was a little girl when she died."

The more Tom listened to Commandant Jourdain the less he liked him. There was something about him that jarred. He was too smooth and at the same time way too pushy – and a mahogany tan in February! The police had sent the locksmith over from the place des Vosges and as soon as he had made the place secure Tom suggested they head back to the hotel. "We can come back tomorrow and start to tidy up."

Apart from anything else, he needed to send an update back to Willi Regan

"By the way, Commandant, is it ok for me to report on the break-ins? I need to file a report and the rest of it would be about the level of interest and the media coverage of the case here in France."

"I suppose it's fine," Jourdain said reluctantly. "It will be all over the news here by tomorrow anyway, so go ahead."

"Let me ask you an on-the-record question, Commandant."

Jourdain swung around and gave a suspicious half-nod, watching Tom closely. "You have asked repeatedly about CountessBratinsky's political connections. Do you think the motivation for this killing is political?"

As he expected, the answer was entirely vague. "At this point it's too early to say but we have not ruled anything out." That last bit in particular would do nicely! Tom could spin it that the police were investigating possible political links to the killing.

Olga and Tom decided to walk back to the hotel, and as they headed down boulevard Saint-Michel Tom stopped to look in some of the shop windows. He pointed things out to Olga more to distract her from thinking about Irina that because of his deep interest in fashion. Like most Irishmen, Tom's idea of being well dressed was a good tweed jacket and a decent pair of shoes. The annual winter sales were on, but the prices still shocked him.

"Hey, Tom – fancy a new look to keep up with Commandant Jourdain?"

"Eight hundred francs for a jacket, a thousand francs for a trench coat –seven hundred and fifty francs for a pair of shoes! How can people afford to eat if clothes cost this much?"

"French people don't buy a lot, but they buy quality – that's why they go for classics. Anyway, I'm sure Willi Regan wouldn't mind if you bought a pair of shoes on expenses."

"Oh absolutely – and I can promise, you would hear the explosion from Paris if I tried that on!"

"Look Tom, that trench coat is eighty per cent off! Try it on. Go on. Don't be such a bore."

Tom tried it on, and though it was clearly way too big, the vendeuse was not giving up. She pulled the belt tight and said, "They're worn loose this year." Tom thought he looked quite dashing as he walked up and down in front of the mirror. "Do you think Bray is ready for this?"

"You just think you look like Inspector Maigret. There's loose and loose, Tom – but you, me and the vendeuse could all climb into that coat and have a party –it's *too* big – put it back."

Tom did as he was told – reluctantly. He needed to get back to the hotel and focus on his report for Willi.

At least he had got Olga to laugh.

CHAPTER 12

Paris 1933

Mr Berenson was old and knowledgeable, and though they never became friends, there was a respect between them, and he taught her everything he knew. Bit by bit Irina learned her trade. Mr Berenson's wife had died and his only son lived in New York and had no interest in the business. When the old man died in 1933, she took over the shop in place des Vosges. The antique trade and a lover with deep pockets were the path to a new life – but no more exiled aristocrats.

Irina had changed. Her father had told her to survive and survive she would: but on her terms. She now selected her lovers in the same way she bought jewels or art – with a calculating eye to the main chance. The men in her life had to be elegant, intelligent, preferably handsome, but above all, rich. Irina knew her value and was fully aware of the effect she had on men. When she chose to, she could be seductive, and she made a point of never losing her oh-so-charming Russian accent.

Irina preferred the role of mistress to Madame and she had absolutely no intention of getting married again. She would never again be dependent on any man. If a man became too pressing in his attentions he would be discreetly replaced. She kept on good terms with all her former lovers. No drama, no conflict: they were gradually moved to the side, but not dropped entirely. In that way she built up a network of contacts who could be called on in moments of crisis. Like when the young Romanian turned up on her doorstep threatening suicide unless she married him. A week later, the police found out that his papers were forged and he was quietly deported.

As the business grew, the apartment over the shop in the place des Vosges became more of a showroom where she entertained clients or occasional lovers. On the first floor she had a salon and cosy dining room, and on the top floor a bedroom with mirrored furniture and a tiny bathroom. It wasn't big but it was stylish. Irina had persuaded a young Irish designer called Eileen Grey that everybody was talking about to decorate the apartment, and the bill was picked up by the rich and very married Marquis de Beaufort whose wife was more interested in raising horses at their chateau in the country. His conservative values and catholic faith were no obstacle to some discreet adultery. With lacquer screens, white carpets and a red chair on a zebra rug, the effect was simple but stunning.

However, Irina's real home was her apartment on the rue du Bac. Nobody knew about it, and when Irina went there, she felt safe and far away from everyone. It was her space, the one place where she could be herself.. It was a typically French apartment, with creaky parquet floors and wooden panelling that gave it a warm, comforting feel. On one side it looked onto an internal courtyard and on the other it overlooked a park, yet it was only five minutes' walk from Saint-Germain-des-Près.

When Irina walked through the door, she switched off the CountessBratinsky, took off the pearls and the Chanel suit, poured herself a whiskey and relaxed. The combination of the fine tweed suit, heavy clip-on earrings and two-tone shoes was like a suit of armour. As she had explained to Olga: "when I'm dressed like this people don't really see me. They see this reassuring image of class and money which makes it much easier for them to hand over 1,000 francs for a bracelet." It also helped to keep people at a distance.

Some people didn't know where to place Irina on the social grid. She was a shopkeeper but also a Countess. She was French in every way that mattered but also foreign. More worrying for some of the ladies, she was both beautiful and divorced. The result was that they either fawned over her or were dismissive and rude. Irina worked with grim determination to wear down their resistance and watched in amusement as they slowly melted in the heat of her charm. Aristo or nouveau riche they were all motivated by the same things: money and status. Seduction was an art that Irina excelled at: elegant surroundings, delicious food, fine wine - and the irresistible smell of freshly minted money. Not even the haughtiest dowager could resist the magnetic pull of a Rothschild at one of Irina's elegant suppers in the upstairs dining room in the place des Vosges.

Gradually Countess Irina Bratinsky became a name in Paris society. Sometimes she and the marquis were invited to dinner or they had supper in the place des Vosges and then went out to one of the nightclubs that were springing up all over Paris in the 20's and 30's. One evening out of the blue he suggested going to *la Vie Parisienne*, the coolest club in Paris.

"Suzy Solidor has a new show – it should be fun. We can go and look at the queers and the freaks." For the first time Irina looked at Jean de Beaufort in the cool light of indifference. In his early sixties, Jean de Beaufort had a smooth well-worn patina of class and sophistication, like the smooth leather of a well-used pocket book. He also had all the snobbery and blinkered vision of his class. In truth, Irina was beginning to tire of the marquis and anything was better than another evening of his endless wartime reminiscences so she jumped at the chance.

Irina considered herself a woman of the world but despite everything that had happened she had led quite a sheltered life and nothing had prepared her for the clientele of *La Vie Parisienne*. The club had been a brothel during the war and some people thought it hadn't really changed that much. It took a second glance before she realised that the handsome young man at the door with the pencil moustache was really a girl and the glamorous woman behind the bar with the *décolleté magnifique* had the suspicion of a five o'clock shadow. The music was loud and the air was full of smoke and a perfume that was heavy and cloying - and vaguely herbal. Nobody was quite what they seemed: boys and girls, boys and boys and girls and girls.

"My oh my!" said the marquis. What is the world coming to? Maybe it wasn't such a good idea to come here. Not our kind of people."

On the dance floor two men were dancing the tango while a young woman in spangled tights dangled on a rope from the ceiling, twirling slowly in the spotlight. Irina clapped her hands and laughed out loud.

"Well, I love it!"

As she looked around the room Irina noticed that the portraits though different in style were all of the same woman. There was a water colour by Cocteau and even a sketch by Picasso. The marquis explained: "Every artist in Paris wants to paint her but she will only agree on condition that she can hang the pictures here. They say she has one of the best collections of modern art in Paris, if you can call it art." Irina looked around her in amazement. The marquis was amused at her reaction: "it's what they call *le style haute fagotte international*," he added dismissively. The marquis was really starting to get on her nerves. She dearly wanted to smack him – very hard! "Time for you to go back to visit your wife in the country," she thought. At that moment the lights dimmed and a spotlight focused on the small stage at the front of the room. Suzy Solidor was tall and blond and if not exactly beautiful she was certainly striking with the angular looks and athletic body that drew all eyes. She was wearing a silver sequinned halter neck dress that clung to every curve of her body. Her back was entirely bare and she was wearing long black opera gloves. She certainly had presence. The effect on the audience was hypnotic. Irina noticed that even the marquis was captivated. After three or four songs the music faded and the lights went back up and Suzy began a circuit of the room greeting people by name and introducing herself to new patrons. Eventually she arrived at their table as the marquis moved away to greet someone he knew, leaving Irina and Suzy sitting together.

"Soooo, the beautiful Countess Bratinsky comes to *La Vie*."

"You know my name?"

"I make it my business to know everybody – especially if they are as pretty as you! But tell me, what on earth are you doing with that living fossil? You should dump him and have some fun;"

The come on was so outrageously blatant that the only thing Irina could do was laugh.

"You see what I mean," said Suzy. "That's better already." When the marquis came back Suzy gave him her full attention. Anyone who ordered bottles of Dom Pérignon champagne was worth a few minutes of her time. As she got up to go she held out her hand for him to kiss and discreetly trailed the tip of one finger up the inside of Irina's arm in a long fluid caress that briefly touched the curve of her breast. No one else even noticed.

The effect was instantaneous. Irina shivered as a bolt of electricity went from her toes to the top of her head before settling somewhere in the pit of her stomach. As Suzy walked away she looked back and winked.

"I hope we'll be seeing you again."

Her remark was aimed at the marquis but Irina got the message.

#

Paris is a big city but in the days and weeks that followed Irina seemed to bump into Suzy every time she turned round. First they met at the Chanel fashion show and ended up sitting beside each other on the front row as model after model drifted past in one tasteful tweed suit or little black dress after another. Suzy leaned over and whispered into Irina's ear,

"My mother would love this – but God it's boring. We should have gone Schiaparelli. More fun!"

Irina wanted to laugh but just then she felt Mademoiselle's beady eye on her from her perch halfway up the staircase and did her best to look serious. When the show ended Suzy blew her a kiss and rushed off to the club with her usual breezy wave. "See you around, kiddo." It felt as if the air had gone out of the room but then she met some of her regular customers from the shop and had to switch on her official charming smile.

#

A week later Irina was standing with her head on one side trying to make sense of a Picasso painting when a voice behind her said "isn't it wonderful?"

Irina turned to find Suzy standing behind her with a group of friends.

"Well, no actually," said Irina "There's something cruel in his pictures that makes me uneasy. I don't think he actually likes women, but at least I now know where to go if I want a portrait of me with one foot sticking out of my ear "

They both laughed and Suzy casually linked Irina's arm as they walked around the exhibition chatting. Irina was very conscious of the heat of Suzy's body though the thin silk of her dress and the smell of her perfume. Something fresh and citrusy - almost masculine – but she tried not to think about that as they drifted along from picture to picture. Afterwards she could barely remember what they had seen. With their blue eyes and bobbed blonde hair they could almost have been sisters and as they came round again towards the door a woman came across to say hello to Suzy.

"Tamara de Lempicka, let me introduce you to Countess Irina Bratinsky. Tamara is a painter and she's done the most divine picture of me."

Suzy sounded fake and brittle. Irina could feel the cool eyes taking her in and after a while she began to feel embarrassed under the intensity of her gaze.

"You're Russian? I lived in Petersburg once upon a time. My first husband was Russian. In another life we might have known each other." All the while she kept looking at Suzy and Irina. "You two look like a pair of Botticelli angels, only not so innocent. I'm going to paint you both."

Irina immediately tried to change the subject. She knew Tamara de Lempicka by reputation and that she was one of the most fashionable portrait painters in Paris - and expensive. Before she had time to protest Suzy had agreed that they would call to the artist's studio the following Wednesday.

"Are you mad," Irina protested. "I can't afford a port...."

"Leave it to me!" Suzy muttered under her breath. "I'll tell her that it's to go on display in the club and it won't cost us a penny."

"You, are very naughty," Irina whispered as Suzy went off to join her friends.

"I try," Suzy laughed. "Anyway, see you Wednesday. 3pm sharp. Don't forget."

#

You had to admit it. Suzy Solidor was a force of nature and there was no point trying to resist her. Most people didn't even try and allowed themselves to be swept along in the tidal wave of her energy. Irina spent the morning arranging pieces of jewellery in one of the glass cabinets at the front of the shop. After she had changed the same display for the third time she finally gave up, closed the shop early and went upstairs to lie down. One part of her was looking forward to the sitting with Suzy and de Lempicka while the other part of her wished that Suzy would forget the whole thing. True to her word, at five to three the bell rang.

"Get a move on: we can't be late for the Baroness with the Brush'

Irina jumped into the front seat of Suzy's silver grey Bugatti and clung on tight as the car swerved off in the direction of de Lempicka's studio in the 14th arrondissement.

"What do you mean?"

"De Lempicka was her first husband but then she married some rich Austrian aristocrat – can't

remember his name. A journalist christened her the Baroness with the Brush. I don't think she was best pleased. "

But I thought….

"What the eye doesn't see the heart doesn't grieve over.'

Just then, the car pulled up outside de Lempicka's house. Like its owner the house was sharp, angular and very smart. They crossed the garden courtyard and up the dizzying spiral staircase to the studio. De Lempicka greeted them at the door. She was wearing black silk trousers and a sleeveless tobacco coloured gilet over a black polo neck, her hair scraped back in a severe chignon. This was a different de Lempicka to the sultry diva in the gallery. After a few minutes small talk it was down to work. She was brisk, businesslike and very focussed. Irina barely had time to take in the double height space with its enormous window looking out over Paris before she was being positioned on the sofa with Suzy half turned towards her. De Lempicka worked mostly in silence apart from the scraping of the brushes and the occasional instruction -turn this way - look here.

After a while she threw down her brushes in exasperation

"It's not working - it's all too stiff!"

Irina looked at Suzy not knowing what to do. She could feel

the tension in the air. Before Irina could say anything de Lempicka said, "Let's move over here to the light."

The sun had moved to the front of the building and there was a pool of light broken up by occasional patches of shadow from neighbouring buildings. This time she positioned them with their backs to the window, half in sun half in shadow. There was a screen of tall buildings behind them. She stood in silence for a moment smoking, analysing the geometry of the composition.

"There's still something missing."

Suzy was wearing a draped Grecian style dress with narrow shoulder straps. De Lempicka reached out with the point of her brush and flicked the straps down off her shoulders. The dress fell to her waist showing her breasts.

On the other side she reached over and flicked just one strap off Irina's shoulder. Irina glanced in surprise at Suzy who shrugged and said nothing.

"Now, look towards each other. That's much better – now hold that. "

Irina felt increasingly self-conscious and uncomfortable as she sat looking at Suzy. Irina could see from the ripples in her stomach that Suzy was trying hard not to laugh. De Lempicka kept on painting in silence but as the afternoon progressed and she was happy with the work they could hear her humming to herself. It was an old Russian folk song that Irina remembered from her childhood.

They had a cigarette break at 4.30 but de Lempicka wouldn't let them look at the picture. By 6 o'clock the light was beginning to go and they had to stop. This time she turned the easel round to face them. The portrait was still unfinished but between the geometric planes of the buildings and the curves of the bodies wrapped in diaphanous silk, de Lempicka had captured a moment in time: a moment of anticipation on the cusp of something happening.

CHAPTER 13

Paris 1976.
Back at the hotel Tom and Olga decided on an early dinner and a good night's sleep.

They were having coffee when Tom sat bolt upright. "It's the shoes!"

"What on earth are you talking about?"

"Commandant Jourdain's shoes!"

Olga was deep in thought trying to remember the good times with Ana and Masha and Tom had interrupted her train of thought.

"Dear God, Tom, we're trying to find out who murdered my grandmother and here you are obsessing about Commandant Jourdain's shoes. I told you; you should have bought the bloody things."

"It's not that; – tell me, what policeman can afford seven hundred and fifty francs for a pair of shoes, not to mention all the rest of it. There's something shifty about him, he's always watching and listening."

Tom was starting to get on her nerves.

"He's a policeman for God's sake, Tom. It's his job. Anyway, he's very senior. Senior officers are probably well enough paid here to dress well. You're over thinking this and the simple fact is you don't like him. Now, can we please talk about something else? I have to meet Irina's lawyer in the morning and Jourdain's boss wants to talk to me. I've asked Maître Berenger." to come along in case I get another grilling."

"Maître?"

"It's what lawyers are called in France. He was Irina's lawyer. Anyway, I for one am off to bed. So stop obsessing about Jourdain and get some sleep. I'll see you in the morning."

Tom sat over a beer in the bar for a while letting his mind settle and looking back over the last few weeks. Out of the blue here he was in the middle of a big international story in the heart of Paris. It was exciting but more than that he felt a sense of freedom that

THE BRATINSKY AFFAIR

he had never known before. He could breathe. Nobody knew who he was and certainly nobody had ever heard of his father or Willi Regan for that matter. Bray was a million miles away. He knocked back the rest of his beer and went out for a walk round the square. The trees were coming into leaf and there was a freshness in the air that he found exhilarating. He could feel the city humming with life around him. He started to laugh. He remembered one of his teachers who was famous for getting things slightly wrong. "At your age the world is your lobster," was one of his favourite expressions. Tom had never known whether he said it by accident or on purpose. Still smiling he went back to his room and spent the next hour roughing out a report for Willi before he rang it through.

From Tom O'Brien in Paris. He got a real kick out of writing that.

The French media are carrying wall to wall coverage of the murder of the late Countess Irina Bratinsky in the aptly named Russian Village in Kilquade, County Wicklow. Most attention has focused on the late Countess's connections at the highest levels of France's political and social elite, and there has been some comment on her Russian background, given recent political tensions over missile testing in the Pacific. The police have not ruled out a political connection to the crime. A well-placed source in the French police has suggested that there is increasing frustration within the force at the lack of progress in the investigation being carried out by the Garda Síochána.

Maître Berenger's office was not at all what Tom had expected. He had pictured something dark and fusty. Instead, it was in a ten-storey office block of glass and stainless steel. When they went through the automatic doors there was a gentle whoosh of air followed by, silence, except for the occasional ping of the lift as it went up and down. A sleek but aloof receptionist showed them immediately into Maître Berenger's office, where the glass and steel effect had been softened by wood panelling and expensive rugs.

MaitreBerenger was also a bit of a surprise. He was a tall well-built man of about 40 wearing a beautifully cut dark grey suit, the jacket of which showed just enough immaculate white cuff to display the dull gold of his cufflinks. His dark brown hair was beginning to show a fleck of grey at the temples and he still had the remains of last summer's tan. He spoke perfect English, in a perfect English accent. Tom couldn't help staring and found himself blushing slightly as they shook hands.

After the formalities of condolences and introductions and the offer of coffee which Olga declined, it was down to business.

"Miss Radcliffe, we can keep all this simple, as your grandmother's will was very straightforward. Simply put, she left everything to you. As you know, there is the shop and apartment, plus contents, in the place des Vosges; the apartment in rue du Bac and finally the house in Auteuil plus equities and investments.

"The house in Auteuil! – no, surely - that's not correct - Ana's house was sold after she died."

"Indeed not. Your grandmother was a shrewd businesswoman. She never wanted to go there but she kept the house and it is now worth a lot of money. It has been on a long-term lease at a very good rent – someone from the US Embassy, I think – I have it here – let me see – ah yes, Mr Richard Dolby III. He's the Defence Attaché."

Olga looked at Tom in astonishment.

"And finally, there is the account in Switzerland. I can provide you with a letter proving that you are the designated heir, which will allow you to transfer the funds to a bank of your choosing. Ah, and I almost forgot. There is the bank account in the Credit Lyonnais on rue Monsieur le Prince – and this." It was the key to a safe deposit box. "And here is the letter to enable you to access the account and the box. All in all, subject to final valuation and allowing for tax, your grandmother's estate comes to something in the region of two-and-a-half million francs, NET. Congratulations."

"I had no idea." Olga's face had drained of colour.

"You are a fortunate young woman and of course if you need advice on investments I, or any of my colleagues, will be only too happy to help."

"I'll bet" thought Tom. For a nice fat fee!"

THE BRATINSKY AFFAIR

Maitre Beranger looked at his watch. "Time to go, if we are to make our appointment in time."

Maître Berenger was nothing if not efficient and in a matter of minutes they were speeding along in his Mercedes to police headquarters for their meeting with Commandant Jourdain and his boss. As they drove along, Olga filled Maître Berenger in on her previous encounter with Inspector Fitzgerald and his insinuations.

"My advice: remember that this is a criminal investigation not a social visit, give factual answers, do not offer any opinions whatsoever, and do not volunteer any information. And if I put my hand up to fix my tie it means *say nothing*."

Once they turned in under the arched entrance of the Préfecture de Police the impressive façade soon gave way to a series of endless corridors with cracked linoleum, brown paint and the persistent smell of stale tobacco. When they were eventually shown into a smoke-filled office Olga stopped dead.

Commandant Jourdain introduced them: "Commissaire Divisionnaire Boyer, and – I think you know Inspector Fitzgerald."

"Miss Radcliffe, nice to see you again." Fitzgerald looked surprised to see Tom and asked Jourdain, "What's a bloody journalist doing here?"

"He stays or I go" said Olga firmly without waiting for Jourdain to intervene.

Jourdain and Fitzgerald exchanged looks then both nodded in unison. Boyer took the lead as they went back over the same old territory – Irina's business, her background, and her family connections. "Tell me again about your grandmother's business."

"But I've already told all this to Inspector Fitzgerald and again to Commandant Jourdain. Do I have to go over all this again?"

"Please, Miss Radcliffe, humour me." He gave a thin smile that showed his yellowed teeth.

"She was an antique dealer specialising in Russian art, especially Fabergé. In fact, she was an internationally recognised expert. Increasingly she was working more as a consultant and lately she had done some major projects – for exhibitions in the Metropolitan Museum in New York and the Louvre."

"And your grandmother was very well connected." Boyer put the photograph of Irina at the Hôtel Matignon Ball on the table. "Do you recognise these people?"

"Well, no - I mean I didn't but I do now – Inspector Fitzgerald told me. The PM and the French Head of Intelligence."

"Indeed." Then he put a photograph of Irina with a handsome young man on the table. "Does this man mean anything to you?"

"Absolutely nothing."

"Let me explain. One of our officers found this photograph in your grandmother's apartment and recognised him – he had worked on the case at the time. Dmitri Shuvalov was a small-time Russian crook, a dealer in drugs and stolen goods, and something of a gigolo. He was fished out of the Seine with his throat cut about ten years ago."

Tom and Olga just looked at each other. Tom was frantically trying to send her a telepathic message: "say nothing!"

"Where is this going, Capitaine?" Olga asked.

He put another photo on the table. This time the photo showed Dmitri Shuvalov with a much older man. "This is Oleg Kerensky, an attaché in the Russian Embassy and a known KGB agent. He is also suspected of having underworld connections both here and in Russia. We have been keeping an eye on him for a long time."

Then he laid down a fourth, obviously more recent photograph, of Irina deep in conversation with Kerensky in the shop in place des Vosges.

And a fifth photograph: Kerensky leaving the shop, with a blurry figure in the background. "If I am not mistaken that, is you in the background, Miss Radcliffe, is it not?"

Out of the corner of her eye Olga and Tom caught the rapid movement of Maître Beranger's hand going up to his tie.

"It seems to be, but I have no recollection of this man coming into the shop. People were in and out all the time."

"Would it surprise you to know that your grandmother, Countess Irina Bratinsky, was on an international watch list on suspicion of receiving stolen antiques from Russia?"

As she struggled for an answer Olga thought back to her grandmother's funeral. "So that's why Semenov, was in Ireland

THE BRATINSKY AFFAIR

for the funeral."

Tom thought back to his first sighting of CountessBratinsky in Kelly's pub in Bray. It was all starting to make more sense now.

Maître Berenger jumped in like a shot. "Is Miss Radcliffe being questioned as a suspect in this matter? If not, I strongly object to this line of questioning."

"Let's not get ahead of ourselves here, Maître Berenger, I am simply outlining, for the benefit of Miss Radcliffe, our present line of enquiry. Now, let me tell you what, with the benefit of forty years of police work, I think is the story." Olga could see Commandant Jourdain rolling his eyes; he had clearly heard that line many times before.

"As we know, the Russians use both honey traps and money traps to pull people into working for them. I think Kerensky used this Shuvalov to trap your grandmother into dodgy deals. Then he blackmailed her into reporting on her friends in high places. An older investigation into an international ring dealing in stolen antiques started people looking at Shuvalov, and that led them to your grandmother. At the time, the intelligence lines were buzzing with rumours of a mole operating in the Hôtel Matignon and they put two and two together. A tale as old as time: *cherchez la femme.*"

Jourdain sat watching all this in silence without taking his eyes off Olga.

Boyer finished triumphantly: "I think that the Russkies realised the game was up and to protect other assets decided to tidy up some loose ends – one of which, sadly, was your grandmother. Is there any proof? Not a shred. Do I think that is what happened – absolutely."

Inspector Fitzgerald sat there looking smug and said nothing. It was Maître Berenger who came to the rescue once again. "The little grey cells are clearly working overtime, Commissaire. Agatha Christie couldn't have done any better. But as you yourself said, you don't have a shred of proof, so this is an interesting theory, nothing more. Now, if you don't have any further questions for Miss Radcliffe we will wish you good afternoon."

Before he could usher her out Olga turned back to Boyer.

"Commissaire, there is one thing you don't know. In fact, I only found out about it this afternoon but in light of all this you probably should know about it. My grandmother owned a house in Auteuil which is currently leased to the Defence Attaché in the US Embassy. It may be relevant to your enquiries." Given the stunned silence and the look of astonishment on their faces, she might as well have taken the pin out of a live grenade and tossed it into the room.

When the door closed behind them Boyer looked at Jourdain: "Keep an eye on her. I want to know her every move and everything about her." He ignored Fitzgerald.

\#

After a few minutes fussing with menus and drinksin Maître Berenger's favourite restaurant they all subsided into silence. It was Tom who spoke first.

"So, what happens now? It all sounds plausible but they have no real suspect, apart from this Kerensky character, who may or may not be connected to the actual killing, and no evidence that would stand up in court, or print for that matter."

Olga was staring down at her plate, the food untouched. "I can't believe what I heard. It's so over the top. Irina, my grandmother, a crook and a spy! I feel I should wear pearls, call myself Mata Hari and take to travelling on the Orient Express! None of this gives us the full story. I mean, if what they say is true, all of this spy stuff has been going on for at least ten years. So why kill Irina – and why now? Despite the fact that Irina has clearly been under surveillance for quite some time they don't have any clear handle on what is going on. Or at least they aren't telling us."

Maître Berenger took a sip of wine: "As far as I can tell it's like this. The police have got their man, so to speak, in that they supposedly know who killed your grandmother. Shuvalov is long dead and Kerensky is probably flying back to Moscow at this very moment, so that door is closed. The intelligence services have got their mole, or will insist that is the case. Do you hear that swishing noise?"

Tom and Olga looked at him blankly.

"It's the sound of evidence being frantically swept under

carpets in the Matignon and the Elysée. As far as they are concerned it will be a case of, Irina who? They will be hoping that all this goes quietly away, but, if the story refuses to die, there will be an unfortunate leak from Commissaire Boyer's office revealing your grandmother's 'business' activities and suggesting that the murder was the result of a falling-out among thieves. I would give it roughly forty-eight hours before that little nugget of information surfaces. Failing that, as the murder conveniently took place in Ireland, they will blame the lack of progress on the incompetence of Inspector Fitzgerald and his colleagues."

Olga erupted. That's all fine and dandy, but what am I supposed to do? They still don't know what the person who broke into our house, attacked my father and trashed Tom's office was looking for. And don't forget, they ripped up Irina's shop and apartment after the murder. Am I supposed to go around waiting for someone to jump out of the bushes and attack me? Am I another loose end to be tidied up? I would like to have my quiet, peaceful and very ordinary life back, thank you very much." With that she stood up, threw down her napkin and walked out of the restaurant.

Tom made to go after her, but Maître Berenger held him back. "Let her go. This is a huge amount to take in. She'll feel better if we leave her alone for a while. Meanwhile, a pity to waste this delicious wine. He moved closer to pour another glass for Tom.

"Are you and Miss Radcliffe dating?" he asked quietly as he poured the wine.

"Absolutely not", Tom spluttered, spilling some wine on the crisp white table cloth. "Why do you ask?

"I just wondered. After all, she is very pretty and you came all the way to Paris with her."

Tom was immediately aware of his physical presence – the fine cotton of his shirt that had a faint sheen like silk and the discreet smell of his cologne, woody with a hint of citrus and something musky underneath. Their knees were almost touching. "How old are you, Tom?"

"Twenty three, why?"

"I think it's time to stop fighting it."

"I don't know what you mean,"

"Oh, I think you know exactly what I mean." Tom was furious with himself as he blushed to the roots of his hair. He needed to escape from the situation.

"I think I should probably go, I have an article to write. Thank you for lunch, MaitreBerenger"

"As you wish, but you could at least call me
. After all, you at least are not a client."

As they got up to go he took out a slim leather wallet and handed Tom a card.

"This is my private number. Call me if you want to talk." As they shook hands to say goodbye he put his hand on Tom's shoulder. Tom did not pull away.

Definitely, not in Kansas now, Toto, Tom thought as he headed off towards the Luxembourg Gardens. He needed to walk and be by himself for a while.

#

Olga kept walking without caring where she was going. She stopped to look in shop windows but didn't register anything she saw, and flicked through books that later she had no recollection of looking at. Finally, she came to the intersection of Saint-Michel and Saint-Germain and decided she needed some comfort food.

Everything that she knew, or thought she knew, had been turned upside down. What was true? What was a lie? Irina had been a devoted if slightly distant grandmother and now, here she was, a spy and a crook. What was it all for? Why allow herself to be dragged into all this after everything she had already endured in her life. Was it just the money? Olga began to feel that she had never known her grandmother and now she began to question how her mother and even Ana fitted into this sordid drama. As for her father he would feel totally vindicated in his ambivalence about Irina. One part of her wanted to walk away and forget any of this had ever happened but like Irina, Olga was stubborn. Someone was playing games and she was going to find out who it was.Olga went into the Cafe de Cluny and ordered a hot chocolate that arrived under a mountain of whipped cream. As she stirred the chocolate round and round to dissolve the cream she wondered *why did I ask for cream, I hate it.* The cloying taste of the sweetened cream made her feel slightly sick. Olga sat without drinking the chocolate, looking at the elaborate floral pattern on the saucer and letting the hot cup warm her hand as she stared into space and replayed all the crazy things she had heard.

The Café de Cluny was a great place to meet someone. Situated on a corner, the glass wall of the terrace went all the way round the building so if you sat in the angle, you could see anyone approaching from three sides. If you wanted to dodge them you could skip out the side door into rue de la Harpe and get lost in the crowds of students mingling outside the many cheap Greek and Turkish restaurants.

Olga was vaguely aware of two men sitting in the far corner deep in conversation until she realised that one of them was staring at her. It took her a moment to recognise him from the photographs she had seen earlier. It was Kerensky, and the man beside him was Commandant Jourdain. Kerensky stood up and moved towards her as Olga ran for the door. She didn't know what would happen if they caught up with her, but she wasn't going to wait to find out. She ran as fast as she could, dodging people on the crowded pavement. It was vaguely in her mind to get to the metro at the bottom of Saint-Michel, when out of the corner of her eye she saw a red taxi light as it pulled up to the kerb.

An elegantly dressed lady was getting out, shopping bags on one arm, a poodle on the other. Olga almost knocked her down as she jumped into the back of the cab. The woman looked mortally offended and muttered something about *les jeunes de nosjours*, but Olga didn't care. She slammed the door shut and banged the lock down. *"Vite!Vite! Police urgence!"* Olga's French had evaporated under the stress, but the driver got the message and the taxi pulled out into the traffic as Kerensky reached the kerb.

As the taxi disappeared from sight Kerensky walked back up to Café de Cluny, where Jourdain was pacing up and down in a panic. "What am I supposed to do now? She's clearly going to blab. I'm well and truly screwed."

Kerensky looked at him calmly. "Don't worry, we'll figure

something out. They may suspect something but they can't prove anything. She's a stupid girl who overreacted. She's never even seen me so how could she be sure. Now, let's go and have a drink and forget all about it." They walked on a few hundred metres and as they turned a corner into a quiet alley between two streets, Jourdain realised that Kerensky wasn't following. As he turned, he saw the gun.

"What the fuck?"

"Sorry, Jourdain," said Kerensky, and shot him twice. Jourdain fell against the wall and slid down, ending up slumped on the footpath with his head on his knees. His overcoat hid the patch of blood just above his heart. With a bit of luck people would think he was drunk, at least for a few hours. It had been a mistake to meet in such a public place but Jourdain had rung him in a panic shouting that the investigation was getting too close. He had always thought Jourdain was a light weight. All he had to do was sit tight, say nothing and wait for the storm to pass. As for the girl, what could he do? The police would be watching her so better leave well enough alone, for the time being. It would be a good idea for him to get offside. Kerensky thrust his gun back into its shoulder holster and walked slowly off in the direction of the nearest metro.

\#

For a minute Olga didn't know where to go. No point going back to the hotel – too risky – and she had no idea where Tom was. There was only one option, police headquarters. At the reception desk she asked for Commissaire Boyer, but the officer on duty looked at her disdainfully as if she had asked to speak to God Almighty. "You have an appointment?" he asked in that tone used on small children or very stupid people. Olga was thinking she might make a run for the stairs when the lift opened and Inspector Fitzgerald walked out. He seemed mightily surprised to see her as she rushed over and started to gabble about what had happened. Fitzgerald led her over to a window recess.

"Slow down, and in words of one syllable tell me what has happened."

When she described in detail meeting Kerensky and Jourdain,

THE BRATINSKY AFFAIR

he took her upstairs and left her in an interview room with a baffled young policewoman. Commissaire Boyer appeared a few minutes later amid a flurry of activity. He glanced once in her direction but didn't even have the courtesy to come over and speak to her directly. Instead he issued a series of curt commands and went back into his office, banging the door behind him. One of his senior officers was either a criminal or a spy, possibly both. There'd be hell to pay. With a year to retirement he could see himself down at his country cottage, fishing on the banks of the Loire. The way things were going this might happen sooner than expected. His secretary stuck her head round the door: "The Minister's office on line 3."

After about half an hour Olga saw Fitzgerald coming down the corridor towards her looking pleased with himself. He had realised early on that the French were going to hang him out to dry for the lack of progress in the investigation but they certainly wouldn't be able to do that now. The chickens had well and truly come home to roost.

"The Commissaire has issued an order to pick up Jourdain and an arrest warrant for Kerensky – though he probably has diplomatic immunity. Now, let's get you back to the hotel. This officer will stay with you until we know what is happening."

\#

Tom had walked around for a couple of hours: down the rue de Rivoli, through the Tuileries Gardens and up into the Luxembourg Gardens. By then he was beginning to flag and decided to go in search of somewhere he could sit down, have a cup of coffee and watch the world go by. He strolled along the boulevard Saint Germain looking aimlessly into shop windows until he found himself standing outside the Salamander shoe shop. He laughed to himself. Olga was right; he was becoming fixated on shoes but since he had arrived in Paris he had noticed two things about Parisians; their clothes always looked immaculate as if they had just come back from the dry cleaners and their shoes always looked new. He was still standing there smiling to himself when he realised that someone inside was smiling back at him. He peered more closely through the tinted glass and realised that Maitre Bérenger, he couldn't quite bring himself to say Jean-Philippe, was sitting inside waving at him. Too late to run away so he went in.

"Hi Tom; Twice in one day. It must be fate!"

was trying on a pair of mountain boots.

"Clearly not for the office." said Tom trying to say something witty.

"I'm going on a hiking holiday in the Pyrenées next month and I'll need to break them in. What about you?"

"I think this is a bit out of my price range."

"Nonsense!"

He pointed to a pair of ox blood loafers that another customer had left on the floor.

"They look like your size – no harm in trying them on."

They did fit and surprisingly, they were very comfortable. As he walked up and down in front of the mirror Tom could see Maitre Beranger watching him, smiling and nodding approvingly.

"They suit you. We'll take the boots and these" he said to the vendeuse, over Tom's protests.

"I insist" he said. "Think of it as a souvenir of your first visit to Paris." As he handed the bag to Tom their hands touched briefly. Tom noticed his eyes for the first time: green with a fleck of brown and breathed in the familiar scent of citrus. He held the bag in front of him to hide his embarrassment.

"I'm meeting friends for dinner in a while but let's go and have a quick drink first."

They walked upto Saint Germain des Près and sat on the terrace outside one of the cafes. The fresh air gave Tom a chance to get his emotions under control. They were both facing out to the street so they didn't need to sit face to face.

Tom ordered a beer and Maitre Berenger had a pastis.

"How did you get to know Ms Radcliffe?"

"Pure chance. I'm a journalist with the local paper. After the fire I went up to have a look at her grandmother's house and she turned up. Neither of us really knew what was going on and we've been helping each other out since then – the blind leading the blind."

"Must be interesting, being a journalist?"

THE BRATINSKY AFFAIR

"Not really - it's small town stuff but I really want to be an investigative reporter. That's why I jumped at the chance to come to Paris."

"City lights and all that?

"Not so much. I want a shot at something bigger – new – different?"

Out of the corner of his eye he could see Maitre Berenger watching him. It was very easy to talk to him, even though they had only just met. That was probably why.

"I know I'm lucky," said Tom. There's a whole future laid out in front of me and all I need to do is reach out and take it, but I want something more. Am I being greedy?" He was talking to himself as much as to Maitre Berenger. He was thinking about Olga, Tess back home – his father .

"So, you have to choose." Maitre Berenger turned and looked Tom in the eye. "That's the hard part. I know from experience"

There was a note of sadness in his voice and Tom wondered what the story was. He looked around him thinking: *here I am sitting on the terrace of a café in Paris, one of the biggest cities in the world, following my first big story and I don't know what I want.* The buzz evaporated.

"I need to get going. Olga will think I've got lost."

"And I need to get going too or I'll be late for dinner. You have my number; call me if you want

to talk."

They stood up and shook hands before going their separate ways. At the last moment Tom turned back into the café and went to the bathroom. He put on his new shoes. To hell with it! He could at least pretend to be a Parisian.

#

Olga was drinking coffee in the lobby with the police officer when Tom wandered in around 6pm. He was wearing his new shoes and carrying his old brogues in a fancy bag with the Salamander logo on the front.

"Nice shoes, Tom, Salamander no less! I see we're going for the cheap shops! But while you were out shopping I had to run for my life."

Tom looked at her in amazement. "What on god's name are

you talking about? Are you OK?" "You better sit down, a lot has been happening. Turns out you were right about Jourdain. He was up to his neck in it." Tom sat open mouthed as Olga described what had happened. "The Commissaire has issued an order to bring Jourdain in and arrest Kerensky. And Tom, if you say, I told you so, I may have to resort to violence." The excitement about Jourdain at least meant that Tom didn't need to give any details about his shopping expedition.

Olga realised that she hadn't actually eaten all day and was absolutely starving. Now that Olga was no longer alone the police officer moved off to keep a discreet watch from the lobby. When she left, they went into the bar and ordered a drink. By this stage the barman knew what they wanted – Redbreast with ice, two cubes.

They sat talking about what was likely to happen next as they looked at the menu. Then the barman came over. "A call for Mademoiselle Radcliffe."

Olga came back in a few minutes looking even paler than before. "That was Fitzgerald. They found Jourdain. He's dead, shot. They found him in the laneway behind the Café de Cluny. Kerensky certainly didn't waste any time. God in heaven, Tom that could have been me! What is going on? What can be so important that at least three people have been killed for it? Did Maître Berenger say something about all this being brushed quietly under the carpet? Fat chance! This will be all over the newspapers in the morning."

Tom rushed upstairs to grab his typewriter. This really was breaking news.

THE BRATINSKY AFFAIR

CHAPTER 14

Paris, Summer1939

After a few years Irina managed to buy a cottage in Auteuil, where Ana lived with Masha. She rented it first, before buying it at a knock-down price in 1938.With war on the horizon the old couple who had lived there for thirty years wanted a quick sale before they headed south. Cottage was something of a misnomer since it was in fact a small villa built in the eighteenth century by a rich aristocrat to house his very young mistress. With its secret gardens and discreet villas Auteuil had kept its village atmosphere and was the perfect place for Masha to grow up. This arrangement also gave Irina the freedom to live alone in the city and be her own person. For Ana, this was the first time she had felt at home since leaving Russia. She liked nothing better than pottering in her garden. In fact, Irina thought she spent more time in the garden behind its high red brick wall, than in the house, growing all her favourite fruit and vegetables. Dill and horseradish for sauces; blueberries, strawberries and raspberries for jam, and tomatoes and cucumbers for salad. There was even a special corner for beetroot and potatoes. And all autumn she spent pickling, canning, storing food as if she were preparing for the Russian winters of her girlhood. The memory of the hunger they had endured during the war had never left her and she liked to keep the larder fully stocked to cover all eventualities.

Ana had the gift of nesting. Wherever she lived, even if it was one room, she always managed to create a warm, happy atmosphere. It was the small things that made a difference – a colourful shawl thrown over a chair or a posy of flowers in a teacup. She was an inventive cook who could turn the simplest ingredients into something delicious. There was always something simmering in a pot, even if it was only vegetable soup, and, as often as not there would be someone sitting at the table by the kitchen window, drinking tea or eating soup, usually someone from the old days in need of comfort or company. Over time the cottage in Auteuil became a magnet for the many lost souls Ana met at the orthodox cathedral who needed to talk to someone who shared their grief and sense of loss. With them there was no need for explanations. They understood instinctively how she felt.

Ana seldom spoke about the past, but Irina knew that she always kept a collection of the poems of Ana Akhmatova by her bed as an emotional touchstone. Ana was not deeply religious but on the table opposite her bed there was a crucifix and an icon of the flight into Egypt. The question of what had happened to Victor and Pavel was never touched on but every year on 5 January, the anniversary of the day they had left Russia, Ana and Irina would go to the orthodox cathedral in the afternoon and light a candle. There was no discussion and afterwards Ana would spend the rest of the evening alone in her room. In January, 1939, Irina arrived as usual to take her mother to church. Irina was feeling jumpy. She hadn't seen Suzy since the sitting with de Lempicka and they had planned to meet up later that evening for a drink. When she walked into the kitchen in Auteuil she found two old ladies sitting at the kitchen table with Ana, eating soup. Irina's heart sank as it looked as though the ladies were settled in for the afternoon. Irina looked at them blankly but fortunately her mother came to the rescue. "You remember Countess Brassova don't you and her friend Princess Odoyevsky.

"Yes, of course, Irina stumbled, "how nice to see you again," but she was too agitated thinking about Suzy to really pay attention and it took her a minute to remember where she had met her before.

Irina looked at the woman in amazement. In the face of this beaten-down old woman she could find no trace of the woman once considered the most beautiful woman in Saint Petersburg. She couldn't have been more than sixty but she looked haggard. She had caused a spectacular scandal when, as a twice divorced woman, she had married the Grand Duke Michael. Irina remembered the last time she had seen her. She had gone to The Passage, the most elegant department store in Saint Petersburg, to buy a ribbon for a dress. She couldn't decide between the pink

THE BRATINSKY AFFAIR

or blue and was holding each ribbon up to her face in turn when she heard a voice behind her.

"You must buy the blue: It goes perfectly with your eyes."

She had looked up to see this beautiful and elegant lady wearing a chinchilla coat and a wide-brimmed hat standing behind her smiling.

"You're Ana O'Rourke's daughter, aren't you? –You're just like her. Please, give her my regards. At that moment her chauffeur came to collect her parcels and she went off with a smile and a wave of her elegantly gloved hand. There was no trace of that refined elegance now. Her clothes were shabby and she looked as though she hadn't eaten for a week. Irina noticed the slight indentation on the engagement finger of her left hand where she had once worn a spectacular diamond ring. To cover her confusion Irina turned to Princess Odoyevsky.

"I don't believe we've met before."

"No, I don't think so, and yet the name O'Rourke seems familiar – such an unusual name!"

Irina wished they would go. She had just turned to say something to her mother when the princess said:

"Now I remember."

All three women turned to look at her.

Irina could see the grief in her eyes that this sudden memory had stirred.

"I had gone to the Peter and Paul Fortress to try and bring food for my brother, but the guards just shouted at me and left me sitting in the freezing hall for hours. I was afraid they would arrest me too but I sat there listening as they called out the names of the prisoners - hoping to hear my brother's name. At least I would have known he was alive. As I listened, I heard, O'Rourke Victor and O'Rourke Pavel called out. I remember, because I was listening so intently and the names were so unusual. They didn't sound Russian.

The next day I went back but the guards wouldn't even let me through the gate. They said that if they saw my ugly face again they would arrest me too. Later, I was told that all the prisoners in that wing had been shot to make room for a new intake of prisoners. The next day I decided to leave Russia." The princess's mind had gone back to another time and she was so focused on her own grief that she didn't realise the impact of her words, as she asked:. "Were they relatives of yours?"

There was complete silence. Ana got up and left the room. Irina's instinct was to follow her mother but she had to stay with the ladies. Countess Brassova turned to the princess: "My dear, you have the sensitivity of a log of wood. That was Ana's husband and son. We'd better go." She gave Irina a sympathetic hug and the two old ladies tottered off down the garden path. As they left Irina gave the Countess the bag of food that Ana had put aside for her.

First Irina rang Suzy to tell her she wouldn't be able to make it and then went up to her mother's room and sat beside her on the bed as they both wept without saying a word. It was Irina's turn to offer comfort. The next morning, they went to the cathedral to light a candle as usual and this time they stayed for the whole service.

#

There were also periods of light relief. To Irina's surprise the Irish Ambassador – or to give him his correct title, Envoy Extraordinary and Minister Plenipotentiary to France – had become a regular visitor. Ana and Irina had bumped into him one day on the Avenue Foch before things with Egon had finally fallen apart. He loved the idea of this member of an old Irish family from Russia having washed up on his doorstep in Paris and he would occasionally invite them for tea in the legation. He collected Sèvres porcelain and duchesses and he adored Ana. He took her under his wing and got a great kick out of introducing her to the other aristocratic French ladies with Irish connections. When the Duchess de MacMahon invited them for lunch even Irina was impressed. She did have to admit that he had wonderful taste and with her eye on the prospect of an Irish passport she gave him the full benefit of her charm and pulled out every Ireland related story that she had ever heard her father tell. Who knew what the future might bring and it would be a good idea to have an escape route to a politically neutral country.

THE BRATINSKY AFFAIR

However, most people got bored with the sad stories of once upon a time. Irina's focus was now firmly fixed on business. And when she went to Auteuil it was like stepping back into the past. She always came away feeling guilty about neglecting her mother and Masha and as a result, she went there less and less. Ana rarely said anything, never reproached her, but sometimes she would look at her sadly and say, "Masha misses you." But there was always a dinner or a deal that was too important to miss, and as Irina's business developed, money became a substitute for love.

\#

And then there was the added complication of Suzy. At the end of their sitting de Lempicka had offered them a drink but Irina needed to escape as quickly as possible; she didn't know what she was feeling and needed some time on her own to process her thoughts. When Suzy insisted on driving her home Irina wouldn't hear of it.

"No honestly I need to get home to make tea for Masha. And my mother is going out to visit a friend. You stay and enjoy the drink."

"At least let me call you a taxi," said de Lempicka .

Suzy could sense Irina's agitation and said nothing as they walked to the door of the apartment.

"Are you ok?"

"Yes, really, I just need to get home."

As soon as she closed the door of the taxi Irina sank back against the worn leather and breathed deeply. She didn't know whether to laugh or cry. Over the next week they chatted once or twice on the phone but Irina made sure to keep things firmly focused on the superficial. Sometimes she felt an almost physical need to talk to Suzy but when they were on the phone together she didn't know what to say. Suzy didn't push it.

After the departure of the late and unlamented marquis, *La Vie Parisienne* gradually became the final stopping off point at the end of an evening for Irina and her friends. Usually Irina went there as a part of a group of like-minded people who enjoyed the bohemian atmosphere and wanted to let their hair down and have some fun away from the stuffy atmosphere of polite society. For Irina there was safety in numbers. Occasionally one of the group might venture into forbidden territory but not Irina. Suzy would always be there hovering in the background watching to make sure that things didn't get too rowdy as the champagne flowed. Irina didn't drink very much but occasionally one of the group might have to be laid down on a sofa to recover or sent home in a taxi. It was a balmy night in early summer when her friend Justin, another dealer from the place des Vosges, called her up and begged her to come out for the night. His wife had dumped him for a rich American and he wanted to drown his sorrows. When he arrived in a taxi to pick her up it was clear that he had already been drinking. When they arrived at the club he finished one bottle and ordered another, gradually getting louder and louder. Irina tried to calm him but he kept drinking and crying. Finally, Suzy stepped in.

"I think it's time your friend went home. Let's put him in a taxi and then we can relax and have a quiet drink."

By the time they got Justin safely into a taxi and gave the driver a handsome tip to make sure he got safely back to his apartment it was already 4AM and the staff were beginning to close up for the night.

"Let's go upstairs and leave Marie-Ange and Pierre to close up. She saw Irina's hesitation and shrugged.

"It's as you wish. If you prefer, Pierre will get you a cab from the corner."

Irina knew she was crossing a line but she followed as Suzy led the way. Behind the bar there was a hidden door that led onto the back stairs. They went up two flights and into Suzy's private quarters. The apartment wasn't what Irina had expected. It was simple, modern and luxurious . The panelled walls were the palest shade of grey, the floors gleaming parquet and the furniture had the sleek lines of an ocean liner. There was nothing to distract from the spectacular art on the walls.

Suzy poured them both a whiskey and handed a glass to Irina.

"I keep the best pieces up here" she said as she saw Irina staring at the now finished double portrait of them by de

THE BRATINSKY AFFAIR

Lempicka.

"What do you think?

"I think I don't know what to think. It's so strange to see yourself as someone else sees you. I never think of myself as looking like that"

"Like what ?"

"I don't know: angry, lost maybe."

For a moment nothing was said and they stood looking at each other. If Irina had expected to be flung on a chaise longue and ravished that was clearly not going to happen. Suzy reached behind her head and pulled the bow of her halter-neck dress which fell to the floor in a glittering cascade of sequins. Underneath she was completely naked.

They continued to stare at each other until Suzy broke the silence. '

"It's your choice."

Irina was trembling as she crossed the room and slowly reached out. She repeated Suzy's gesture from the first night they met and ran her finger up Suzy's arm, gently touching her neck until she ran her finger around the outline of her lips. Suzy arched her neck and took Irina's finger between her teeth in a mock snarl.

"I think we could be more comfortable in the bedroom, don't you?"

Irina smiled and let Suzy lead her by the hand to the bedroom at the back of the apartment. Like the living room it was a symphony in shades of off white and cream. As they stood by the bed Suzy took her in her arms and kissed her for the first time.

"I'm not really sure what to do," said Irina. "I've never done this before – with a woman that is?"

"No worries, whatever happens, happens."

Suzy pulled Irina down onto the bed and wrapped her in her arms

"You worry too much," she said as she ran her fingers up the inside of Irina's thighs, across her stomach and over her breasts slowly and gently, barely touching her skin. Suzy could feel Irina's intake of intake of breath as she crossed from one erogenous zone to the next. The tingle of the first caress grew steadily from the pit of her stomach until her entire body felt like one enormous pleasure zone. When the orgasm came she clung to Suzy as if her life depended on it. Afterwards they kissed and caressed, talking. For the first time in her life Irina told someone the whole story of the escape from Russia, the rape, the disappearance of her father and brother and the nightmare they had experienced in their flight across Europe. Suzy just let her talk until she had exhausted herself and they both fell asleep.

THE BRATINSKY AFFAIR

CHAPTER 15

Paris, March 1976
The next morning Tom ran down to get the early morning papers. *L'AffaireBratinsky*, as it was now known, was the front-page story in all the leading newspapers. The murder of Commandant Jourdain and the search for Kerensky had highlighted the role of the Russian Embassy and shifted the focus away from the murder of Irina onto the intelligence failures in the Prime Minister's office. Some journalists were beginning to portray Irina as an innocent victim lured into the world of espionage and then eliminated when she was no longer useful. Partly true, partly a work of fiction, but a convenient way to spin the story.

Tom spent two hours on the phone to Willi Regan, then to Irish radio and the BBC.

His latest article led with the dramatic headline:
Special Report by Tom O'Brien in Paris
"L'AffaireBratinsky" Takes Dramatic New Turn: Spies, Diplomats and Political Scandal

The murder of Commandant Jourdain, the officer in charge of the investigation into the murder of CountessBratinsky in Wicklow, has exposed a Russian intelligence network operating between National Police Headquarters, the Elysée and the Hôtel Matignon, and possibly involving both the President of France's staff and that of the Prime Minister. Members of the opposition and satirical publications such as le Canard Enchaîné are calling for heads to roll in what they describe as "a catalogue of corruption and incompetence."

Tom and Olga were going over the papers when Inspector Fitzgerald arrived. Strangely, he seemed much calmer, and even nodded hello to Tom. "Kerensky was seen getting onto a flight to Moscow this morning so I think you can probably relax now, though you should keep your wits about you in case. As for the investigation, the French are saying it's case closed. Boyer has been moved off the case and the new man, Corot, obviously wants to bury it. He hardly had time to talk to me this morning and asked me when I was going back to Dublin."

"But what about the Jourdain/Kerensky connection and the break-ins?" asked Olga.

"They're not interested. The Minister of Justice and the Head of Intelligence are fighting for their political lives and as far as they are concerned the murder of CountessBratinsky and the break-ins are a minor inconvenience detail. The Minister may well have to resign. I will hang on for a few more days and see what I can dig up but I will probably head back to Dublin by the weekend. The truth is we may never know the full story. You should probably think about heading home soon, too. There's not a lot more you can do here."

After Inspector Fitzgerald left Olga remembered that she had to go and get some francs. She also needed to go to the Credit Lyonnais over on rue Monsieur le Prince, near Saint-Michel, to sort out Irina's affairs. If she kept busy she wouldn't have time to think about what was going on around her. The late March chill was beginning to fade and the sun was shining, so they decided to walk over and enjoy the change in the weather.

Finally, Tom was getting a chance to enjoy the beauty of Paris. At the bottom of boulevard Saint- Michel they stopped for coffee on one of the many outdoor terraces to watch the world go by. Since they had arrived in Paris there had been so much going on that they had had no chance to sit down and breathe. Tom looked at Olga as she sipped her coffee. He could see that the strain was beginning to tell in the way she looked nervously around her every few minutes and kept flicking her hair out of her eyes.

"Olga, are you ok?

"I'm absolutely fine. Why do you ask?" The brittle tone of her answer said all too clearly that she wasn't fine at all.

"Well, maybe Fitzgerald is right – and it's time to call it a day. This all started out as a straightforward investigation and now here we are in the middle of an international conspiracy. Do you not think we are a bit out of our depth here?"

Olga looked at him.

"Getting cold feet, Tom? You said you wanted to be an investigative journalist. So, this is your big chance. You can go if you want, but I came here to get answers and I'm not going home until I get them."

For the first time he could the steel in her character.

"I'm just worried about you, Olga. This isn't exactly holiday of a lifetime!" To change the subject he asked casually "Did you get a chance to speak to Maître Berenger?"

"I had a quick chat with him this morning – he sends his regards, by the way. He said he would call over to the hotel this evening with some papers for me to sign. He was shocked about Jourdain, and of course he had read all the details in the papers. Wanted to know if I was ok, if I needed anything. In the end he more or less said 'told you so," that's the way Paris works'. As he put it,'*Sauve qui peut*' – or less politely put, when the shit hits the fan it's every man for himself. Anyway, how is Dear Willi Regan?"

"Willi is beside himself with excitement. It's a long time since *The Wicklow Herald* featured in breaking news. He said the best part was when the foreign editor of *The Irish Times* had a hissy fit wanting to know how, as he put it, "a provincial rag like the *Herald* got on top of such a big story." Willi took great delight in telling him that if he got his backside off a bar stool in the Kildare Street Club, he might know what was going on. But even he is beginning to wonder how much longer this will last. Must need somebody to do the Farming Today column."

They both laughed and the tension between them subsided.

When they got to the bank after lunchtime Olga presented the letter from Maître Berenger." and within minutes they were being ushered into a private room and offered coffee. The manager himself came in to offer his condolences and to know how he could be of help. Olga explained that for the moment she wanted to review the account and check the contents of the safe deposit box. The manager placed some papers on the desk in front of her and called one of his assistants to take them downstairs to a private room while they waited for the assistant to bring the box.

"I have a feeling Irina was a valued customer," said Tom.

"You have no idea!" said Olga as she flicked through the

papers. "The smaller account has a hundred and fifty thousand francs in it. Clearly the housekeeping account!"

The young woman came in and placed a large safety deposit box in front of Olga. She hesitated for a moment before she opened it. Inside there was a copy of Irina's will, share certificates, various property deeds, and a jewellery box containing a pearl necklace, a locket and a pair of diamond stud earrings. There was also a letter and a faded leather-bound diary with the monogram of a crown and a sword on the front. And a photograph of a finely-decorated sword.

Olga read the letter, hesitantly translating from Russian as she went.

My Dearest Olga

If you are reading this it means that the worst has happened and you will already know more about the sordid details of my life that I ever wanted you to know. I hope that you can forgive me and that this drama will die with me.

In this box you will find a pearl necklace, a locket and a pair of earrings; these are the last surviving pieces of Ana's jewellery, the emergency fund jealously guarded in the hard times, and I know that she would have wanted you to have them and to wear them in memory of her. I know she adored you, and one of my few consolations is that she died before your mother got ill.

Olga stumbled over the words as she read. She picked up the locket, and held it in her palm as she read on.

You know that Masha and I did not always see eye to eye, but despite all that there was a bond between mother and daughter that nothing could ever break. To your father I owe a debt of gratitude because I know he made Masha happy, which is more than I was ever able to do.

My life has been a struggle for survival and I have made many mistakes. But worst of all I allowed myself to be trapped into betraying everything I have ever believed in. The diary is Ana's. She wrote it during our escape from Russia. Every day she wrote a letter to her beloved Victor, knowing that he would never receive them. In the beginning she hoped that they would be reunited, but by the time we reached Paris she realised that that was a lost cause. She wrote the last letter after we arrived in France after which she never opened it again. My father was not a heroic man; in many ways he was weak; but theirs was a great love and I hope that one day you will find the same.

Olga looked up at Tom, tears sparkling in her eyes. As regards the photograph, that connects to our family history. Some time ago Kerensky came to me asking for my help in finding this sword. But of all the military swords hanging on museum walls, I have no idea why this one is special. A presentation sword with a few diamond chips? Why would this be of any interest to anyone and why would I know anything about it?

I can think of only one answer – Pavel and the story of the Battle of Leipzig that Ana repeated endlessly to Masha. As far as I knew my father and brother disappeared into the camps after they were arrested and died there. I never tried to find out what had happened to them, it was too painful. More recently I was told that they had been shot in the Peter and Paul Fortress. That was the end of the story as far as I was concerned.

Someone said 'The past is a foreign country; they do things differently there'. I have clung to that, and all my life I have tried to avoid looking back. I advise you to do the same. There is nothing to be gained from going there. Everything I have, I leave to you in love – take it – use it – be happy and forget the past. Remember me with kindness in all my human frailty.

Your loving grandmother

Irina

PS Whatever is going on is connected in some way to Russian intelligence. Be warned, Olga, these people are dangerous and unscrupulous, so whatever it is, have nothing to do with it. If Oleg Kerensky makes contact with you there is only one thing to do – run!

When Olga had finished reading the letter, she sat for several minutes without moving, tears running down her face. "I wish I had got to know her better. Now, it's too late and another part of me is angry that Irina got herself caught up in this whole saga instead of focusing on the people closest to her. What a waste of a life." Olga sat and wiped the tears away.

It was only then that she opened the locket. It contained the photographs of a man and a woman, taken at what looked like their wedding, obviously her great-grandparents, Ana and Victor. She looked at Tom.

"That's it! That's what was missing in Irina's apartment. In the icon corner there was always a photograph in a silver frame of Ana and Victor with two children. One was Irina and the other, presumably, was poor Pavel. But of all the things that could have been taken – why that?"

There was only one answer, Tom thought: Pavel. Everything that has happened is in some way connected to Irina's brother.

Olga took the locket and the diary and put the rest of the jewellery back in the box.

"Come on let's go – I need to get out of here!"

The safety box was locked and handed back as the manager ushered them out with profuse offers of assistance. They went back to the café and as they waited for the waiter to bring their drinks. Olga started flicking through the pages of Ana's diary. After a few minutes she said, "Tom? Don't look up now, but in a minute glance around and look at the man sitting on the terrace of the café across the street. See if you recognise him."

Tom looked up and glanced around as if checking for the waiter. "There is something familiar about him but I can't place him."

"I'm pretty sure he was at Irina's funeral. Count Tolstoy said he was from the embassy – the Russian embassy, I mean. Safe to say I don't think it's a coincidence."

After a few minutes they finished their drinks and headed in the direction of the metro, where it would be easier to see if they were being followed. When they reached the bottom of the escalator Tom glanced discreetly around and, sure enough, there was their man at the top. When they got into the train Tom could see his face reflected in the glass of the carriage as they hurtled through tunnels. He was pretending to read a newspaper, but Tom could see in the reflection that he glanced up every time the train stopped to make sure they were still there.

It was after four thirty when they got back to the hotel. Tom

THE BRATINSKY AFFAIR

tried to ring Inspector Fitzgerald but the receptionist in his hotel said she thought he had gone back to Dublin.

They were on their own.

\#

Tom had to talk to his father. There was something he remembered from his research about the O'Rourke family that he couldn't quite remember and that was niggling at him. He went up to his room and had a slightly tricky conversation with his father, who wanted to know the details of what exactly he was doing, why it was taking so long and when he would be home. It was a relief to get off the phone. Then he called Thomas Douglas, the librarian in the Chief Herald's office back in Dublin. He was in luck; he had caught Douglas as he was packing up to go home.

"Hi Thomas, I don't want to keep you, but there was a chapter in the book you read me, about the role of Count O'Rourke de Breffny in the Battle of Leipzig. Any chance you could pull that out for me? There's something I want to check."

Tom scribbled furiously as Douglas read out the section. Finally, something was clicking into place that might make sense of all this. Tom wanted to rush up and tell Olga immediately, but she needed a rest and he would keep it as a surprise to be revealed later. Neither of them had any appetite so they headed out for a walk along the Seine in the glorious early spring sunshine. There was a kiosk selling crêpes on the corner and they bought two of the delicious slightly crisp pancakes and strolled along the embankment. It was a relief to be out in the fresh air. Finally, Tom couldn't contain his excitement any longer. "You know that old sword in the photograph – the one Irina didn't know that much about? I've found something."

"What, don't tell me, its solid gold and studded with rubies!"

"Not quite – but almost. As far as I can see, it belonged to Napoleon and was the one he was wearing at the Battle of Leipzig."

"But why is that so special? Every soldier in the world at that time had a sword and every antique shop in Paris has at least two of them hanging on a wall, and nobody wants them at any price."

"Think about it. This sword was specially made for Napoleon. It is gold, inlaid with silver. It has his monogram on it, and he was carrying it at the crucial battle that was the beginning of the end for his empire."

"But how did my ancestor get his hands on it?"

"According to the book in the Chief Herald's office, the Russians played a key role in the battle, and your ancestor – General Count O' Rourke, Baron de Breffny, to give him his full title – led the brigade which turned the tide against the French. When the French retreated, the Prussians captured the emperor's campaign tent and the sword. Afterwards the King of Prussia presented it to the general in recognition of his bravery."

"But why would someone kill for it?"

"Every museum, historian or collector in the world would give their eye teeth for it, and according to Thomas Douglas in Dublin, the Chief Herald, the last sword that could definitely be linked to Napoleon to come on the open market was sold for $2.5 million. That was several years ago, and he says that if a similar sword came on the market now it could fetch up to $5 million."

"But it was probably sold years ago. The whole story of the sword is family legend."

"I doubt it." Then Tom noticed that Olga had brought Ana's diary with her. She hadn't wanted to take the chance of leaving it in the room.

"You don't know that much about the history of your family, do you?"

"My mother shut all that Russian family stuff away – except for anything to do with food. She and Ana would spend hours in the kitchen concocting recipes. My earliest memory is of me sitting at a table in the garden of Ana's house in Auteuil eating cherries while they decorated a cake for my birthday. Irina, of course, was too busy to come."

"So you don't know what this is?" He pushed the diary across the table

"Of course, it's Ana's diary."

"And this?" As he opened the book to the flyleaf

"It's a coat of arms."

THE BRATINSKY AFFAIR

"Yes indeed – it's the O'Rourke de Breffny coat of arms, the central image of which is a crown – and an arm wielding a sword which matches the sketch of Napoleon's sword in the book in the Chief Herald's Library! That's why someone would want it so badly – the history –the intrinsic value, the family provenance and the direct link to a crucial moment in the life of Napoleon. The bad news is that someone seems to want it very, very badly, and that someone seems to think that even if you don't have it, you might have information that would help them find it."

Finally, all the stress that had been building up over the previous weeks burst out. "This is absurd. What does any of this have to do with me? I don't have any information. I don't know if this Pavel is dead or alive, he would be at least 70 by now, and for all I know this could all be a load of wishful thinking. There's too much going on. Tomorrow I have to start clearing up the shop and the rue du Bac apartment and start thinking about what I am going to do with them. Plus, I have to contact the bank in Geneva and sort out all the tax stuff, and I haven't seen Dad in weeks. As far as I'm concerned, Pavel, or whoever it is, can take the sword and stick it, pointy end up, where the sun don't shine!; here you look after the diary, I'm going back to the hotel, I need a rest. They walked back in silence and Olga went straight up to her room

#

Tom picked the diary up and took it with him back into the bar; he might as well take the time to get to know this woman at the heart of the mystery. It was just as well he had taken that course in Russian and even though his Russian was rudimentary it was the spidery handwriting that was more of a challenge.

It wasn't a diary, more of a sketch book. The first few pages were drawings: a house in a park surrounded by thick forest, a pair of ponies grazing in a field, a watercolour of an old church with gilded domes and pink walls against a blue sky. The first diary entry proper was Christmas 1916: details of visits by uncles and aunts, presents given and received, minor disagreements.

The main focus of the diary was family life. He read notes on a sick child, a cure for whooping cough, worries about Victor, who had been sent to the front. Surprisingly, apart from that, there was little mention of the war; apart from the occasional mention of someone else they knew who had been sent off to fight.

Every page was accompanied by a sketch or a caricature, and here and there a recipe had been pasted in: lamb pilaff, piroshky meat pies, fish soup, spiced Russian tea. He had to look piroshky up the dictionary to see what it was as none of this delicious sounding food had ever graced the family table in Bray. But as the days wore on the entries became more sombre. War and rumours of war and food becoming short. Every day Ana went to help in the local hospital for wounded soldiers where drugs, especially morphine, were almost unobtainable and everyone was trying to ignore the reports of political turmoil from the city and the front.

She described the fear in the eyes of wounded soldiers who were getting better, as they dreaded being sent back to fight. A whole page was devoted to the day the Empress and her daughters came to visit the hospital. She described how clean linen and flowers appeared out of nowhere for the visit and how the Empress was surprisingly friendly and down to earth, not at all what she had expected. On the opposite page a card had been pasted in with a sketch of a cat sitting on a wall watching a bird on the branch of a tree. It was simple and charming and signed, *with thanks, Anastasia*.

The entries became more and more sporadic. "Now there is fighting in the city, armed mobs in the street. How to keep the children unaware of what is going on? Then one day, a celebration – "Victor has returned, wounded but getting better", while outside the fighting between striking workers and the soldiers was getting more intense with every passing day.

February, "the Tsar has abdicated: Dear God, let there be an end to this terrible war and we can begin to rebuild." As spring turned into summer there was a sense of fading hope and growing concern for the future. It was not safe to go out in the streets and the final straw came when the windows of their house were broken and Victor was attacked in the street. "This cannot go on!"

THE BRATINSKY AFFAIR

The entry for 10 August 2017, read: "Finally, we have decided to leave the city and go to the country for the summer. The schools are closed, there is constant fighting and there are queues for food everywhere. Hopefully in Tsarskoye Selo there will be some peace and the children will be able to go outside and get some fresh air. I long to walk in the forest and feel the soft grass under my feet. I dream of fresh mushrooms. Heaven knows when we will be able to come back – maybe October if the schools are open."

Tom got the impression of a warm, affectionate woman with a dry sense of humour trying hard to maintain a sense of normality for her son and daughter as the world fell apart around her. On every second page she worried about Victor. Where is he? How is he? Clearly Victor and the children were the entire focus of her life.

She certainly sounded completely different from Irina. Tom was so engrossed in his reading that apart from a cursory glance when they walked in, he paid no attention to the couple sitting at the other end of the bar, and didn't notice the light reflecting on the lens of the camera tucked carefully under the flap of the woman's handbag.

The next morning Tom was on his second cup of coffee by the time Olga appeared. She sat down opposite him. "Sorry for the rant last night. Everything built up. I can't help feeling that in the middle of all this drama I'm forgetting about Irina."

"Don't worry about it. You know what? We can only do so much. It's not our job to catch the criminals. This is a story about your family and what happened to it, like so many other families. Let's just take the story as far as we can and leave it at that. We can't expect to unravel all the angles of a story that covers a revolution and two world wars. Irina was right. At a certain point we may have to let it go." Olga didn't look altogether convinced. He poured her a cup of coffee. "Here, you need to eat something. I didn't eat all the croissants.

They took their time walking back to rue du Bac in the sunshine and took a few minutes to go into the medieval church of Saint Germain des Prés. Olga wanted to light a candle for Irina and Ana while Tom sat in the silence. They were about to leave when the organist arrived to practice and as they walked out into the sunshine, they were accompanied by the swelling sounds of a Bach toccata. Tom knew that Olga was postponing the moment when she would have to walk into her grandmother's apartment and face her absence. As they passed the Deux Magots and Café de Flore, Olga filled Tom in on all the famous people like Sartre and Hemingway who used to hang out there in the 1920s and 30s. "You can see all kinds of everything here," she said. "It's the best free show in Paris."

At that point Tom caught the eye of one of a group of young men sitting at one of the front tables wearing full make-up and elaborate eye shadow. He couldn't help staring. The man winked at Tom and laughed before turning back to his friends. Olga caught the exchange: "You could at least *pretend* to be cool, Tom!"

A few minutes later they arrived at the apartment. As they walked up the staircase Olga was silent, and as they opened the door to go in she said "You know it's not only about Irina. It brings home to me that they are all gone, Ana, mother – now Irina. Now, there's me and my father. As long as they were alive there was this connection to a whole other world and now it's gone. Mother rejected it but at the same time she could never cut herself off from Russia completely. It's like hearing a conversation in another room. At a certain point you have to decide whether to join in or ignore it and walk on by. Now I don't know if I will ever have that chance." She squared her shoulders and took a breath. "Anyhow, enough of this – we have a job to do"

There was another conversation Tom needed to have with Olga, but he had been putting it off. Now was as good a time as any. "Olga, you know at some point soon I'm going to have to go back to Dublin – this adventure will have to come to an end."

"Yes, I realise that, and you have no idea how grateful I am that you came. I couldn't have done this on my own. Still, it would be great to have your help over the next couple of days while I put things in some kind of order. I'm hoping to persuade my father to come over for a few days, if he feels up to it."

They started in the kitchen and the connecting dining room, which were largely untouched, and after an hour's tidying they began to look normal. The drawing room and the bedroom were a different story. Tom offered to do the drawing room while Olga dealt with the more personal things in the bedroom

First, he arranged things in piles to find a logical home for them. Books and records and piles of art catalogues were reasonably easy to sort out. From the bedroom he heard Olga exclaiming – "My God there must be 40 years of couture clothes here. We could put on a fashion retrospective. Surely someone will be interested in all this."

At one point she appeared in the doorway wearing a silver turban. "It's the one Irina wore to the New Year's Eve Ball in the Hôtel Matignon. Fabulous, but I don't think I have Irina's panache, somehow." Nevertheless, she went back to work still wearing the turban, with the feathers bobbing up and down.

After a while Tom noticed that there was silence from the other room. When he went in he found Olga standing in Irina's dressing room staring at a painting on the wall. It was a picture of two young women sitting on a sofa and staring intently at each other against a geometric background of skyscrapers. It could have been New York but it was clearly Paris. Olga took the picture down and turned it over. *Irina Bratinsky and Suzy Solidor, 1939, by Tamara de Lempicka.*

"It's an Irina I never knew; she looks so young – so beautiful. Why did she hide it away? As for Suzy Solidor – no idea who she is."

"I can answer that' said Tom smugly.

Olga looked at him in surprise.

"How come?"

Tom went over to the book case and picked up a bundle of records.

"I found these scattered all over the floor. It seems Suzy Solidar was a nightclub singer from before the war. Quite a big name by the look of things. There's an intensity in the picture, the way they look at each other. They were obviously close. Do you think they ..?

"No – please - don't go there! I already have enough mysteries in my grandmother's life. It's like an archaeological dig. Every time I uncover one layer of mystery I find another one underneath. Do you really think…. I mean…. my grandmother? Olga kept glancing from Tom to the picture.

"Your granny was obviously quite a gal" said Tom and he started to laugh.

"Anyway it's a fabulous picture. I would never part with it and I'm going to put it over here on the fireplace so I can see it while I'm working. There's obviously a story there. Now back to work!"

As they continued the carpet emerged bit by bit from under the chaos of papers and documents. Tom focused on the bookcase in the corner by the window. Everything had been scattered to the four winds, but it wasn't as bad as it looked and gradually the home that had been Irina's sanctuary came back into view.

With most of the wreckage cleared, Tom reached down to pull out a stack of papers wedged under the desk. Pushed in against the wall he found a slender vanity case. Inside was a bundle of letters tied with faded blue ribbons. He immediately recognised Ana's handwriting. As he went through the letters he became so engrossed that he didn't realise Olga was standing beside him.

"What have you found?"

"Letters from Ana – and photographs."

Underneath the bundle of letters was a photograph album.

He handed the album to Olga and she flicked it open. A photo of Ana as a young woman, probably taken before she got married. She looked young and serious and stared directly into the camera. She was wearing a straw boater and a tailored linen jacket over a shirt with a stand-up collar and a tie – clearly a studio portrait. The second photograph was a formal portrait of Ana with the children, taken some years later. She wore a silk blouse with a collar of embroidered daisies and a ruched silk skirt which trailed to the ground. Her hair was piled up in curls on top of her head and she sat in an armchair with a child standing on either side of her.

THE BRATINSKY AFFAIR

The girl on her left is all in white, with a ribbon in her hair. The boy, a few years younger, is standing on a stool wearing a knee-length lace dress and has his hair in ringlets. They all look serious, as if they had been warned by the photographer not to move or speak. Under these formal portraits was a jumble of more casual pictures: people playing tennis in a garden; a group of young people having a picnic by the seashore, an old lady sitting by a window sewing while a small baby played at her feet.

At the bottom of the box there was a photograph in a silver frame. It showed a family group sitting in cane chairs on the terrace of a country house in what looked like late summer. The photograph missing from the icon corner had obviously been cropped from this larger version. To the left was a door into what looked like a conservatory. Behind the family a path led up a hill to a chapel in the distance. On the right was what looked like part of a formal French garden with box hedging and roses. A picture of a vanished world.

Olga picked up the photograph. Despite the country house setting, things had clearly changed when this was taken. Ana had a kerchief on her hair and wore an apron. You could see a pair of work boots peeping out from underneath her skirt. The children were barefoot and wearing smocks –and Pavel has had his head shaved, perhaps to avoid lice in the summer heat. Victor had a rough shooting jacket on, and there was a hunting rifle propped against the table.

"It must have been taken that last summer," said Olga. "A group of elegant aristocrats waiting for their world to end."

She suggested a break for lunch and they went into the kitchen where she had laid out a picnic lunch on the heavy kitchen table. Comté and brie and country cheeses, some paté and two mini quiches, fresh French bread and a bowl of cherries. Even a bottle of wine. They sat and picked at the food, but neither of them was in the mood for eating. Looking at the photographs had induced a feeling of deep sadness.

"I have heard the story so often that when I look at that photograph now, I almost feel I was there," said Olga. "I was only six when Ana died but I have such vivid memories of her warmth and kindness. Mum and I used to go to stay with her in Auteuil. Sometimes Irina would appear, sometimes she wouldn't.

"But Ana was the centre of our lives. If she wasn't digging in the garden she was cooking in the kitchen and she had endless patience for a little girl who wanted to follow her around and do whatever she was doing. If she was making a cake, she would always let me lick the wooden spoon and would leave a spoonful in the bottom of the bowl for me to scrape out."

Tom remembered the same with his mother. The scent of warm scones and apple tart when he came home from school. It seemed all families deep down were broadly the same. He must get back to his dad soon, he thought.

Olga sliced off a piece of the Comté and lifted it onto Tom's plate with the knife. The scent of the cheese came up to him. "I can remember sitting on her knee as she read me a story. Of course, I got the famous story of our hero and the battle of Leipzig, and if she was in a nostalgic mood, she would tell how she and Irina escaped from Russia – except that she made it sound like an adventure. Isn't it funny, I can remember the feeling of that house, but I could only describe it in the vaguest most general way."

Tom was half listening as he ate. What a strange family story she had.

Olga poured them a glass of red to go with the cheese and raised her glass as she looked at Tom: "to absent friends."

They sat in silence for a minute and then she said, "Can I ask you a question?"

Tom looked at her in surprise – "yes, of course."

"Now, I know this is none of my business and nothing to do with anything but, are you gay, Tom?"

Tom put down his glass in shock.

"Jesus; Olga where did that come from?"

"Oh nothing, just a feeling. I thought I caught a vibe between you and MaitreBerenger and then with the boys sitting outside the café earlier."

Tom could feel himself getting redder and redder. In the end he put his head in his hands and stared at his plate. Tears weren't far away.

Olga moved round to sit beside him and put her arms around him.

"Look at me, Tom."

Tom raised his head.

"It's no big deal, you know. Half the guys in my glass were gay and in Sotheby's every second man seemed to be gay. I mean, what's a girl to do? So?

Tom took a deep breath before he spoke. "I think so – I mean yes – probably - but I've never done anything about it."

"Well, maybe it's about time you did."

"That's easy for you to say, Olga. You've no idea what it's like living in a small town where people know everything about you. I live with my father and he would be horrified and as for Willy Regan, let's not even go there."

"You might be surprised, Tom" and she leaned in and kissed him on the cheek.

"Now that we've got that out of the way we can concentrate on being friends. Let's call it a day," said Olga. "It's only 2PM but I think we both need a break and this place gives me the creeps. I'm not sure I could ever imagine living here after what has happened, more so even than the shop, because it is so much more personal."

As they headed back to the hotel Olga took Tom's arm and they strolled along in a companionable silence. As they went up the stairs into the hotel Tom handed the diary and photographs to Olga: "Here, can you take these? I think I'll go for a walk."

Olga looked at him.

"Are you sure you're ok?"

"Yes, really. I just need some air, and a bit of time to myself."

CHAPTER 16

Paris, Spring, 1939
This was fun! For the first time in years Irina was doing something for the pure hell of it. The business was growing steadily: she was finally able to pay the bills, look after Ana and Masha and even start putting some cash aside. When one of the younger members of the Peugeot family fell madly in love with Irinashe discreetly failed to mention her time working on the assembly line in the family factory. Meanwhile, every so often there would be a discreet knock on the door of the apartment in the rue du Bac in the early hours of the morning and Suzy would appear in a cloud of smoke and Je Reviens perfume. Sometimes Suzy would pull up in her Bugatti sports car and they would drive off for picnics in the forests near Fontainebleau leaving Monsieur Peugeot waiting for a phone call from Irina. On some evenings Irina would drift along to the club and sit at the bar waiting for Irina to finish.

Even Ana noticed that there was something different about Irina andover lunch in Auteuil she asked her straight out:

"You seem happier, my dear – lighter in yourself. Is there something I should know? Have you finally found someone to compensate for Egon?" Ana still felt guilty about pushing Irina into that disastrous marriage.

"No mother; don't worry, if there is something to tell, you will be the first to know," and then changed the subject to Masha's performance in school. Ana was not convinced but she was glad to see that the weight that Irina had carried since Egon left had finally lifted. Meanwhile, between Monsieur Peugeot, running the business and making time for Suzy, Irina had no time to worry about the imminent prospect of war. Nevertheless, when it happened, the invasion of France, the collapse of the government and the occupation of Paris it was suddenly like being back in the middle of the revolution. However, like many Parisians, once the initial shock had worn off Irina focused on keeping her business going.

THE BRATINSKY AFFAIR

As a Russian with anti-communist credentials the Germans left her largely alone. A lot of people needed to turn valuables into hard cash and Irina was smart enough to know that the market would pick up after the war, no matter which side won, so she kept some of the best pieces locked away for a better time. In the meantime, if a Jew needed to sell jewels, she knew he would take whatever price she offered, because he had no choice. And when a German soldier came in with a diamond ring or a bracelet to sell, she didn't ask any questions.

Life was so chaotic that in the first months of the war Irina and Suzy saw very little of each other and Monsieur Peugeot was busy keeping the Germans who had taken over his factory happy while discreetly finding ways to help the resistance. It was a Friday evening when Irina decided to call into *La Vie Parisiennce*. She hadn't heard from Suzy for weeks and was beginning to worry. 'Marie-Ange' was in her usual spot at the till when Irina asked for a whiskey and sat at the end of the bar where she could see everything that was going on. She looked around her in amazement. It was early in the evening but the club was full. As her eyes adjusted to the dim light Irina realised that half the men in the bar were in uniform – German uniform - and Suzy was on stage singing Lili Marlene. Irina looked at Marie-Ange and raised an eyebrow; Marie-Ange shrugged.

When she finished her number Suzy spotted Irina at the bar and crossed the crowded room towards her. She was half way across when a tall German officer stood up and kissed her hand. Irina could see Suzy shaking her head as he invited her to join his group of senior looking officers. She paused just long enough to have her picture taken with the German officers and their French friends. They clinked glasses in greeting when she finally sat down beside Irina. Making sure she wasn't overheard Irina muttered under her breath:

"Suzy, what on earth is going on? Paris is occupied and this place looks like an R and R centre for the German army, not to mention that the other half look like a bunch of spivs."

Suzy's reaction was immediate and angry.

"Now, don't you start?"

She had obviously been getting the same heat from other people and the pressure was getting to her.

"What do you want me to do? – put a sign up saying No Germans Welcome? 'Marie-Ange' here has a wife and five children and Pierre is the only one in his family bringing in a wage. There are ten people who depend on this club for their living so spare me your high moral tone. What am I supposed to say – thanks and goodbye and see you after the war: that is if you don't starve or get sent to a labour camp in the meantime. We have to live; you of all people should know that. Anyway, I don't see any sign of you putting up a notice saying 'closed for the duration' and do you really think nobody knows about your discreet little diamond deals?"

"I know that Suzy but...

"But nothing; business is business and now, if you'll excuse me, I have a club to run. She stood up and continued her tour of the club meeting and greeting as she went with a smile and offering toasts with her glass of champagne. There was a flash as Suzy posed in the middle of yet another smiling group.

Irina took a final look around the bar and saw a face she recognised. She realised that he in turn was watching her with the sharp watchful eyes of a predator. He was one of those people who sit on the sidelines waiting for the right moment to make their move. He had moved into the apartment that belonged to a Jewish family who lived across the street from Irina. Here he was in the middle of a group of German officers drinking champagne and smoking a cigar. He caught her eye and raised his glass in silent salute. Irina did not feel reassured.

\#

While never actually a collaborator, Irina noticed that certain people In Paris were becoming decidedly cool. After the argument in the club Irina and Suzy avoided each other for a few weeks until finally they agreed to meet for coffee one afternoon. They were sitting in the late afternoon sun when two German officers came up and started chatting to Suzy. Irina recognised one of them as the tall officer she had seen kissing Suzy's hand in *La Vie Parisienne*. After the officer moved on Irina noticed that the other people sitting on the café terrace were glaring at them with open hostility. A tall elegantly dressed woman and he: husband who had been sitting at the next table got up to leave. They threw some coins in the saucer and as they passed the woman spat at them. "dirty collaborators!"

The following week when her neighbour, Madame Marchand, cut her dead in the street Irina knew it was time to make herself scarce for a while, and decided to move with Ana and Mashato Bordeaux. Out of sight out of mind seemed like a good idea. When she told Suzy she was taken aback by her angry reaction.

"What are you running away from - me or yourself?"

Irina didn't know what to say; she tried to explain that she needed to protect her family but Suzy wouldn't listen.

"What, you think you'll be safe hiding in the shadows with your fancy friends. You know something, Irina: half your so called friends are sleeping with Germans and as for that bitch Coco Chanel, don't get me started."

"Suzy, it's not like that. We're not like you. You're French - we're Russians and if we say or do the wrong thing they can deport us back to their Bolshevik friends without even thinking."

For some reason this seemed to make Suzy even angrier "Oh poor Irina, it's always about you. Those horrible Bolsheviks took your palace and kicked you out with only your second best tiara and a handful of diamonds stuffed up your tush. Well, let me tell you something sweetie – some of us never had a palace to start with and anything I got I earned slinging my ass from here to Biarritz. I'm not giving up anything I've earned and I'm certainly not going to play some fake patriotic game with some so called resistance guy who's calling me a German whore while he's busy doing black market deals on the side and putting the squeeze on me."

Irina looked at her in shock and Suzy realised that she had done too far.

"Look, Irina I'm sorry it's just that…."

Suzy reached out to take Irina's hand but it was too late. Irina stood up and turned to go.

"Good luck Suzy. I hope your German friends don't let you

down."

\#

Bordeauxwas full of soldiers and there were road blocks everywhere because of Bordeaux's strategic importance. Irina thought that if things got too tricky they could cross over into the Free Zone or lie low in the countryside. For Ana and Masha, it was like an adventure, but for Irina it was more pressure to provide for the family without her circle of influential friends whispering secrets in her ears and pouring profits into the snap purse in her crocodile handbag. And she missed Suzy. There was only one thing to do – keep her head down and focus on business.

Meanwhile a steady flow of refugees trying to get to the Spanish border meant that there was always the possibility of a deal to be done over a quiet drink in the bar of the Grand Hotel. Irina was extremely generous to Emile, the head barman, who would tip her off if there was a likely client. They were usually people who were trying to leave France and who needed to keep below the radar of both Vichy and the Germans. In time, Irina and Emile developed a system. A lady would appear with her husband, wearing a ring or a bracelet or a pair of earrings. Over a drink a price would be reached following which the ladies would disappear to the bathroom where a discreet exchange would take place. Irina would appear wearing a new piece of jewellery and the couple would leave with an envelope of cash. The next day Emile would receive his cut.

Some of the people Irina knew in Paris had also moved south, and after a while life settled into a calm but boring routine. War or no war there were always some people with the knack of turning the situation to their advantage. There were the Flash Harry's who liked to splash their black-market cash on something shiny for their girlfriends – or who wanted to convert cash into something more solid that could be tucked away for a rainy day. During the day Irina chased up any bits of business she could find, and in the early evening she took her usual seat at the end of the bar in the Grand Hotel. Emile knew everything that was going on in the city and became her main source of information.

One beautiful September day Emile brought her usual glass of Chablis. As he set the chilled glass in front of her, he nodded over towards a table at the window. "They want to speak to you."

Three people: a man, a woman and a girl, probably a few years younger than Masha. As they had their backs to the sun Irina couldn't see their faces properly initially. When her eyes adjusted to the light, she saw who it was. The hair was greyer and he was thinner but otherwise Egon was unchanged.

Irina walked over.

"You're looking well, Irina." He stood up to greet her but fortunately didn't offer to kiss her. "This is my wife, Marie-Laure, and my daughter, Mathilde – Matti."

Irina nodded a greeting– "Madame – Egon" – and smiled at the girl.

Strangely, as she looked at this family group Irina didn't feel angry or bitter, indifferent more than anything else. At the same time there was no point prolonging this, so better to get it over with. "Emile tells me you asked to see me. What do you want?" It was abrupt, but the time for niceties was over.

"I need your help. I need cash. I heard there was a woman who might buy diamonds, and when I came here, I realised it was you. A friend told me there's a ship from Marseilles to Martinique and if we can get there we can travel on to the United States. My wife and daughter need to… get out – the sooner the better."

Irina smiled grimly. Then she looked at the girl and her mother. Not their fault. Rumours were already beginning to circulate about a coming round-up of Jews in Bordeaux and Egon's wife and daughter would be in real danger. There was always the chance that some conscientious citizen would tip off the Gestapo.

The new CountessBratinsky was exceptionally beautiful, and her daughter had the same dark eyes and lovely complexion. Despite the difference in colouring, Irina saw a resemblance between Masha and this beautiful young woman. One fair, the other dark, like the fairy-tale, but – the same mouth and the same tilt of the head. After all, they were sisters. Out of the blue it made her want to cry.

Despite the war, everything in Bordeaux was available, at a price, and Irina made a point of knowing who was buying and who was selling. "You're too late – that ship has sailed – literally. The Allies have closed that route. Your only option now is over the Pyrenees to Spain – on foot."

"Does that mean you'll help us? We can p…"

Irina cut him off. "It doesn't depend on me." She nodded to Emile as though to order another drink and he came over, flapping his napkin into place over his arm, and bowed to her, with a half-bow to Egon. His eyes swept over the woman and her daughter.

Irina murmured, "My brother, Count Bratinsky, wants to take his family on holiday – and soon. Somewhere sunny."

"That could be expensive."

Egon made as though to take his wife's handbag

"Not here!" Irina hissed. The door swung open to the sound of male laughter. Two men came into the bar, a high-ranking SS officer and a well-dressed civilian. The men nodded a polite greeting as they sat down on the other side of the room. Irina recognised the civilian immediately: he was vice-prefect Maurice Papon, one of the top Vichy civil servants in charge of the Service for Jewish Affairs. He was also in charge of transport; in fact, the pair was probably discussing the planned round-up of Jews in Bordeaux at that moment. She said nothing of that to Egon and Marie-Laure.

Papon was always nice to her, excessively so in fact, but he made her shudder; there was something reptilian about him that she found repulsive. Emile went over to take the men's order and Irina decided it was time to leave. The German was staring at Marie-Laure, making no effort to hide his admiration. That was part of the problem. She was not a woman to pass unnoticed. She would be remembered.

"It's time to go. I will see you here tomorrow – same time."

The next day Egon and Marie-Laure came by themselves and Irina could feel the stress that they tried to hide. To all intents and purposes, they were a normal handsome couple out for a walk on an autumn evening, but Irina noticed the way Egon was smoking cigarette after cigarette and the nervous smile that flitted across Marie Laure's face.

"I spoke to Emile. There's a lorry travelling to Saint Jean de Luz tomorrow evening. Come to the rear of the building here, before curfew. He will fill you in. It's better if I don't know the details. Take only what you can carry and be warned, it's a tough hike – dress for the mountains, and wear strong boots."

Irina slid an envelope across the table to Egon. It contained a thousand dollars. "Keep the diamonds – you'll probably need them."

Egon started to rise. "No…"

"It's not for you – it's for your daughter. After all, what would I say to Masha – that I handed her sister over to the Gestapo?"

He hesitated. "How is Masha?"

"She's fine – she's with Ana." Irina had wanted to say "…and she has almost forgotten that she ever had a father" – but what was the point?

Marie-Laure had kept her eyes down throughout this exchange and now she looked up at Irina. "Thank you."

There was nothing more to be said.

CHAPTER 17

Paris, March 1976

It was a mild, sunny afternoon and Tom had no clear idea where he was going. Today he had no interest in window shopping or museums; it was just a relief to be out in the fresh air. Spring was already well on its way with the symmetrical lines of chestnut trees coming into leaf and the magnolias already in full bloom. Dozens of people were strolling about enjoying the sunshine: tourists posing against the backdrop of the Louvre and couples holding hands. From somewhere out of sight he could hear the music of a carousel. He sat down on one of the uncomfortable metal chairs beside the pond and watched children pushing model sailing boats out in the breeze under the watchful eye of their parents. That would never be him. A lot had happened in a few days: his conversation with Olga and his meeting with MaitreBerenger. He felt trapped inside this emotional prison of his own making. He knew what he wanted to do: the question was whether he had the courage to do it. It was a lot to process. On a whim he took out MaitreBerenger's card.

The café outside the park gates was busy but the telephone box down at the back was quiet as he dialled the number. He could hear his heart beating as the phone rang on the other end and he was about to hang up when a voice answered: "Hallo, Berenger."

"It's Tom."

There was a momentary pause.

"This is a nice surprise. I wondered if I'd hear from you."

Tom didn't know what to say. He felt foolish.

"I shouldn't have called – I'm sorry, I shouldn't have bothered you!"

"Tom, relax, it's ok. I'm glad you called. Where are you?"

"I'm in the café beside the gate into the Tuileries."

"I can be there in five minutes – ten max."

Tom felt a surge of excitement as he sat pretending to read the newspaper that someone had left behind and looking at his watch every two minutes. It felt like an eternity but it couldn't have been more than ten minutes before he saw Maître Berenger striding along the footpath towards him. He looked stylish in his navy suit, white shirt and his sunglasses.

"You look well, Tom, how are you?"

Now that the moment had come why had he called MaitreBerenger. He couldn't look at him.

"It's just that I was thinking – I mean… after our conversation - and then I told Olga about me and…..

He looked up and MaitreBerenger could see the tears.

"I should go. This was a mistake!

"Tom, first things first. My name is Jean-Philippe so can we please get that out of the way, ok?

"Ok!"

"We need to go somewhere we can talk properly – my apartment isn't far. We can go there if you want?"

Jean-Philippe's Mercedes was parked in a narrow side street a short walk away and in a few minutes the was car humming along the boulevards as Tom wondered if he had made a complete fool of himself. Jean-Philippe kept the conversation moving on safely neutral topics: the investigation, his impressions of Paris, what he'd studied at college, until they arrived at one of the large nineteenth century buildings with a glass door that clicked shut behind them as they went into the courtyard. Neither of them spoke as they went up in the lift. The apartment itself was bright and airy with a mix of modern and antique furniture and mostly modern art.

"You look like you need a drink" Jean-Philippe said as he handed Tom a whiskey and they settled in the large comfortable sofa, a safe distance apart.

"So, Tom 0'Brien, tell me, why are you so upset?"

"It's just that all of this is so sudden – I mean, I've known for years.

"What exactly have you known for years, Tom? You need to finally find the words to say it."

Tom took a deep breath. I know I'm gay but I've never done anything about it. There have been a few moments in the past when something could have happened but it never did. I was always too afraid. And now I keep thinking about my father – what my mother would think - and the people in the job - and then Olga....

"You thought maybe your attraction to the lovely Olga would make it all go away. I tried that, Tom. It didn't work and ended in a very expensive divorce!"

"Yes."

This time there was no holding back the tears and they poured down his face.

"Come here, you silly boy." Tom felt Jean-Philippe move closer and pull him into his shoulder. It was the first time a man had touched him who wasn't his father or brother or a close family friend. Tom tried to relax as Jean-Philippe massaged the muscles in his neck that were rigid with tension.

"The first thing you need to realise is that whatever you do has to be your choice. It doesn't matter what other people think. Most of them couldn't give a dam anyway and your family, if they love you they will accept you. The golden rule is, if in doubt, say no. It's your life and you have to take control."

As Jean-Philippe kept talking Tom became more and more aware of the heat of his body and the smell of his cologne. Jean-Philippe reached out and ran his finger down the line of his jaw, down his neck and onto his chest. Tom leaned in. The kiss was slow and intense and threw Tom into a frenzy of passion that came out of nowhere.

Jean-Philippe held him back at arm's length.

"Are you sure? asked the big bad wolf."

There was no answer except more kisses and the realisation that for the first time he didn't feel afraid. For some reason he trusted Jean-Philippe . One by one the buttons of his shirt popped open and clothes were flung aside until they were both naked. Was this how sex was meant to be? A handsome naked man taking him in his arms, long muscular legs, skin on skin, mouth on mouth in a blur of desire. There was no time for second thoughts. For the first time in his life Tom felt unreservedly happy and at ease.

The light was beginning to fade when Tom glanced at his

watch. It was almost seven o'clock.

"God almighty, Jean-Philippe, Olga will think I've been kidnapped by aliens or murdered by the Russians."

Jean-Philippe lazily opened one eye and watched Tom getting dressed.

"You do have a beautiful body, you know."

Nobody had ever said that to Tom before. He glanced down.

Jean-Philippe laughed. "My shy Irish lad! Do you think there's a possibility of another spontaneous phone call in the middle of a busy afternoon?"

Tom leaned in to give him a kiss, something that a week ago would have been out of the question but which now seemed entirely natural. "You never know your luck, now quickly, will you drive me back to the hotel before they send out a search party?"

☦

Olga got into bed but after ten minutes tossing and turning it was clear she wasn't going to sleep. Better to do something useful and focus on Ana's diary The leather cover had aged into a deep mahogany colour but the pages were still crisp and fresh after all this time. They exuded a faint perfume of lavender and as she turned the pages a sprig fell out onto the sheet, scattering flower heads. It was the perfume she most associated with Ana. There was always a bowl of dried lavender on the side table on the upstairs landing and Ana used it in sachets to keep the sheets and pillow cases fresh and safe from attack by moths.

It felt like an invasion of privacy to be reading her private thoughts, even after all this time.

ANA'S DIARY
TsarskoyeSelo AUGUST 1917

"Every day we hope for good news, but every day the news is worse. One day there is a rumour that the Germans have crossed the border and will take Petersburg in days. We don't know whether to celebrate or mourn the final collapse of our country. Then for days there is nothing.

The peasants have taken over the land and it is dangerous to leave the park around the house. There is the risk of running into poachers or army deserters. Victor has told us to stay close to the house, and sometimes he sits up at night with the old hunting rifle he has so far managed to hide from the search parties, despite the risks. It's a choice between being murdered by robbers or arrested for hoarding weapons.

At dark every evening he pulls over the shutters. I can hear them banging closed one by one until the house begins to feel like a prison. He has reinforced the front door and the shutters on the windows along the terrace with sheets of metal salvaged from the old barn and cut portholes so that he can shoot out. Rumours arrive from the city – the Bolsheviks have seized power. How has it come to this?

Looking back, it was inevitable that things had to change, but now it seems that the country has flown out of all control. Day by day the violence is getting closer. Yesterday a group of Red Army guards came to search the house – supposedly looking for weapons. They turned things upside down but left in the end, taking some bottles of brandy but without doing any real damage.

It seems that our lives are hanging by a thread, depending on the mood of men with guns. If there is an officer in charge you may survive. If they are drunk and out of control you may die. And they know exactly where your weak spots are.

As he left, the officer in charge said, "You have a very pretty daughter." Anything can happen but I will not let this fear eat away at me. This morning, we heard that last night robbers broke into the home of old Komarov, less than three miles away. They tortured him to reveal where the gold was hidden and then burned the house around him when they didn't find any. He had already used everything he had to get his son released from prison.

It's inevitable: we will have to leave. I look at Irina and Pavel and tell Victor that we have to go, for the children's sakes. If we don't go now, it will be too late. But for Victor leaving Russia is like an act of treason. He says things will settle down, but I live in a state of permanent dread of what will happen next."

THE BRATINSKY AFFAIR

Olga read on: the garden, Ana making a joke of fighting with the slugs and rabbits that eat the food she is growing. A season goes by.

"Autumn is here. Today we have made the decision to go. The final straw was the order for all aristocrats and former landowners to register. Whatever we do to adapt they will come for us in the end. I wake up in the night listening for the sound of gunfire or boots on the stairs. If we can make it to Finland we have a chance. Bit by bit we have been selling pictures and furniture for food, so the house already has a half empty feel and there is an echo in the hall that was never there before. Now, it makes no difference what happens to the house, as we can only take what we can carry. I was twenty when I married into this house and now we are being hunted out like animals.

There is always someone watching so, under cover of darkness last night Victor took the bags to the gamekeeper's shed in the woods, beyond the chapel. We will go for a walk in the woods tomorrow afternoon, picking mushrooms and berries – nothing unusual for the casual observer to see and then we will disappear quietly into the forest. It is bitterly cold but so far, the snow has held off, and we may get at least as far as Tallinn before the first fall. The alternative is to go via the city, but the situation there is too dangerous. Victor has made me promise over and over – if we get separated – run – don't look back. I look at him and say we can never be separated.

Olga got up to switch on the light and sat down, gripped by this story. It was the first time she had known anything of what daily life was like for Ana and Irina in those days.

HELSINKI, FINLAND December 1917

Irina has finally gone to sleep. The room is small and dirty but at least it is dry. She doesn't say anything, but I can tell she has been crying. Neither of us says anything very much these days, each of us wrapped up in our own misery. There are some things I cannot talk about or even think about. It has taken us a week to make a journey that would normally take a day by train, sleeping in barns, hiding in a church at the sound of approaching traffic.

The old priest in one village allowed us to sleep in the vestry for a night. It was bitterly cold but at least it was out of the wind. The next day he told us we had to go. "Someone is bound to see and report you," he said. "These days you can never tell who is on what side. Heaven help us in these Godless times." He gave us a loaf of bread and part of a comb of honey. I asked for his blessing and we knelt in the snow as he made the sign of the cross over us. We avoided the villages where possible except when we absolutely needed to buy food. Even then we had to be careful only to offer small coins, not gold. If anyone thought we had gold we wouldn't live to see daylight.

One day, a farmer with a horse and cart passed us. He nodded to us to get up. Nobody asks any questions these days. It's better not to know. In the evening we came to his rundown cottage with a couple of outbuildings. He said we could stay in the shed for the night. His wife stood at the door glaring at us, and afterwards I could hear them arguing inside. Later a little girl appeared with a bowl of thin soup and some bread, but she ran away when I spoke to her. There are still some people with generous hearts willing to share what little they have. This simple act of kindness restored my faith in humanity. We left at first light without even saying goodbye. I remember them often in my prayers.

The real danger was when we crossed over into Estonia. For weeks there had been rumours that Estonia was going to declare independence and there were red guards everywhere. When I saw the checkpoint on the main road my heart sank. I wanted to sit down on the side of the road and weep with exhaustion but I looked at Irina and knew I had to keep going. I saw a group of women with baskets and bags heading for the temporary barrier that had been slung across the road. They looked like peasants who had been bringing food to sell at the market and were now heading home. I noticed that none of the women was under fifty. All the young women had been left safely at home and these village women had been smart enough to keep some food to bribe the soldiers. We tagged along hoping that nobody would pay any attention to us. At the last minute I heard the dreaded words:

"You there, stop – papers!"

THE BRATINSKY AFFAIR

The soldier in question looked about nineteen, hardly old enough to be carrying a gun. His two companions seemed more interested in chatting with the women and cadging cigarettes. When he spoke to me I thought I would vomit.

"You don't recognise me do you?" he said softly. "You gave me an Easter cake once after the midnight service."

It was only when I looked at him closely that I recognised him. His name was Ivan and his father, Dmitri, had been a steward on the estate for many years. I remembered that he had a beautiful tenor voice, and when I thought back to that moment of music and celebration with the choir singing and candles glittering against the gold of the icons I thought my knees would give way. Normally I would have given him a gift but now the tables had been turned and he was the one with the power. I felt lost and broken until I felt Irina's hand gripping my arm to give me strength.

He glanced over to see where the other soldiers were and then he said: "keep going and get as far away from the main road as possible. There are troops on the move day and night. Go through the forest if you can. Don't stop in the first village, there's a Red unit there and they could be trouble." With that he handed back the papers and smiled at Irina as we passed. The thought crossed my mind that he was doing this more for her than for me.

By the time we reached Tallinn our feet were swollen and our faces were scorched with frost. We needed to rest, and I hoped beyond hope that Victor and Pavel would catch up with us. When we finally got on the boat to Helsinki we stood at the stern and watched as the coastline faded into the night. I knew in my heart that we would never see Russia again.

Inside I feel dead. I can't talk to Irina about what has happened. If we stop to think we might not be capable of moving on. We are like two machines endlessly repeating the same motions without feeling. Even when I expected the worst I always thought we would face it together as a family. We are caught between the fear of what is coming behind us and the fear of what lies ahead. I can only imagine what is happening to Victor and our son. Pavel looks older than his age but he is only twelve. I have to keep strong for Irina. They will escape and they will be able to follow us. I must hope. I pray mechanically without faith.

I am exhausted but I cannot sleep and instead I sit by the window and watch the falling snow. Out of nowhere come the words of the prayer for the dying that I whispered to my mother as she breathed her last: Holy God, Holy Mighty, and Holy Immortal, have mercy on us. I cannot bear to think that maybe in some prison my husband and my son may be facing death. But I won't think of that. We must keep going.

I continue to repeat the ten words of the prayer, but the words are empty and my mind won't rest, playing the same scene over and over again. We had come to the edge of the woods when we heard shouting and the noise of a horse drawn wagon pulling into the forecourt in front of the house. A dozen men. Victor and I crept over to the chapel at the top of the hill and hid behind the balustrade where we could look down to the house without being seen. It was clear the soldiers were drunk. They were singing and shouting and waving bottles of vodka.

My heart froze for a moment. One of them was the leader of the group who had searched the house before. He was the one who had said how pretty Irina was. He stood on the steps and looked around. I felt he was staring straight up at us, but then he turned and kicked in the door. I prayed they would assume we had fled. We could hear the sound of breaking glass. A chair came flying through the dining room window in a shower of broken glass, followed by a clock and my grandfather's marble bust of Catherine the Great.

Two of the men came to window and started to use the bust for target practice before going back inside. There were still some cases of wine and brandy in the cellar, and I hoped that maybe they would take them and go. Once the word got out that we were gone, people would descend on the house from all around and rip it apart looking for anything of value they could eat or drink or sell for food.

After a couple of hours things got quiet and the men staggered out in a bunch, shouting and laughing. One of them was carrying

THE BRATINSKY AFFAIR

the silver samovar from the dining room; another was carrying a pair of candlesticks that we had decided were too big for us to carry. The cart drove off in the direction of the main road and in a few minutes everything was quiet as before.

I told Victor that we needed to get away quickly in case the soldiers came back but he insisted:"I need to get the food from the kitchen. It's in a bag in the pantry behind the false door. With any luck they won't have seen it. If we don't have food we won't last long and we need to save our money."

I begged him not to go but he was adamant and then Pavel insisted on going with him.

Victor handed me the sword. "Hold onto this until we come back. Don't worry, they're gone. Everything will be fine. I will be back in a few minutes, and then we can go."

We waited for an age and then I heard the shouting. Next minute three more soldiers came down the steps pushing Victor and Pavel in front of them down the avenue.

They were gone. I stood and screamed but it was too late. There was no one left to hear. We sat in stunned silence before we finally summoned up the courage to go down to the house. If we were caught, so be it. At least we would all end up together. But now the house was completely empty. The doors had all been left open and inside there was a smell of alcohol and urine, with broken glass everywhere. The staircase and the rooms on the ground floor were in flames but so far the fire hadn't reached the kitchen in the wing. We needed to move.

They had shot at the portrait of the Old General on the first landing and through the smoke I could see the canvas hanging in shreds. The kitchen had been torn apart in the search for food. The door into the back scullery was wide open and had screened the hidden door to the old pantry where I kept the food. The bag of bread and apples and dried meat was still where I had left it. We couldn't delay. Enough of the old deference had survived to keep the villagers away from the house over the previous weeks but if they arrived now they would tear the place apart. We wouldn't stand a chance.

Irina and I went back up to the shed and repacked the bags, making sure we took anything we could eat, wear, or sell. The sword was too bulky, and anyway would attract too much attention. In the end I decided I would leave it with the old General. He could be relied upon to look after it.

I looked at Irina "We have to go"

"But what about Papa and Pavel?"

"They will catch up with us – they know where we are going."

Irina sobbed. "No, I won't go without them, I want my papa."

I took her by the arm. "Irina, darling: I know, I know, but if they find us they will kill us. I promised your father that if we were separated, we would keep going. We have to go." In my own mind I thought death would be the least of it if we were caught.

By now it was getting dark, and with luck we would be well away before anyone came to the house."

There it was: the reference to the Leipzig Sword. At least up until that point, it had still been with the family."

THE BRATINSKY AFFAIR

CHAPTER 18

Bordeaux: May 1944

On a balmy evening in late May Irina walked into the bar of the Grand Hotel. Summer had arrived early and the fan circling slowly overhead was having no noticeable effect on the temperature, it just moved the cigarette smoke around. Irina looked at the clientele. The usual mix of off duty army officers, a smattering of more senior Germans and some women whose make up and silk stockings suggested the nature of their contribution to the war effort. The city was tense as rumours circulated of an expected allied landing. Time to move somewhere further south, close to the sea perhaps, only problem was most of the ports were occupied by Germans.

It would be good for Masha who had evolved from a sulky teenager into a rather beautiful young woman. Irina would have to take Masha in hand. Ana was getting too old to keep a firm grip on her rebellious daughter and the last thing she needed was a wartime romance with some handsome soldier without a penny to his name. As Irina pondered what to do she looked around: no sign of Emile. She settled into her normal seat and watched as the receptionist crossed the bar towards her: "The manager would like a word with you in his office, if you wouldn't mind, says it's urgent."

When Irina stepped through the double doors there was no sign of the manager but Emile was in front of her, tied to a chair. He had been badly beaten. The door closed behind her.

"No point trying to run, Irina, it won't do you any good." It was Gerard Granot her would be rapist from Paris.

"Hope you still have my gun, Irina, I'd quite like it back."

"If I had it, I know what I'd do with it," Irina replied.

"What, no kisses after all this time?" He pushed her forward into the room with the barrel of his revolver.

Nearing sixty, Gerard had not improved with age. His fleshy charms had run to fat and his receding hair had been slicked into a greasy comb over. She hadn't noticed before how he kept licking his lips and their wet flabbiness made her feel sick. His taste in aftershave hadn't improved either.

"Well now, isn't this a turn up for the books – the beautiful and, from what I hear, rich CountessBratinsky. I have been watching you, Irina and I know all about the deals and the people smuggled over the border, including your ex-husband and his Jew wife and daughter. Emile here has been very informative."

Irina looked at Emile. One eye was already closed and his nose would never be straight again. She could tell that he was barely conscious.

"You shouldn't believe everything you hear. Now, spare me the chit chat. If you were going to hand me over to the Bosch you would have done it already. You clearly want something, so spit it out."

"Straight to the point like a true business woman. I want cash and a lot of it. Our German friends are getting a little jumpy and now might be a good time to do some travelling."

"What, - no more Jews for you to round up and fleece?"

Gerard barely looked at her as he struck her across the face, knocking her onto a chair facing Emile.

"I want 100,000 francs. You have one week."

"Why would I do that?"

"There is a train leaving for the east on Saturday. If I don't get the money your mother and daughter will be on it.

"But we're not Jews!"

"You're Jews if I say you are. Jew – Jew lover, doesn't matter. You're not French and anyway Bratinsky/Skaminsky, sounds kind of Jewish to me, so, who cares. The Gauleiter isn't fussy. We just need to make up the numbers and well, the way things are he'll probably just shoot the lot of you to be sure. On the other hand, your daughter is beautiful. Masha, isn't it? I saw her in the cathedral. I'm sure she'd be very popular in a military brothel. In fact, I might take her there myself."

Irina looked at him "Rape still your speciality then, Gerard? You really are a piece of scum."

He hit her again.

"Sticks and stones, Irina. I couldn't care less. Just get the

THE BRATINSKY AFFAIR

money."

Irina looked at Gerard and realised she had no choice. "How will I contact you when I have the money?"

"Just leave a note at the main desk in headquarters telling me when and where, no other details. Remember – one week!" Gerard picked up his hat to go and adjusted his gaudy tie. As he walked out the door, he turned back for a final parting shot "See, Irina – that wasn't so difficult but if you think I'm joking just ask our good friend Emile here," and he twisted Emile's dislocated shoulder for emphasis. Emile screamed.

As soon as he left, Irina and the duty manager took Emile upstairs to one of the empty rooms. After the local doctor had reset his shoulder and finished cleaning him up he began to come round.

"How do you know that piece of garbage?"

"Let's just say our paths crossed in Paris. It wasn't pleasant."

"I can imagine. What will you do? You can't pull a fast one on a man like him - he's dangerous, Irina - best buddies with Papon and in and out of Gestapo headquarters like a yoyo. He blackmails Jews and when they have no more cash, he hands them over to the Gestapo anyway. Tries to play both sides - feeds the odd bit of information to the resistance but nobody trusts him. He's a complete snake and he won't let go."

Irina poured them both a glass of the manager's brandy and for a minute they just sat sipping their drinks.

"What can we do? Go to the police? He is the police and the Germans would shoot us as quick as look at us. He thinks he has all the cards. There's only one thing to do. Gerard Granot needs to disappear."

"Easier said than done. If they link it back to you, we'll all end up in front of a firing squad – if we're lucky."

"There's no choice. As you said, he could take the money and still sell us down the line. We have to make sure that there is no way of linking it back to us."

\#

At 08.00 am on the following Thursday morning a note was delivered for Inspector Gerard Granot as the shifts were changing in police headquarters. The place was in chaos with junior officers kicking out the drunks so they could get home to bed. The members of the new shift were standing chatting or drinking the disgusting ersatz coffee while the cleaners were going around sweeping up the debris from the night before. Afterwards, nobody could remember when the note was delivered or who had delivered it. Nobody had paid any attention to the old lady who went around collecting the dirty cups and emptying the rubbish bins in the offices. The note, found on his desk afterwards, just said: Cathédrale de Saint André, Thursday, 2pm. Nothing else - No signature.

\#

Now that the one o'clock mass was over the cathedral was almost completely empty except for a lingering smell of incense and the sound of a door banging somewhere in the depths of the ancient building. The sacristan had just extinguished the candles and a spiral of smoke was wafting up towards the lofty ceiling. Irina, dressed in black, was wearing a large rather old-fashioned hat that cast a shadow over her face. She had pinned the veil into the brim so it wasn't noticeable. She heard the door swing open and watched as Gerard walked down the main aisle towards the high altar with his usual arrogant swagger. He clearly thought he was still some kind of matinée idol but he had at least had the good grace to take off his hat? As he approached, Irina turned off towards the side chapels knowing he would follow her.

She stopped beside the chapel of Saint Anne, furthest from the main body of the church.

"What's with all the black, Irina – you going to a funeral?" and he laughed his usual greasy laugh.

"As it happens, I am – after we've finished here. Gerard was so intent on getting the cash that he barely glanced around him. Over on the right there was a coffin in one of the other side chapels. A small group of mourners dressed in deepest black were on their knees mumbling the rosary. The coffin had a wreath on it: *Mort Pour La Patrie.*

Death was such a daily ritual in Bordeaux that people no longer paid any attention to funerals. Every day there was another round

THE BRATINSKY AFFAIR

up of Jews, another public execution of people suspected of supporting the resistance or in random reprisals for the latest resistance attack. They were glad to survive another day. The mourners had their backs turned to Irina and Gerard and the babble of prayers would cover up their conversation. There was no one else in sight.

"Have you got the money?"

"Of course. How do I know you'll keep your promise and that Ana and Masha will be safe?"

"You don't. You'll have to take my word for it as an officer and a gentleman," he smirked.

Irina swallowed her anger and handed over the package wrapped in brown paper. She watched closely as he tore it open. Apart from a few hundred franks at the beginning the rest was folded up newspaper.

Gerard ripped the paper apart and flung it up in the air with a howl of rage.

"What stupid game is this? I warned you. Think you can mess with me? I'll show you!" He was so angry and focused on Irina that he didn't notice the slight movement behind him as Emile stepped out of the confession box and pulled the garrotte tight around his neck. Irina calmly watched his face turn purple as his heels drummed on the cathedral floor and his pudgy fingers clawed helplessly at his neck.

"Big mistake, Gerard to threaten my daughter." There was a sudden smell of excrement as his bowel voided. It was all over in seconds. Irina did not feel one ounce of pity. It was him or her family.

Emile whistled and the mourners from the neighbouring chapel stood up and opened the coffin. In a matter of seconds Granot's body was in the coffin and hoisted aloft by four dark suited mourners.

"Are you sure he's dead?" Irina asked.

"Probably," Emile grunted. "But if he's not he will be shortly."

As the coffin moved off down the aisle towards the main door it was followed by the now heavily veiled Irina supported by an apparently overwrought Emile clutching a handkerchief to his face.

As they came to the main door there was a sudden flurry as the sacristan rushed over. "What's all this? Nobody told me about a funeral!"

When Emile hissed that if he didn't piss off, he'd live to regret it the sacristan scurried at speed back into his office. The shock was softened by the hundred frank note Irina handed him.

"Your discretion is much appreciated at this difficult time."

The man slipped the money into his soutane and scuttled off into his office, casting a nervous glance at Emile as he went. The office door closed with a bang. Irina had to suppress a burst of hysterical laughter.

As they reached the bottom of the steps a hearse and a large black car pulled up. Two SS officers saluted as they passed. The coffin was loaded into the hearse with great dignity and Irina and Emile got into the back of the car. The coffin would be on its way to a small graveyard on the outskirts of the city where it would be buried under a false name.

The rest of the plan needed to happen like clockwork. Emile had taken Gerard's, wallet, ID, cheque book and keys. Irina's instructions were clear. Emile's brother Serge, who was enough like Gerard to pass muster, was to go to the bank and empty his account. Then, they were to go to his apartment and pack up all his stuff. His wife was in Paris so there wasn't much chance of being intercepted. Finally, Irina handed Serge a card with the address of a hotel in San Sebastian that was to be left somewhere visible and a map of the Pyrenees. "Leave this somewhere in the apartment, near the door, as if it has been accidentally dropped."

At 15.15PM precisely, Irina made a dramatic entrance into the bar of the Grand Hotel wearing a figure hugging bright red dress with a plunging neckline. Nobody could see how fast her heart was beating or the bead of sweat that ran down between her shoulder blades.

At 15.30 on the button "Gerard" was withdrawing all the cash from his bank account while Irina was the focus of all eyes in the hotel bar. "Gerard" had been instructed to ask the bank teller the time so that if questioned afterwards he would remember the time exactly.

Emile was in his normal spot behind the bar.

"Good evening, Countess. The usual?"

"No, I'll have a whiskey. Make it a double!" Her hand shook as she lifted the glass.

Gerard would not be missed for a few days and even then, with a bit of luck, his colleagues would accept that he had done a runner to Spain. He wasn't the type of man who would be much missed.

As she sipped her drink Irina thought that now was probably a good time to consider moving back to Paris.

CHAPTER 19

Paris, April 1976

Olga had been so engrossed in the diary she hadn't realised how much time had passed until she realised it was getting dark. She went over to close the curtains as a silver grey Mercedes pulled up in front of the hotel and she realised that it was Tom stepping out of Maitre Beranger's car.

"Well, well."

Olga was stepping of the lift when Tom arrived in reception; He looked happy and relaxed. She decided to have some fun with him.

"Nice walk, Tom? -Where did you go? Anywhere interesting?"

"Yes, lovely – very nice." He didn't know what to say and hoped to escape up to his room without having to answer any questions. Olga was having none of it.

"You, Tom O'Brien will sit and you will tell me everything."

"I don't know what you mean."

"I saw you getting out of Maitre Beranger's car."

"Ok, I confess, I bumped into Jean-Philippe and we went for a drink."

"I see – so it's Jean-Philippe now - no more Maitre Beranger.". You don't waste any time, do you when you get going. Where did you 'bump' into him?"

"Olga, you're worse than a policeman. Ok. We went back to his apartment and spent the afternoon there."

"Tom I'm glad. No, don't tell me anymore. I don't want the gory details. Spare my maidenly blushes! Anyway, as it happens, you're not the only one with news. While you've been gallivanting around the city I've been at work. Listen to this," and she pulled out the diary and read out Ana's description of their escape.

"The question is, said Tom. "Who was the old general and what did he do with the sword?"

"I'm not sure I care that much about the sword anymore. I find it difficult to think of someone I know and loved in that desperate position. How do people find the strength to keep going at times like that? I have been thinking about Ana and Irina all afternoon and trying to picture that terrible journey. Ana would never talk about it. She would say *you have no idea what it was like. Be glad that you don't,* and then she would change the subject."

She hesitated. "I want to go out to her grave and say hello after all this time. You needn't come – I'm quite happy to go by myself. She's buried out in the Russian Cemetery in Sainte Genevieve des Bois – it's not far. You might want to link up with ."

"There's no way I'm letting you out of my sight – we'll go together. I would be quite interested to see a bit more of Paris and Jean-Philippe can wait – for a while."

≠

The weather was getting brighter and sunnier with every day that passed, and they enjoyed the leisurely twenty-minute stroll across place de la Bastille and up to the Gare de Lyon. When they walked up the steps in front of the vast façade of the main station Tom felt quite intimidated. "I love this station" said Olga "When I come here I just want to get on a train and go - somewhere – anywhere."

As they crossed the main concourse Tom looked up and saw the neon sign for Le Train Bleu restaurant. "Look, Olga," he shouted over the noise of the trains. "Maybe we'll meet Hercule Poirot."

"As long as you don't mention Death on the Orient Express."

Within minutes they had their tickets and were standing on one of the lower platforms, ready to head out into the suburbs. By the time they boarded the train, the morning rush was over and they had the compartment more or less to themselves. After a while Tom couldn't help feeling disappointed. As they left the tall apartment buildings of the city behind the houses got shabbier and more sprawling the further they went. Blocks of cement-coloured factory buildings interspersed with small chalets, each with its own sad-looking garden. Maybe it was because the sun had gone in and everything looked grey. By comparison Dublin didn't look so bad after all.

In less than an hour they were pulling into the station in Sainte-Genevieve-des-Bois, and Tom realised that the most interesting building in the town was the station itself with its pots of flowers and faded nineteenth-century charm. The rest of the town was pretty nondescript, with an occasional café or bakery. Tom was beginning to feel let down until they walked up to the gates of the cemetery itself.

Beyond the wooden gates he could see a white church with a blue dome topped with a gilded cross, and up ahead, a long avenue, flanked on either side by dozens of graves topped with Russian Orthodox crosses. Some graves were meticulously cared for, while others were disappearing beneath nests of ivy. In among the famous names, an occasional photograph of a man in elaborate military uniform or a coat of arms whose gilded lettering had virtually disappeared. Here and there a simple wooden cross with no name or a wound of earth with no other memorial. Many of the people buried here had left everything they had known and loved behind in Russia and ended up living in Paris on the charity of others or working for a pittance.

They found Ana's grave at the far end of the cemetery sheltered under a tall laburnum. Ana had bought a bunch of white lilies at the kiosk outside the cemetery, and when Tom caught up with her she was standing staring at the simple black marble slab inscribed in gold letters:

Countess Ana Maria O'Rourke de Breffny
1878 – 1958
Beloved wife of Count Victor O'Rourke de Breffny
Mother of Count Pavel O'Rourke de Breffny

At the foot of the grave someone had left a fresh wreath of pink and white roses. The accompanying card was simply inscribed 'П'.

Olga took the card and showed it to Tom before putting it in her handbag.

"What's up?" Tom asked

"I'm surprised that someone would still remember Ana after all this time. Looks like the letter N. It's a bit smudged so I can't read it properly. I have no idea who that could be. I'm sure most

THE BRATINSKY AFFAIR

of her friends are dead and gone now, but I am glad that someone still cares enough to bring her flowers. I have nothing but fond memories of her. I suppose I should get the headstone amended to include Irina. It seems sad that she should be left out."

"Let's go and sit over here for a while; it's so peaceful here."

Olga had put the photograph of Ana, Victor and the children into the diary and stuffed it in her handbag. She took out the diary and read Ana's description of their last day together out loud, as it seemed the best way to remember her. They were sitting looking at the photograph when Tom asked, "Who built that chapel in the photograph?"

"It isn't really a chapel; it's more of a crypt or a mausoleum."

"And who is buried in it?" he asked even though he thought he already knew the answer.

"It's the older generation, including the man who built the house, General Count O'Rourke de Breffny, the grand old man of the family, and his wife and their children."

Tom remained completely silent.

"What is it? Did I say something?"

Tom took the diary from Olga and flicked back to her description of their last moments at the house and read it out loud again: *"Irina and I went back up to the shed and repacked the bags, making sure we took anything we could eat, wear, or sell. The sword was too bulky and anyway it would attract too much attention. In the end I decided to leave it with the old General. He could be relied upon to look after it."*

"So now we know or at least we think we do."

On their way back into the city they were silent. They were both grappling with the same question: what next? In the end they decided to head over to Saint-Germain and have dinner in Brasserie Vagenende. The head waiter greeted them like long lost friends and gave them a good table tucked in a corner where there was no chance of their conversation being overheard.

For once they didn't say anything about Ana or Irina, or the dilemma that was facing them. They concentrated on good food and wine and books and music and travel – anything except what was weighing on their minds. Olga wanted to know if Tom had heard from Jean-Philippe but he carefully side stepped that issue.

After dinner they took their usual route down boulevard Saint-Michel towards their hotel. They would walk part of the way and then pick up the metro at Châtelet if they felt tired. Halfway down, they stopped to look in the window of the Nouvelles Frontières travel agency. It was offering Easter deals in Rio, Bangkok, Machu Picchu, Sidney. They were about to turn away when Tom noticed card pasted directly onto the window: Moscow/Saint Petersburg: one week 1,000 francs: special price due to last minute cancellations. Visas included – three places only available.

He looked at Olga. "Are you thinking what I'm thinking?" But before Olga had time to say anything Tom was in the shop, which was open late, to get the brochure.

"At least let's have a look at it" he said in reply to Olga's look of astonishment."

Back at the hotel Olga said, "This is crazy. We don't know where we are going or what to do once we get there – if we get there."

"First things first. Let's see what exactly Nouvelles Frontières is offering?"

The offer was for one week in Moscow, Petersburg and the surrounding region, including a one-day trip to the complex of Romanov palaces at Tsarskoye Selo. "Didn't you say that the O'Rourke estate was not far from the palace?"

"I remember Ana talking about all this, but it's a bit vague. They had a house in Petersburg and the estate in the village of Pushkin not far from the palace at Tsarskoye Selo. Ana said it was a short carriage ride from the palace. The men in the family tended to be in the army, so it was close to the palace and army command, and not too far from the city. It was the place they loved most, though they also had a huge estate somewhere near Minsk where they went for the summer and to hunt in the winter, though neither Ana nor Irina went in much for country life."

Tom had a bright idea "What about those letters in the box. Maybe there is an address in one of them?"

Olga went up to her room and returned a few minutes later with

THE BRATINSKY AFFAIR

the bundle of letters. Several were addressed to:
 Countess Ana O'Rourke de Breffny
 Babalokovo
 Tsarskoye Selo

When Tom looked at the detailed map in the brochure he found that it looked it as though Babalokovo was only a ten or fifteen-minute walk across the park to where the old de Breffny estate stood, or more correctly had stood. "But, Tom, for all we know the whole place has been obliterated. Between the combined effects of the Bolsheviks, the Nazis and sixty years of neglect, the chances are there will be nothing left to see. Even the palace itself was burned down during the war and had to be rebuilt."

"There only one way to find out."

"You're not serious!"

"The way I look at it, it's a choice. Either you follow it through to the end – or as far as you can go – or you take Irina's advice, forget the whole thing and get on with your life."

"I can't decide like that – I need to sleep on it. Anyway, what about Willi and your father – not to mention my father and Maitre Be, sorry Jean-Philippe."

"Jean-Philippe would lose his mind and my father would arrive with handcuffs. Better not to tell them. After all if we travel as part of a normal tourist group we can be in and out before anyone is any the wiser. We just need to keep a low profile."

The next morning Olga came down to breakfast looking pale but determined. "Ok, let's do it. But on one condition. We go to Russia, we try to find the house, and if there's nothing there that's the end of it. We walk away. Ok?"

Tom toasted her with his *café au lait*. "Agreed!"

CHAPTER 20

Paris 1944
Irina could always tell which way the wind was blowing and after the Gerard Granot episode her instinct was telling her not to hang around waiting for someone to start asking questions. With a bit of luck the confusion of the allied advance and the German retreat would cover her tracks. The one thing Irina was sure of was that from here on in nobody was ever going to get in her way. She did wonder how Suzy was faring now that the tide of the war had turned. She had had no news of her for months and in any case she was too busy getting her own life back on track. The shop on place des Vosges had been completely vandalised and though the apartment on rue du Bac had been occupied by a Nazi official it wasn't really damaged. The furniture was gone but that was a minor detail. The house in Auteuil had survived best of all, though Ana's meticulously maintained garden had turned into a jungle. All in all they were very lucky.

One afternoon Irina was down on her hands and knees in the shop trying to scrub scorch marks off the parquet floor where people had been stubbing out cigarettes. She looked up and there was Suzy peering in through the window. Irina got up and opened the door for her.

"Come in. This place is still a shambles. There's no electricity but I can offer you a drink if you like."

"No thanks. I'm heading out of Paris for a while. You probably heard the club is closed. Marie-Ange told me you were back and I decided to come by to see if you were here."

The conversation was stilted as if they had never known each other.

"How have you been, Irina?"

"Fine. Like most people, surviving, but at least the war is over."

"Sweetie, I wanted to say how sorry …

Irina cut across her.

"I'm not your sweetie – I'm not, anybody's sweetie!"

"That's a pity. I thought you might like to escape from Paris for a while. The beaches are open again."

"It's too late for all that and I have a business to get back on track. Anyway what to do, life goes on. And you? Are you in trouble?"

"Oh, me and half Paris! But don't worry about me, I have insurance."

"What do you mean – insurance?"

"Remember all those annoying photographs I got Philippe to take for me in the club?"

"What about them?"

"And remember all those important Vichy people and the black market guys who wanted to smooze the Germans. Where did they go for fun and to do their deals? *La Vie Parisienne* of course: and I have every single one of those photographs. Such a pity if they ended up in public! My good friend the Judge only had to move my file from one pile to another. I'll get a slap on the wrist and then after a year or two life will go back to normal."

"Be careful, Suzy, blackmail is a dangerous game. You might pull that stunt on the wrong person". Irina couldn't help thinking of Gerard with his heels drumming on the stone flags as he choked. "Do you need money?"

Suzy laughed. "That's the one thing I'm not short of. But friends? That's a different matter. I better go. I'm driving down to Nice this afternoon. I have an apartment there."

Suzy was silent for a minute and they stood looking at each other.

"We did have fun didn't we, Irina?"

"Yes, we did."

"I'll see you around kiddo!"

Suzy walked off down the street and Irina went back to scrubbing the floor trying not to think of what might have been.

#

A week later a parcel was delivered to the rue du Bac. When Irina opened it – it was the double portrait of her and Suzy by Tamara de Lempicka. The card said: love always – Suzy. Irina hung the picture in her dressing room in the rue du Bac but never mentioned it to anyone.

As life began to get back to normal Emile's resistance contacts stood Irina in good stead and when a leading member of the resistance needed cash, she was only too willing to help him launch his political career. When he subsequently became a minister in the post-war Provisional Government, he was suitably grateful. The beautiful CountessBratinsky became a regular guest at receptions in the Prime Minister's official residence, the Hôtel Matignon, in the Elysée, and more importantly still, at the private suppers afterwards where the news of the day and the latest scandals were discussed. Irina became the go to jeweller for members of the political elite.

Helping out on the Committee for Refugee Children and organising some high-profile fundraising events improved her reputation and at the same time made her some new and influential contacts. Since half the members of Parisian high society, and the government, were busy re-writing their war time curriculum vitae she didn't have too much to worry about. Irina's number one priority was business and for her the post-war period presented its own unique opportunities. France had been stripped bare by the departing Germans and it took the next decade for the economy to pick up again. As to how some people seemed to have so much money after 5 years of war and occupation that was none of her business. Irina could always be relied on to advise on a suitable gift for a wife or what was more appropriate for a mistress. "Discretion is my middle name, she would murmur reassuringly to her clients: "*Monsieur, Je suis unetombe.*"

\#

Back in Paris there was one major problem on the horizon for Irina: what to do about Masha? The simple fact was that Masha was spoiled. Ana adored her only grandchild but she still clung to the old fashioned idea of what was appropriate for a young girl of her class. For her, the priorities were that her granddaughter, Countess Maria Bratinsky, should dress nicely, speak several languages and play the piano. If she learned to cook, so much the

THE BRATINSKY AFFAIR

better. The idea that her Masha needed to think about a career never crossed her mind. Irina had hoped that the nuns of the Assumption in Bordeaux would instil some discipline into her wayward daughter but to no avail. Masha had used her combination of charm and impeccable manners to glide through school with the minimum of effort. "If I had beaten her like a gong and locked her up with an enclosed order of nuns, it wouldn't have made a blind bit of difference. She wouldn't have learned a thing and they would probably have elected her Mother Superior," Irina would say to friends later on. It didn't matter what she did, Masha would neither lead nor follow. Inevitably it ended in tears. One morning Irina was sitting on the terrace of Lipp's Brasserie on boulevard Saint-Germain, having coffee with a client, when she saw Masha whizzing past in a sports car convertible with a handsome young man at a time when Irina knew she was supposed to be attending lectures in the Sorbonne. Still, she couldn't help smiling. It was good to see Masha finally having some fun. She pictured herself at Masha's age trekking across borders and scrambling for food. There were some things she didn't want to remember. Irina had been successful because she had no choice but she doubted Masha had that instinct for survival and she certainly didn't understand how things could fall apart from one day to the next.

A different tack was clearly needed. Masha was intelligent but she didn't want to study and had so far shown no interest in developing a career. At one point Irina had thought that Masha might take over the business but although she loved the money and the lifestyle she wasn't prepared for the discipline and hard work that running a successful business entailed. Irina wanted to see her settled one way or the other. Marriage was the only option. Irina herself had never wanted to be a hard-nosed business woman. When she married Egon she had thought that her life would revolve around her husband, two or three children and her comfortable home. Comfortable for her of course meant an apartment in Paris, a house in the country and staff to manage both. Circumstances had decided otherwise. Now, Irina spent a fortune organising parties, buying clothes and making sure

Masha got invited to the smartest dinners and weekend parties. But nothing doing. Ana laughed. "Darling, it didn't work for you and it won't work for Masha. Remember Egon! If you try to force her into some "suitable" marriage it will be a disaster. You should learn from my mistakes and let her find her own way."

Irina and Ana were sitting in the kitchen one Sunday morning when Masha burst in excitedly. She was in love and she was getting engaged. "His name is William, William Radcliffe a decorated RAF pilot and diplomat. You'll love him." Irina doubted that very much. This was her worst nightmare, that Masha would just drift along and then when she got bored decide she was in love and rush into some disastrous marriage. She should have listened to her mother. She didn't. Instead she exploded and the fight was nasty.

"With your looks and background you could have anyone you wanted, do anything you want. The truth is you don't know what you want. You're spoilt and selfish and now, you want to throw everything away and marry this nobody. Well, don't come running back to me when it ends in tears." Masha had never forgiven her for that.

In the weeks that followed Irina tried everything to keep them apart but nothing worked. She used all her wiles on the British Ambassador to have William sent back to London but that made things even worse. A month later Masha announced that William was being posted back to London and she was going too. They were going to be married. One afternoon Ana called in unexpectedly to the shop. They were chatting over tea when Ana brought up the subject of Masha. "You're fighting a losing battle with Masha. You have to let her go or lose her altogether." For once Irina took her mother's advice and reluctantly took on the role of mother of the bride. The wedding in Saint Germain des Près was everything you could have expected. The bride wore Dior, the flowers were beautiful, the champagne cool and crisp, but it was far from being the joyous occasion Irina and Ana had hoped for. After Masha left for London both Ana and Irina went into a period of mourning. Irina worked day and night and Ana dug obsessively in her garden. Nothing helped. Their little world

THE BRATINSKY AFFAIR

had revolved around Masha and now she was gone.
\#

In the years that followed Irina worked non-stop to build a profile as the leading expert and dealer in Russian art and antiques, especially the works of Fabergé. Most people wanted the diamonds and the bling but what Irina loved most were the small carvings of animals in Siberian jade. She loved their simplicity and the sheer genius of the workmanship as well as the way they nestled in the palm of the hand. However, the more successful she became the more vulnerable she felt. She had never forgotten the hungry years not knowing where the next meal or the next generous benefactor would come from. Money became an obsession. But now, there were fewer and fewer old ladies with carefully preserved relics of old Russia whom she could help to dispose of their treasures. One by one they were dying off, and by the early 1960s it was clear that Irina needed a new approach.

She still went to the Orthodox cathedrals in Paris and Nice from time to time, to be seen and to keep up her contacts. Irina cultivated the old aristocrats over tea in L'Orangerie and encouraged them to reminisce about the good old days. If she sensed a deal in the offing, lunch in the Georges V would be an occasion to dress up in their smartest clothes and best jewellery, if only to show that they could still pull it off. At the same time, this gave Irina a clear idea of who still had what. Of course, they were always happy to gossip about who was having money troubles and might need to sell off an interesting piece. Irina would follow up by inviting them to her Christmas and Easter receptions, so that they would still feel part of a world that had forgotten them as they slipped from uncountable wealth to getting by, and onwards into true poverty.

In the end, when they needed to sell, their dear friend Irina was only too willing to help. Irina would do them a favour by taking these "old-fashioned pieces" off their hands. She would sell them on for multiples of what she had paid making sure to cover her tracks by selling them in London, or better still New York, where there was a large Russian community willing to pay top dollar for good pieces, especially pieces with a story. Usually, the old ladies were embarrassed to be seen selling heirlooms and wanted it done discreetly with no questions asked. That suited Irina fine. And if from time to time a friend of a friend needed to dispose of a piece of more dubious provenance; who was she to ask questions.

By the sixties the economy was booming and Irina's business was on the up and up. In 1962 Irina was out for dinner with friends when she met Dmitri, a handsome and much younger barman in Raspoutine, who had some enterprising contacts back home in Russia. The fact that he was easy on the eye was no great hardship. Irina sat at the mirrored bar waiting for her friends to arrive. Not bad for fifty-one she thought. Half a century! How in God's name did that happen? She had to say she thought she still looked pretty good. Maria Callas's surgeon had done a good job. Anyone in the know could see that she had had work done but it was so subtle as to be almost invisible. She was still lost in her thoughts when she heard a voice.

"What can I get you, Countess?"

The voice startled her out of her day dream and she found herself looking at a handsome young barman with jet black hair and a dazzling smile.

"Martini with a twist."

She watched as he deftly picked up the bottles to mix her drink. At one point the phone behind the bar rang and she overheard the conversation.

"That's no good, man, it's 4 carat stone – it has to be worth double that. Christ, go back to him – see what you can get – I need the cash and quick."

There was a note of panic in his voice. She knew that feeling. As he turned to put the glass down in front of her, Irina looked at him and smiled.

"Money troubles?"

He glanced around to make sure the manager was out of earshot. "You better believe it. My mother is ill back home and I'm trying to get some cash to her. I need to sell this ring. It was her engagement ring. She gave it to me when I came to France."

THE BRATINSKY AFFAIR

Irina was pretty sure the story was a load of hooey – more likely a drug or a gambling debt. It may have been someone's engagement ring but probably not his mother's. "Let me see the ring. Maybe I can do something for you."

Dmitri handed the ring over. It was indeed a nice ring - as he said - a 4 carat marquise cut diamond.

Just then Irina's friends arrived and she discreetly handed the ring back. "Come by the shop tomorrow and we'll talk."

The dazzling smile he gave her was almost worth the outrageous price of the drinks in Raspoutine.

And so, it began.

Every so often a prize piece of jewellery or a painting would disappear from a provincial museum in Rostov or Odessa and after a suitable time lapse be 'discovered' in an auction room in France or Ireland, after which it could be sold on with a new paper trail. In the beginning Irina believed or at least went along with the story of noble families disposing of hidden family treasures until in the end she decided it was better not to ask any questions.

The shop in place des Vosges was her official profile, and kept her on the guest list for parties and receptions, but the real money was to be made in the shadows. From time to time there would be a discreet knock on the side door after the shop had closed and a package would be handed over. Smaller pieces she sold on directly – after all, a diamond ring is a diamond ring – but larger pieces that might be recognised would be broken up, and her good friend Maurice would reset them in modern settings. Once the item was safely sold on, the money would be split fifty-fifty. Irina soothed any residual qualms of conscience with an occasional large cheque to a charity that looked after exiled Russians who had fallen on hard times.

The system worked well, and profitably, until one day in the spring of 1965 Dmitri disappeared. Irina went to the bar early in the evening, knowing it was a good time to catch him on his own. When she asked if Dmitri was on, the barman shrugged his shoulders and continued drying glasses. "Haven't seen him in a week –didn't show up – no message, nothing. No loss, if you ask me. Maybe he has a new boyfriend."

"Boyfriend?" Irina squawked, choking on her martini

"Oh yes, that's our Dmitri, all things to all men – and women."

Irina finished her drink and left. The barman nodded to the man sitting in the red velvet alcove on the other side of the bar. He came over and slid a bundle of discreetly folded notes across the counter before he headed out after the Countess.

THE BRATINSKY AFFAIR

CHAPTER 21

Paris, March 1976

Things fell into place surprisingly easily. Tom and Olga went to the agency, handed over their passports and filled in a bundle of forms. Tom put himself down as a teacher of English as a foreign language, not a journalist, and Olga put herself down as an art historian. That was it; in four days they would fly to Moscow. In the interim they continued the clean-up of the apartment on rue du Bac, and when that was finished they started on the contents of the shop and the apartment on place des Vosges.

Olga asked Tom to make an inventory of the contents of the shop while she worked on the apartment. Fortunately for him most of the things were labelled and all he had to do was transcribe the details into a notebook. Before Irina was murdered, Olga had thought of working in publishing, and had even had a few interviews but now she wasn't sure. The one thing she did know was that she had zero interest in being an antique dealer. In all probability the valuable contents of the shop would be sold but she could deal with that when they came back from Russia.

≠

The big problem for Tom was what to say to Jean-Philippe. As they walked back to Jean-Philippe's apartment after dinner on the Thursday evening Jean-Philippe could sense that something was up.

"What's wrong? You seem preoccupied. Don't tell me you've gone off me already?"

"Don't be silly," Tom said, and leaned in to give him a quick kiss as they turned a corner. "It's nothing. I'm thinking about what happens next is all: work, this whole Bratinsky thing… and us …and going back to Ireland."

It wasn't altogether a lie, but it was still only half the story.

Jean-Philippe turned to look at him. "You want my advice? Stop worrying. You're young, so just let yourself enjoy this big adventure. And, don't worry; I'll be here to catch you if you fall!"

Tom now felt even worse. Fortunately for him, Jean-Philippe was going to New York the next morning for ten days for a big corporate merger he had been working on for the previous two years. As he had to be up at dawn to catch his flight they just had a passionate snog on the sofa and a lingering kiss before Tom walked back to his hotel. As he strolled along he realised that de didn't want to go to Russia. He wanted to stay in Paris with Jean-Philippe. Was this what love felt like, this mixture of nerves and excitement? One thing was clear: every time they said goodbye Tom found himself thinking about when he would see Jean-Philippe again.

Even so, there was no backing out now. He had pushed Olga into travelling to Russia and now he had to see it through. He felt like a complete shit but he promised himself that he would make it up to Jean-Philippe when they got back from Russia.

≠

On the Saturday before departure there was a meet-and-greet session organised by the travel agency. It was an opportunity to meet the other members of the group and for the travel agency to mark their cards as to what to do and what not to do in Russia. There were about 40 people on the trip, as mixed a group of people as you could hope to find. There were the two couples in their fifties, lifelong trade unionists from one of the biggest trade unions in France who were clearly trying to suss out political fellow travellers; a couple of teachers from a left wing lycée in Corbeil-Essonnes, and several civil servants. Then there was the elderly museum curator, Serge Alloncle and his very grand wife, Chantale, who clearly thought that they should be travelling with a much more exclusive group. She always had a look on her face as if somebody nearby had just farted.

Finally, there was a charming retired antique dealer from Blois, Henri Dufour and his equally charming wife, Françoise, who had taken a shine to Tom and Olga. They were well into their seventies and were still clearly mad about each other. One was never seen without the other. Most of the people in the group had never been to Russia before and there was a general feeling of excitement tinged with nervousness.

THE BRATINSKY AFFAIR

Helene, their tour guide, was a glamorous woman in her forties who had clearly been everywhere and seen everything. Nothing fazed her. She specialised in top-end cultural tours, and with her carefully coiffed red hair, her fur coat and high heels she looked the part, especially as she moved in a cloud of Shalimar perfume and chain-smoked Sobranie Black Russian cigarettes. The only thing missing was a cigarette holder. She focused on laying down what the travel group jokingly referred to as 'the law according to Helene.'

She stood up on a small platform at the front of the room to give them a long spiel on their behaviour in Russia. "You will inevitably be approached by touts offering to give you ten times the official exchange rate for roubles, in exchange for Dollars or Deutschmarks. Under no circumstances should you do this. The money you bring in will be recorded, and on the way out the value of any purchases will be checked. If you have spent more than you brought in, customs will know that you have been dealing on the black market and you will be in trouble – especially with me!

Everyone laughed obligingly.

"Not only that, but everything you have bought will be confiscated and the whole group will be delayed. You could end up paying a fine or missing your flight – which would be very expensive. Under no circumstances should you discuss politics, ask political questions or in fact say anything remotely political at all. As far as you are concerned everything in Russia is wonderful."

"There will be no wandering off on solo expeditions, and you should assume that the group is being monitored at all times. In the hotel you should assume that the room is bugged, even if it isn't. The same goes for telephone conversations. In addition, bring toilet paper, a plug for the sink, basic medicines and small gifts such as soap and sample bottles of perfume which can be used as tips." She hopped down from the platform and picked up her glass of wine.

"It feels like a school trip," said Tom,

Olga giggled and said, "I hope there won't be an exam at the end of each day – I have a terrible memory."

They were given a glass of sharp wine and a bundle of brochures on shiny paper. That was it. Forty-eight hours to lift-off.

The day before the flight they were both wound up. Tom had called his father and Willi to say that he was finishing up some things in Paris and would be home the following weekend. If he had felt bad telling a lie to Jean-Philippe, he felt even worse lying to his father. Olga told her father a version of the same story. They both knew that if they told the truth there would be a storm of protests, so they said nothing and both felt guilty. That evening they decided to go to a film to ease the pressure. The one thing about Paris is that if you are interested in cinema, any great film that has ever been made will be showing somewhere.

When they turned onto place Saint-André des Arts they noticed that a film in a season of Russian movies was running in one of the cinemas: *Andrei Rublev* by Tarkovsky, the story of Russia's most famous icon painter by one of Russia's most famous film directors. Tom's heart sank. Secretly he would have preferred a Bond movie, but what the hell, he couldn't let the side down and have Olga think he was some kind of peasant. The cinema only seated about a hundred people, and as they settled into their seats Tom noticed that the audience was divided into one block of people at the front of the cinema and another at the back.

Olga explained what was going on. "You see those people at the back? Those are the White Russian aristocratic exiles or their children. The people at the front are the lefties – the socialists and communists. Both sides are interested in Russian culture, but never the twain shall meet. We could probably re-enact the Russian civil war right here."

As Tom took in the two groups, he noticed that the Whites were much more formally dressed, and there seemed to be a lot of hand-kissing going on. Up front, the lefties tended more towards Che Guevara t-shirts and ponchos from Chile.

"It was Irina who pointed it out to me, and it seems to be the same at every Russian cultural event," Olga muttered in his ear.

To his surprise, Tom found the film stunning – especially as it leaped from black-and-white into a vibrant colour sequence showing Rublev's icons. Looking at the film about 15th-century Russian life, Tom wondered whether life had changed much for the peasants since Olga's grandparents had fled the country. It was a strange film – but he found himself surprisingly moved by it.

Their flight was early the next morning, but they were both reluctant to go back to the hotel and face the inevitable packing. After the movie they went to the Italian restaurant next door. It had a cheap set menu and the interior embodied every cliché ever invented in the history of Italian restaurants: red-and-white gingham tablecloths, candles in Chianti bottles, a waiter wearing a red waistcoat who had a heavy black moustache and spoke with a singsong Italian accent. The food was good, especially the lemon tart, and as time passed the waiter became more and more friendly until by the time they were paying the bill his Italian accent had disappeared completely.

As they sat over coffee Olga asked him "Tell me about you and?"

Tom looked embarrassed.

"Now don't go all shy on me. I'm interested. Are you happy?"

Tom smiled. "Yes I am. I mean, this is still all a bit of a shock to the system. He's kind, as well as sexy and he makes me laugh. He can come across as all high powered and lawyery but in reality he's very down to earth. Wants to cook dinner for me when he gets back from New York."

"I'm glad to hear it. Now could you do a girl a favour and find another handsome, sexy, successful and charming lawyer – for me!"

"Is there no one in your life?"

"Nothing serious. Public school boys who think they're doing you a favour by asking you out or young politicians on the make who think that going out with Sir William Radcliffe's daughter will help their career. For the moment I'll focus on sorting out my career. And you, do you think this 'thing' will go anywhere?"

"It's way too early to say. I'm still adjusting and happy to take it one day at a time. One thing I do know is I'm lucky to have met someone like him."

"A toast? – Carpe Diem," said Olga.

"Carpe Diem!"

Now it was time to go back to the hotel and prepare for the inevitable. In their innocence, Tom and Olga were unaware that they were being shadowed every step of the way.

\#

As they gathered their luggage in the lobby of the hotel there was a momentary panic when Olga couldn't find her passport, then she realised she had deliberately left it in a prominent position on the dressing table so she wouldn't forget it. As they checked out, Olga made sure to ask if they could reserve the same rooms for a week's time;

The receptionist was chatty. "Off anywhere nice then?"

Olga had started to say " a short visit to Rus… when she caught the glare from Tom, and hastily changed the subject. They were both jittery, and it was only when they arrived at the airport and some of the people they had met at the briefing session greeted them like old friends that they started to relax. No turning back now.

THE BRATINSKY AFFAIR

CHAPTER 22

Tom and Olga's Aeroflot flight had turned for the approach to Sheremetyevo Airport. As the plane began its descent they could see huge expanses of water – rivers, lakes and reservoirs broken up with large stretches of dark green forest. The landscape was vast and open to the horizon until they began to see blocks of built-up areas as they descended into Moscow.

Their guide, Helene, marched them through security in full Mother Superior mode. Everything had to be checked: luggage, visas, currency control, and customs. The entire group was watched through plexiglass screens at every step of their slow progress through the system. What Tom and Olga hadn't seen was that as they were approaching the final gate one of the more senior security men checked the name on their passports against a list in his hand.

His phone rang, and a voice on the other end grunted, "Let them go," and with a curt nod he waved them through.

Friendly chap! thought Tom, but for once he was wise enough to shut his mouth and keep moving. As they came out into the main terminal Tom and Olga looked around at the flights listed for Ekaterinburg, Vladivostok, Murmansk and Krasnoyarsk, places they had either never heard of, or had only read about in novels by Tolstoy. They felt like two little hobbits creeping into Mordor, but as far as they knew they were completely unobserved. The coach to take them into the city was filled with excited chatter as the group relaxed after navigating their way through the fearsome Russian security system.

Tom and Olga had agreed that they would pretend not to speak or understand Russian. They would follow like the rest of the group then, when they got to Tsarskoye Selo they would conveniently get lost and make their way from the palace across the Alexander Park to the location of the old O'Rourke estate, if they could find it. Hopefully a few hours would give them time to suss out whether anything remained of the house and more importantly the chapel. They could grovel to Helene afterwards.

Better to ask forgiveness rather than permission. In the meantime follow the herd.

They rubbernecked and Tom pointed out the sights to Olga as the bus drove into Moscow and they finally made their way up the vast expanse of Tverskaya Street towards the Kremlin with its multiple lanes of busy traffic. Olga was fascinated both by the huge modern skyscrapers and the sheer scale of some of the late nineteenth-century apartment buildings. The bus pulled up at the hotel and they braced themselves for another bout with Russian officialdom.

"Look!" Tom told Olga. "That's the Bolshoi Theatre up the street!"

Once inside everything worked efficiently, if slowly, and eventually they were given the keys to their rooms. The Metropole still had an air of palatial grandeur, despite evidence of a slightly faded 1960's makeover.

Tom was unprepared for the marble columns and gilded furniture of the lobby or the double-height glass ceiling of the main dining room. When he had been in Russia before, he had been staying in student hostels and university dormitories. The highlight of that trip had been a visit to a cooperative farm. This was quite an upgrade. As the mirrored Art Deco lift took them up to their rooms Olga joked, "Looks like socialism might have something to recommend it after all."

The rooms were huge, but comfortable and clean, if spartan. Tom could feel himself beginning to let his guard down. At least for the next few days they could relax and be normal tourists. Dinner in the main dining room was a long-drawn-out process with a lot of toing and froing between dining room, reception and the kitchen involving the exchange of dockets. Nevertheless, the food was good, and they sat on velvet chairs beneath the opulent stained-glass ceiling waiting patiently for it to be brought by the unsmiling waiter. He looked as if he had been there since before the Revolution and while they were waiting, Tom read Olga amusing titbits out of the guide book about the history of the hotel.

"Can you believe it? Rasputin held orgies here in the

THE BRATINSKY AFFAIR

Metropole? And the first Soviet constitution was written here in a matter of days because the drafters were locked in their room and told they wouldn't be allowed out until it was finished."

"I hope at least Rasputin didn't stay in my bed!" said Olga

"Pay attention. There will be a multiple choice quiz every evening over dinner to see whether you have been paying attention during the day."

"God in heaven, Tom, You're worse than Helene."

Tom continued relentlessly. "Lenin harangued his followers in this dining room, and it has been known to happen that every so often drunken visitors have ended up in the fountain, over there in the middle of the room, after too much Crimean champagne."

"Now, Tom, would you ever switch it off? I'm tired and hungry and if I had a pearl-handled revolver I might be tempted to use it."

After dinner Tom wanted to go for a walk round the block to get a sense of where he was. As a student of history and politics he was fascinated to be staying within walking distance of Red Square and the Kremlin, which he had only seen during his university years in rigidly controlled speed tours. It was even exciting to see the sinister Lubyanka Square on the map. As he crossed reception, he spotted Helene on patrol and decided that maybe it wasn't such a good idea and bed was a better option.

Breakfast the next morning was surprisingly good: tea and rye bread and butter, eggs and pancakes with fruit. Helene warned them, "Stock up on breakfast, as there's a lot to see and lunch will be on the hoof. Also, don't wander off. If you do get lost head back to the hotel as I won't be coming to look for you."

In Red Square, Tom and Olga stood in awe at the immense breadth of the square with the domes of the Kremlin Palace peering over the red walls of the fortress. Tom had to remind himself of the purpose of their visit, andkept looking around to see if anyone was following them. The only people he could see were tour groups like themselves listening attentively to their guides, bands of soldiers taking photographs outside Lenin's tomb and groups of children more interested in buying ice cream.

Four cathedrals and a palace later Olga muttered to Tom, "I

have lost the feeling in my feet and I think I'm developing an allergy to churches, and this is only day one! There's so much gold I need sunglasses indoors" By the time they had completed the tour of the Grand Kremlin Palace and the Armoury with its collection of court costumes and a dazzling display of imperial jewels they were both wilting. In the middle of the gilded throne room Olga turned to him and said "Can't you imagine Irina swanning around here in her heyday?"

Though they hadn't realised it, Helene was behind them and overheard their conversation.

"Who was Irina? She sounds interesting."

"Oh, an old friend of my grandmother's, said Olga – "She was very grand and very glamorous – French."

"Oh, I thought maybe you had Russian connections, especially with a name like Olga. In fact you look kind of Russian, don't you think?"

"Ach no, not at all" said Tom cutting in. "Bog Irish, through and through, even though her father is a Brit." And he gave Helene his most roguish smile. She laughed and walked on.

Olga gave him her - are you out of your mind look: "Bog Irish!!!"

The next part of the tour was a visit to the Bolshoi that evening after an early dinner. Since they arrived Tom had been wearing his standard uniform of a khaki anorak, jeans and boots while Olga had been wearing a navy reefer jacket and jeans with the jeans rolled up to the top of her comfy boots. Comfort and warmth were the priorities. But this was the gala opening of a new production of Spartacus that was due to travel to Paris later in the year and Helene had told them to dress up. "Don't let me down. There will be a lot of important people at the performance tonight.'

Tom came down to the hotel lobby before seven. Most of the group were already there, the men in suits and the women in little black dresses. It had gone seven and Helene was beginning to look at her watch when Olga stepped out of the lift. As she crossed the floor every head in succession swivelled to follow her.

Helene said: "You certainly took me at my word when I said dress to impress." There was admiration edged with a slight element of snark in her tone. She herself looked great, even if her elegant black wrap dress lacked the drama of the one skimming Olga's figure.

Olga went up to the bar, smiling at Tom. "It's my tribute to Irina and Ana, and my mother." She was wearing a dress from Saint Laurent's 'Petersburg Nights' collection, a black velvet skirt almost to the ground with a jewelled peasant belt, such as no peasant had ever worn, and an off-the-shoulder blouse with balloon sleeves in electric pink. Her hair was swept up in an elegant chignon and she had Irina's sable cape draped over her arm. "I found the dress in Irina's closet with the label still on it. She never got the chance to wear it."

Tom noted that she was wearing Irina's Fabergé egg pendant hanging from Ana's pearl necklace. The silver locket with the pictures of Ana and Victor was pinned at her waist. "Don't you clean up well," he said. He, as usual, was wearing his one and only navy suit.

"Is that a compliment or should you be suitably punished?" she asked, and picked up the glass of champagne he had ordered for her.

"You know perfectly well that's an Irish way of saying you look drop dead gorgeous." He felt comfortable saying something like that to Olga now that things were out in the open.

It was a short walk to the theatre, but it was chilly and Olga was glad of her fur, even as she walked up the spectacular double staircase in glittering white marble. This was imperial Russia on steroids: gold, marble – more gold – chandeliers the size of a tank. . Tom and Olga were standing chatting to the Dufour's when out of the corner of her eye Olga saw Helene coming towards them accompanied by a tall, elegantly dressed man. She had the air of a cat about to present a particularly plump mouse to its owner.

"This is Mr Ivanov, Director of the Bolshoi, and he wants to wish you a special welcome to Moscow." She had obviously used all her contacts and charm to pull off this introduction. Mr

Ivanov was tall and lean, and judging by the way he moved had probably been a dancer in his day. His long hair was swept back loosely and his unstructured black jacket was casual yet stylish. He had that bohemian chic look that takes a lot of money to pull off.

Here we go again, thought Tom. Should have bought that suit in Paris! Back in Bray Tom had always tried to get along attracting as little attention as possible. Since arriving in Paris he was beginning to feel that he wanted to cut a dash. He found himself noticing what people were wearing and how they carried themselves. He no longer walked around with his shoulders hunched up with tension.

After the introductions the group settled down to chat over drinks. Madame Dufour in her excitement turned to Ivanov. "I was saying to my husband that our lovely Olga here could pass for Russian – with her colouring and especially wearing this beautiful dress – don't you think?"

"I'm sure that must be the case, you would be perfect in the role of Ana Karenina – Are you sure you don't have a Russian grandmother Miss …"

"Radcliffe – Olga Radcliffe. I'm boringly English, I'm afraid." Olga was becoming more and more uncomfortable at being the focus of his attention; especially as there was something in the appraising way Ivanov looked at her that made her think he knew more than he was letting on. As if that wasn't bad enough, Mr Dufour chose that precise moment to start gushing. "Olga, I wanted to say how wonderful you look, and what beautiful pearls. I thought only royalty wore pearls of that quality these days."

"They were my grandmother's." She could feel Ivanov taking in every word of the conversation. Fortunately the bell rang just then summoning them to their seats. Olga looked for Tom and saw him behind her, chatting to Ivanov.

Minutes later as they were walking into the auditorium Ivanov turned to Tom and said casually in Russian, "You are English, Mr O'Brien, yes?"

Tom rose to the bait and instinctively started to reply in

THE BRATINSKY AFFAIR

Russian, rejecting such an outrageous slur. His Russian was a bit stilted but it was clear that he understood and spoke at least some Russian. It was a trap and he had walked straight into it. He assumed a blank look and tried to backtrack but the damage was done.

"Ah good, so you speak Russian, Mr O'Brien, that makes life so much easier!"

"A few phrases," said Tom. "You know, to ask for directions and say please help, I'm lost!" He laughed unconvincingly. He wanted to kick himself for being such a fool. He had zero prospects as a spy.

Ivanov nodded knowingly before suavely resuming the conversation in English.

When the lights went down Olga tried to focus on the spectacular auditorium with its multiple levels, the magnificent royal box and the wonderful dancing, but she couldn't concentrate. Ivanov was sitting on their left and Olga could see that his head was slightly turned in their direction so that even though he was looking at the stage they were constantly in his line of sight because of the curve of the auditorium.

"Tom, I don't think I can do this, he's onto us."

"Relax, it will be all right – remember what Irina said – shoulders back – head up – smile. He may be a snoop but he knows nothing, he's fishing. We have to keep calm and stick to the plan."

A sharp shush from Helene told them to be quiet. The rest of the performance passed in a blur, and both of them were glad when they were able to make their escape back to the hotel. Ivanov had invited them for supper but Olga pleaded a headache and the need for an early night.

Tom could see the look of incredulity on Helene's face as if to say "what kind of idiot turns down an invitation to supper from the Director of the Bolshoi!" She on the other hand, was only too happy to accept as were the Dufours and the Alloncles. It was noticeable that Ivanov had managed to winkle out the grandest members of the group. The trade unionists and the librarians were discreetly ignored. *Quite an operator*, thought Tom.

Back at the hotel they sat in a quiet corner of the bar to relax by themselves.

"Tom, I'm serious. I don't think I can do this. I'm not cut out for espionage."

"If I'm honest, neither am I," said Tom. "Ok, how about this?. Sleep on it, and if tomorrow morning you feel the same way we can call the whole thing off and finish the tour as normal tourists."

"It's a deal," said Olga. "Thanks, Tom, you're a brick… and now I need to get out of this ridiculous dress and get some sleep. We have to be up at five to get the train to Saint Petersburg."

THE BRATINSKY AFFAIR

CHAPTER 23

Paris 1968

As long as the Soviet Union was securely locked up, Irina had felt reasonably secure. She had always known there was a possibility that one day someone would walk out of the past and she would have to confront the reality of what had happened long ago. As a result she mostly preferred not to appear in society photographs but then, when a journalist from the *New York Times* wanted to do a feature on exiles who had made a new life for themselves she couldn't resist it. This was the ultimate validation of her success, and it might bring in some wealthy new clients to replace the old ladies. *Time for a change? she thought – I could even open a shop in New York?*

As she told the journalist, "People don't understand what it is like to leave everything you have ever known behind, or what it takes to create a new life from scratch, or how it feels to be a permanent outsider – the one who never quite fits in. I want to tell my own story." The problem with opening the door to the past is that you never know what will emerge and Irina found herself confronting things she hadn't thought about in years. She hadn't expected the feelings of guilt and loss that swept over her. The loss of her father and brother, her inability to save them and the gulf that she had allowed to grow up between her and Masha. For the first time she realised that while she had recreated a facsimile of a perfect life she was alone. Everything came out in a rush of raw emotion. Irina was completely taken aback when the NYT put her picture on the cover of the weekend magazine and devoted 4 pages to the interview. In retrospect it was not a good idea to draw so much attention. It would invite too many questions.

A few weeks later a well-dressed man walked into the shop. She knew immediately he was Russian: something in the way he carried himself and in the slant of his face. He was muffled up in a heavy black overcoat and a cashmere scarf, but the shaved head and the tattoos across both knuckles told her what she was dealing with: one of the new generation of thugs who had survived the kill-or-be-killed life of the camps and now operated as hired guns in the shadowy underworld of Brezhnev's Russia. From time to time one of them would show up in Raspoutine. She would feel them watching her and discreetly quizzing the barman as to who she was. One of them sent over a bottle of champagne which she had politely declined.

Too loud and too much gold jewellery, better to steer clear.

He spoke French but the accent was unmistakable. "A friend told me that sometimes you have interesting things for sale." The voice was surprisingly cultivated.

"Are you looking for anything in particular?"

"Maybe something like this" – and he put three photographs on the table. "Three of a kind – isn't that what they say in poker?"

Irina looked at him and then down at the photographs.

She knew what they were immediately. The photographs were the last three pieces she had got from Dmitri: a pear shaped natural pearl on a platinum chain, a large oval sapphire brooch surrounded by three concentric rings of diamonds and a frog carved out of Siberian jade. The quality was so good that she should have suspected something. But she had been greedy.

"All these pieces have been reported stolen from museums in and around Leningrad."

Irina steeled herself. *Don't show anything, bluff this out –keep calm.*

"And your point is?"

"We know you handled the sale and we know who bought them. I doubt very much if these distinguished pillars of society would be happy to find out that you have been selling them stolen property."

Irina paused for a moment. "I bought them in good faith and nobody can prove otherwise."

"Maybe not, but think of the scandal. Your rich friends wouldn't like it and something tells me the invitations might be a bit thin on the ground after that."

"What exactly do you want?"

"Information."

"And how can I have information that would be of interest to you, or… anybody else, for that matter."

"Come, now, Countess, let's not play games." As he said it, he lingered on the word *Countess,* giving it a subtle, ironic emphasis. "We know all about your visits to the Hôtel Matignon and the Elysée and the intimate suppers when everyone else has gone home. I'm sure the conversation must be… interesting."

Dropping the names of the official residences of the Prime Minister and President of France had only one meaning. They had been watching her and knew her every move.

"So you think that after all this time – after everything I've had to do to get to this point in my life – I'm going to become a puppet dancing to your tune? I think not."

He leaned towards her. She could smell the cologne he wore, Teak by Shulton, light, oriental, masculine, repulsive. "She recoiled instantly as the smell took her back to the room in Helsinki. She thought she might be sick but managed to hold it together.

"That's very principled of you, but in the end of the day it's your choice, Irina. You don't mind if I call you Irina, do you? 'Countess' seems so formal – and I think we are going to be seeing a lot of each other. You can call me Oleg." He rose and bowed ironically from the waist. "Oleg Kerensky." She wanted to slap him down and tell him that only head waiters bowed from the waist.

"I'd rather d…"

He cut across her. "Oh please, Irina, don't be so melodramatic. You are a survivor, like me – and we survivors will do whatever it takes to survive. After all, we 'former people' have to stick together."

Irina looked at him in silence. The words 'whatever it takes to survive' were like a door into the past. She could hear her father's voice the last time she had seen him – "Survive, Irina. Whatever it takes, survive."

"You and I have absolutely nothing in common."

"That's where you are so wrong. I clawed my way out of the camp and you clawed your way to the top of the heap here in

Paris. We are not nice people, we both smell of shit. I bet you wake in the middle of the night dreaming of Russia, don't you? I can see it in your eyes, the ache for something you will never get back. Apart from all that, you don't have a choice. It would be terrible if the beautiful CountessBratinsky, friend of presidents and prime ministers, turned out to be a common thief. I don't think prison would suit you one little bit. And there's your daughter to think about."

She froze. "My daughter?" To her rage, her voice was trembling. How could this be happening to her again? In her mind's eye she could see Gerard's piggy face as he choked in the cathedral in Bordeaux and if she could have, she would have obliterated Kerensky without a moment's hesitation. It was as if he could read her mind.

"No magic solution, Irina. As I said, it's your choice. All you have to do is listen carefully, and, if you can, steer the conversation in directions that might interest our masters. Then you will write a report."

Her shoulders slumped and she spoke softly. "How will I contact you?"

He looked around at the stock on display. "Put the bust of Robespierre in the window and I will know you have something for me – I can't imagine anyone is ever going to buy it." Robespierre, the man who chopped off aristocratic heads. When she had found it at the auction, she thought it would be a bit of fun to put it in the window surrounded by the flotsam and jetsam of exile. Now it didn't seem one bit funny.

As he went out the door, Oleg – if that was his name – paused for a moment. "One thing. There's no point trying to find Dmitri. He's gone away, and he won't be coming back."

Later that week, Irina was sitting in a café drinking her morning coffee and flicking though the newspaper. She stopped. There, in the middle of the page was a picture of Dmitri, except he no longer looked anything like the handsome Dmitri she had known. When she read the headline, she felt sick:

Body Fished from Seine Believed to be Well Known Drug Dealer

THE BRATINSKY AFFAIR

She read on: *"The deceased, Dmitri Shuvalov, was known to the police and was suspected of dealing in drugs and stolen property. His throat had been cut."*

Irina stood up, paid the bill and walked back to the shop. The message was clear. There was no way out.

\#

As the sixties moved into the seventies Irina sent in regular reports: the aftermath of the Cuban missile crisis, the situation in Indochina, competition over missile testing or relations with China or Germany. After a while, things settled down and life carried on as normal. A lot of her reports consisted of rumour and speculation, but Oleg seemed happy enough, except when the student riots erupted in 1967 and revolution seemed to have broken out on the streets of Paris. Then he wanted daily updates. When the very chatty wife of the American Ambassador became a customer and started inviting Irina to lunch things got even easier.

It was the quiet time between Christmas and New Year in 1976 when, at one of their tête-à-tête teatimes, Oleg produced a photograph. Irina stopped breathing. She knew immediately what it was, but she needed time to process what she was seeing – to work out what was going on. Why this? Why now? She couldn't ask Oleg anything; he would use any questions as an opportunity to manipulate her further. She had to wait for him to show his hand.

"A friend is interested in acquiring this object and he thinks you might be able to help."

Irina looked at the photograph closely, as if studying the object in detail. It took every ounce of her control to continue breathing normally. She looked him in the eye as she handed back the photograph.

"It's not my area – I don't see how I can help you –sorry. Anyway, I've been trying to contact you for weeks. I've done what you asked all this time but now I'm getting too old and too tired for all this stress. People have started asking questions. I need to get out." Irina sank back; "I don't know what's going on, but someone is sniffing around and I don't like it."

Oleg lifted the teapot from the samovar where it was simmering. He poured, replaced the teapot, sipped. "Remember Dmitri, Irina – be careful what you wish for. The KGB doesn't have a retirement plan."

Irina braced herself to ask if he was threatening her. He spoke first. "Think of it as a friendly warning."

At that moment two ladies came into the shop and by making a big fuss of looking after them she was able to cover up her shock. As soon as he left, Irina took a taxi to rue du Bac and made a series of calls to some of her best placed contacts. One of her oldest admirers from the past, the sublime Didier, had gradually moved up the ranks and was now head of a department in the direction générale de la sécuritéextérieure – France's foreign intelligence service. Hopefully he could find out what was going on.

She would go to the Prime Minister's New Year reception, then fly to Ireland and stay there for a few weeks. January was a dead month in the trade anyway, so no one would comment on her absence. While Irina waited for Didier to ring back she scribbled a quick note to her granddaughter, Olga, in England:

Dearest, Going to Ireland for a while – if anybody starts asking questions, you know nothing.

When Didier called her back the news was not reassuring. "Someone from Intelligence has been asking questions. Odd! You seem to be becoming famous, perhaps too famous. Irina, are you in trouble? Is there anything I can do?"

She laughed lightly. "No, nothing. The Louvre is putting a major Fabergé exhibition together. A lot of the pieces have to be shipped across Europe and everything has to get security clearance, even me! Normal procedure. Anyway, thanks for that, but let me know if you hear anything else. I'm going away for a rest – I'll call you when I get back."

Irina was so agitated that she didn't notice the slight click on the line as she hung up.

Irina knew that she was safe only as long as she was useful to Oleg and his friends. If things got tricky, what could she do? Throw herself on the mercy of the Prime Minister? If it was a choice between saving her or avoiding a political scandal, he would throw her to the wolves without blinking an eye. Run to Moscow? With her background and name they weren't going to roll out the red carpet. Spending her old age in a labour camp was not appealing. The implications were clear: carry on as usual or run – at the risk of ending up like Dmitri.

In the meantime, don't get spooked: lie low and wait for things to develop. Out of the blue Irina remembered hunting deer with her father in the Caucasus. They had spent the day trekking through the forest when towards evening they finally spotted a stag. She could almost feel her father's hand on her shoulder: "Down! Be still. Don't move or even breathe. Be patient: watch and wait to see which way he goes. Then aim and fire? One shot. You can't afford to miss." If only!

Irina's wasn't going to hang around like a sitting duck waiting for the enemy to appear. Two days after the Prime Minister's party she packed a suitcase and called a taxi. Nostalgically, she still maintained the old Russian custom when going on a journey: sit for ten minutes quietly before you leave, so that you start your trip in a calm frame of mind. It didn't work.

As she sat, she randomly noticed a magazine. It happened to be the supplement from the *New York Times* with her interview. As she idly flicked through it she stopped at one section – and as she read it, the penny dropped. There was only one explanation and it spelt nothing good. The taxi arrived and she grabbed her bag and ran out the door. She stopped long enough to drop the letter to Olga in the post box on the corner, and jumped into the taxi to the airport. She was in such a rush she failed to see the figure standing in the doorway on the other side of the street, or the car that followed at a discreet distance.

CHAPTER 24

Paris

It was the following Tuesday when Inspector Fitzgerald walked into the lobby of the Hotel Victor Hugo and asked for Miss Olga Radcliffe. The French police had gone silent and it looked as though the investigation into the murder of Countess Bratinsky was going to die a gradual death: filed under case pending. In a few days the eye of the media would turn onto a new crisis or scandal and life would go back to normal. That suited him just fine. The Radcliffe girl and O'Brien would be out of his hair and if he played his cards right Semenov might bring him into the team investigating the stolen antiques. He hadn't a bull's notion about antiques and he didn't want to make a fool of himself but he had time yet to do some reading. As it turned out he was out of luck.

The dour male receptionist he spoke to was having a bad morning. The newspapers had arrived late and two members of staff had rung in sick.

"Yes?" he asked in that tone of barely suppressed contempt that is part of the Parisian DNA.

"Can I speak to Miss Olga Radcliffe?"

"Checked out."

And Mr Tom O'Brien?"

"Same."

Fortunately for the Inspector, at that moment the friendly and very pretty, Head Receptionist arrived and caught the tail end of the conversation. After briskly sending her colleague off to sort out the papers she turned and smiled at the Inspector.

"Oh, you're looking for Mr O'Brien and the young lady? They checked out on Monday but they'll be back again on Sunday," she said.

"Did they say where they were going?"

"I think they're off to Moscow. When they were checking out I noticed the tickets on the counter.

Inspector Fitzgerald looked at her stunned. "Russia! Sweet

THE BRATINSKY AFFAIR

Mother of Divine Jesus!"

"I beg your pardon, sir?" said the receptionist in a slightly affronted tone.

"Oh nothing, nothing," he muttered. "You've been very helpful." Fitzgerald rushed out of the hotel heading for police headquarters. He needed to find out what those two young fools were up to before they got themselves into real trouble and more importantly before they screwed up Semenov's investigation. Semenov had explained how he needed to keep the investigation quiet until he had identified all the players in the network and was ready to make his move. The last thing Fitzgerald needed was an international diplomatic incident and his bosses asking how he had let the situation get so out of hand. The French police would just shrug their shoulders in helpless ignorance and he would be left to shoulder the blame. Fortunately Semenov was at his desk when he rang.

"The birds have already flown so there's nothing we can do to stop them but I'll find out what I can." He rang back a couple of hours later. By the end of the conversation Fitzgerald's blood pressure had gone up several points. Semenov had managed to find out that Tom and Olga had travelled to Moscow via Tokyo with Nouvelles Frontières. He read the details of their itinerary out to Fitzgerald over the phone. The next piece of information set off all the alarm bells. "Kerensky is back Moscow and he and his cronies have a finger in every criminal pie in Moscow and Petersburg. Whatever is going on, if he finds out they're in Russia I wouldn't give much for their chances. You need to get over here, Fitzgerald. If I intervene to pick up two foreign tourists it'll be a big scandal and there'll be a lot of explaining to do. I don't want anybody else here to know what I'm doing. Best thing would be for you to track them down and haul them back to Paris before any harm is done, or better still Dublin. Officially, you'll be here as part of the investigation into the stolen antiques, on a fact finding mission. Just keep it quiet. I'll contact the embassy in Paris and sort out the visa."

Fitzgerald reached for the phone and dialled the number of the Chief Inspector in Wicklow. An *Garda Síochána* weren't known for their generosity in doling out cash for foreign trips but if this case exploded it wouldn't just be Fitzgerald's ass on the line. The Bratinsky Affair was a policeman's worst nightmare: crime, politics and espionage all mixed up together.

Fitzgerald sat looking at the phone, pouring cups of coffee he never finished and wondering what to do. Finally it rang. Semenov had pulled out all the stops for the Gardaí. He had his visa, he had his ticket, and he had an allowance to get around Moscow. But now he had another problem. If Tom contacted his father Fitzgerald needed John O'Brien to warn him that he was in danger and to tell him to sit tight and do absolutely nothing until Fitzgerald got in touch. With a bit of luck he could contain all this. Nothing for it. After what he'd heard, he would have to tell John O'Brien what was going on. The phone rang for at least a minute before Tom's father picked up.

"Mr O'Brien, Inspector Fitzgerald here – yes, fine – how are you? We have a problem. Tom and Miss Radcliffe have gone to Moscow. Thing is, they don't know what they are walking into."

The line from Ireland crackled. "And what exactly are they 'walking into?"

"Kerensky, a man we think is behind at least three murders, including CountessBratinsky and Commandant Jourdain, is back in Russia. But that's not the worst part. His boss, his real boss as far as we know, is part KGB colonel, part crime boss. He's known as the Colonel and he's a killer, the kind who doesn't blink before pulling the trigger. Nobody knows how many people he has killed and he is politically connected at the highest level. He works from the shadows so he can never be held directly responsible but he has a finger in every criminal pie in Moscow and Petersburg. Kerensky is his fixer." He had expected an outburst of anger or emotion. Instead there was a few seconds pause and then he was taken aback by the series of specific and clinical questions from O'Brien.

"Where are they now?"

"Moscow, but heading to St Petersburg."

"Are they in any immediate danger?"

"Not that we can see at the moment but we have no real idea

what is going on until I get there."

"What are the options?"

"I'm in touch with my Russian colleague, Major Semenov, and I'm on the evening flight from Paris to Petersburg the day after tomorrow"

"Can you get me on the flight?"

"The flight is not the problem but there's not a snowball's chance in hell of you getting a visa in time."

"What about your Russian friend, Semenov?"

"I'm sorry, he had to pull in all his favours to get my own visa sorted, and now we don't have time."

John O'Brien thought before replying. "It's like this, Inspector, Tom is my son and he's in trouble. The choice is, get your friend Semenov to sort the visa or you can read all about this in tomorrow's *Irish Times*. Tom told me all about Jourdain, the moles in the Matignon and the Elysée and the cover-up. If you don't want to read the full, unedited version in all the papers, including the juicy bits Tom left out – sort it. If I don't hear from you inside the next hour my first call will be to the RTÉ news desk, then the BBC and whoever else I can get hold of."

"But ..."

"But nothing!"

The line went dead.

Fitzgerald cursed inwardly, wondering, what he had done in a previous life to get caught up in this three-ring circus. Tom O'Brien wasn't the only one with his eye on wider horizons. Inspector Edward Fitzgerald, Eddie to his friends, had no intention of sticking around Bray for the rest of his career. For a boy like him, from a small farm in County Wexford the Gardai had offered the chance of a career. His older brother would get the farm in due course and it looked like his younger brother was heading for the church, God help him. There was no money for college so he didn't have much of a choice.

Eddie Fitzgerald was smart and ambitious and so far he hadn't put a foot wrong. The arrival of Semenov on foot of the Bratinsky murder had started him thinking. It was a big case and the international coverage and the involvement of the Russian police would do him no harm at all. Now it looked as if things were hotting up again. If he played his cards right a transfer to Interpol might be on the horizon. Then, who knows: as long as that little pipsqueak O'Brien didn't mess things up for him. "God's blood," now he had the father to deal with as well. Thought they were so smart because they had been to college and that he was some sort of clodhopper. Time would tell. Trusting Semenov was a gamble but as far as he could tell he was a good guy.

He rang Semenov back and filled him in.

"I know but I've no choice: either he gets to tag along or he goes to the media and that's the last thing we need at this point. He's a history buff and I heard he did a degree in art history so we can bill him as our resident expert on the antiques trade in Ireland. He should know enough to be able to bluff his way along. The main thing is the visa. Do you think you can swing it?

"Won't he have to go to London to get the visa? and you don't have time. "

"No, there's been a new Russian Embassy in Dublin since last year"

"Ok, I'll do what I can but you better drill him on what to say."

John O'Brien was on the first train to Dublin the next morning to get to the embassy and fill in the forms. The Embassy on Orwell Road in Dublin was cold and forbidding and the waiting room with its heavy old fashioned furniture looked as though it hadn't changed since the 1950"s. He handed over the papers to the receptionist and waited. He wanted to jump up and down and shout that they were wasting time while his son was in danger but there was no point. That would only make things worse.

Finally the door into the inner office opened and the First Secretary came out holding the papers. John stood up not sure whether to be chatty and friendly or wait for the Russian to speak first. He opted for silence.

"How do you know Inspector Semenov, Mr O'Brien"

"I don't know him really. I have a degree in art history and I have been helping the Irish police with their investigation into various stolen Russian antiques that have been showing up on the

THE BRATINSKY AFFAIR

Irish and European markets. I discovered the first case of a Fabergé box a few years back. Semenov wants to bring a few people together to pool information."

"And why would this require you to travel to Russia at a moment's notice? Doesn't seem like a matter of life and death."

"There has been a break-through in the case and Semenov wants to move before the trail goes cold."

Fitzgerald had warned him: "don't overdo it or you'll trip yourself up. Tell him just enough to sound convincing and let Semenov do the rest."

The First Secretary looked at him nodding silently before walking over to a desk by the window and stamping his passport.

"One week!"

He was on his way.

CHAPTER 25

The Russian Village Wicklow January 1976
The house in Wicklow offered Irina a respite from networking and making money. It was the name Russian Village that had first attracted her when she was in the area for a country house auction. She had thought it was a joke when someone told her there was a Russian Village in the middle of Wicklow. The house, with its cedar shingle roof and black-and-white wooden trim, reminded her of the old wooden house they had had in the forests near Minsk. They used to spend the long hot summers there before the war when the days were endless and time meant nothing. She remembered the picnics, swimming in icy streams and galloping madly through the trees on one of her mother's ponies with her brother. The house in Wicklow was the first place that had ever felt like home since she had left Russia and it even had central heating, unusual in Ireland at the time! In the winter with snow on the ground and the wind blowing from the east it might almost have been Russia.

Her father, Count Victor O'Rourke, Baron de Breffny, used to joke that he was Irish, descendant of a long line of Irish soldiers, to which her mother would inevitably reply: "But darling, you couldn't even find Ireland on the map." How ironic, then, that with the family having fled to Russia to escape persecution in the seventeenth century, she had now come full circle to find a place of refuge in Ireland in the twentieth century. More and more Irina was thinking of retiring to focus on herself and make the most of what was left of her life. Let Kerensky do his worst. Problem was, he was capable of doing just that and she had to think of Olga.

When Irina closed the door of the house in Kilquade she felt a sense of relief as she switched on the heating, lit the fire in the drawing room and poured herself a large whiskey. She had never liked vodka, though at times she needed it to enhance her Russian pedigree and always made sure to have a bottle of Stolichnaya prominently displayed on her drinks table.

THE BRATINSKY AFFAIR

Irina sat by the fire and stared at the portrait of her mother over the fireplace as the memory tapes began to play. She hadn't realised how much she would miss Ana until she was gone. Strangely she felt closer to her mother here in Ireland than anywhere else. Irina raised her glass in a silent toast to her mother.

'Looks like it's you and me on our own again after all this time, mother. You're the only one who never let me down. I should have given you the time you deserved but I was too busy running away, looking for something that could never replace what I already had. We should have had this conversation a long time ago. Who knows, maybe we'll be able to pick up the threads sometime in the future, as long as you don't judge me.

We're the same you and me. We both married handsome, charming men who couldn't adapt to changing times: losers both, but we loved them anyway. You always said that family was more important than anything else. And now, what's left of it? Me and a granddaughter I hardly know. And yes, I know, what about your darling Masha. I don't know where I went wrong with her but you have to admit, mother, she was a brat: beautiful and charming but also selfish and spoiled. And whose fault was that? You never could say no to her – or Olga for that matter. It's a wonder that girl has a tooth left in her head with all the cakes you made for her."

A few of the old family photographs had survived the wars and the revolutions and Irina had placed them on a small side table near the fire: her mother and father on their wedding day, her grandmother sitting on the balcony of the house in the Crimea; Masha and William on their wedding day: Olga as a baby.

"And what amixum gatherum of a family we are: Father, part Irish, Egon, Russian, my daughter, French and my granddaughter, English. Tell me, mother, what am I?I could have locked that door and thrown away the key but where would that have left me? Probably feeling even more alone than I do now. I have all of that stored up in me and I couldn't let it go. It's who I am.

Still, you were right on one thing: I should have found

somebody else after Egon left and made a new life for myself. I suppose I could have married Yuri: You would have liked that, wouldn't you, mother? Right family, right class. Yes, he was kind and generous, but weak like all the others. You should know that better than anyone. After all, it was your money that kept us afloat, and it would have been the same if I had married Yuri – a disaster.

You never met Suzie! That would have been a shock to the system if you'd known. Or did you? For a woman who never went further that the bakery on the corner or the cathedral on a Sunday, you always seemed to know everything that was going on in the Russian community? You remember Sofia, my opera singer friend? She used to joke that that clutch of old hens sitting at the back of the church had one of the best spy networks in Paris.

But Suzy wanted more that I was able to give. Maybe that was my problem: that I was never able to share. I was always so afraid that people would discover my secret – the hole at the heart of my life. You know what I mean, don't you, mother? You understand exactly what I mean. I've seen that haunted look on your face when you think of them. You know, I sometimes wake up screaming and I am back there, beside the chapel, looking down as the soldiers take Pavel and father away.

We wasted so much time when we could have been happy together. All those business deals and people who were so important. In the end what did it matter? I was trying to put the shattered pieces of the past back together. I told myself it was for you and Masha but in reality it was for me, locking away the pain in a vain attempt to create a perfect imitation of a lost world. Ok, I admit it: that's not completely true. I suppose by now you know all about Dmitri and Kerensky and all the nasty little deals. I did say, don't judge me, didn't I? Truth is, it was exciting. I got a real kick out of putting one over on all those smug upper class French men who thought I didn't know what I was doing. It became addictive.

It's so easy to let people slip through your fingers, especially the good ones. You remember Madame Rostand don't you? Then

THE BRATINSKY AFFAIR

there was Sofia and of course there was Suzy. Why did I shut her out? She's living somewhere in the south of France and only comes up to Paris every once in a blue moon. It was all such a waste: one missed opportunity after another. At least Sofia got lucky. She met a wealthy retired diplomat with a passion for music who swept her off to his villa in the south of France and doted on her until the day he died. I still see her from time to time when I'm in Nice.

You know something mother, Masha was right to walk away and build her own life. She married her William, and was happy in her own way. I thought losing father and Pavel was the worst thing that happened in my life until Masha got cancer. At least you were spared that. She was just like you. She had no ambition and preferred a quiet life in the country with her chickens and horses. I remember the last time she came to Paris before she got too sick to travel. We sat in the garden in Auteuil chatting and reminiscing. She teased me about all the times I tried to marry her off to one chinless wonder after another.

We stayed in the garden until it began to get dark. In the half light I could see how thin and pale she had become but I didn't want to face reality even though I could see her fading away before my eyes. I thought if I didn't acknowledge it, it wouldn't happen but I can remember every detail of that evening. I put a shawl around her shoulders when it began to get cold and I could feel how thin she had got through the delicate fabric. We went into the house together :I cooked dinner and Masha pretended to eat. I knew then that that was probably the last time we would spend together, just the two of us. At least we had made peace and put all the arguments of the past behind us. All the money in the world couldn't save her and after she died I couldn't bear to go back to Auteuil. I've rented the house but don't worry, I made sure your beloved garden is well looked after. And I still have your book of Ana Akmatova's poems on my bedside table: that way I don't feel so alone. I remember you used to say: 'one day you're thirty-five and the next day you're seventy five and you wonder – where did it go?' I laughed, but you were right.

Don't look away! I have to tell you this. I'm sorry I couldn't save them. I blamed you for not doing anything and you blamed me because you had to stay and protect me instead of running after them. What could we have done to stop it? You, a middle-aged woman and me, little more than a child.

And now this business with the sword. Kerensky is too dangerous to trust so there's no point asking him, but there must be some connection between him and our family. Is it possible after all this time, do you think? Could he be alive? I'm afraid, mother. I'm afraid that all the walls will come tumbling down around me again. I don't know what to do for the best."

Irina got up to put another log on the fire and sat staring into the flames remembering, and thinking.

THE BRATINSKY AFFAIR

CHAPTER 26

Moscow – Saint Petersburg - March 1976

At five-thirty next morning Helene was standing in reception with a checklist on a clipboard, and all the luggage lined up in the hall. Tom and Olga barely had time to grab some black tea and rolls before they were ushered out into the coach to the station. The early train from Moscow to Petersburg only took five hours, and Helene had block-booked seats.

Tom took out his maps and brochures to read up on the city of Peter the Great. They were both feeling jittery the closer they got to their goal. He had been trying to follow their journey on the map, but found he couldn't concentrate and sat looking out the window as the train hurtled through the industrial suburbs of Moscow into the countryside beyond, which seemed to consist mainly of vast expanses of forest and empty fields. From time to time the train slowed as they passed through small villages that looked half abandoned. He had left the brochures in English and Russian spread out on the table between them. In an ideal world they would have stopped to visit medieval Novgorod along the way but the closer they got to their goal the less interest they had in the touristic aspects of the trip. They had to keep focused on the mission.

Olga picked up one of the brochures and was flicking through it when something struck her. She rummaged in her handbag and finally came up with the card that had been attached to the wreath on Ana's grave. She put the card signed with the letter П on top of the brochure

"Tom – quick, have a look at this."

The urgent tone in her voice woke him out of his comatose state.

"Have a look - It's not N – its П – It's Russian fo…"
"P– Pavel! How could we have been so dim! So he is alive –

and has been recently in Paris" said Tom. Good old Uncle Pavel – you could invite him to dinner."

"Great-uncle, – the one no one ever spoke about, not even Ana, from what I can remember. Suddenly I feel scared, Tom. Maybe this trip wasn't such a good idea after all."

"Do you think..." Tom went on carefully. "Do you think he could be involved in all this?"

"What are you saying – you think he could have murdered my grandmother? Murdered his own sister?"

"A sister he hadn't seen in almost 60 years."

Olga sank back against the banquette, her face pale. "But why, after all this time? What can be so important? This whole thing is starting to creep me out. The more I think about it the more I want to go out to the house to be able to say we've done it and then set off for home. I don't even care if there's nothing there."

There was nothing Tom could add as secretly he was feeling much the same. Russia was a different world and they had no idea what they were doing. In Paris their plan had seemed so simple and logical. Now, it looked dangerously stupid.

The train pulled into Moskovsky station in St Petersburg bang on time. If Moscow was impressive St Petersburg was like stepping into an imperial fantasy, with domes and cupolas everywhere and huge buildings painted yellow and ochre and pale green. It was both familiar and very exotic at the same time. The streets were so wide that even huge buildings were dwarfed by the immensity of the sky that hung so close overhead.

When Helene ushered them into the Grand Hotel Europe in St Petersburg Tom felt that he was stepping back in time. If he had met a Romanov Grand Duke coming out of the lift he wouldn't have been surprised.

"Chop-chop!" said Helene, clapping her hands. "No time to dilly dally and would you be so kind as to check your luggage onto the coach?" Helene could switch between English and French without blinking an eye but some of her expressions sounded a bit old fashioned, as if she had learned her English by reading Agatha Christie novels. They rushed through check-in and barely had time to drop the bags in their room. A couple of hours sleep would have been better than hitting the tourist trail. The room was luxurious in a slightly dated way while the marble bathroom could only be described as opulent. The enormous bathtub with its dolphin taps could have been used to refloat the Titanic, but Tom didn't have time to appreciate all this luxury. He needed to get back down to the lobby.

Tom was nervous about carrying the diary with him. After all, it was their only real evidence about the existence of the sword and what had become of it. As he went into the bathroom he heard the tell tale squeak of a loose board. When he knelt down he could see that the saddle of the bathroom door was loose, and he was able to swivel it round, revealing enough space to take the diary. He stood back up. The hiding place was invisible.

They gobbled an early lunch and were herded back into the coach to head for the Winter Palace and the Hermitage museum. By one o'clock they were standing on Palace Square waiting for the rest of the group to gather and looking across at the vast expanse of the Winter Palace. Tom stared at the pistachio-coloured building that stretched as far as the eye could see. He felt puny and insignificant compared to the scale of the building and the vastness of the square, but that was probably the intention of the builder.

"I thought Buckingham Palace was huge but this is gi-normous,"said Olga. "It was the biggest empire in the world so they probably felt they deserved the biggest palace. Glad I'm not paying the heating bills."

Helene, unsurprisingly, had clear and brisk instructions. "The palace is 750 feet long and has 1,500 rooms and seventeen staircases, so if you get lost, tough! We are going to see the state apartments after which you will have two hours to wander around on your own. Be back at the entrance at five-thirty."

The Jordan staircase leading up to the state apartments was a blaze of dazzling white and gold rising three levels to the painted ceiling. "Hard to believe Nicholas 11 and his family processed formally down this staircase in their glory days just a few years before they were shot and dumped in an unmarked grave," said Olga.

They wandered on, gazing at the wonders and chatting. "I might feel sorry for the children, but from what I've read, he was no great loss," Tom batted back.

"How can you say that about God's Anointed?"

"Because he was an idiot and…

"It was a joke, Tom!"

"Cosy it ain't. I doubt if there's a single comfortable chair in the whole place. Not hard to see why there was a revolution! I can feel my republican hackles rising."

"Never took you for a radical."

"Dad is very much a republican. It must run in the blood. The Russians weren't the only ones storming the barricades in 1917."

Tom's eyes began to glaze over as they passed through gilded room after gilded room. "Impressive certainly – beautiful? – not so sure. There's only so much of this stuff I can take!"

Finally Helene announced, "We now come to the Military Gallery celebrating all the generals who fought in the wars against Napoleon." This was what they had come for. As they stepped through the double doors into the double height space Tom whistled. "Never expected it to be so huge."

"Impressive, isn't it?" said Helene. "Apart from the Emperor of Russia, the Emperor of Austria and the King of Prussia there are three hundred and twenty portraits of the individual generals who fought against Napoleon."

They were halfway down the hall when Tom couldn't stop himself blurting out

"There's our man!"

Helene looked at him "Who?"

Tom stopped, flustered, and reached for his patriotism to cover his blunder. "General Count Joseph Cornelius O'Rourke de Breffny, an Irishman in the service of Russia. Handsome chap isn't he? Did you know that he led one of the critical charges against Napoleon's army at the battle of Leipzig and helped turn the tide against the French? My father is a history buff, and when I told him we were coming to St Petersburg he told me to be sure to look out for him. You see, we Paddies get everywhere."

At that moment he spotted the full length portrait of the Duke

THE BRATINSKY AFFAIR

of Wellington farther down the hall. Out of the corner of his eye he could see that Olga was getting weepy, and so he kept waffling on to keep Helene's attention focused elsewhere. "There he is, another Paddy, the Duke of Wellington, born in Dublin. Sure, they couldn't have beat Napoleon without the Irish!" and he discreetly steered Helene along by the elbow, leaving Olga to focus on her distant ancestor.

The General stared out of the picture. A pale complexion, dark hair and eyes and a wavy moustache. Despite the gold braid and the rows of medals it was a typically Irish face, such as you might see anywhere in the west of Ireland. It was an oddly emotional experience for Olga to look into the eyes of her ten-times great-grandfather, but she kept quiet, not wanting to draw attention to herself again. She preferred to let Tom do the talking. There was a bench opposite the picture, and Olga sat there for a few minutes staring, looking for any family resemblance. She had heard the story of the General's adventures a hundred times but looking at the portrait made it real for the first time.

In the distance she could hear Tom burbling on. "And did you know that Count O'Rourke also helped to defeat the Turks in Serbia, and the local people even built a statue to him? Imagine that."

Olga could see from the look on her face that Helene was bored out of her mind and trying desperately to escape from Tom's interminable monologue. Eventually she made her excuses and escaped to speak to the other members of the group.

As Tom came back to Olga he could see that tears were still not far away and felt he needed to do something to lighten the mood. "I can see a definite similarity between you and the General – I think it's the moustache!"

Olga hesitated for a second before laughing and taking a swipe at Tom with her handbag as he skipped out of reach. "For that, Tom, dinner's on you, and I am having champagne! That'll teach you to be so smart."

\#

They fell into step and, arm in arm, continued their tour of the Hermitage. At one point Tom smiled to himself as he heard

Madame Dufour whisper to her husband, "such a nice young couple," as they passed. If only they knew. Tom and Olga walked through room after room of priceless paintings without really seeing them. They were both thinking about the next day when they were due to visit the complex of palaces at Tsarskoye Selo an hour outside St Petersburg. If luck was with them, they would finally find if there was anything left of the old O'Rourke estate. As they walked back out into the square they could see the rest of the group starting to gather beside the coach. Tom needed to clear his head and decided to walk back to the hotel while Olga took the bus with the rest of the group. "I saw on the map that the Cathedral of the Saviour on Spilled Blood is on the way back, and I want to have a look around."

"Not for me" said Olga. "My batteries are dead. I'll see you in the bar at seven, and don't forget, dinner is on you, Mr O'B, and, it's going to cost you!"

It was a relief to escape the oppressive splendours and overheated atmosphere of the palace and to be out in the fresh air to get a feeling for this amazing city. It was a beautiful evening and Tom started to relax as he crossed over the Moyka River and continued along the bank. He saw the sign for Pushkin's apartment but kept going. Young couples walked along holding hands and groups of students sat on the grass chatting. It could almost be St Stephen's Green in Dublin, he thought, except for the scale of the buildings around him and the amount of open space. After about fifteen minutes Tom could see the multicoloured domes of the cathedral looming up ahead. He wasn't that interested in visiting the church, it was just an excuse to get a bit of time on his own after days couped up with the same group of people. He missed Jean-Philippe and still felt guilty at having lied to him.

He was so busy admiring the facade of the cathedral that he didn't notice the two drunks until they appeared in front of him.

"Hey, buddy, got the price of a drink? A cigarette? Marlboro, yes?

One of them crashed into Tom sending him stumbling towards his pal, and they began a game of catch-catch that became increasingly threatening. On one of the rebounds Tom felt a hand reaching for his wallet but managed to pull himself away and ran towards the cathedral. There were so many tourists taking pictures that he knew he'd be ok if he got that far. When he heard no sound of footsteps behind him Tom chanced a look behind and saw that the two guys were back on the bench smoking and staring in his direction.

By now he didn't care if it was the last church in the universe, but he went in anyway and sat at the back to catch his breath. The church was closing, and as the crowds gradually thinned he started to get a sense of what it had been like as a church. Awesome! That was the only word for it. Every inch of the walls was covered with glittering mosaics telling stories from the bible; Tom didn't have the energy to walk all the way round but it was worth it just to sit and contemplate the spectacular mosaic of the Risen Christ in the dome. By then it was almost a quarter past six: time to head back to the hotel. On his way out he stopped to light two candles: one for Irina and one for his mother. He felt it was the least he could do. Once outside he glanced around. No sign of the two thugs.

†

It was almost 7pm when Tom walked into the bar. He ordered a vodka and sat down to wait for Olga. He was still unsettled after the incident in the park, but at least the thugs hadn't got his wallet or his passport. At seven-thirty there was still no sign of Olga. At eight, he went over to reception and asked them to call her room. No answer. She probably fell asleep he thought, and went up to check on her. "Not surprising that she's tired after everything she's been through," he thought to himself.

There was no answer when he knocked on the door. He called, "Olga, are you there?" Again, no answer. He thought maybe she was in the shower, so he knocked again, harder this time. As he did so the door swung open and he could see that the entire room had been turned upside down. No sign of Olga. When he checked his own room next door it was the same story. "What in God's name had happened to her?" He was about to rush down to reception when he remembered the diary. In a panic he ran over to the bathroom and prised up the loose board. At least the diary was still there. *Better leave it there for the time being.*

Tom walked slowly down the stairs thinking what he should do. If he called the police it might make matters worse, but he had no choice. As he crossed the lobby a young receptionist came over and handed him a letter.

"For me?"

"Yes, the gentleman was most insistent that I was to give it to you – nobody else."

Tom ripped open the envelope; it was a single page.

48 Fontanka Embankment: if you want to see Miss Radcliffe alive come to this address this evening. Bring the diary that's in your inside left pocket. Don't call the police.

Tom's hand instinctively patted his breast pocket, but nothing there. The incident in the park
made sense now. They weren't two stupid drunks. They were after the diary, which also meant that someone was watching his and Olga's every move.

Helene came out of the bar and saw him. She came straight over. "Are you all right, Mr O'Brien? You look like you you've seen a ghost." Tom did his best to brush her off but she hung on, determined to find out what was going on. She clearly smelt a rat.

In the end he lied. "I think I have a migraine coming on so I am going outside to get some air and then I'll go straight to bed."

"Well, if you need anything…"

Tom had no idea if Inspector Fitzgerald was in Paris or Bray, and no way of getting hold of him. There was nothing for it, he would have to call his father and ask him to contact the Inspector. Tom booked a person-to-person call to Ireland and sat in the mahogany phone booth in the lobby waiting for the operator to connect him. It felt a bit like a confession box but other than that he was too agitated to take in what was going on around him. A bride and groom had just arrived, accompanied by a gypsy orchestra. Suddenly reception was a riot of music and roses and laughter. Normally he would have been in the middle of it but now it got on his nerves.

THE BRATINSKY AFFAIR

He could hear the phone ringing, and in his mind he could picture Mungo flopped in front of the fire waiting for Tom's father to take him out for a walk. The phone kept ringing until finally the operator came back on to say, "I am sorry, caller, but there is no answer from that number." He would have to go it alone. He ran back up to the room to get the diary and sat down for a few minutes to check where the Fontanka Embankment was on the map and think about what he was going to do. In the end there was nothing he could do except follow instructions. As he stuffed the diary into his pocket he scrunched the letter up into a ball and pitched it towards the waste paper basket – missed. Then, mindful of Willi Regan's watchword, he picked up the flashlight and walked out of the hotel.

It only took twenty minutes to reach the Fontanka Embankment. The address turned out to be on a corner not far from the huge Vladimirsky Church. He could see from the front that the main door and windows were boarded up but there was a laneway down the side of the house. There was a yard behind the house but the huge metal gate was securely locked. To the right of the gate a flight of stone steps led down into an old cellar, a door propped open, darkness beyond.

Tom climbed cautiously down, and crossed the empty cellar into a warren of small rooms smelling of damp and decay. A door opened into a narrow set of stairs that took him up into what had been the main part of the house. There was virtually no light here. He switched on the flashlight. Silence. In the torchlight he could see that the floor had collapsed in places, and he heard water dripping. There was a splash and something with scrabbling claws scuttled away.

He came up into the entrance hall of the house. It had been an impressive building at one time. The series of interconnecting rooms on the ground floor were empty, except for occasional pieces of broken furniture. In one corner the flashlight picked up a piano that had crashed onto the floor. Its legs had been sawn off, probably for firewood and the carcass of the piano had been left on its side with the strings hanging out, too heavy to carry. Opposite the front door a wide staircase swept up to a gallery that ran along the front of the house. On the right hand side a row of floor-length windows faced onto the canal and patches of moonlight shone on the dusty floor. On the other side doors opened into a series of bedrooms. As Tom walked down the hall he flicked the flashlight into each empty room in turn. In one, there was an old iron bedstead with a collapsed mattress, in another a marble-topped washstand had been pushed up against the window to keep the shutters closed. In a third room, the ceiling and chimney had caved in and soot had settled on the strands of cobweb forming a glittering jet curtain.

At the end of the gallery there was a partially open door and he could see Olga sitting in a patch of light, her arms tied behind her back. He rushed towards her and in the same moment heard a step behind him. The barrel of a gun pressed against the back of his head.

"Move, slowly, straight ahead."

Unlike the rest of the house, this room was clean, with a fire burning in the grate and a few candles stuck in bottles. A table with one chair – a chessboard with a game half played, a bottle of vodka, a single glass.

"Sit"

Tom's hands were tied behind his back and he was shoved down to sit beside Olga. He had seen this set up before, in Bond movies but now it didn't seem one bit entertaining. He recognised the man from the photographs. Kerensky stood behind them, between them and the door.

"Are you ok?" Tom whispered.

Olga nodded.

"I should have listened to you," said Tom.

THE BRATINSKY AFFAIR

CHAPTER 27

Russian Village, Kilquade January 1976

As the flames blazed up, Irina remembered another fire she had watched with Ana, a lifetime ago. To all appearances it had been an afternoon like any other, a family walking in the winter sunshine, enjoying the peace and pine scented tranquility of the forest. In her mind's eye she could still see Ana and Victor walking slightly ahead holding hands as she and Pavel ran through the trees competing to see who could find the most mushrooms. Ana had brought a flask of hot tea in one of the new thermos things and they sat on a fallen tree in the middle of the forest listening for birdsong. The smell of cinnamon and cloves always brought her back to that moment of stillness in the eye of the storm. It was the last time they were together as a family.

Everything changed in an instant. They heard shouting in the distance as Ana and Victor ran over to hide behind the balustrade in front of the chapel to see what was happening down at the house; "Stay there," Irina, Ana whispered frantically: "Watch the bags." After a while Irina saw Victor and Pavel go down to the house and for a few minutes there was silence, then more shouting. Irina ran over and stood beside Ana as they watched Victor and Pavel being marched away.

That was the day her childhood ended. She remembered what her father had said to her as they dragged the bags up the hill from the house to the old shed beyond the chapel. "You're the strong one, Irina. Whatever happens, you have to survive to look after Mama and Pavel." But Irina was too young to understand what was happening as she stood looking down on the shattered house with tears rolling down her face calling "Papaaa" into the darkening silence.

Ana grabbed her by the arm. "We have to move quickly; the soldiers could be back any minute and if it isn't them it will be some of the people from the village. They will have seen the smoke and come to see what they can scavenge. If they find us two here alone we won't stand a chance."

In a matter of days the house would be a charred skeleton like so many others in the area.

Irina remembered looking back with Ana as they walked away from the house that had been the heart of their family life for so long. They could see that the whole centre of the house was on fire and as they reached the brow of the hill they heard an explosion. Irina's last view of the house was to see the glass dome over the staircase landing exploding and the flames leaping up into the evening sky. After the roof crashed in and the flames began to die down she and her mother moved away through the woods to begin the long trek to the coast. More than two hundred years of fighting and struggling and building, reduced to ashes in a few minutes. Ana put an arm around Irina's shoulder. "It's time to go. We have no choice."

\#

During all the years in Paris Irina had never dwelt on the past or wallowed in the nostalgia that obsessed so many of the Russian exiles. The title was a useful tool, but she was much more interested in the here and now, making money, surviving. Now, out of the blue, here was the past knocking on her door again. Maybe it was time to disappear. Who would miss her?

Like all refugees Irina was haunted by the fear of needing to escape. Sometimes, when she couldn't sleep, she would lie awake thinking about what she would take in her one suitcase if she had to run again. After Kerensky appeared on the scene it became an obsession. She had kept the Swiss bank account for years, but now she began to move all her spare cash there, and sold off most of the pieces of superb jewellery that she had kept locked away in a safe deposit box in the bank.

The Irish passport in her maiden name of Irina Ana O'Rourke de Breffny was sitting on her desk. It had taken a lot of smoozing and several generous donations of pictures to the National Gallery of Ireland to pull that off. Her father would have been amused. She could become Ana de Breffny. It would help her to lie low for a while if things got too complicated. On a sudden impulse Irina picked up the phone and made a provisional

THE BRATINSKY AFFAIR

booking for first class flight to New York for the end of February. It cost a fortune but now was not the time to economise. The money would be no good to her if she were dead. She hadn't finally made up her mind to run yet – but it was an option and she could change the ticket at a moment's notice if she needed to. Having an option helped to steady her nerves. Anything was better than sitting around waiting for something to happen.

In the morning Irina went down to the shop in the village and stocked up. Mrs Kelly in the small grocery shop seemed to regard Irina as something close to royalty and always made a fuss of her when she went in. It amused her, and Mrs Kelly was such a nice woman that Irina always played along. "You know, Countess, I come from a good family myself. I have one cousin a priest and another is a TD." Irina smiled: "I'm sure you do, Mrs Kelly: you can always tell." She picked up her shopping as Mrs Kelly beamed.

For the next two weeks Irina tried to switch off and forget about things. She went for walks, cleaned the house and sent New Year greetings to all her clients who would think it odd if they didn't hear from her. Everything needed to go on as normal. There was no news from Didier in Paris and Irina hoped that things were beginning to settle down. By the third week of January, the house was sparkling and all the paperwork had been done. Bill Egan had called in for a drink: there was an auction coming up and there were a few pieces he thought she might be interested in. Apart from that she had seen no one. Irina was beginning to go stir crazy and decided that work was the only way to take her mind off things. The Vorontsov family collection was being sold off at a big auction in Paris and Maison Drouot had asked her to do the catalogue. It was amazing what they had managed to hold on to for so long: jewels, portraits and porcelain, photographs from before the Revolution, icons, silver, monogrammed cigarette cases, even a dance card that still had its tiny silver pencil attached. Irina and Ana had gone to their house for dinner when they had first arrived in Paris. The Vorontsovs were one of those Russian families who spent as much time in

France as in Russia and had managed to transfer a lot of money out of the country before the war. Evidently the cash had finally run out.

There were a few interesting pieces she would probably bid on herself. Irina became totally engrossed, and as she worked, she occasionally played with the gold egg she still wore on a fine chain round her neck. Around the top of the egg was a finely worked snake with its tail in its mouth, a symbol of enduring love. On the front was a small ruby. Her father had given it to her the Easter before the war started. It was Fabergé, the only piece she had always refused to part with, whatever the cold or the hunger.

Survival was still the goal. By Sunday she had completed a first draft of the catalogue and started laying out the pages. As the day wore on to evening Irina kept working, stopping only to switch on the lamps and stoke up the fire.

Her house in the Wicklow Hills was off by itself at the end of a narrow lane way. Each house stood by itself in a large garden surrounded by trees so that it was not visible from the road. People here kept themselves to themselves and unlike Paris there was no nosy concierge watching everything that went on. From time-to-time Irina remembered old Madame Rostand the concierge from the Avenue Foch who had been kind to her. She didn't know why she called her old Madame Rostand as she probably wasn't much more than ten years older than Irina. Somehow, she always seemed to belong to an older generation. Irina wondered if she was still alive. The building had been sold several times over the years and the last time Irina had gone past, it had been turned into a bank.

Much as Irina loved the peace and solitude of the house in Wicklow, the countryside had a limited appeal and after a while she yearned for the buzz and excitement of Paris. The commission from the Metropolitan Museum in New York to advise on their jewellery collection had opened a new avenue. When she got back to Paris it might be time to pull the shutters down on Bratinsky& Co. With a bit of luck she could wave goodbye to Kerensky as well.

THE BRATINSKY AFFAIR

CHAPTER 28

Air France – Paris- Saint Petersburg flight
Fitzgerald collected John O'Brien off the early flight from and Dublin. He needed this extra passenger like a hole in the head but he had no choice. Once they had done their check in for the flight to Saint Petersburg and got rid of their luggage they settled down for a cup of coffee

John O'Brien decided there was no point avoiding the issue.

"Look Inspector, I know it's a pain in the neck having me tagging along, but what am I going to do? Sit at home and wait for a phone call. You have a job to do and I'll try not to get in your way but if, as you say, Tom is in danger I need to be there."

"Well; I can't say I'm thrilled but you're here now, so we'll make the best of it. Officially I'm here to liaise on the investigation into stolen antiques and you're here as my expert witness. You have a degree in art history you have been tracking antique auctions and it was you first spotted the pattern of antiques from Russia tuning up randomly in Irish auctions and then turning out to be worth a fortune –surprise surprise. Stick to that story and you'll be all right.'

But what if they ask me specific questions? ;

Fitzgerald handed him a folder

"What this?" O'Brien asked as he opened the folder and started leafing through a set of photographs.

"Semenov gave it to me. All these items have been sold at auction in Ireland, France or Italy in the last five years."

"And?"

"And, all of them were stolen at some point from provincial Russian museums where they don't keep very good records. Same ploy every time. Find a small auction house, plant the object which is then 'discovered' during the sale of the contents of a small country house and low and behold it emerges with a new paper trail onto the legitimate market. On the back of each photograph you'll find a description of the object, where it was found and where it originally came from. During the flight you can read up on them and then you'll know nearly as much as

Semenov does. You'll see three of the pieces turned up in Ireland."

"Don't tell me, Egan Auctioneers?"

"Not exclusively;"

"How did you know the Countess was also doing business with Egan back in Bray? As far as I can see he seems to have been offloading stuff for her for years and vice versa.'

"That smarmy low-life. There have been rumours about him for years, mostly local tittle tattle, but nothing that would stand up. I'll be taking a close look at him when we get home.

"Now, tell me, why is pal Semenov being so helpful? Why is he so interested in the Bratinsky case?"

"Semenov couldn't care less about the Bratinsky woman. As far as he's concerned she's just some dodgy dealer who got in with the wrong people and got her comeuppance. He's only interested in her because her connections may lead him to some of the other players in this ring. The other angle is political. Russia has just opened a new embassy in Dublin and there's talk of Aeroflot starting transatlantic flights from Shannon. The Russians want to play niceynicey with Ireland, at the moment."

"How does any of this affect Tom? What makes you think he's in danger?"

"As for the danger, there's not much doubt about it. If they get tangled up with Kerensky they're in trouble. You've read the papers so you'll know the basics. CountessBratinsky has got herself pulled into spying for the Russians. We have Kerensky in the frame for the killing but why he killed her and why he killed her now we have no idea. It's all guess work. What we do know is that Kerensky is the fixer for this guy the Colonel. As for Tom and Olga and this mad dash to Russia, do you have any idea what that's all about?"

"I helped Tom with his research. All I can think of is that when he was trying to flesh out the background to the Countess he discovered the Irish connection to the O'Rourke de Breffny family and their life in Russia. For him it was just background to the story for the paper and then he found the reference to a sword that had been presented to an earlier Count O'Rourke during the Napoleonic wars."

THE BRATINSKY AFFAIR

"A sword! Who cares? Not exactly a weapon of mass destruction is it?" Fitzgerald laughed.

"If it belonged to Napoleon and is worth between 2.5 and 5million dollars a lot of people would be interested."

"My giddy aunt!" said Fitzgerald

"It's not just the money. If you remember your history, the Russians defeated the French in the Napoleonic wars and given all the recent sabre rattling, if you'll pardon the pun, about ballistic missiles it could be a useful propaganda tool. You can imagine some Russian general holding it up saying; *you want to take us on. Try it. Remember what happened last time.*"

Thanks for the history lesson professor, Fitzgerald thought to himself. *Bloody teachers. They never miss a chance to hold forth.* For the rest of the flight they focused on what was to happen when they hit the ground.

"When we get in, Semenov has set up one or two meetings to cover our tracks so I'll go with him to police headquarters and you can stay in the hotel. I'll only bring you in on this if I have to."

Once the plan was clear they both subsided into their thoughts, apart from sporadic bursts of conversation. Fitzgerald sat looking out the window trying to gather his thoughts. He glanced over at John O'Brien sitting on the other side of the aisle. *For such a smart well educated man I wonder does he know his son's a queer?* he thought to himself. One of the young Gardaí had seen Tom hanging around the seafront and put two and two together. Fitzgerald felt smug having one up on John O'Brien. O'Brien was a decent man but Fitzgerald couldn't help resenting the way people in the town looked up to him and treated him with respect, whereas he had to fight for every bit of recognition he got. *These university boys think they're a cut above everybody else.*

±

Major Semenov picked them up at the airport. Fitzgerald was right about Semenov. He was a good guy, as least as far as that goes in the murky and often brutal world of the Russian police. He tried as far as possible to stay out of the ongoing turf war between the cops and the criminals, in which it was increasingly difficult to tell who was who. His job investigating the theft of stolen artworks was an elite specialist force that protected him from having to make a decision about which side he was on. That's not to say he was averse to the occasional backhander if the price was right and it didn't put him in the line of fire.

When they arrived at the hotel the first thing Semenov did was to call Tom's and Olga's rooms. No reply. The phone kept ringing until it rang off. When there was no reply to the loud knocking on both doors he went back down to reception and asked for the keys to the rooms. The receptionist gave him a blanket refusal until he flashed his badge and after a nervous look at her colleague she handed the keys over.

A quick glance told them both rooms were empty. Once Fitzgerald and John had dropped their bags Semenov and Fitzgerald headed off. "I'll take Inspector Fitzgerald here to headquarters and get these meetings over with." He said to O'Brien. "You stay put and we'll be back to you as soon as possible. With a bit of luck they've just gone off on a tour. If there's no sign of those two useful idiots check out their rooms and see if you can get any sense of where they might be." From the tone of his voice it was clear that he was in charge now.

After he had dumped his bag and washed his face John O'Brien took the keys and went exploring even though what he wanted to do was crawl into bed and pull up the covers. He was exhausted. The first room was clearly Olga's judging by the clothes in the wardrobe and the makeup on the dressing table. Everything looked completely normal. Tom's room next door was just the same. He could see nothing that would give him any clue as to what was going on. He began to feel discouraged. What could they do? No point running to the authorities. Tom and Olga were here under false pretences and even he and Fitzgerald could have their bluff called at any moment. There was even a chance that he and Fitzgerald had got the wrong end of the stick and come all this way for nothing. He sat down at the desk where Tom had dumped a bunch of tourist leaflets and fliers. Nothing of any interest. Better go back to his own room and have a rest before the others came back. He stood up to go and dropped his key. As he stooped to pick it up he noticed a

THE BRATINSKY AFFAIR

scrunched up piece of paper lying beside the waste paper basket. Something about it caught his eye – it was written in English.

It was after midnight when Semenov and Fitzgerald came back. John O'Brien was sitting in the bar with a drink and struggling to stay awake. He slid the letter across without saying anything. Semenov nodded. "I was afraid of something like this. I know where the house isis but we can't go near it without backup. Best time to go in is just before daylight. It will take me a couple of hours to get things organised. You two say here until I get back."

Fitzgerald and O'Brien objected in unison.

"You think I came all this way to sit in a bar when Tom's life is in danger."

Semenov erupted. "You don't have the slightest idea about what a shit storm is going to come down on us. You're here on the basis of some cock n bull story about stolen antiques. O'Brien and the girl have got themselves picked up by one of the biggest criminals in Russia who is also best friends with the KGB and you think we can just wander along and ask nicely, "what's going on here, chaps?. I don't have time to argue with you so you will do what you are told, you will stay back and out of sight, and you will do nothing until I give the word!"

±

The house on the Fontanka looked deserted. Fitzgerald could see the police cars discreetly pulled in at either end of the street but apart from that there was no sign of life. On a signal from Semenov the ram took out the front door and within seconds the police were swarming through the building. The sound of heavy shod feet on the stairs and doors banging could be heard all over the house. There was no resistance. The few men they found drinking coffee in the back of the house surrendered without a struggle. The door into the room at the end of the upstairs corridor swung open - empty, though judging by the embers still smouldering in the grate and the smell of recently extinguished candles they had missed them by minutes.

"What now?" asked Fitzgerald.

"I have no bloody idea!" said Semenov kicking the door as they headed back towards the stairs. "They probably got a tip-off we were on our way."

As they passed one of the supposedly empty bedrooms they heard a sound of movement. Semenov led the charge and they found a kid, barely twenty by the look of him, frantically trying to smash his way out of a window at the back of the house. Semenov grabbed him and pinned him against the wall: "Where did they go?"

The kid was clearly terrified but whether of them or the rest of the gang, impossible to say.Semenov repeated the question and when the kid still refused to answer he took out his gun and whipped him across the face with the barrel, opening his cheek. The gleam of white bone was visible in a spray of blood and saliva. The kid screamed.

"Jesus, Semenov what are you doing?" shouted. O'Brien

"You, shut the fuck up. You're on my turf now. We do this my way."

He muttered to the kid through clenched teeth: "I'll ask you one more time. Where did they go? If you don't tell me I'll rip the other side of your face open and no woman will ever look at you again."

Between the blood and the screams the kid was incoherent. Semenov raised the gun again.

"Babalokovo. They went to Babalakovo."

"Where in God's name is that?"

"It's an old ruin of a place out in Pushkin, beyond the palace. The Colonel's family had a place there, back in the old days."

Semenov threw the kid on the floor and nodded for the other cops to take him away.

"Let's move. We need more back up and I need to cook up another work of fiction to cover all this. The way this is shaping up I could spend the rest of my career policing polar bears in Siberia, if I'm lucky."

John O'Brien looked at the kid as he was dragged away and felt sick.

THE BRATINSKY AFFAIR

CHAPTER 29

Wicklow, January 1976

Against the backdrop of pine trees and following the light dusting of January snow, Irina's house almost looked like a Russian dacha. The drawing room, the only grand room, stretched across the back of the house and with its beamed and vaulted ceiling above the bay window it was the perfect place to enjoy the evening light and the view out towards the forest. She had decorated the house simply but with some of her favourite pieces. Rugs from the Caucasus, rare blue-and-white Gzhel ceramics beautifully made in the villages south of Moscow, and a small but valuable collection of paintings.

Irina liked to leave the windows partially open so she could smell the pines. Nobody ever believed her when she said she could smell snow, but when the wind came from the east, she could pick up the almost imperceptible traces of snow in the air: the smell of Russia in winter. The two French windows opened onto the garden, and as the daylight faded the patches of light stretched almost as far as the tree line. Sometimes deer would come into the garden from the forest and she would sit watching them as she thought about recent events. Irina hadn't been in Ireland for several months and the garden was starting to look a bit neglected. She would feel better after a few hours pruning the roses and the flowering shrubs that clearly needed their annual haircut. *Maybe she would come for Easter and she and Olga could try to make up for lost time. It might even be an idea to invite William Radcliffe as well, though that would be hard work.*

Irina failed to notice the solitary figure standing in the trees beyond the light, or the leaf that had blown in through the window. When she felt the cold draught she knew immediately she was not alone. She looked up and there he was, standing across from her, staring at one of the paintings. There had been one by the same artist in the house in Petersburg. It was Ana's favourite; she had always hung it in the dining room where she could see it during dinner.

"Hello, Irina. A Russian Village in Ireland? Who would have thought? You know, for such a smart woman you can also be so stupid. Did you seriously think New York was an option? Maybe you could hide for a week or two, but in the end, I can find you anywhere. All it takes is a phone call."

The phone – that was it. Her mind raced back to the call: the hum in the background – and, as she replayed it in her mind, the slight click before she hung up. She had been unbelievably stupid.

"What do you want, Kerensky?"

"We have some unfinished business. I think you know what I'm looking for."

"I don't know what you're talking about." Irina's mind flicked through the house: too far from the knives in the kitchen; he was between her and the heavy fire irons…

"So predictable! Don't waste my time. When I have finished, you'll be happy to tell me anything I want to know, so you might as well save yourself the trouble, and the pain."

"I don't have it and I don't know where it is."

"Yes, you are lying"

"Why is this so important?"

"Now, if I told you that, I would have to kill you. Let's get down to business." He smiled. It was not a friendly smile. He reached into his inner pocket and took out a photograph and showed it to her. It was a picture of Olga coming out of Sotheby's offices in London with a group of friends.

"On the other hand I could ask Olga. She might be more forthcoming." The knife materialised out of nowhere and as he stared at her he slowly sliced the photograph into thin parallel strips that curled in a small heap on the carpet. The anger surged. They always knew the weak point to press. How many times did she have to fight this same battle? Kerensky hadn't come all this way for a quick chat and she could see only one outcome. Once he got what he wanted to know, she would be of no further use: that much was clear. *A pity Emile wasn't nearby with his garrotte.*

Irina had got a jib door set into the wall between the two

bookcases that ran the length of one wall. It led into the back hall, and if she could get there, she had a chance. The old revolver she had taken from Granot all those years ago was in a box on the hall table – and it still worked. She kept it oiled and loaded in case someone came to the front door late at night, but she hadn't reckoned on coming face to face with a killer in her own drawing room.

She pushed over the table and made a run for the door – but too late, he was already on top of her. The first punch winded her. With the second she felt something crack in her jaw and she fell to the floor. As she attempted to crawl away, she saw that the paper knife had fallen on the floor and as he moved in to catch her by the hair, she grabbed it and lunged up with all her strength. She got him in the shoulder. Not enough to block him, but enough to send him into a frenzy of rage.

Kerensky snatched up the malachite globe on the table and swung it once in a reflex action. It hit Irina on the side of the head and she hit the ground instantly. Kerensky had killed enough people to know that she was dead. The side of her head was smashed in and a pool of blood was slowly spreading out over the carpet.

He sat down at her desk and flicked through the pages of the catalogue she had been working on. One by one he turned out the desk drawers, and the bookcase, then every other drawer in the house, going through everything systematically. Nothing. After a few minutes he went through to the garage and returned to the kitchen with Irina's spare can of petrol.

He sloshed it around the house from top to bottom, soaked the sofa, crumpled some sheets of newspaper and soaked them too, and threw back a match. He stopped to watch the fire take hold, went out through the front door and walked slowly back to where he had parked the car behind the church. No one around except for an old lady out walking her dog. She politely wished him good evening as she passed, and he thought about that for a moment but decided to let it go. She wouldn't remember anything except a figure in black driving a grey Mercedes. In a few minutes the car would be a burnt-out shell and he could walk the mile or so to the station in Greystones before he got the train back to Dublin.

This was not the plan. Maybe it was as well to tidy up loose ends but the boss would not be happy.

THE BRATINSKY AFFAIR

CHAPTER 30

Tom and Olga could do nothing except wait. A man walked in and sat at the table, facing them. In his seventies: tall, muscular, shaved head and dressed like a soldier. He picked up one of the black chess pieces and made a move, then another with one of the white. After a while he looked up. "So, here we are at last, and you will give me what I want or there will be consequences. No threats, consequences."

Unbelievably he spoke English with a hint of an Irish accent. He was watching them both closely, and caught Tom's surprised reaction to the accent. "When we were children we had an Irish nurse. The Empress had an Irish nurse for the four Grand Duchesses so it became the fashion. My mother thought it would be amusing to resurrect an Irish connection, not that she was at all interested in the Irish link one way or the other. She did it to tease my father. The nurse spoke English to us all the time so the other servants wouldn't understand. Strange: I can see her face and I remember her voice but I can't remember her name. She stayed until the riots started and then she ran away too." He moved the black bishop and took a white piece. "Enough reminiscing. I assume you know who I am?"

Tom replied. "Count Pavel O'Rourke de Breffny, blackmailer and murderer."

"I see" said Pavel "Mr O'Brien will have his little joke. But you're not in Bray now" and he nodded to Kerensky who stooped and punched Tom hard in the gut, making him retch.

"The problem, for you, is that you have absolutely no idea who you are dealing with. Pavel Orork, by the way, not O'Rourke. I can make the two of you disappear like that!" He clicked his fingers. "Nobody will ever know what happened to you and nobody will ever find the bodies. What did you think? That you could waltz in here, take the sword and fly off home again with a nice adventure story to tell your snotty rich friends in Dublin, London or Paris. Not very smart."

"Tell me, Olga, what did you think would happen when you

came back to Russia– that we would rush to greet you with open arms– offer you back your palace– open the champagne? Idiots!"

Pavel Orork took a sip of the vodka. His voice was equal parts charm and menace and as he spoke it was as if he had waited for the last sixty years for this opportunity to unleash all the bitterness that he had kept locked away. "For you people, being Russian, it's like something you wear to a fancy dress party – you put it on and take it off when it suits – it has no meaning."

Olga tried to speak but he cut her off. "Don't say a word, because people like you know nothing and understand nothing." There was no emotion in his voice; only bitterness, ice. "What did you think happened when they took us away? Do you have any idea what they did to us?"

Olga blurted out "You can't blame me for what happened to you fifty-eight years ago, for God's sake! I'm not Irina!"

"I do. Not one of you ever bothered to ask, what happened to us? Not my mother, or Irina or your mother or you. Four generations of indifference. You were all too busy getting on with your lives. Did Irina ever use her political connections to try and find her little brother? Not once. I have seen the files and I know. Did she ever ask her good friend the Minister for Foreign Affairs to find out what had happened to her father – and to me? Never."

"They thought you were dead!" said Tom.

Pavel made a choking sound. "Let me tell you what happened. I was twelve years old when we were arrested, but I pretended to be fifteen so they wouldn't separate us, because I knew my father wouldn't last a week on his own. They locked us in the school for three days with no food and no water. I kept waiting for my mother to come and bribe a guard to get us out, like some of the other women did, but she never came. Some prisoners got food from family outside, but not us. We had to beg or starve: eat slops or die."

He kept drinking shot after shot of vodka but the alcohol had no noticeable effect. "Then there was a trial. That's what they called it. The judge was a former coal miner. As soon as he heard 'Count O'Rourke de Breffny, that was it. Straight to prison. I was lucky they didn't shoot me there and then. I don't know who was worse, the guards or the prisoners. The guards hated us all and the ordinary criminals hated us 'politicals' even more. It was a question of die today or die tomorrow. If the cold didn't kill you the hunger might or one of the other prisoners."

He raised his hand as if to sweep the pieces off the chessboard but changed his mind and topped up his glass.

"Father got typhus and I thought he would die, but against all the odds he lived. Then they sent us to the labour camp. Do you have any idea what happens to a pretty blond twelve-year-old in a place like that? The first time, they held me down and made my father watch as they raped me. It was fun for them, but also power – they liked to make me scream. They did it to show that they could do anything, and that we were nothing. They made us cut logs in the snow. If we didn't make our quota they beat us. If we did make the quota they beat us anyway, because they didn't like us. They stole our food and if we complained they beat us again. Every day I could see Father getting weaker. I wrapped him in bits of rags and put him as close to the fire as I could. I gave him my food, I stole food for him, and I traded my body for medicine. But one morning when I woke up I looked over and I knew immediately by the grey colour of his face that he was dead. He survived in that camp for two years.

Now I was on my own and I had a choice – kill or be killed. I was fifteen when I killed a man for the first time. He tried to take my food but I had taken a piece of metal off the bunk and sharpened it in the fire. I stuck it in his brain and watched him die. Then I took his belt and his shoes and his jacket. Nobody cared; he was another dead convict. But they began to be afraid of me.

And where were my mother and Irina? In Paris, drinking champagne and going to parties."

"But it wasn't like that you don't—"

"If you tell me I don't understand I will kill you here and now. I've seen the photographs! CountessBratinsky at the races, CountessBratinsky at the opening of an exhibition. The noted beauty. The celebrated, businesswoman.

They probably hoped I was dead. It was probably easier that way to close the door and forget we ever existed. But I did survive. I survived the camp and I survived the war, and I swore that I would get back everything that was mine and I would kill anyone who got in my way. Because I am Russian – not like you people – you are nothing– you don't know where you belong. Russian, French, English - mongrels all of you - you don't know who you are."

Pavel stopped, staring at them – no, beyond them.

"How many people have I killed? I have no idea, and I couldn't care less. I became a spy. I spied on the other prisoners and I spied on the guards. I used information as currency. I traded it for food, for sex, for more information, and I took control of my life. Now, I spy for the government, I spy on the government and I spy on people like you. And every step of the way I accumulate more money and more power.

In the beginning I didn't know who I was dealing with. Kerensky's job was to find someone close to the government in Paris who could be persuaded to work for us. He told me he had found this greedy Russian woman who was friends with lots of powerful people. Greedy, and stupid, he said. We set a trap and she walked straight into it. I thought she was just another jaded Russian exile who could be manipulated. It was only when I saw the interview in the *New York Times* that I realised who she was."

Pavel stood up and walked over to the fireplace. He kicked one of the logs that had fallen down back into the fire, and turned back to face Olga.

"Do you know where we are?"

"I have no idea."

"This is the old O'Rourke house – your ancestral home. Now I own it, and I own the other buildings on this street. The taxis outside your fancy hotel – they pay me. The expensive girls sitting at the bar, waiting for rich foreigners, they pay me too, because they all know what will happen if they don't. I have a share in every deal done in this city, and I have more money than you can ever imagine.

THE BRATINSKY AFFAIR

And now, you will give me what I want."

As he stepped closer to Olga any hint of charm was gone.

"We don't have it!" shouted Tom in an attempt to distract him.

Without a second's hesitation Pavel smashed him across the face and knocked him flying. He kicked Tom in the back and then dragged him upright again.

"You don't speak until I tell you to speak. But, since you are so anxious to speak, go ahead, Mr Tom O' Brien, Mr would-be journalist with the not so well-known *Wicklow Herald*. You see, I know everything about you. I know where you work, I know where you live and I know that your father's dog is called Mungo. I know where he takes Mungo for a walk and I know how easy it would be to kill him – or you."

He reached into Tom's inside pocket, took out the diary and flicked through it. "Now – where is it?" His tone was calm, almost gentle, but menacing.

"We don't know for sure."

"Be very, very careful what you say next."

"It's true" said Olga "It's in the diary. Ana describes the last night on the estate and what she did with the sword when she and Irina left – she says she gave it to the old General– read it for yourself."

"We think it's in the crypt," said Tom, "but that's all we know. That was our plan: to try to go there tomorrow to see if there is anything left of the chapel."

"You think it's in the crypt!" Pavel said, enunciating every word very slowly.

"Please let us go," said Olga. "I have no interest in the sword: we just wanted to follow Irina's story through to the end. .Let us walk out of here and we will say nothing to anybody, I swear."

Orork said nothing. he took the diary and left the room. Kerensky followed.

\#

They heard a key turning in the lock, then nothing, though in the distance they could occasionally hear the sound of footsteps on the stairs and people coming and going. It sounded like a group of men, though it was hard to say how many. Neither Olga nor Tom spoke. It was as if one of them spoke they might fall apart at having to confront the situation they were in.

After what seemed like an eternity, though it could not have been more than a couple of hours, they began to see a faint line of light across the top of the shutters. Outside the door they could now hear a flurry of activity. Kerensky and two other men came in. Nothing was said but they blindfolded Tom and Olga and dragged them to their feet.

"Move."

They were marched back down the corridor, but instead of continuing down the main staircase they tuned to the right and went down what in the past had obviously been the service stairs. From what he could gather, this side of the house was in much better condition. The floors felt more solid, and as they went down past open doors Tom could hear men chatting. At one point he even smelled a delicious whiff of fresh coffee. Finally he felt air on his face and knew that they were out in the open. They were forced into the back of a van and the door was slammed shut.

"Tom, I'm scared. I think they are going to kill us."

"Don't worry, Olga, it's fine. If they were going to kill us they would have done it already." Tom was far from believing his own words.

They waited for five or ten minutes until the two men got into the front. The engine started and they drove off slowly. Tom could hear the rev of a car following closely behind them.

The drive lasted for at least forty minutes before Tom could feel them bumping over rough ground. The van stopped and after a few minutes the door opened and they were pulled out. Kerensky pulled off the blindfolds but their hands were still tied.

"How are you feeling?" he whispered to Olga.

She flashed him a brief smile, "I'm fine." She looked pale and tense. Dawn was breaking. The air smelt of pine trees and early morning dew and the birds were beginning to sing. Tom looked around him and saw that they were in a clearing in a forest with stacks of cut timber and the tracks of heavy machinery. Another car pulled in behind them and Orork and Kerensky got out. They and the two men who had driven the van were wearing military uniform. There was a rough track up ahead and from time to time he heard a car passing in the distance so he knew that there was a main road somewhere behind them. He was trying to get his bearings so that if they got a chance they could make a run for it. All the men were carrying sub-machine guns, except for Orork, who had a revolver tucked into the waistband of his trousers.

Kerensky came towards them and jerked his head. "Move. "

The road curved on up through a forest of pine trees, but here and there he could make out an occasional beech or chestnut tree that had been swallowed up in the forest. They came to a pair of fallen stone gate piers, barely visible among the grass and weeds. The gate itself was long gone and the path now turned up a slope where the ground was rougher. At one point Olga fell and Kerensky dragged her to her feet.

"Can you not at least untie us, for God's sake?" said Tom. "How can we run? We're in the middle of nowhere."

Pavel didn't reply but nodded to Kerensky who pulled out a knife and cut the ropes. Tom rubbed his wrists, then took Olga by the hand, as much to reassure himself as her.

They came out into a clearing and ahead Tom could see the bulk of a large house outlined against the sky. As they got closer he could see that it was a ruin. The house consisted of a large central block with a pillared two story portico and wings jutting out on either side. It reminded Tom of the many abandoned country houses he had seen in Ireland. Even the style of the architecture was similar. The fire had clearly been concentrated in the main part of the house. The roof had fallen in and there was still a pile of charred timber and fallen masonry in what had once been the stairwell of the house where a tall tree had taken root. One wing looked reasonably intact and had clearly been used as a store.

Kerensky pushed the partially open door and gestured them inside with the barrel of the gun. Leaves had blown in and weeds were starting to grow in the cracks in the stone floor, but it was still recognisably a kitchen. There was an enormous wooden table in the middle of the room with a couple of benches on either side. Empty bottles and tins had been abandoned on the table. Probably the men working in the forest having lunch, thought Tom. Strands of ivy were winding in under the eaves of the roof and there was a pervasive smell of rot. In a few more years it would be a ruin like the rest of the house.

Pavel sent two of the men to do a recce and sat down on the bench across from them. He reached into an inside pocket and took out a photograph. It was the same one Tom had found in Irina's apartment on the rue du Bac. "I suppose you smart people know where you are?"

"Babalokovo," said Olga. "Ana's home."

"My home!" snapped Pavel. "And soon I will get it back."

"Was it worth killing your sister for?" asked Olga

"That was unfortunate, but Irina was nothing to me. She was a traitor to this family, this country – even to France, the country that sheltered her. Irina and my mother abandoned us. They ran away and never looked back. She had no loyalty to anybody but herself."

"But why do all of this for a stupid sword?"

Orork stood in front of Olga and almost spat at her. "Stupid? *Stupid* sword? You are a stupid little girl from England.. You read a couple of books and you think you understand Russia. When everything has been taken from you and you have been abandoned by everybody you cling to one thing, the one idea that has any meaning. After my father died that was me, and Russia, in that order.

"The General's sword is all of that in one thing. Our family fought for this country, built this country, and no one will take that from me – not you, not Irina, not the Party, nobody. You think you can march in here and take what you want? As the Americans say, over my dead body."

If only, thought Tom.

The two men came back in and gave the all-clear, and Pavel sent them back out to guard the vehicles. Tom and Olga were forced out at gunpoint into the forecourt of the old house. Up ahead, Tom could see the outline of an overgrown avenue of trees that led up to a drum-shaped temple with a shallow dome on top. It was clearly the mausoleum they had seen in the photographs. They walked up the slope with Orork and Kerensky coming behind, guns drawn.

"Olga, I don't like the look of this. Listen to me. If you get a chance, take it and run – don't look back -go."

"Jesus, Tom! Don't say that. It's history repeating itself."

The mausoleum was an elegant Greek temple in miniature. A series of columns went all the way around the temple, and below the dome was an elegant swag of what looked like plaster roses.

"Here it is" said Orork. The tomb of General Count O' Rourke!"

"In," said Kerensky, pointing with the gun.

Two steps led up into the building, with the remains of a broken balustrade on either side just as Ana had described it. The door was hanging off its hinges, and as they went in they found themselves in what been a small chapel. Directly in front of them was a large window above the remains of what had been an altar or tomb. To the left of the altar a narrow staircase descended into what they assumed was the crypt. Four other windows flooded the space with light even though they were partially boarded up.

In between the windows there had been a series of memorial plaques, and though these had been obliterated, a few pieces of marble with fragments of lettering clung stubbornly to the brickwork. The chapel had been used as a wood store and there were stacks of rotten logs against the walls. Judging by what looked like axe marks on its surface, the altar itself had been used as a chopping block, or worse.

Tom looked around to see if there was any way out.

Pavel intercepted the look. "Don't waste your time. If you so much as make a wrong move Oleg has orders to shoot to kill."

"Now what?" asked Tom. "At this point you know as much as we do "

"You better pray that I find what I am looking for, otherwise…" Pavel nodded to Kerensky to check out the crypt below. He came back up almost immediately.

"Nothing."

The graves had been looted and the chapel stripped during the hungry 1920s as starving people searched for anything that could be sold for food, even the clothes of the dead.

Kerensky was coming up out of the crypt when he caught his toe on the top step and fell heavily. As he fell, he dislodged one of the marble slabs, revealing a recess underneath. The end of a red tassel was immediately visible. "There's something here!"

Pavel was on him in an instant, and in the same moment Tom grabbed Olga by the arm and made a run for the door. Pavel spun on his heel and fired immediately, hitting the ceiling above their heads.

They stopped and clung together.

"Put your hands behind your heads and sit there on the step. One more stupid move and I will kill you both. You won't get a second warning."

They sat facing the door while Pavel stood over Kerensky as he grappled with the stone slabs. He dragged out a long box covered in faded blue velvet and handed it to Pavel. As he opened the box all eyes were fixed on the glittering blade. Napoleon's Leipzig Sword, abandoned when the Emperor fled the battlefield.

The sword was steel encrusted with gold, a symbol of power and strength. The pommel was gold, set with diamonds, while the scabbard was black leather edged with more gold. When he pulled it from the scabbard the curved steel blade inlaid with gold and silver sparkled in the sunshine. It looked beautiful, and deadly.

"Some people say it's worth $2 million, some say $4 million, but to me that's irrelevant. It represents everything our family stood for, everything that was taken from us. Beautiful! A curved cavalry sword, finely balanced, razor-sharp, perfect for lopping off heads."

He stroked it lovingly.

Tom felt increasingly nervous. Orork was clearly building up to something.

"You see Kerensky here?" He pointed with the tip of the sword. "He's a loyal servant, but he makes mistakes, too many mistakes. Losing Commandant Jourdain was careless, but bringing the intelligence services down on us by killing my sister

THE BRATINSKY AFFAIR

was downright stupid – and dangerous. If anyone was going to kill Irina it should have been me. I wanted to tempt her back to Russia and confront her after all these years. Now that can never happen."

Kerensky stood up to speak, but, with a single movement Pavel pivoted and the sword arced through the air, severing Kerensky's head in a spray of blood.

"That's for my sister, treacherous bitch though she was."

The severed head rolled across the floor, landing almost at Olga's feet. Tom and Olga sat in silence, trying hard not to vomit.

"Blood will out, isn't that what they say? Now, it remains to be decided what to do with you two. Unfortunately, dear Olga, family or not, there is only one way for this to end. You know that don't you?" He raised his gun.

As Pavel was speaking Tom caught a flicker of movement among the trees outside and glanced towards the door. Pavel stepped forward into the light from the window over the altar to take closer aim. At the same moment there were two shots and he fell sideways.

Tom took his chance and launched himself on top of him, kicking the gun towards the door and grabbing the sword as, to his amazement, four heavily armed policemen burst into the room. Tom was even more astonished to see Inspector Fitzgerald and his father coming in behind them.

Orork was not, dead. He had been hit in the shoulder and chest, but he was still conscious as the police prepared to drag him away.

"You should have killed me when you had the chance. No Russian prison will ever hold me, and I will come for you, I promise you that. You are a dead woman. And as for you." He pointed at Tom. "I will enjoy killing you and every member of your family."

Tom's father and Fitzgerald had come to the front of the group, with a third man Olga now recognised as the Russian police officer she had met in Wicklow. Semenov.

John O'Brien stood looking at Pavel for a minute before

stooping down and picking up the gun. "You're quite right, that would be a dangerous mistake. Thing is, you're not the only one who fought in a brutal civil war and survived;" Before anyone could stop him he pointed the gun at Orork and shot him in the head. Then, John O'Brien dropped the gun and walked back out into the sunshine. In the stunned silence that followed Tom looked at Olga: "stay here, I better go after him."

Tom followed his father out and found him sitting on the broken balustrade staring into the distance. "I can't believe it has come to this. I just shot a man in cold blood." he was visibly shaking.

"Dad, I'm sorry I dragged you into all this. I should have told you what was going on from the beginning. Now I've landed us in this mess. I never realised what you went through in the war."

"It's not something I like to remember. I was young and it seemed exciting… and right now I want to forget it. You can see for yourself, Tom, war makes monsters of us all."

Olga had followed them out and was walking back towards the ruins of the house.

She turned back to look at the chapel and the surrounding forest. This was the last view Ana and Irina had of their home before they left forever. John waved to her to join them. "Come and sit by me, Olga. Seems strange to be doing formal introductions in the aftermath of a murder, but anyway, nice to meet you, finally."

Olga walked over and sat between Tom and his father on the broken balustrade. Inspectors Fitzgerald and Semenov had been deep in conversation with the Russian officers and now came over to join the group.

"If it isn't the three musketeers," said Fitzgerald "The three of you should be locked up, but I'm not sure if it should be jail or the loony bin. What in God's name possessed you to…and as for you two! Oh, what's the point – it's done."

He turned to John "And you're not out of the woods yet, O'Brien. We still have the problem that you shot dead a serving and much decorated colonel of the KGB."

"Who was a murderer and a blackmailer, a kidnapper holding

me and his great-niece to ransom, and God knows what else," said Tom.

"All true, but at the moment that's beside the point. It's like this. I've been talking to Semenov here and he says there is no way in the wide world that the Russians are going to accept having a KGB colonel and hero of the Great Patriotic War exposed as a criminal and a psychopath and killed in a shoot-out with two foreigners. Not to mention the fact that he was in cahoots with every political and military boss in the country as well. Killing him is like a declaration of war. The only thing saving us is that a lot of people hated Orork and had their eyes on his empire. It would suit them for him to disappear quietly into history. We have to agree a story before the drums start beating. But we think there is a way out. What we will agree is this. Miss Radcliffe, and her pushy little friend here, came to Russia to look into her family history. She made contact with her newly discovered great-uncle and they decided to come here to pay their respects at the tomb of their mutual ancestor. Lo and behold, they discovered the sword. When he heard how much it was worth Kerensky tried to grab it for himself. A fire fight erupted in which he shot General Orork and John shot him trying to save the General."

"Are you crazy?" Tom said. "It's ridiculous, no one will believe it. I can see the headline: Man Attacked by Headless Corpse."

"Very funny – now, shut up and listen, for once. They will believe it because it suits them to believe it. That inconvenient detail will now be airbrushed out of history, and not only that but you, Tom O'Brien, will get the opportunity to write up this story, in which you will interview Inspector Semenov and extol the dedication and courage of the late General Orork, descendant of an ancient and distinguished Irish family, for the national and international press. Apart from that you're going to have to pay off Semenov's men and it won't be cheap."

"You mean bribe them," said Tom.

"Not to put too fine a point on it, yes. and as far as the murders of CountessBratinsky and Commandant Jourdain are concerned,

Kerensky was a rogue agent acting on his own initiative and there will be no mention of espionage or a possible mole in the Hôtel Matignon – *none*. This way, everybody will be happy."

"What, and cover up this tissue of lies?"

"Your choice. That, or your father will be charged with murder and spend the next two years in a Russian prison waiting for his case to come to trial – and after that –who knows?"

"But that's blackmail!" said Tom as his mind flashed back to his last conversation with Bill Egan. The words hoist and petard came to mind.

"You can look at it that way or, you can view it as a deal that allows you, your father and Miss Radcliffe to walk out of Russia, no questions asked;- and gives you the opportunity to write a story that the international media will eat up!"

Tom looked at his father. John O'Brien shrugged. "There's no other way. You wanted to see your name up in lights, Tom. Well, there's a price."

"There's one detail – what about the sword? What happens to it?" asked Olga. "After all, that's what this was all about."

"You know," said Fitzgerald, "I couldn't give a flying fuck what happens to it."

Olga thought for a minute. "There's only one place for it. We should present it to the Military Gallery in the Hermitage, where it can go on display along with the portrait of the General. It's caused enough grief, and I for one never want to see it again. In the end, Ana did say she was giving it to the old General to look after. He can keep an eye on it in his home city."

THE BRATINSKY AFFAIR

CHAPTER 31

Tom and Olga walked back into the lobby of the hotel later on Friday evening accompanied by Tom's father, Inspector Fitzgerald and Semenov. They found Helene pacing up and down in a rage. She pounced as soon as she saw them, and without drawing breath launched into a tirade of questions.

"What in God's name happened to you two? Do you have any idea how much trouble you are in? Where have you been? Do you know that half the police in Petersburg have been looking for you? And I had to send the rest of the group off with another guide while I looked for you."

When she finally drew breath she looked at Inspector Fitzgerald and John O'Brien. "And who are these people?"

"It's all right, Helene, we're fine," said Tom, "But thanks for asking. By the way, look what we found" – and he pulled out the sword.

She took a step back and for once - had nothing to say. "What is going on?" she asked after she got over her surprise.

"It's a long story, so let's go into the bar and have a drink. With all your wonderful contacts we're hoping you can help us organise something special before we head to the airport on Sunday afternoon." Over a round of dry martinis, Tom gave Helene a highly selective version of recent events.

She listened open mouthed.

"This is an international story that will have every photographer and news agency in St Petersburg, not to mention the rest of the world, clamouring for access. You know your friend from the Bolshoi, Mr Ivanov? Do you think he could use his contacts to help pull a presentation together? Miss Radcliffe wants to present this historic sword to the Hermitage in the Military Gallery, in honour of her famous ancestor Count O'Rourke de Breffny. Could you handle that?"

Tom could hear the wheels clicking in Helene's head as she calculated the advantages to her.

"No problem at all," she said with enthusiasm. She turned to

Olga. "I knew you two were up to something. And I was right, you are Russian."

"Irish, actually," said Olga, and she winked at Tom.

Despite the pressure of time, with the combination of Helene's charm and Ivanov's contacts the reception in the Hermitage on Saturday evening was a triumph. The Director of the Hermitage was virtually in love with Olga, and kept referring to her as Countess O'Rourke. When she corrected him for the third time to no avail she decided to give in and enjoy being Countess O'Rourke for the duration.

It was a coup for the museum, and nobody wanted to ask any searching questions though there were a number of men in dark suits who kept a close eye on what was happening yet had no interest in joining the conversation. This time, when Ivanov and the museum director suggested supper in the Hermitage's private dining room, Olga and Tom were only too happy to accept. As for the rest of the group, they treated Tom and Olga like celebrities and basked in their reflected glory, as well as enjoying the copious amounts of champagne. Ivanov gave Tom a knowing look but said nothing.

As the party began to wind down Tom took his father by the arm.

"Let's take a walk up the gallery and say good bye to the General. Anyway there's something I want to talk to you about. They walked up the long gallery and sat facing the portrait of General Count Joseph Cornelius O'Rourke de Breffny.

Tom had been dreading this moment and now it was here he didn't know where to start.

"Dad, there's something I need to tell you, about me. I...."

"No, you don't. You mean that you're gay! I know, I've always known. You young people! You think you invented sex."

Tom looked at his father, speechless.

"When your mother and I talked about it …."

"Jesus, Dad! You - and Mama as well!"

"You won't remember, you're too young but your mother had a younger cousin, Thomas. He was gay and when the family found out there was a big hoo ha. The Parish Priest was called in and there was talk of sending him off to Canada. He couldn't handle it and he committed suicide. Hi mother went out to the yard one Sunday to feed the chickens and found him hanging in the barn. She never got over it. Your Mam always said that was the worst day of her life. Nobody ever talked about it. It was all hushed up. When we talked about you she said. "He'll come to it in his own time. If he does, all we can do is to be there for him. I'm here, Tom. I've always been here, waiting for you. I'm your father."

By this time they were both in tears. At that moment Tom saw Helene and Ivanov coming down the gallery towards them.

"Better shape up now. And join the party." As they headed off to the restaurant Olga came over to Tom.

"You, ok?" and squeezed his hand.

"I'm fine, absolutely fine."

$\neq$

When they headed to the airport on Sunday afternoon, Inspector Semenov saw them though security and as they headed to the boarding gate he whispered discreetly to Tom, "It might be better if you didn't come back to Russia for a while. A long while."

As the plane cruised over the endless expanse of forest in the middle of Russia, Inspector Fitzgerald and John O'Brien were sound asleep across the aisle while Tom focused on his next instalment for Willi Regan.

"What did Willi say?" asked Olga.

"I think he was genuinely relieved to hear from me, even got quite emotional. But in true Willi Regan fashion he wants a two-page spread covering the story from beginning to end, he wants a lead for the front page and he wants exclusive first pick of the photographs from the presentation in the Hermitage. He certainly wants his pound of flesh."

Olga leaned over to read what Tom had written. "Not bad for a beginner."

CHAPTER 32

EPILOGUE

When they arrived in Orly Fitzgerald and John O'Brien were taking a connecting flight back to Dublin and Tom and Olga were heading into the city. It was an emotional moment between Tom and his father.

"I'll be home by the weekend, Dad and we can spend some time together."

John O'Brien gave him a tight hug and hurried off to departures before the tears started. Fitzgerald gave a brisk nod to Tom and shook hands with Olga

"I will need to get a formal statement from you Miss Radcliffe to close the case but that can wait for a while. Maybe we will see you back in Bray," he added.

He was clearly fishing but Olga just smiled and said, "That would be lovely."

As they went through arrivals the first person Tom saw was Jean-Philippe standing with his arms folded and doing his best to look angry.

"Well, well, the wanderers return. "Nice to see you Tom, and Miss Radcliffe or should I say Countess O'Rourke?" There was a definite note of sarcasm in his voice. He held up a copy of Le Monde which had a double page spread of photographs from the reception in the Hermitage.

"How did you know when we were arriving?"

"You're not the only one with contacts, Tom, and you weren't exactly flying below the radar. In the end when I couldn't get hold of you my office managed to track down Fitzgerald's superior and he told them. We can drop your luggage off at the hotel and then we are going to my place for dinner where you will explain yourselves. Meanwhile, I will consider which of you two I will beat first."

"You can't beat me, Maître Berenger," said Olga. "I'm your client!"

"Your grandmother was my client. You are a legitimate target." There was a hint of a smile as he said it. "And, for God's sake, can you please call me Jean-Philippe ?"

THE BRATINSKY AFFAIR

END NOTE

'The Bratinsky Affair follows a line from the collapse of the Imperial regime in Russia to life in wartime France and the post war period of rising social and political tensions in the 1960's. 'The Bratinsky Affair' is a murder mystery but it's also a story about the choices that people make and the price they have to pay in every instance. It shows how easy it is to let the really important things in life slip through our fingers.

In 1607, when Hugh O'Neill, Earl of Tyrone and Hugh O'Donnell, Earl of Tyrconnell and their followers fled to France and then Rome it was the end of the old Gaelic way of life in Ireland. In the years that followed generations of young men escaped the repression of the Penal Laws in Ireland by joining the armies of Spain, France, Austria and Russia. Known as the 'Wild Geese' many of them achieved distinction under foreign flags. By one estimate, over 100 Irish men were field marshals, generals, or admirals in the Austrian Army alone.

The O'Rourkes of Breffny were one such family. While 'The Bratinsky Affair' is in every respect a work of fiction it is rooted in fact. The family members were descendants of ninth-century kings of <u>Connacht</u>and ruled the ancient kingdom of *Breifne* until they were dispossessed in the Elizabethan wars. By the start of the Napoleonic wars Joseph Cornelius O'Rourke had risen to the rank of Count O'Rourke de Breffny in Russian service and was owner of a vast estate near Minsk and one thousand serfs.

In the course of his career he received two golden swords for bravery, one of which was encrusted with diamonds but neither of which had any connection to Napoleon. That was my embellishment. There is however a portrait of him in the 'Military Gallery' in the State Hermitage Museum in Saint Petersburg. There is also a monument to him in Serbia commemorating his participation in the Battle of Varvarin against the Ottoman Empire. As for the diamond studded sword it's probably hanging in a dusty antique shop somewhere waiting to be discovered.

JIM LOUGHRAN

The characters of Ana and Irina are pure invention while Tom O'Brien, though fictional, reflects certain elements of my own experience as a young gay man finding my way in Paris in 1976.

The General's descendant, Count Edward O'Rourke, inherited the fighting spirit of the O'Rourkes. As the first Bishop of Danzig he came into conflict with the Nazis in the years prior to the outbreak of World War 11. As far as I have been able to find the title is now extinct. However, if any of you know differently I would be happy to hear from you. You can contact me by e-mail at walkinstown97gmail.com.

FURTHER READING

Among the dozens of books I have read on the build up to and the aftermath of the Russian Revolution of 1917 these three are outstanding in their grasp of detail and ability to capture the human cost of the cataclysm. For readers whose curiosity is piqued about wartime France and the history of the O'Rourke family, I also include suggested further reading.

The Whisperers: Private Life in Stalin's Russia by Orlando Figges - Allen Lane.
Former People: The Final Days of the Russian Aristocracy by Douglas Smith - Pan Books.
The Romanovs: 1613-1918 by Simon Sebag Montefiore - Orion Books.
Vichy France and the Jews by Michael R Marrus and Robert Paxton - Basic Books.
Vichy France and Everyday Life: Confronting the Challenges of Wartime, 1939-945 by David Lees (Author, Editor), Lindsey Dodd (Author, Editor) - Bloomsbury Academic.
Irish Brigades Abroad: From the Wild Geese to the Napoleonic Wars by Stephen McGarry

The History Press.Irish Identity *The O'Rourkes in Russia*
http://www.irishidentity.com/geese/stories/orourkes.htm

The Russian Village

THE BRATINSKY AFFAIR

https://airrynna.livejournal.com/110041.html

The Russian Village
https://www.independent.ie/life/home-garden/homes/presidential-retreat-with-a-russian-influence-on-the-market-for-11m-in-wicklow/41113028.html

Patrick Comerford - *A Polish bishop with Irish ancestors who stood up to the Nazis*
https://www.patrickcomerford.com/2018/03/a-polish-bishop-with-irish-ancestors.html

Printed in Great Britain
by Amazon